Inspired By True Events

The Bitter Half

a Dichotomy of Trust & Betrayal

Simon

Leadstart
INKSTATE

ISBN 978-93-90463-02-2

First published in India 2020 by Inkstate Books
An imprint of Leadstart Publishing Pvt Ltd

Sales Office:
Unit No.25/26, Building No.A/1,
Near Wadala RTO,
Wadala (East), Mumbai – 400037 India
Phone: +91 969933000
Email: info@leadstartcorp.com
www.leadstartcorp.com

Disclaimer: The views expressed in this book are those of the Author and do not pertain to be held by the Publisher.

Author Disclaimer: This novel is inspired by true events, but it is a work of imaginative fiction. While the backdrop of the book is a creative recreation of true events, the characters themselves are derived solely from the Author's imagination. Resemblance to any persons living or dead is purely coincidental. Any reference to actual persons, places, buildings or products is unintended and should not be inferred to be otherwise unless explicitly stated by the Author.

Editor: Shayoni Mitra
Cover: Saurabh Garge
Layouts: Kshitij Dhawale

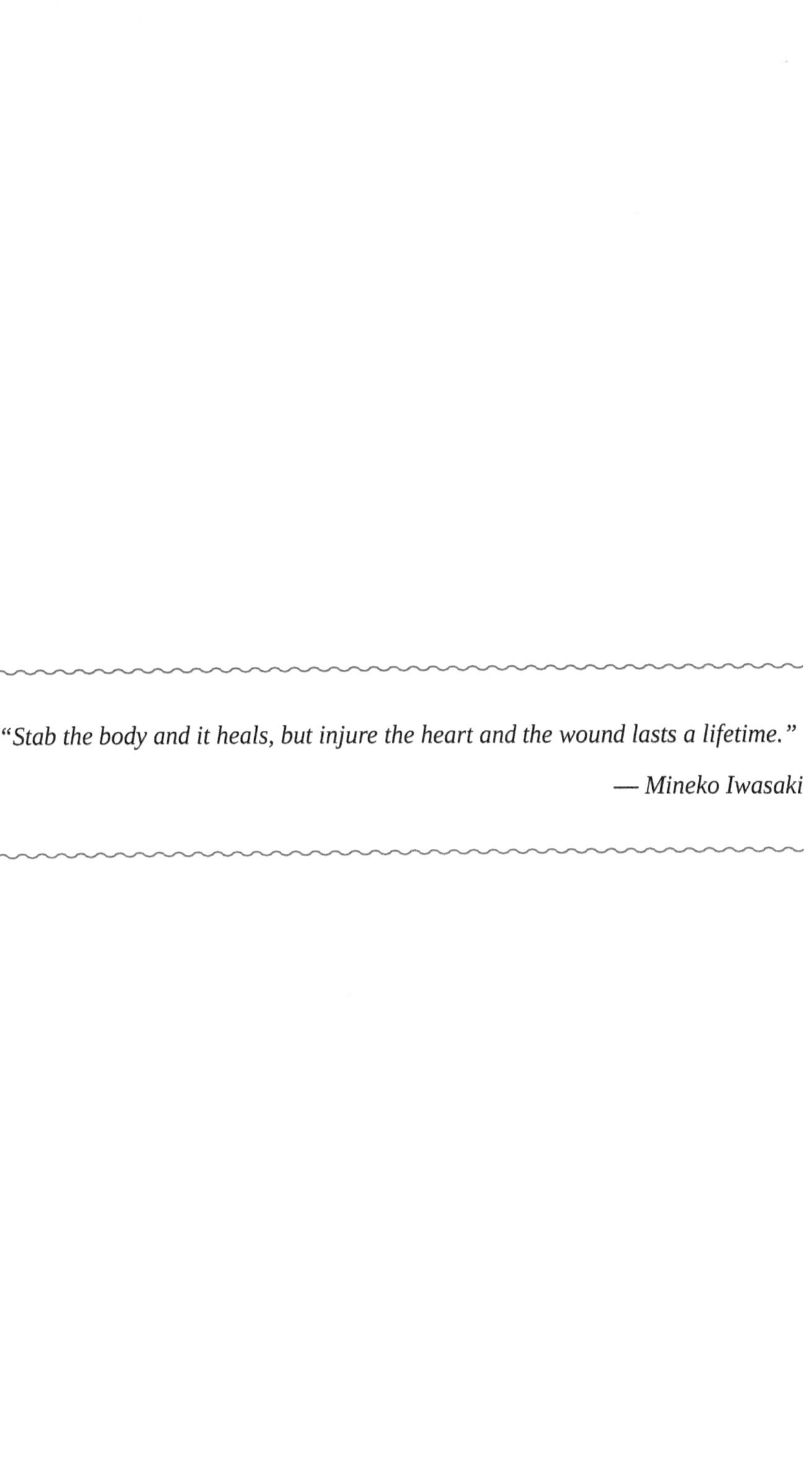

"Stab the body and it heals, but injure the heart and the wound lasts a lifetime."

— *Mineko Iwasaki*

ABOUT THE AUTHOR

Simon is a Mechanical Engineer with Masters in Business Management. He has been a Consumer Insights professional throughout his career and has served Market Research biggies like KANTAR-IMRB and Nielsen before leading and managing roles at some of the renowned corporates and start-ups in BFSI, Real Estate and eCommerce segments. Meeting consumers and listening to their preferences and viewpoints helped him craft stories for Brands he has handled, which later got transformed into his passion for storytelling. *The Bitter Half: a dichotomy of Trust & Betrayal* is his debut novel, which is inspired by a set of true events.

He is based out of Mumbai, and is a passionate quizzer who likes to explore varieties of cuisines. He is also in absolute love with Spanish flicks and retro Bollywood numbers.

ACKNOWLEDGEMENT

Writing a book can be a lonely pursuit and at times you miss the forest for the trees. In light of this, I am immensely grateful to my family, friends and loved ones who helped make *The Bitter Half: a dichotomy of Trust & Betrayal* possible.

A heartfelt gratitude to my dearest *Dadu*, Late Naliniranjan Das, who imbibed the art of storytelling in me during my childhood days. Those *Perry Mason* series by *Erle Stanley Gardner*, gifted by my grandfather back in 80s, formed the foundation of learning to weave words into the fabric of a storyline.

My mother has been my biggest critic; never imagined her to be a task master in making me rework each and every chapter of this book to fit the plot. Thank you *Maa*.

A big shout-out to my beta reader, Manie Dhir for ironing out those initial inconsistencies in the narrative. I thank my editor, Shayoni Mitra for meticulously morphing the manuscript into its final version.

For police procedurals and judicial proceedings, I am indebted to my school friends from Kolkata Police, Calcutta High Court and Bombay High Court for their technical inputs. I also appreciate the zeal with which my student – Trishanu Paul agreed unanimously to appear on the cover-page and thereby bring out the essence of the storyline.

Finally, I am grateful to the folks at Leadstart Publishing for providing me the opportunity to bring my work to you.

Last and certainly not the least – I am thankful to all my dear readers, who will complete this book. I hope you enjoy reading this as much as I enjoyed writing it.

ONE
2014

Haldia, West Bengal, India

The doorbell rang constantly in an unusual manner. Not in the signature style of Sushil Ghosh. And why would he be at the door now? It had hardly been ten minutes that he left for his regular morning walk, followed by which he would visit the *sabzi* market and by the time he returned, it would be at least an hour or so – this is what was running through Chitra's mind, while she hurriedly made her way from the balcony to the living room. But before opening the door she glanced through the peephole and just couldn't believe her eyes. She almost fainted but took control of herself and stepped back…*What would she do now?* Quickly, she rushed back to the bedroom and rang her husband on his mobile.

"The police is at the door. What should I do now? Where are you?" she spoke these words hurriedly and surreptitiously. She was simultaneously shivering and sweating profusely.

"Whaaatt – Police...! But why? Wait, don't open the door till I am there." Sushil disconnected the call and dialled Sudeep on his way back home, and asked him to reach immediately for his cousin sister's rescue.

The Odisha Police had a long and tiring day. The team had to leave Birmirpur Police Station (PS) at around 7:30 pm and had assembled at Rourkela Railway Station by 9 pm. Sub-Inspector (SI) Shamita Mohanty led the team of two constables and one Assistant Sub-Inspector (ASI); while Deputy Superintendent of Police (DSP) Ajay Dash supervised the entire operation. In fact, DSP Dash appointed this young dynamic, dexterous SI as the Investigation Officer (IO) for this specific case. He had instructed his men to reach Haldia early in the morning. Shamita, who was relatively new in the police force went on to become the most trusted subordinate of the DSP. Hardly a year in the job, she often jumped hierarchy to report progress of various cases directly to the DSP, something her colleagues at the police station couldn't stomach.

The team had a quick dinner at the railway canteen in Rourkela before boarding the Howrah bound *Samaleshwari Express* at 10:40 pm. Instructions to the team were loud and clear – serve the notice, seize all the materials and head back to Birmirpur. Haldia being out of their jurisdiction in the neighbouring state of West Bengal, the team had to take special permission from top officials before this visit. DSP Dash got all the necessary clearances and connected with Haldia Township's station-in-charge Rabindra Mondal the previous evening, and requested Mondal to accompany Shamita on this operation.

The entire process of taking permission from one state official to another took a good forty-five days. Unfortunately, by then the Supreme Court of India had passed an order in July 2014 against arrests on prima facie complaints. Shamita, who waited outside Ghosh's fifth floor apartment, was not only irritated but also helpless. Had the paperwork been over before July – she would've already arrested the elderly couple and returned back.

Twenty-four years old Shamita was just two cases old in the system. This was her first case outside the jurisdiction and being the IO, a slight arrogance crept into her approach of dealing with simple things. She signalled Mondal to try and convince Mrs Ghosh to open the door, use his Bengali tongue to build assurance.

"Madam, please open the door, I am Rabindra Mondal from the local *Thana*. I am from Haldia, don't worry, they're here only to serve a notice."

"You may be the Prime Minister, for all I care. There's nobody in the house. My husband has gone for his morning walk. Let him come back and you can serve whatever notice you want to," came a strong voice from the other side of the door.

"Madam, we are the police and you've kept us waiting for the past fifteen minutes!" Shamita yelled, losing her cool.

"How do I believe that you're from the police? These days, robbers disguise themselves in police uniform and break into the house of senior citizens. I request you to wait for some time. My husband is on his way." Chitra gave an equally loud reply.

The entire police team of five were kept stranded outside flat number 505 of Monalisa Apartments. They were all tired and restless yet had no option but to wait. The journey from Rourkela to Haldia wasn't smooth – the night train got delayed and the men in uniform got down at Panskura Station in the wee hours of the morning. Then next, they took a local train till Mecheda Station, wherefrom, Mondal arranged a Mahindra Scorpio for their pickup. Overall the journey duration was a little less than nine hours.

Sushil couldn't even imagine in his worst nightmares, that the police would find their way to his door step. A retired officer from Indian Oil Corporation, he had lived his entire life in prestige and just couldn't think of the enormous amount of embarrassment he and his wife would have to face in front of the neighbourhood. He would hardly have any dignity left after this in the housing society. He was breathing hard and speeding towards Monalisa Apartments, all the time feeling the stare of an invisible pair of eyes – *How will he explain his situation to others? Will anybody believe him to be innocent and guilt free? And how will he regain his status amongst the people who respect him?*

As someone who always led a simple, humble life, Sushil Ghosh came across as a middle-class, senior citizen, who was always ready to help others selflessly. And today, at this juncture he felt helpless and miserable.

As soon as he reached the entrance of the building, he spotted the West Bengal Police's white Scorpio parked a few meters away from the gate. Few curious passers-by had gathered around the vehicle to figure out what was happening. The police vehicle itself had raised enough inquisitiveness amongst the neighbouring buildings. Some peeped out of their windows, while others were at their balcony. It was such an ignominious moment for Sushil. He went past the white Scorpio, almost pretending to ignore it, but was shocked to see Mr and Mrs Chell sitting inside the vehicle and making animated gestures from the rear seat to explain something to the gathered mass.

Sushil purposely didn't take the elevator, instead opted to climb up the stairs till the fifth floor. It allowed him time to give a shape to his thoughts and weave a convincing story as to what led the police to arrive at his door. There were mixed feelings of hatred and tension that riddled him. Generally, it would take him time to reach the fifth floor, but today the same path seemed shorter and he reached his door in no time. The neighbouring Mukherjees had kept their door wide open to figure out what was happening.

"Sorry for keeping you all waiting outside. Actually, my wife got tense. She is all alone and had never expected the police to visit at this early hour of the day," Ghosh said politely before ringing the doorbell.

Flashing his identity card, Mondal said "We are on duty and have been kept waiting for the last forty-five minutes. The Odisha police has come a long way to meet you."

"I am really sorry, Sir." Ghosh said in an apologetic tone.

Chitra finally opened the door. Ghosh asked the police team to give him a few minutes, so that he could quickly arrange for their seating.

"Everything is over! What if they have come here to arrest us?" Chitra asked in a shaky voice before bursting into uncontrollable tears.

"Nothing will happen. Be strong. Let me now ask them to come inside."

The next six hours were a hell of an experience for the elderly couple. The police team from Odisha entered and handed over the notice issued by Birmirpur PS as per Section 41A CrPC of IPC. It was in the name of Sushil and Chitra Ghosh, along with their wards Sumit and Sunita, both residents of Mumbai. The notice stated that an FIR had been lodged on May 2014 u/s 498A, 323, 294, 506, 34 of IPC and the entire Ghosh family needed to appear before the police by the first week of August for questioning regarding the registered case. The Chell couple waiting in the police vehicle below were called in and asked to identify the belongings of their daughter. A *seizure list* was immediately prepared by the IO which had a list of garments, ornaments, cosmetics and other belongings of Moulina, which she carried with her sixteen months back, when she was married off to Sumit Ghosh. All the while, Chitra kept complaining to the officer how they all have been falsely accused by the Chells. The Chells seemed ecstatic about the fact that they succeeded in their mission to get rid of the Ghosh family. They kept telling everybody in the building how their daughter was being mistreated and tortured by the Ghosh family. Everyone in the locality had last seen Moulina and Sumit attend the society's *Durga Puja* last year and nothing seemed to be wrong then. In fact, Moulina used to go out with her in-laws for morning walks, shopping and to the beauty parlour – everything was normal in the family, how could things take such an ugly turn!

After the police team left, the shattered Ghosh couple locked themselves up in their flat for almost a week. Neither did they go out nor did they speak to anybody in the society. Chitra's cousin brother Sudeep Das, his wife and their eight-year-old son were the only visitors. They tried their best to keep the Ghosh couple cheerful, but the entire incident had taken a major toll on both Chitra and her husband's health. Sushil's blood pressure shot up abnormally with increased blood sugar levels, while Chitra went into depression with anxiety, insomnia and lack of appetite.

⸙ ⸙ ⸙

Section 498A which was passed by Indian Parliament in the year 1983, colloquially referred as the Dowry Law, is considered a pure criminal law.

It was formulated to protect married women from their in-laws, but is now being grossly misutilized, mostly to settle scores with their husbands or in-laws. Various High Courts across the nation and the Honourable Supreme Court has acknowlwdged the fact, that this draconian law is being highly misused. As per the NCRB data – over the years, the number of cases registered under this IPC has gone up tremendously, whereas the conviction rate has drastically come down. In fact, 498A is being used as an extortion weapon by many in our country. In spite of the Supreme Court's strict guideline, the police and the system take a lethargic approach in handling such cases. FIRs filed across police stations comprise almost of the same script. Inadequate investigations are carried out for the sake of formality and the chargesheets filed always point a finger towards the husband and his relatives. While the wife has every liberty to file 498A from any jurisdiction, it's the husband and his relatives who get harassed. They travel states, at times countries, to fight for their dignity. Some FIRs have even blamed infants, pet dogs and paralytic septuagenarians as the ones who have tortured the daughter-in-law physically and mentally. Once the case is up for hearing, a public prosecutor represents the wife free of cost, whereas the husband has to shell out a huge amount for his legal expenses. Over and above this, he loses dignity and prestige in the society; precious time of his career; and at times is forced to take the drastic step of ending his life.

The icing on the cake is that, 498A comes with a bouquet of other IPCs slapped on the husband and his relatives. Some of the common IPCs which come as a combo offer are: 34, 294, 323, 341, 354, 379, 406, 504, 506 and section 3 and 4 of Dowry Prohibition Act along with 125 CrPC, section 18 of HAMA et al. If a couple happens to be lucky enough to have a kid from their wed-lock, the husband will be equally unlucky to get charged with additional IPCs related to child custody. While the criminal proceedings commence, maintenance and divorce petitions are also filed by the wife in Family court simultaneously. The harassment for the boy and his family increases multi fold. Both criminal and civil cases run parallelly, and in this entire circus the policemen, lawyers, bailers and a few middlemen become the beneficiaries by default.

TWO
2014

Mumbai, Maharashtra, India

Mid-July is when Mumbai generally starts preparing for its monsoon season, which then goes on to last for next three to four months. There had been a brief spell of morning shower, because of which Sumit couldn't go out for his regular jog. He watered the potted plants in front of the window pane of his sixth floor 1BHK flat overlooking the Santacruz-Chembur Link Road (SCLR) instead. The construction of the SCLR was in full swing, as the authorities wanted to open it up for public before the monsoon. SCLR would become Mumbai's first six-lane-double-decker flyover connecting the Central and Western suburbs, thereby cutting short the travel time by almost thirty minutes.

Sumit was in between jobs and had taken up some freelancing work, while his younger sister Sunita was employed with a private bank. Just last week, he bagged a content writing assignment from a Malaysian firm and the last submission had to be re-worked a bit. Since he had skipped today's jogging session, he planned to finish off the assignment early. It was 7 am and a cup of morning tea would give him the right kick to start with the day's work. He switched on his laptop and by the time it was booting he quickly made two cups of tea. Sunita's share was poured in a flask for the time being, so that she could have it with cookies and sandwiches before leaving for her office.

The last six months had been quite different for Sumit. Moulina had always been an 'early to bed, early to rise' person. She would accompany him for his morning walks and jogs. However, she left for her parents' place in Birmirpur nine months back and since then had been dilly-dallying her return to Mumbai. Married since May 2012, they had spent sixteen wonderful months together. In his wife's absence, Sumit was kind of leading a bachelor's life, yet Moulina captured his mind and emotions. Had she been here at this hour she would have immediately got into the kitchen and made him a cup of tea. Before she got married, she could only make Maggi and fry omelettes. Cooking never interested her. But in the last couple of months before she left for Birmirpur, she was slowly and steadily picking up her culinary skills. Sumit was fond of her tea and *'aloo ka paratha'*.

He checked the time – 7:30 am, time for Dad to go out for his morning walk, while Mom would stay back home and consume every piece of news from *Anandabazar Patrika*. Did the rain Gods usher their blessings on Haldia too? Like every other day, Sumit gave a good morning call to his Mom back in Haldia – Life in a small town is completely different from a fast-paced city like Mumbai. A morning or evening stroll along Haldi River is always blissful, the unlimited cool breeze could rejuvenate any tiring soul. Born and brought up in the port city, Sumit missed the tranquil township situated at the confluence of Hooghly and Haldi River. Given a chance, he would love to go back to his hometown and retire in peace. But at this stage of life, probably Mumbai was the best fit for him. He enjoyed the hustle and bustle of this city that challenged him to keep up with the pace of life every moment.

With a cup of tea in his left hand, he reached out for his mobile phone and dialled his mother – it kept ringing, but nobody attended the call. Without wasting any more time Sumit started working on his assignment. Content Writing was his new found love and he enjoyed every bit of it. A seasoned Digital Marketer with almost eleven years of professional experience, Sumit was a qualified mechanical engineer with a post-graduate degree in marketing management. Before this small break in his career, he had single-handedly managed the digital and social media marketing portfolio of one of Mumbai's prestigious real estate companies.

It was 9:30 am and Sunita had left for her office in Sion. It took her approximately thirty minutes every day, to reach office by autorickshaw. It was drizzling when she sat in the autorickshaw. On her way, she tried calling Mom but the call couldn't be connected – may be due to network issues caused by bad weather conditions.

After finishing with his assignment, Sumit was relatively free. He put on some *Manna De* classics on one of his favourite YouTube channels. He was thinking of calling his mother again, when the doorbell rang. The Nepali watchman was there at the door to inform about a leaking pipe being fixed near the overhead tank. The water supply would get affected and resume only after 3 pm.

So far it had been a not-so-smooth day, and now Sumit had to store adequate water to avoid further complications. It irritated him somewhat. He had not been able to reach his mother's mobile since morning, nor had she called back; something which was quite unusual. *May be, she is busy with household chores* thought Sumit. So, he dialled his father's number. The line was disconnected from the other end just after three rings. "Now what?" Sumit said out loud as he stared at his phone, the irritation building up further. He felt a bit jittery, but in the next moment got busy with a call from a Placement Consultant. Because of his active job search routine, he often got calls from various head-hunters.

Around lunch time, Sunita called her brother to enquire if he had spoken to either Dad or Mom, as it had been a hectic first half for her and she hadn't even got a chance to steal a sip of her favourite coffee. The fact that none of them could reach their parents on the phone, created a bit of consternation.

While browsing the internet, Sumit wondered how to connect to his parents back home in Haldia. He thought of checking with Sudeep uncle who often visited his parents. But then if uncle was in office he wouldn't pick up the phone, as his company had barred the use of mobile phones during office hours. *Nothing wrong in trying whatsoever…*Sumit thought and reached out for his handset and dialled the number.

After almost two complete rings Sudeep picked up the call, and even before Sumit could say anything, he muttered quickly before disconnecting the call, "I am at your parents' flat…the police is here…will call you in ten minutes."

The next ten-fifteen minutes seemed like the longest hours Sumit had ever spent. Anxiety, curiosity, perturbation drove him crazy – *What could have gone wrong? Are Mom and Dad alright? Why were the police visiting? Did his parents get into a fight with someone? What did they do to invite the police? Who would complain against them, and why? What will happen now?* He almost trembled thinking up all kinds of crazy questions. He had to talk to his parents immediately. He wished he could reach out to them right this minute. While all these thoughts were running through his head, the laptop automatically went into hibernating mode due to battery drainage. Sumit didn't even bother to plug in the charger. He had bigger fish to fry now.

Mrs Ghosh finally called her son and narrated the horrific experience. It was like a cyclone which came without any warning and wiped out everything it could…

"Please don't panic, my son. Everything will be alright. We've done no wrong, so nobody can harm us." She sounded calm to Sumit, but he knew his mother was upset.

"But what is it all about, *Maa*?" He asked desperately.

"Nothing is clear yet, but it seems Moulina has filed a complaint against our family and the police has applied some IPC sections based on that. They even handed over a summon notice to us. All of us have to report at the Birmirpur PS by first week of August."

Sumit froze as he heard his mother's words. "What does the notice say?"

"Your Dad will mail it to you by this evening. Here, talk to him. It's late and I should go cook some lunch. Take care of Sunita." Chitra passed on the mobile phone to her husband.

"Don't worry *Babu*, I'll visit Advocate Sikdar to understand these IPCs and plan our next course of action. You stay calm and don't mention anything to your sister until she comes back home from the office." Mr Ghosh sounded a bit worried.

"I'll email you a scanned copy of the police notice by the evening. Just take note of the sections which are imposed on us and look up the internet for more information."

"Did they say or do anything else? *Baba*, please tell me. You are okay, right?" Sumit asked anxiously.

"They seized all your wife's belongings. Moulina anyway had all her stuff packed in a big red suitcase. We just handed it over to the Inspector. Her jewellery was in the locker. I handed it over to your in-laws, they checked and confirmed. The police have given us a *seizure list*. They were also asking for Moulina's academic certificates. But since they are with you, they've asked us to carry the same with us when we visit the police station next month." Sushil informed his son all in a single breath.

"Oh, so Mr and Mrs Chell accompanied the police? Was Moulina with them too?" Sumit's temper rose as he enquired.

"No, she didn't come. But she was clearly instructing her parents over the phone. Chell was telling our neighbours that his daughter had been living a life of hell all through these months and has now found solace back in her parental home."

"Anyway, we have almost twenty days. Let's see what can be done. We also need to know what the complaint is all about, you go and have your lunch. We shall connect on this in the evening." Sumit's father sounded a bit low, before disconnecting the call.

With much difficulty, Sumit calmed his nerves and addressed the questions in his mind – *How could Moulina do this to his family? Who gave her this heinous idea? His family had been nothing but nice to her, all these months. Mom and Dad loved her just as much as they loved Sunita. Never questioned her. Never confronted her…and this was how she is paying them back?*

He quickly dialled his sister to inform her that he just had a chat with both Mom and Dad. There was some network issue in Haldia, as a result neither of them could be reached earlier in the morning. For a while, he just sat with his head down resting on his folded hands over the table. He was clueless about what all had happened with his parents that morning. Had the police come to his flat here in Mumbai, not only would it have ruptured his image and reputation; but he was also sure, the owner would've asked him to vacate the flat immediately.

Needless to say, Sumit had lost his appetite. Around 2:30 pm, he turned on the gas-burner and started to boil some water in order to prepare a bowl of Maggi for himself. Simultaneously, he switched on his laptop after plugging in the battery charger. He spent the next forty-five minutes gathering information on the probable IPCs imposed on them. Though his father was going to send him the exact details by evening, he was running out of patience, thus unable to wait. He went through each and every detail of the sections thoroughly. Shock and confusion loomed over his head as he understood the false accusations it all implied. He just couldn't believe that an FIR had been registered with IPCs which just didn't hold any bearings with the truth – a sense of malaise prevailed.

Later in the evening around 6:00 pm, Sushil Ghosh visited Advocate Sikdar at his chamber.

Prabhat Sikdar was a known lawyer in the Haldia Township area. He had been practicing in the local court for the last fifteen years. He was a real estate expert and was associated with most of the Builders' community in and around Haldia. Though not an expert in family matters cases, Mr Ghosh visited him to gain a basic understanding of the laws and the probable steps they could take as a counter measure of the current situation.

A little above 5'5", half bald, stoutly built Sikdar appeared to be a lazy person. He went through the photocopy of the notice twice, removed his pair of glasses, wiped his eyebrows with his hands and took a pause before finally saying – "Ummm, it's a dowry case Mr Ghosh. It has been coupled with some more serious charges. But in the entire bouquet of charges applied, this 498A would hurt our case the most."

"No idea, Sir. We've absolutely no clue as to why these charges are being pressed on us..." Ghosh was visibly angry. He had spent the last few hours playing the events of the morning in his head over and over again.

"When did your son marry this girl, were there any kind of disputes between them? Or was there any sort of unrest between her and other family members?' Sikdar asked while reaching out for some hard-bound books from the shelf to his right.

"Sir, everything was absolutely fine. We treated her like our own daughter. The marriage happened in the middle of May 2012. For the last fifteen-sixteen months that she stayed with us, everything was normal. We had never even imagined these problems coming our way." Ghosh shuddered.

"Arranged marriage or love marriage? Do you've any grand children?"

"Arranged...we had placed an advertisement in *Anandabazar Patrika* and her family had contacted us. Things took off from there. And no, my son doesn't have a kid."

"Hmm...see Mr Ghosh, I don't know exactly what might have happened, but let me tell you... these days the number of fake cases registered by females have sky rocketed. Don't panic. You'll need to take proper legal advice from an expert criminal lawyer who has experience in dealing with this particular IPC 498A." Sikdar paused while flipping through a hardcover book titled *Criminal Manual: CrPC, IPC and Evidence.*

"But Sir, we've done nothing. We have never even dealt with police, judiciaries, etc." Ghosh sounded perplexed.

"Agreed, but now you've no option. Generally, the purpose of registering such fake cases are to extort money. In that case, the opposite party will approach you directly or indirectly and force you to go for an out-of-court settlement."

"But, Sir…"

"Treat this unfortunate incident as an accident, Mr Ghosh. It's like you were safely walking on the pavement and all of a sudden, a speeding vehicle takes a wrong turn, hits you and flees. What will you do? Struggle and stand up, see a doctor, recover from medical complications and then fight back to teach the offender a lesson."

"What do I do now?" asked Ghosh dolefully.

"Well, first try and get a copy of the FIR. I suggest that you catch hold of a local lawyer from Odisha. He will be able to do the needful. And yes, since it's a police case – never visit the police station without your lawyer, they can do anything. I mean anything…" Sikdar warned.

"What do you mean by *anything,* Sir?! Will they arrest us? But trust me, we are absolutely innocent." Ghosh was alarmed and almost in tears.

"Come on Mr Ghosh, please be strong – I know this is hard, but please gain control over all your emotions. Forget that the girl who has launched a fake complaint is your daughter-in-law. Forget that she is supposed to be the wife of your only son. You have to fight back now. Police isn't a trustworthy community. My suggestion is that you get yourself and your family protected in the form of Anticipatory Bail before visiting the police station." Sikdar tried to console Mr Ghosh.

"Sir, do you know any lawyer from Odisha, who can help us in this case?" Ghosh gained control over himself and asked.

"I am sorry Mr Ghosh, I've no acquaintances or associates outside Haldia. Although I know a few who practices in Calcutta High Court, but that won't help. Even if they agree to defend you, it'll be an expensive affair. So, I suggest you to get someone local."

"Hmm…got it. Thanks a lot for your valuable suggestions and advices. How much do I pay you as counselling fees, Sir?"

"Two-hundred-fifty…"

Baffled with the current happenings Sushil returned to his flat and called up his son to tell him what Advocate Sikdar had to say. He also asked Sumit to meet a specialized family court lawyer in Mumbai and get a second opinion. He then quickly disconnected the call, as he had to rush to the local police station to meet Inspector Mondal and seek guidance. Before visiting the Haldia Township PS, he emailed the scanned copy of the notice to Sumit.

The local police station was about fifteen minutes away from the Ghosh residence. It was 7:30 pm and Inspector Mondal was about to leave for the day but could see that the Ghosh couple was in distress and decided to meet them.

"Nandu, *teente cha bol…*" ordered Mondal to his subordinate.

"Sir, believe us, we are innocent, we aren't criminals, and we've done no wrong." Mrs Ghosh pleaded.

"Aunty, I am just doing my duty. Even I have no idea what went wrong. Last evening, I received a fax from Odisha police and the DSP asked me to accompany his team."

"But the Police madam must be annoyed with me, as I kept her waiting outside." Chitra referred to Shamita.

"No Aunty, I don't see anything wrong in your act. These days the burglars are breaking houses disguised in police uniform, so you had a point."

"Sir, you're of my son's age. We are ordinary citizens and have no idea about the legal complexities of the fake case registered against us. What do we do now?" Sushil wanted to come to the point.

"Uncle, the society is growing more and more complex day by day. Family matters are growing bitter. What I understand is that, you all are being framed in a false case and that all this is being done just to disturb you, harass you and defame you in the society. If you ask me why – the reason is simple, *money.* These cases have no future, it all ends in extortion and out-of-court settlement. Anyway, did the Odisha police call you before registering this FIR?" Mondal handed them their tea before asking.

"No Sir, we had no idea. They just arrived with a team this morning and that was the first time we heard anything."

"Hmm…but as per the guidelines specified by the Honourable Supreme Court, before registering any complain under 498A, the police should call both the parties and hear their points of view. It seems the girl's side is influential…else it's not easy for the police to come and serve notice to a party outside their jurisdiction. It takes a hell of a lot of time."

"What do we do now, Sir? We had never thought we'll have to see such days in our life." Chitra wished she could make Mondal understand her concerns. All these talks of defamation and settlements were new to her. She had only ever wished for her children to be happy.

"Aunty, let me tell you – personally I had gone through all this pain, five years back, when my elder brother's wife decided to walk out of all family ties. Thereafter, she demanded her share in our ancestral property. On being denied the same, she went ahead and launched a false case of domestic violence against my brother. I was then just a Havildar. The mess went on for 2 years, before she withdrew the case and settled for some lakhs of rupees. In the process, I lost my father, who suffered a stroke. So, believe me, I understand what you're going through." Mondal sounded emotional.

"I suggest you should start collecting all evidences to counter the allegations made in the FIR. Take a lawyer's help to get Anticipatory bail before you all give *hajira* at Birmirpur PS. Give Sumit my number. He can call me any time." Mondal suggested promptly.

THREE
2014

Mumbai, Maharashtra, India

Sunita generally returned home from office at around 7:30 pm everyday, but today was hectic. It had been raining for the past one hour and during the rains, it becomes extremely difficult to get a cab or autorickshaw from Sion to Tilaknagar. After getting rejected by four autos and a couple of cabs, eventually she managed to find an autorickshaw that agreed to take her. But her problems did not end there…after reaching her building, she found that the elevator wasn't working and had to climb up the six floors to their residence.

Usually whenever Sunita returned home from office, she rang up her mother and chitchatted with her, giving her an account of the day spent at the office. Today, however Sumit asked her to ring *Maa* a bit late as she planned to go out with *Baba* for some work. All this while, Sunita spotted a strange gloominess in her brother's body language – it was as if, he was hiding something from her.

"Hey *Dada*, is everything fine with you?" she enquired.

"Yeah, why what's wrong? You had a hectic day at the office, so now freshen up, I'll make some tea for you."

"*Dada*, today I was so busy, that for the entire day I couldn't speak to either *Maa* or *Baba*. Tried reaching *Maa* once during the lunch break, but there was no response. I hope you spoke to them," she said a bit concerned.

"Hmm…yes, I told you I did."

Sunita suffered from chronic migraine and it hit her so hard, that at times, the sleeping pills turn out to be ineffective. She often had to tie her head tightly with a scarf, to get rid of the hammering effect. Since stress and anxiety are some of the major triggers for her migraine, Sumit preferred to reveal all the incidents that had happened since morning, slowly, while she was more relaxed over her tea and snacks...

Sunita was shell shocked upon hearing the entire story that had conspired, from her brother. She appeared despondent and crestfallen. She was worried about

Baba's high blood pressure. Deep inside, she always felt that her sister-in-law was complicated and manipulative – but registering an FIR against the entire Ghosh family was completely unexpected. She was now desperate to talk to her parents. Who knew what they were going through? Had she been there in Haldia with them, things would've been different. Aged parents always find strength in their children and today her parents had to fight out all the odds themselves. As children, Sunita and Sumit were frustrated that they couldn't be with their parents.

"Do you have the copy of the notice, *Dada?*" Sunita asked.

"Yes, *Baba* e-mailed it to me. It says that an FIR has been lodged against all four of us."

"Forward the email to me, I'll print some copies from the office tomorrow. I think we should consult a few lawyers here in Mumbai. What do you suggest *Dada?*"

"Yes, even *Baba* asked me to do the same. He met Advocate Sikdar earlier today, but we should hear it from a lawyer specialised in these matters."

Sumit briefed his sister about what Sikdar had to say on the IPCs imposed and his suggestions to combat the current situation. He also shared a list of lawyers who practiced in Bandra family court, which he had already prepared from Google search.

"I see...So, your entire afternoon was spent glued to the internet, browsing all these...wasn't it?" Sunita suddenly got into the motherly mode and questioned her brother.

"Yes, I plan to call some of them tomorrow."

"And what did you have for lunch? Tell me you didn't skip it because of all this mess!"

"Hmm...I had Maggi. I should be fine." Food was the last thing on Sumit's mind. He felt overwhelmed with the recent set of events.

"Let me tell you one thing *Dada*, you can't win a battle on an empty stomach. So please, skipping meals isn't a solution."

"Will you shut up, now don't have to act like *Maa!*" Sumit smiled at his sister.

"Okay, I think I know a lady who practices in Bandra family court. She is our client. Let me confirm this with my colleagues tomorrow and then we can fix an appointment with her. What say?"

"Sounds good. We need to have an understanding of the legal remedies and avail them as soon as possible. *Maa* and *Baba* should be back home by now. You can call them if you want." Sumit glanced at the clock and then at his sister.

Earlier that evening, Sumit browsed through the internet to get an idea of the sections of IPC under which his family had been falsely accused. He also discovered an online forum, where all the victims accused of 498A had come together to share their experiences and provide guidance to each other. He came across a few NGOs who are fighting for the men's cause in the country. After going through a couple of posts on the forum page, he realised that he was in deep shit. The fight was not going to be easy. The proceedings and consequences would hit them hard from all squares – be it emotionally, mentally, or financially. Not knowing what to do, where to start and how to start, he quickly registered himself with the online forum and posted his story in brief, asking for guidance from other members.

It would be unfair not to mention here that luck favoured the Ghosh family even in this period of crisis, however small it may be. If luck hadn't been on their side, Mr and Mrs Ghosh could have been behind the bars by now based on the prima facie complaint. But thanks to their stars, only a month ago the Supreme Court had made some amendments in handling domestic cases and strictly instructed the police force not to arrest the accused immediately. Sumit's ears heated up and turned red due to anxiety. The idea of his parents facing a situation like that gave him goose bumps.

The next day, at around 11 am, Sumit met Advocate Mrinalini Shah at her Sion residence. Advocate Shah was a premium client of the bank where Sunita was employed. And one of Sunita's colleague was the Personal Banker for this lady lawyer. So, getting an appointment with her wasn't a problem, everything fell into place and she agreed to hear the case.

Sion suburban is a place with very few high-rises, and is characterized by buildings not more than four to five stories high, mostly without elevators. The address of the family court lawyer was easy to spot and it didn't take much time for Sumit to find out it's exact location – the 5th building behind the HP Petrol pump on TV Chidambaran Marg had a signboard in black and white '*Shah & Mehta Associates*'.

Mrinalini Shah was an average looking smart lady in her early forties, who loved to flaunt her beachy, mermaid wavy hairstyle. She had been practising law for the last sixteen years and specialized in matrimonial disputes, corporate law and cyber law. She made Sumit sit on a chocolate coloured Lawson sofa placed along the road facing corner of her plush living room. The entire room was well maintained with a couple of wall-mounted oil paintings of Buddha and Ganesha, except her working table which appeared scruffy with files, folders and a couple of reference books and magazines. Two bookshelves stuffed with various legal manuals, High Court journals, Cyber Law books, etc. stood tall behind her chair. The Dell laptop was shut down but plugged in to absorb charge.

"Okay Sumit, show me the papers you have." Mrinalini said as she placed her coffee on the side table next to her.

"Here it is ma'am – the copy of the Notice."

The solicitor puts on her reading glasses and glanced through the piece of paper twice before marking the IPCs with a highlighter "Hmm, a dowry case has been pressed against you and your family. Do you have any idea about these IPCs?"

"Yes ma'am, got a brief idea about all of it through Google." Sumit answered like a kindergarten kid.

For the next fifteen minutes, the lady explained each of those IPCs to Sumit, and the circumstances when they are applied and their implications in terms of punishments and/or fine. Her version sounded exactly the same as that of Advocate Sikdar's – almost like a repeat telecast. However, Sumit listened to her carefully, marking the important pointers mentally.

"Do you have pictures of you and your wife or your wife with any of your family members?" asked Advocate Shah.

"Yes ma'am, I have the wedding photos."

"No that's fine, but apart from that – any family get-together snap or any photo taken while you two went for an outing, that could be within or outside Mumbai? Anything? May be, a video taken?" probed Shah.

"Photo...I'm not so sure, but I must be having a video of her, where she was singing for a competition in Vashi," replied Sumit. He could still remember the day clearly. Moulina was so excited about the competition. Her mellifluous voice, like the sound of a windchime, would travel through the walls and curtains of their home on lazy Sundays. Sumit imagined that same voice instructing Mr Chell on the phone while he was at his parents' house the previous morning and he was jolted back to the present.

"Great, please retain the original format of those photos, videos, etc. You might need them later."

"But ma'am, why?"

"Well Sumit, I've not seen the copy of the FIR, so I am not in a position to comment. But my experience says that since it's a dowry case coupled with these IPCs; the female must have complained about how you all might have tortured her by keeping her in confinement and that's when you'll need these pieces of evidences to prove things otherwise."

"Got it ma'am. So, what should my next course of action be?" quizzed Sumit.

"Get a local lawyer and apply for Anticipatory Bail before you visit the police station and if possible, let the lawyer accompany you." Mrinalini took off her glasses, kept them on the table before taking a long pause and then continued "Please remember one thing, 498A is a game of patience, so don't panic. Be brave and handle situations tactfully."

"Can't anything be done from Mumbai?"

"First thing first, get a bail from lower court. If that is denied, you'll have to move things through High Court. Once that is done, we can think of filing Restitution of Conjugal Rights (RCR) from Mumbai. Your wife will have to travel all the way from Odisha for that," assured Ms Shah.

Now, RCR was something new which Sikdar never mentioned. Sumit noted it down carefully, as he had to gather more information about this. He thanked Advocate Shah, asked for her visiting card and paid an amout of Rupees two thousand towards counselling and consultation charges, before making his way out towards the staircase.

"Sumit, you can WhatsApp me the FIR copy later and also let me know in case you want to apply for an RCR – we'll have to make arrangements for the same." Mrinalini picked up her coffee again.

"Alright ma'am…" Sumit made his way out, thinking that meeting Advocate Shah was a good decision, after all.

FOUR
2014

Mumbai, Maharashtra, India

Back from Advocate Shah's chamber, Sumit felt restless. Turbulent thoughts flowed unstoppably through his head – *Why is all this happening to me? This is the absolute worst time for such matters to spring up without warning. The legal expenses would be humongous – hiring a lawyer, fighting the case, travelling all the way from Mumbai to Odisha, food and lodging. How am I going to manage all these? Dad has retired and I don't have a steady job. Currently the sole earner of the family is Sunita and that too with a meagre salary of an Assistant Manager, the lowest in the company hierarchy. What rotten times are these!*

Sumit's mobile phone rang. It was Sunita "How did the meeting go?"

"It was fine. She suggested almost the same stuff which Advocate Sikdar told Dad. Except for one thing – RCR, which can be filed here in Mumbai court."

"Okay *Dada*, listen…I know a cop who is station-in-charge of Ghatkopar's Pant Nagar *Thana*. Let's go and meet him today evening, what say?"

"Why Police? And, how do you know him?"

"Inspector Ranade's home loan is with our bank, he often visits our branch – that's how I know him; if you agree to meet him, I can call and fix up an appointment. We can meet directly at Ghatkopar. What do you say?" Sunita seemed quite eager to meet the Inspector.

"Ok, but is there any merit in meeting the Inspector?"

"*Dada*, as of now we are in a mishmash. We don't even know where to go, and what to do or for that matter, more importantly, what not to do. Our case also involves more than one jurisdiction. There's nothing wrong in meeting people and listening to their suggestions. Later on, we can compile them all and take a call."

"Hmm…you are right." Sumit finally agreed.

"And as an Inspector, he might have handled such disputes in his career. He can suggest a way forward to us. So, let's meet him, I'll let you know the time."

After ending the call Sumit pondered for a while and thought of his sister's suggestion. At times, his younger sister acted like his guardian, directing him to alternate options when he was clueless, and evoking his ideas when he went blank about something.

Sumit logged into his laptop and searched the internet for details on RCR. Legal terminologies were very specific and at times hard to decipher. Legal practitioners would never use the term 'Application' but refer to it as 'Petition'. He also checked his inbox and figured out that there were a few notifications from the Forum he joined, where he had posted his horrific account the previous night and asked for suggestions from the members. On clicking the link in the email, it redirected him to the forum's page – there were 8 responses to his query. Almost everybody unanimously suggested to quickly hire a local lawyer and file an application for Anticipatory Bail. It was good to see the virtual world coming together for a common cause to help out the men in distress.

Unaware of RCR, Sumit decided to seek opinion from the forum members to understand the pros and cons. However, with contrasting viewpoints from the members' post, he got further muddled.

Sumit's mental state was difficult to explain – just one question kept haunting him…*Why did Moulina do this to him?* A vortex of despondency, anguish, desperation mixed with determination, tenacity, unrelinquishing feeling stormed up in his head. While he was frustrated, feeble and debilitated with his ongoing situation, he was also adamant and unswerving to prove himself not guilty. He was not going to give up. In this maelstrom, he couldn't afford to be emotional, though every corner of his house had some form of his wife's reminiscence or the other. But how could he possibly forgive her in the given situation! Whenever emotions tried to overpower him with those precious moments he had spent with his wife – the very thought of what would've happened if the police handcuffed his parents and took them into custody nullified it all, making him more obstinate, perseverant and determined.

Sunita's call interrupted the flow of his thought. *"Dada*, you've got to reach Pant Nagar Police station by 5:30 pm, I've already given a brief background of the incident to Inspector Ranade."

"Ok, I'll be there."

Sumit ended the call and fiddled with his mobile's contact list for a while and after much deliberation dialled Anup Bose. The phone was disconnected from the other end after three rings and then came a message instantly *"In a meeting, will call u in the evening."*

Sumit and Anup were tight friends since their MBA days in Rourkela Institute of Management Studies (RIMS). While the former stayed in the hostel, the latter was a localite from the railway colony of Rourkela. On weekdays both used to roam around the steel city on Anup's bike and often on weekends after a game of cricket, Anup would stay back at Sumit's hostel room. Besides both being Bengalis, their love for music was also another bonding factor – generally they would end up jamming in the hostel room. Sumit cooked awesome Bengali style chicken curry and other hostel mates along with Anup used to relish the smell and taste of his preparation. College life was funfilled until both friends had to leave for Gurgaon and Kolkata respectively for their first jobs through campus placement, way back in 2004.

After spending almost fifteen months with the first company in Gurgaon, Sumit shifted to Mumbai in 2005 for a better opportunity. And almost around the same time, Anup too quit his job in Kolkata and shifted to Mumbai without any job in hand. He struggled for a couple of months in Mumbai appearing for interviews, braving the overcrowded Virar local, surviving on *vada-pav* and *cutting chai* breakfast. Eventually when he cracked the final interview of a private insurance firm as a Business Development Manager, the HR Head wanted to connect with a couple of senior references from his previous employer as a protocol for the candidate's background verification. That day Anup was almost jacked, but his college buddy Sumit, who was then almost 6 months old in Mumbai came to his rescue. They took a chance – Anup passed on Sumit's number to his HR, stating that it was his team lead's contact. However, the verification call never came, and Anup successfully bagged the job. While Anup used to stay in a PG accommodation in Goregaon East, Sumit used to stay in Byculla's Sussex Road area in a rented studio apartment. They used to meet over weekends, often Anup used to either get chicken or fish from Goregaon market, carry it all the way to Byculla and then get it cooked by Sumit. Bachelor life had its own charms and excitement.

And then in July 2006, the unfortunate incident of serial bomb blast shook the entire city of Mumbai. Seven explosions took place over a period of eleven minutes on the suburban railway, killing 209 and injuring over 700 people. That's when Anup's petrified mother became hysterical about Mumbai being her son's job location and asked him to immediately resign and head back to Rourkela. Though Anup was getting into the rhythm of the city, he couldn't disregard his mother who suffered from hyper tension and nervous breakdown.

After returning from Mumbai, he helped his father in their family business for a while before taking up a job with the Toyota Showroom in Rourkela. Today Anup Bose was the regional sales head of Toyota Motors, looking after the western part of Odisha and operated out of his Rourkela office cum showroom. Three years back, he got married to his childhood sweetheart, a Bengali girl from his neighbouring colony and they were now well settled in life.

Sumit tried connecting with his old friend in anticipation of getting some expert lawyers' contacts from Rourkela.

Outside, it was mizzling steadily. Somehow Sumit managed to get an auto and head towards Pant Nagar Police station, while Sunita left office early for the meeting. The police station entrance was crowded, partly due to passers-by seeking shelter from the ongoing continuous drizzles. Inside, the cabin on the right-hand side, had a brass nameplate '*Raghav Ranade, Sr. Police Inspector*' and had a Havildar stationed outside the smudged glass door.

"*Namaste* Sunita *ji*, how are you?" the six feet tall, strongly built cop greeted Sumit's sister.

"Good evening Sir, I am fine, how about you? I don't see you visit our branch anymore these days." Sunita replied with a smile.

"Oh yes, I was on leave, and then was unwell. Had to visit my native place in Sholapur."

"Sir, meet my brother Sumit. I told you about why we wanted to meet you, right? Please let us know, how we should proceed from here." Sunita put forward her query without wasting any time.

"Hmm…see Mr Sumit, honestly speaking, these domestic cases have now become a regular affair and I regret that this has happened with you too. Its worse that the entire family is dragged into this dirt. Let me tell you something – forget that the girl is your wife and never ever think that she is going to come back. What I'm trying to tell you is that you should wipe out all the emotions attached with her while dealing with this case."

"Sir, this is the Police notice which was served to my parents two days back." Sumit didn't feel like discussing his feelings. He interrupted Ranade and forwarded the photocopy.

"Ok, did the police call you before registering this complain?" enquired the Senior Inspector.

"No Sir, they marched straight into our home in Haldia."

"This is the problem. Honourable Supreme Court has spelled out clear guidelines to the police stations handling these cases, but unfortunately they aren't followed in reality."

"Anyway, most of these cases don't have any future and die their natural death in the form of out-of-court settlement. As per my experience, nearly 95% of these cases are to extort money from the husband and his family. This is a complete mind game and a test of patience. Since money is the main motive, nobody in this world would like to hold up in procuring it. So, use delaying tactics and frustrate the girl."

"But Sir, we've done no wrong," pleaded Sumit.

"*Haan*…so then why worry? The onus is on them to prove whatever they've mentioned in their complaint and that'll only happen during the trails. Till then you keep delaying things and start collecting evidences to counter their claims."

"But Sir, is there a possibility for Odisha police to visit our Mumbai residence too, the same way they had gone to my parents' place at Haldia with a team?"

"*Naah*, it's not that easy to get through Mumbai police in these cases, unless they've maintained strict guidelines and protocols. Here, they've already jumped Supreme Court's order and visited your parents."

"So, Sir…" Sumit was about to ask something, but was interrupted by Ranade.

"Let the police file a Chargesheet, then ask your advocate to play those delaying tactics and frustrate the girl. Once they are harassed by virtue of frustration, they will approach you for mutual settlement and then you'll have an upper hand in this case. Till then just relax and lead a normal life." Ranade finished off these lines in a hurry and said, "Ok, I've to make a move now, there's a suicide case which needs my intervention."

Sumit and Sunita thanked the senior police officer and left the police station.

✣ ✣ ✣

The cops and the lawyers talk of these cases with such ease that it seems as if nothing has happened and it's quite natural. But for a layperson who has never dealt with police or judiciary, its hell. FIR, Anticipatory Bail, investigation, chargesheet, summons, trials, court hearing, etc. made Sumit feel dejected and miserable. But one thing emerged quite evidently from these interactions – Patience is the key to success.

Every 498A case is unique and should be dealt with utmost care. Strategy should be chalked out by studying the opposition's movements. Indian judiciary acts funny – while it opposes dowry, simultaneously it also instructs and fixes alimony – so isn't that technically a reverse dowry?

It takes less than a dollar to file a false case under 498A for a female, just by mentioning some keywords in the complaint like – dowry, domestic violence, physical and mental torture. Whereas it takes thousands of dollars and n number of years for the man to prove himself innocent. In the process, he loses his job, his precious time, his reputation, his status and what not; whereas the girl gets sympathy from the society.

It becomes difficult for the man to accept that the woman with whom he dreamt of building a family, shared his sorrows and happiness, and even his bed, is now the cause of his family's distress. Eventually he has to forget everything and fight for his prestige, glory and stature. However, in spite of it all, even now, men are considered guilty unless proven innocent by the society, and the burden of procuring proof lies on them, not the accuser. The battle is complex, emotional and time consuming.

At around 8 pm, Anup called back "Sorry *yaar*, was in a review meeting, hence couldn't take your call and, thought of chatting with you once I got back home. So? Tell me how is life in Mumbai? What made you call me after such a long time?"

"Well Anup, quickly need your help *yaar*. It's super urgent!" Sumit answered.

"Okay Boss, as you command – but tell me, is everything fine?" Anup was curious.

Initially, Sumit was hesitant about revealing all the details. In fact, nobody likes to go about discussing the nitty gritty details with everyone in these kinds of situations. But then he had no option, so finally had to briefly narrate to his friend about the unfortunate incident and how he was grappling to get a proficient lawyer who could help him out in these difficult times.

Anup thought for a while and then replied "I know someone who had handled some legal matter for our office accounting fraud in the past. But I won't be knowing his area of specialisation and whether or not he can take up these kinds of matrimonial disputes. Nonetheless, you can always talk to him with my reference. If not him, I am sure he can refer someone from his fraternity." Anup sounded a bit concerned about his friend.

"Ya, even that'll do, currently I have nobody from Rourkela to approach for this mess." Sumit sounded a bit relieved.

"Okay, I am messaging Advocate Basant Panigrahi's number to you. Call him in half an hour and check with him. In the meantime, I'll call and brief him about your situation."

"Sounds good. Thanks, *yaar*!"

"Take care, Sumit. Call me whenever." Anup ended the call.

Sumit didn't want to waste any time. He has just twelve days in hand to get Anticipatory Bail from the session court and then appear before the IO. God knows where it would lead him next. At around 9 pm, he called up the mobile number forwarded by his friend. While he tried the number, Sunita stood anxiously behind him. The phone kept on ringing but nobody attended the call.

Five minutes later, he dialled the number again, this time the number appeared to be busy on another call. Sumit ran his hand through his hair in frustration.

Around 9:15 pm, his phone rang…

"Sorry Sumit *Babu*, I was on another call with my client." Advocate Panigrahi's raucous and thick voice sounded apologetic. "Your friend Anup did tell me about your case. It would be great if you can quickly tell me what has happened and what all documents you have." The lawyer went straight to the point.

Sumit narrated the entire incident – by now it was like reciting a fifth standard poem, which one mugged up before the oral examination. The lawyer listened carefully, asked a few questions to clarify his doubts and finally asked Sumit to WhatsApp the Police notice.

"Sir, will you take up this case? I mean, do you deal with matrimonial cases?" Sumit asked diffidently, as he was sceptical.

"Sumit *Babu*, I am a criminal lawyer and have dealt with these cases in the past, so you just relax and let me take over this case. First I'll go through the notice, then on the basis the FIR number, I'll have to pull out a copy of the complaint and finally file a petition for Anticipatory Bail on your behalf – your job will be done, you don't have to worry." Panigrahi assured.

"Sir, are you sure the court will issue us Anticipatory Bail?" Sumit was still not convinced.

"I am 99% sure it'll be done. Even if they object, you don't have to worry, we'll get it done from the High Court." Panigrahi reassured.

"Sir, we have to apply for the bail quickly, as we have only ten-twelve days in hand. And Sir, for the filing, do I've to be present there physically?" Sumit wanted to know every detail.

"Sumit *Babu*, ideally your presence is required but we'll manage. You have to provide me with a scanned copy of the full signature of your family members, along with scanned copies of everybody's voter identity card. Without these I won't be able to initiate the process."

"Sir, I request you to start drafting the petition. By tomorrow morning all these will reach your inbox. And Sir, please don't mind if I ask you silly questions – we've never dealt with the judiciary in the past, so I have literally no clue about the procedures."

"No problem at all – first you have to sign a *Vakalatnama*, then I'll draft the petition and file the same for a court hearing and you all will be issued Anticipatory Bail, that's the process flow." Explained Panigrahi.

"What's *Vakalatnama*, Sir and how do I sign it?" Sumit sounded perplexed.

"Well, it's a document where you give me permission to fight your case in the court. Something similar to Power of Attorney. My juniors will replicate all of your signatures and that's why I need those scanned copies." Panigrahi explained calmly.

"See, Sumit *Babu*, I shouldn't say this – it's like blowing one's own trumpet, but then, since we have not met and you know nothing about me, let me give a brief background of my professional career...I've been practicing criminal law in Rourkela session court for the past twenty years. I am also associated with some of the renowned High Court lawyers in Cuttack. My father retired as an SP of Western Range of Orissa Police and my wife is a Senior Inspector at Uditnagar PS, due for her promotion as Assistant DSP. So, you can imagine the kind of connections I have in Rourkela. I am sure my wife will also know the officers of Birmirpur PS, where your case has been registered. That's why I am asking you to simply relax and let me do my job. I'll get your bail easily and then let's see how quickly we can wrap this up. I must say, you're lucky enough to get me on-board for your case. I've won criminal cases with negligibly less evidences. These family court matters are just nothing. You simply don't need to worry."

Sumit was listening to Panigrahi all this while and then took a deep breath and felt a sense of hypnotic relaxation within. He was convinced that all his worries were going to end soon, someone in the form of a Messiah would surely surface and be his family's saviour.

Shaking himself out of his reverie, he asked the advocate "Sir, I am confident that you'll be able to get us out of this entwined situation. Now, can you please let me know your fees?"

"Sumit *Babu*, I plan to file three petitions – first one for your sister and mother, second one for your father and finally yours. Generally, in these cases the husband remains the prime accused and we have to shuffle the petition along with others in different time periods. These are all lawyers' tactics to ensure that all the accused members get bail."

"Sir, the case is now all yours – do whatever deems fit. Please let me know the fees and the procedure to make the payment." Sumit sounded a bit relaxed.

"Per petition, I generally charge INR 15,000. Since you're a friend of my client, the entire Anticipatory Bail petition for your family will cost you INR 40,000. Pay me fifteen grands now as an advance, the balance you can pay me later after getting the bail. I'll message you my HDFC bank details, you can do an NEFT."

"Okay Sir, but I request you to please start drafting the petition tonight itself, so that we are on time. I'll add your details as a beneficiary to my account and once the bank accepts and confirms it, I'll transfer the amount, which will probably feature only by morning. So, by tomorrow morning, you'll get both, the scanned document as well as your advance," assured Sumit.

"Another important thing Sumit *Babu* – preferably avoid calling me in the morning hours of a weekday, as I generally remain busy in the court. Incase of any urgency, you can either text me or WhatsApp me. Evenings, post 7:30 are the best time for a call," clarified Panigrahi.

"Sure Sir, noted."

FIVE
2011

Birmirpur, Odisha, India

It was celebration time for the Chells of Birmirpur, not that there was only one family with such a surname but it was just the way Sanat thought about his kinship. His elder son, Lokesh had bagged a new job in Faridabad and before joining office, he was there for a brief visit to his native place. The new company has given him a good hike and was also a good brand in the KPO sector.

Lokesh was always a careerist. After his B. Com, he started looking out for a job. But Birmirpur was not where he had dreamt of initiating his professional life, nor did he want to stay back. The family business was slowly declining then and he didn't want to risk his future. Instead, he appeared for various interviews in the adjoining cities of Bhubaneswar, Ranchi, Jamshedpur and even Kolkata. His mother never wanted him to move out of Birmirpur; her concerns were another story altogether…

It all happened when Lokesh was in fifth grade at St. Martha's Convent School, Birmirpur and was representing his class in an inter-school cricket tournament. He had always been passionate about cricket. But that afternoon, a speeding ball hit his right eye, leaving him with a drooping eyelid for rest of his life. After moving to NCR, his ptosis treatment was being done at AIIMS. He got it operated once, but the nerves failed to respond and his right eyelid still sat awkwardly above his swollen cheek, as if melting down from where it was supposed to be.

Lokesh visited Birmirpur approximately once in every eighteen months. Each time, he would carry little gifts for all his siblings and cousins. This time around, he brought a yellow coloured handbag, an umbrella and a wallet for his *Didi*, younger sister and younger brother respectively. And some chocolates for his cousins.

As soon as he entered his house, Lokesh looked around for his mother. While he maintained a formal relationship with his father, he was very close to Maya. He hugged her and secretly handed her some cash from his savings.

"*Dada*, which all movies do you have on your laptop?" Lina asked Lokesh in excitement. This was the only time of the year when she got to lay her hands on a laptop.

"Check that *My Movies* folder on the desktop. I have some of the latest Hindi and English movies for you guys," replied Lokesh while twiddling with his phone.

Lalit, who was busy with his new gift from Lokesh, snatched the laptop from his sister to figure out which latest Hindi movie his elder brother had downloaded. Lina started wailing and protesting like a kid, *"Dada,* this isn't fair!! *Bhai* has now taken control over your laptop. Please ask him to return it to me, else I'll complain about it to *Baba."*

"Lalit, what's this? Bring the laptop to me, I'll put on a movie and then you two can sit and watch it. You both only have time until *Di* comes in. Then we will all have lunch together."

"*Di* is on her way, will take another half an hour," replied Lalit obediently.

Some of the 2011 Bollywood hits were already loaded in his laptop, of which Lokesh played *'7 Khoon Maaf'.* Lina would've liked to watch *'No One Killed Jessica'* while Lalit preferred *'Delhi Belly',* however, both agreed to watch these along with their *Di* later in the evening.

Summers in Birmirpur are always extreme and atrocious with an average temperature of 45° C plus. Every year, the government declared early morning sessions for schools, colleges, and administrative works; so that by noon everyone could head back to the comfort of their homes and avoid the extreme heat waves. March, April and May are the unbearable summer months in these parts of Odisha.

Moulina never liked the summers. It was mid-April and her day started as early as 4 am. It took roughly 70 minutes for the local bus to reach Rourkela from Birmirpur. By chance, if she missed the 5 am bus, she would get late by almost half an hour, which she couldn't afford, as the first session in Rourkela Municipal College was allotted to her.

Eleven months back, due to recommendation from her father's friend, she had bagged this job of a part time lecturer. It was a huge pain for her to travel back and forth everyday and deliver lectures to the students of Classes IX, X and XI; but there were no other alternatives. With M.A. in English as her qualification and no prior work experience, this was the best she could possibly get in the Rourkela area. End of a normal month would fetch her a pay cheque of a meagre eight thousand rupees, whereas during exam seasons she would earn two thousand extra.

Though morning bus rides were smooth and less troublesome, the return journey to Birmirpur during the afternoon hours was equally vexatious and tiresome – overcrowded bus, slow-moving traffic at Vedvyas junction, irritating passengers made her impatient and infuriated. At times, she felt like ditching these daily struggles and getting married to a well settled guy in some metro city. She was fed up with this slow moving semi-urban life.

Today, Moulina's bus tyre got punctured. At 2:30 pm, the heat waves outside were so extreme that any living being could get dehydrated in no time. The dry hot air created a burning sensation on the skin. It was one of those mad afternoons when Moulina felt disgusted with everything. When she finally entered her room, she found her siblings gathered around Lokesh's laptop enjoying a movie indoors. It irked her even more to see them comfortable indoors while she was sweating outside, doing her day's job.

"Why is the cooler throwing hot air?" snapped Moulina. "Isn't there anybody around to pour even a single bucket of water into the cooler? Everyone is so engrossed in movies, am I the only stupid one to go out and work for this family?"

"*Di*, we all were waiting for you only." Lokesh politely uttered those words before hitting the pause button of his laptop. "Lina, go and get a glass of water and some Frooti for *Di*, please."

Lalit quietly slipped out of the room to fill the Cooler.

"What's this? You all have messed up my room. Look at the bed-sheet, why is that magazine lying below the table?" yelled Moulina again.

"*Di*, just relax, we will re-arrange your room as it was. Now quickly freshen up, let's have lunch together." persuaded Lokesh.

Sensing that she might have tyrannized her siblings with her tantrums, Moulina calmed down a bit and asked her brother, "When are you leaving for Faridabad, Lokesh?"

"*Di*, we'll talk about it later, I have one full week to chew your brains!" guffawed Lokesh.

The Chells were three generations old in this small town of Birmirpur. Almost five decades back, Deepten Chell left his village in Bankura, a district of West Bengal, for Birmirpur, in search of work. Back then, Birmirpur was known for its mining industries and sponge iron factories. The vicintiy had some of the largest limestone and dolomite quarry of the state.

After some initial nugatory jobs in the mines, Deepten thought of getting into business, as those petty jobs would never earn him a fortune. He had basic business acumen and in no time gauged the market need. With factory workers flocking in from the neighbouring states of West Bengal and Bihar (now section of Jharkhand), there was an acute need of fresh water fish to supplement a fishetarian's daily meal. Deepten started a shop at the *Chowk-Bazaar* and sold *Rohu, Katla, Bhetki, Magur, Chingri*, etc. which were being supplied by the local *adivasis* from their daily catch from the nearby Ludki River. From selling fish he ventured into supplying fish and then later entered into the transport business.

Everything fell in place for Deepten; luck was on his side. He had to trade off some of his ancestral farm land in order to finance his first mini-truck for the transport business. This time around, he felt the need of a reliable business partner, with whom he could scale new heights. At this juncture, Rathin Burman came in as a blessing. He was Deepten's neighbour in Bankura and also a sworn brother. Being inspired by Deepten, Rathin left his village to assist his 'elder brother' in his newly setup transport business.

Though the surnames Chell and Burman were considered as lower caste in their village, Chell was higher up in the caste hierarchy than Burman. This played a role in Rathin being inspired by Deepten.

Business for the 'brothers' went on smoothly and steadily. It was during this time that Rathin decided to change his surname from Burman to Chell – an act which would prove his loyalty towards his 'elder brother' and a chance to climb up the caste ladder and pose equality. The move was strategic, which Deepten as a down-to-earth man never bothered to ponder over.

Due to high concentration of mining works, both the 'brothers' realised that transportation business can further be diversified into the crusher business, where they could undertake the crushing operations as a third party contractor. Both the Chells channelized their contacts to bag contracts from BSL Mines. The Bisra Stone Lime Co Ltd., commonly known as BSL was a PSU under the Ministry of Steel. It was a profit making unit then and distributed contracts amongst the localite for crushing and mining jobs. It was a win-win situation for both the parties.

Once the 'Chell brothers' started minting money from the crusher business, there was no looking back. Both the brothers got married and started their family. Deepten birthed four daughters and one son, while Rathin had one daughter and four sons. The families were close to each other and were doing well. And to cement it further, Rathin took another strategic step to strengthen the family ties – he put forward the marriage proposal of his elder son with Deepten's elder daughter. An affable, amiable Deepten was ecstatic and elated with the proposal. That's how Sanat and Maya Chell got married. However, the same proposal was again put forward by Rathin for his second son's marriage with Deepten's second daughter after a couple of years – to which Deepten complied too.

After getting all of his four daughters married, Deepten breathed his last, leaving his only son without a business portfolio. Deepten's wife also passed away after fifteen months of her husband's death. Eventually, leaving Rathin as the sole beneficiary. Finally, all his strategies paid off. He mourned his dear 'brother's' demise, but had his eye on the future of his kinship. Rathin slowly started building *The Chell* family. His sole focus was on the crusher business and he deployed all his four sons into it.

Rathin wanted all his sons to stay together, united in the business. He had bought an acre of land and constructed a large two storied house with provisions made for the extended family. The Chell house stood tall, bang opposite to the Birmirpur Railway station. It had a pond in the backyard, surrounded by banana plantation, Palmyra palm and some bushy trees.

Sanat was cunning and conniving – the only characteristics he inherited from his father, Rathin. While all his brothers Sarat, Partha and Palash believed in harmony and hard work, Sanat was always devious and scheming. Being the eldest, he had always been an authoritarian and believed in the fact that his younger siblings were meant to obey him irrespective of their opinions on any matter. Sanat's adamant, oppressive, despotic nature didn't go well with his brothers and their wives and finally they parted ways in business. While all three brothers jointly continued to manage the crusher business, Sanat was left out.

The Chell family grew gradually. The large house was all chirpy and eventful, it was like a picnic spot every day. With nine grandchildren around, Rathin Chell felt like a *Santa Claus*. He was aging gracefully and was proud to be the fulcrum of a growing family, but was unaware of the little cranny that had developed amongst his sons.

All the brothers, except Sanat wanted to move out of Birmirpur and settle in Rourkela – citing their children's education and better future. Birmirpur had limited options to offer, whereas the steel city had reputed educational institutes, along with a good number of hobby classes. Rathin tried every emotional trick possible to hold back his sons, but the brothers had already made up their minds.

Though kids' education was just one of the reasons, the reality was that Rathin's *daughters-in-law* were all claustrophobic to Birmirpur's environment. The semi-urban town didn't have a basic lifestyle – there was nothing to do on weekends. The days were spent locked within the four walls of the Chell mansion. There wasn't any shopping mall, nor a theatre or even a decent eatery to go out to for a family dinner. If they could afford it all, why remain deprived of these pleasures? Another major reason was, of course, Sanat Chell. His bullying nature didn't go well with the brothers and their wives. Sarat, Partha and Palash took up an entire three storied building on rent at Rourkela's Civil Township, each floor being occupied by a brother and his respective family separately.

With this shift, the families started enjoying late night movies, kitty parties, more socialization, pizza parties at home, weekend shopping and what not. They all felt a sense of freedom in their new residence. Once in a fortnight, one of the brothers would visit Birmirpur with his wife and kids. Eventually a nineteen-member family at Birmirpur, shrunk to just eight members.

On the contrary, Sanat was of the opinion that it was wiser to remain close to his father because it would make him appear as the most trustworthy, reliable, responsible son as compared to the younger ones.

SIX
2011

Birmirpur, Odisha, India

"Today at *Rawdon Bengali Association*, Mrs Mullick was asking me about our Moulina's whereabouts. I had once asked her to search for a suitable groom for our girl. It seems she has some lead, as most of her relatives now reside in Bangalore." Maya informed her husband while handing over a cup of evening tea.

"Why do you have to even ask for help from people in Birmirpur? Didn't I tell you before that people over here are envious, they cannot see others happy?" an irritated Sanat responded.

"Moulina is thirty now! Exactly how much longer are we going to wait? Unless we start looking out for prospective grooms, do you expect them to surface out from the middle of nowhere?" revolted Maya.

"Maya, just leave this task to me. I am trying my best and will surely do something by this year end. Didn't we try our luck with Dr Sanyal from Kolkata?"

'Year-end, huh!! And on the other hand, if everything goes fine, your niece will get married in a couple of months, at the age of twenty-eight. Do you have any knowledge of that at all?"

"I am aware of it, but I don't want my daughter to get married to a *school teacher*. I want her to have a secured future. Our Mouli will get married to some MNC Executive who draws a six-figure salary every month and has a stable job. I'll find her a boy, it's my promise."

"Do whatever you want, you've never listened to any of us anyway...Your brothers left you alone here in Birmirpur because of your mulishness," grudged Maya.

A visibly vexed Sanat left his unfinished cup of tea and reached out for his mobile phone to call *Pandit ji*, his trusted astrologer from his native village in Bankura...

"*Pandit ji, Namaskar* – when will the *Kundali* and *janam-patrika* be ready? It's been a while since I asked you for it. These days without a matching *Kundali*, it's extremely difficult to initiate talks."

"*Namaskar Beta!* Give me a couple of days more. By the end of this week, Moulina's *perfect Kundali* will be ready. It is a big responsibility. I have to be very careful with those two dates, which you've given me. That is why this is taking time."

"Okay, you get this week to finish it off, but not a single day extra – I'll personally come and collect it from you. I also need to consult you on two more things…about Moulina's post-marriage life and my future business prospects. Things aren't going my way in the business."

"*Beta*, let me inform you something about your daughter's original *Kundali*. There's one *Kundali Dosh*, for which she is unable to get a suitable boy. She'll have to give up non-veg and convert into a complete vegetarian. Certain *Pujas* need to be performed until her engagement is finalised," warned *Pandit ji*.

Being the first girl child of the Chell family, Moulina had always been very special to her father. Sanat had been a protective father all through her teenage years. He was aware of the fact that his daughter might get distracted during her growing years and hence kept a close vigil on her during her college days. His beautiful petite daughter got all the attention from boys of her age and Sanat wasn't comfortable with it. He drew some strict lines for Moulina, which she wasn't allowed to violate – *no boyfriends, no affairs.*

Being an overprotective father, Sanat always accompanied his daughter to her college and tuition classes. He always made it a point to drop and pick up his daughter from college. He kept all details of her college friends. Moulina never got to own a mobile phone, because her father felt that mobile phones were the means to keep in touch with *male* friends. Instead, she had to share her father's mobile number, in case any of her friends wished to get in touch with her. Sanat was even against his daughter sporting any western wear or jeans. Moulina had never tried a denim outfit because her father felt it to be an obscene garment. There had been enough instances where Sanat had proved beyond doubt that he had overdone his protective stance towards his daughter…

Once, Moulina missed the college bus and was seen talking to a guy at the bus-stop. This was reported to Sanat by one of his *informers*. The very next moment, Sanat came on his bike, asked Moulina to ride pillion and without uttering a single word, took her home and caned her black n blue. She didn't even get a chance to speak her piece. Sanat had his own set of *informers* in the form of shopkeepers, watchmen and other petty workers; who silently kept an eye on his daughter for him.

In another such incident, one college guy had passed on a note with an *"I Love You"* message to Moulina, which Sanat later found in her closet. The very next day the boy was beaten up like a dog by a gang of *adivasis*, sponsored by Sanat.

Sanat never wanted his daughter to master the internet, as he was of the opinion that dating sites and chatrooms could be the major distractors. Among Moulina's friend circle, Sanat was popularly known as her *Bodyguard* rather than her father.

Since childhood, Moulina was an adorable kid, whose innocence and pristine look made everyone go *Awwww…how cute!!* Almost everyone would pinch her chubby cheeks affectionately and make them go apple-red. Unlike her father, who had a pitch-black complexion, Moulina inherited her mother's pale yellow skin colour, flawless and smooth. She grew up to become a 5'6", fair skinned, attractive girl, who would never go unnoticed. Her smooth, silky, straight hair, mellifluously soothing voice and alluring candy-pink lips had some secret admirers in her college.

Sanat never wanted his daughter to settle down with any *Tom-Dick-Harry* by indulging into a college love-affair and hence was cautious. Everybody in Birmirpur, was well aware of Sanat's rogue behaviour towards anybody who could be a possible threat to his daughter. Somewhere within this protective shell of her father, Moulina had mixed emotions – at times she felt that she has been brought up under some *Talibani fatwa*. While her cousins led a liberal life in the neighbouring city area, her father chose to stay back in a semi-urban area with a forlorn, backward lifestyle. She tried complaining about it to her father, but somehow Sanat emotionally manipulated his daughter and kept assuring her that she could have her life in her own hands once she got married.

Every father-daughter quarrel eventually ended up in Sanat treating Moulina to *phuchkas*, which she loved a lot. All through, she had always been her *Daddy's blue-eyed girl*. Sanat also was partial in treating his other sons and daughter. Among her other siblings, Moulina was made to believe that she was probably the *only* daughter of Sanat and used to get a queen-like treatment. In the process, Moulina grew up with the mis-conception that her siblings were meant to obey her and give into her totalitarian dominance. Sanat often told her, he saw himself in her; that he was exactly like her when he was her age. Moulina felt obligated to obey and respect her father every time she heard this.

⁜ ⁜ ⁜

"Baba, I've kept this month's pay-cheque on your table. Please deposit it to the bank accordingly." Moulina informed her father one morning.

"Did you get paid for those extra exam hours this month?" enquired Sanat.

"Yes *Baba*. By the way, Lina wants a mobile phone. Please withdraw some cash for it. We'll go and buy it from Rourkela when we visit uncle's house next week."

"Why!! What will Lina do with a mobile phone? I told her that she'll not get a phone till she graduates. Do you want to spoil your sister?" an infuriated Sanat replied.

"*Baba,* why don't you keep those orthodox approaches towards life to yourself? Today everybody has a mobile phone, it's a necessity. The bus-driver, watchman, *pan-walla*, every bloody guy has a mobile phone these days and it's only you who feels that mobile phone will spoil our career! How illogical and ridiculous is that?" Moulina blasted.

"You never allowed me to get a mobile phone in my college, when everybody in my class had one. Had I still been financially dependent on you, I would've had to beg you for a phone." Gauging his daughter's aggravated mood, Sanat responded, "You will realise this only when you become a parent. Do whatever you want for your sister."

Almost after half an hour, when the dust settled, Lina quietly entered her *Di's* room...

Even though Moulina bullied her little sister, the girls shared a strong bond. For Lina, her elder sister was a stubborn, short tempered, Daddy's girl; for whom *Baba* was the only one who mattered, even if the truth was that he was a strict conformist and bourgeois person. Their *Baba's* conservative, unprogressive approach was imposed on them since childhood, which is why all four of them were less confident, and unsmart as compared to their cousins. Their younger cousins owned the latest smart phones, whereas her *Di* only had a Nokia feature phone.

"*Di,* you didn't have to fight with *Baba* for my mobile phone. We know how hidebound he is."

"Which is what I dislike. He should realise that this world is changing fast and he can't just hold on to his old school thoughts. Why isn't the restriction same for Lokesh? In fact, *Baba* himself had gifted *bhai* a mobile phone on his first job!" argued Moulina.

"Forget it *Di*, mobile phone isn't a priority for me. I can manage without it. Instead, please buy me some cosmetics and accessories. I've listed them all. Coming week when we visit Rourkela, let's go shopping." Lina sounded ebullient and happy.

"If you're sure, okay."

"*Achha Di*, why don't you open your own bank account and save your hard-earned money? Why do you have to hand-over the entire sum to *Baba*?" Lina had wanted to ask her this for a long time.

"Why? What's wrong in it, Li?"

"I hope you're aware that since last six months, *Baba's* business is down with almost no income. He uses majority of your funds in running this family."

"Yes, I know that the BSL Company has shutdown a few of its mining units and that has badly affected *Baba's* business. His brothers have maintained silence as well as distance on this, and aren't willing to help him recover from this slump. Which is why, it is my duty to contribute in whatever way I can in such times."

"Agreed *Di*, but you should also have some savings for your wedding. Last year a huge amount was spent on *Maa's* fibroids operation and that has dried down all of *Baba's* savings. Today, when there's a financial crisis, none of our uncles nor our grandpa is willing to support *Baba*."

"Uncles and grandpa cannot be blamed for this. I know, they all dislike our *Baba* for his nature but would never say it out loud. Anyway, it's my responsibility to support my family...so let it be, Li." Moulina didn't want to discuss the topic any further.

"Ok *Di*, so you've your moral obligation towards the family, but tell me one thing, has *Baba* performed his responsibility towards this family? When I compare ourselves to our uncles' families, I feel we are just living a substandard life in this filth." Lina's frustration was evident in her voice.

"Hmmm...my little sister is now a grown-up girl. You talk like a Granny, Lina." Moulina chortled.

"Well *Di*, I understand all these complexities but I rarely open up about them. Whenever I visit Rourkela, I often overhear our uncles and aunts making a mockery of *Baba*. They keep raising the same concern - *How will Sanat get his daughters married?* And *Di*, honestly speaking it is a serious concern. These days, weddings are an expensive affair and one has to spend that much money to keep up with the reputation of *The Chell family.*"

"Oh my Granny, stop worrying about my marriage. It'll happen only when it has to happen." Moulina comforted her little sister.

"I know *Di*, you don't want to hear anything against *Baba*. But the truth is that he has murdered all our dreams and aspirations for his own interest and selfishness. Today, even after being an ex-All India Radio artist, you can't pursue your career in music. Why? Because he thinks that the music line is full of muck. This is the only reason why Lokesh *Da* stays away from *Baba*. Today Lalit *bhai* is a school dropout. Why? Because there's no one to guide him and chalk out his career path. Our lives are an utter mess." Lina poured out her worries to Moulina.

"Aahh...that reminds me...this time during *Durga Puja* at Rawdon Bengali

Association, the Puja committee has requested me to sing for their opening ceremony." Moulina tried cheering up her sister. "And by the way, isn't it time for your favourite TV serial to be aired on StarPlus? *Chal, chal*...let's see, what happens to your favourite character." Moulina dragged her sister out of her room.

While the TV telecasted the popular daily soap, Moulina was actually submerged in her thoughts. Whatever Lina said, were some of those harsh and vexatious, bitter truths. These excruciating thoughts weren't new to her. They always prevailed at the back of her mind like an undercurrent, and gradually kept eroding her inner self. She had been ineffectual in handling this dichotomy. She strangulated her own dreams and aspirations, which now appeared to be a chimera. All this just to keep her *Baba* happy and cheerful. She was also aware of the fact that he had fooled her into thinking that his business was going fine, whereas the reality was that she was the sole breadwinner of the family. While her uncles and aunts had invested a considerable amount of their income in various life insurance policies and mutual funds, her *Baba* had not thought of any such investment which could be utilized for their future. Today if some unforeseen, unfortunate incident happened – Moulina's family would have nowhere to go. And the root cause of all this was her father's obstinacy and perversity. Somewhere deep inside her heart, she felt that fatherhood isn't just about conceiving a child with a woman, but much more than that – and her *Baba* had completely failed to live up to those responsibilities.

SEVEN
2011

Birmirpur, Odisha, India

"Maya, this evening we are going to Rourkela. Almost after three long years, we'll have a family dinner together. Sarat and Palash are throwing a joint party." Sanat informed his wife with exuberance.

"But why this celebration, all of a sudden?" exclaimed Maya.

"Don't tell me that you're unaware of the good news, Maya!"

"No, seriously, I've no clue, why would your brothers treat the entire Chell family?"

"Well, that's because Sarat's daughter Pinki got through NIFT's Fashion Designing course in Delhi, whereas Palash's daughter Isha will be attending Ambedkar College of Engineering in Bhubaneswar." Sanat replied in full excitement.

"After so many years of staying together, I still fail to understand you. You are ecstatic about your nieces' career progress, but have you ever thought of your own children's futures?" confronted Maya. "You never allowed your girls to get out of Birmirpur and Rourkela, Lina's postgraduate admission is still pending and our youngest brat has no intentions of completing even his basic education and…"

"What do you want me to do, Maya? If Lalit isn't willing to continue his schooling, if there's no college with Hindi as a postgraduate subject for Lina, then how is it my fault?" yelled Sanat.

"Don't shout at me, that won't help! Have you ever paid attention to the rest of our kids? It's always Moulina for you, as if she is your *only* child and the rest are your foster kids. Even for her, you've failed to find a perfect groom!" Maya started snivelling.

Sanat could feel the pressure pile up on his shoulders – both within the family and outside. Almost everybody had that one common question for him *"When will Moulina get married?"* Two earlier attempts of getting a *suitable* groom for his daughter got foiled. Out of which one went as close as exchanging of engagement rings among the two families. The boy was from a reputed Bengali family based out of Bhubaneswar, having some film background. Within a week, the marriage was called off. Nothing much is known about the incident except the fact that Sanat was the one to back out. Their neighbours in Birmirpur also had no clue about this incident. Eventually, people forgot about it and the episode was hushed up. After six months of this incident, Dr Sanyal's only son from Kolkata saw and liked Moulina and they proposed an engagement. However, Sanat felt that it wasn't a suitable match and didn't proceed further.

Somewhere, deep in his heart, Sanat didn't want to lose his darling daughter by marrying her off. His unconditional love and affection for Moulina sometimes made him judgemental when it came to shortlisting a groom. He wasn't mentally or emotionally prepared to marry off his daughter so soon. He loved his daughter more than himself and was of the opinion that the best phase of a woman's life is well spent with her father, rather than her husband.

However, Sanat's critics in Birmirpur thought otherwise. They felt that he is purposely delaying Moulina's marriage, as his financial condition wasn't as sound as he projected it to the outside world. And in such condition if Moulina got married, probably his only source of income would dry up.

Back in Bankura, Sanat's sister had almost finalised a groom for her daughter. The dates for an engagement ceremony were being sought after and would also be finalised soon. Rathin fully approved of this marriage. In fact, he also financially supported the wedding – something which made Sanat very uncomfortable.

"Sanat, did you book my tickets?" Rathin reminded his son.

"No *Baba*, it is holiday season and train tickets are almost unavailable."

"That's why I had asked you to do the bookings well in advance, hadn't I?"

"Yes *Baba*, but I was busy. So, I couldn't."

"Busy with what? Your business is almost doomed. Also, I don't see any progress in Moulina's wedding arrangements – what is keeping you busy?" an irritated Rathin responded.

"I'll get you a *Tatkal* reservation when the time comes. Now, for God's sake please don't start all over again. I am aware of all the developments and trying my level best to improve my condition," stated an irritated Sanat.

While Sanat faced all the brickbats, his daughter was quite composed and unflustered about her own wedding. She believed that one cannot make an enforced, obligatory entry into the institution of marriage, and that it'll automatically happen in due course of time.

Moulina's *amour-propre*, self-obsession and pride came from the fact that she was the prettiest, most charming and alluring among her friends circle as well as within the Chell clan. She knew that it was just a matter of time when things would fall into place and she would get married to a Mr Right.

Moulina always wanted her married life to be like a six-lane-highway drive – smooth, elegant, adventurous, without any speed breakers. She was fed up of the narrow, dusty lanes of Birmirpur, full of potholes leading to an irritated bumpy ride of life. Those invisible pair of eyes staring at her and judging her every move was simply asphyxiating. She wanted to move out of this hell and settle down in a bigger city. She wanted to lead a more liberal life and be appreciated and loved by her partner. She wanted to break free from her father's cocoon, get rid of all inhibitions, unlock those bilboes and lead a soothing, comfortable life.

She was very close to Sushweta ma'am, her colleague at Municipal College, who treated Moulina like her own daughter. The experienced geography teacher had lost her only daughter a decade back in a road accident and since then, had been practicing spirituality and elementary palmistry. Being Moulina's true well-wisher, she often shared spiritual tips that helped her get rid of all anxieties and negativities. After having a close look at Moulina's soft pale-yellow palms, Sushweta ma'am had once pronounced – "You've got late marriage in your cards, so don't worry about it. It'll be an arranged marriage and your to-be-husband will be a gem of a person – good at heart and will take utmost care of you. He would never leave you in distress ever. You might have issues in adjusting with his family, but you can get rid of those minor glitches by practicing spirituality."

Like any ambitious girl, Moulina asked ma'am inquisitively "Will I be able to resuscitate my dreams and aspirations after my marriage?"

"Oh yes, your husband will be very cooperative and supportive. You will be able to achieve whatever you crave for, only if you have the patience in you. The moment you lose your forbearance, you'll have to face the consequences. Also, remember one key thing – since your husband will be your support system, you will have to align yourself according to him. The minute you go against him, you will have to deal with the repercussions alone. Within two-three years of your marriage, expect a period of litmus test; be heedful about your actions at that time."

Moulina felt so happy at that moment, she couldn't register the depth of the lady's words.

Sanat, on the other hand was sincerely trying to get a suitable *rishta* for his daughter. He had asked Lokesh to create Moulina's profile at *BharatMatrimony.com*. Apart from this, Sanat diligently scanned through every Sunday issue of *Anandabazar Patrika*'s matrimony section. The online profile created, was a basic one, free of cost.

He preferred responding to suitable ads published by the groom's side, rather than publishing his own requirements.

"Lina, get me today's *Anandabazar Patrika*, and the green cover diary from my room," called out Sanat.

"*Baba*, where's your green diary?"

"Ask your mother. I've noted down a few contact numbers in it, will start calling them now," informed Sanat.

Maya heard the conversation from the kitchen. "No need of doing that! For last week's ad, you want to call and check this week? I've been telling you to post an ad as per our requirement, but you don't even want to shell out a few thousands for that. How will you manage to spend in lakhs for our daughter's wedding? At times, I feel the remarks made against you by others are absolutely true – you've become a pauper and an indigent…" an irritated Maya remarked.

"Will you stop taunting and let me do my work?" replied Sanat quite sternly.

Sanat had circled two advertisements from last Sunday's newspaper, but since both were from Bhubaneswar, he wasn't keen on calling them. He had clichéd views on the lifestyles of tier two cities and knew that his Moulina would never be happy in such places. His parochial mentality was beyond any explanation – while he never allowed his daughters to move out of Birmirpur during their college days, he was now very clear on getting them married off to any of the metro cities for a privileged lifestyle. May be as a penance for his inability towards his responsibility as a father or just as a social snob!! He had already started dreaming of bragging about having a son-in-law from a metro city.

This Sunday's paper scan seemed futile to Sanat – the first two pages didn't generate anything, the third page was full of advertisements of Astrologers and *Pandits* who did matchmaking, computerised horoscopes and all kinds of rubbish. He was about to finish off with the fourth page, when a small featured advertisement caught his attention. Sanat read it twice, before noting down the details in his diary.

The ad read: *Mumbai based Bengali boy. MBA, BE working with MNC, handsome salary. 33 yrs 5'8" seeks simple, good looking, graduate girl within 30 yrs. Call 03224-818187.*

8 pm on a Sunday evening seemed to be the perfect time to connect with the matrimonial advertiser. Sanat carried his diary and mobile phone to the bedroom and locked it from inside, while his wife and two daughters remained busy watching a Hindi movie on Zee Cinema.

"Hello, *Namaskar* – this is Sanat Chell from Birmirpur. I wanted to discuss about the advertisement published on today's *Anandabazar Patrika*. Is this the right time to talk?" Sanat sounded a bit shaky.

"Yes, please go ahead. Where did you say you are calling from?" a polite, gentle voice enquired from the other end of the phone.

"Birmirpur – it's in Odisha, outskirts of Rourkela. In fact, just 40 kilometres from Rourkela."

"I see… and who are you?"

"I am the girl's father. I wanted to discuss about a match for my elder daughter." Sanat didn't want to reveal much without getting affirmative gestures from the other side.

"Before you proceed, let me inform you that my son stays in Mumbai…so I hope you are okay with your daughter shifting to Mumbai? Else there is no point in wasting time."

"Yes, I am aware of that, and I am fine with it."

"No, you should also ask your daughter, she needs to be fine with it. The reason I am particular about this is that, many parents back-off due to the location. Hence, it's better to clarify everything at the beginning." The man at the other side was adamant.

"You are absolutely correct. By the way, who am I talking to?" asked Sanat.

"I am Sushil Ghosh and you've dialled our Haldia residence. Well, yes now tell me what you would like to say."

"Yes Mr Ghosh, this is for my elder daughter – Moulina. She is around 29 years of age. Slim, fair, good looking and possesses a Master's degree in English. She is also a trained vocal artist and has been conferred *Sangeet Visharad* in Hindustani classical vocals and *Sangeet Bibhakar* in Odissi vocals. She has also been a certified AIR artist at Sambalpur Radio station." Sanat narrated it all with utmost pride.

"That's fantastic, your daughter is truly talented – is she currently working somewhere?" Sushil asked calmly.

"Yes Sir, she has joined a college in Rourkela as a part time faculty."

"Hmmm, I see – let me also inform you that we are primarily looking for a girl who would largely manage the family. And that too for the initial period of shifting and adjusting to the new city. Thereafter, it's completely upto the new couple. If they feel like working together, they can do so. However, my son earns a handsome salary and hence, there won't be any need of a supporting income. Yet, we are open to the idea, if the girl wants to do something and follow her passion."

"I absolutely respect your views Sir. Family comes first. Once you're well set and adjusted, you can look out for other things," replied an elated Sanat.

"Correct Mr Chell. By the way, what do you do for your living?"

"Sir, we are a reputed business family in Birmirpur. I, along with my three brothers manage our father's business, who is now almost seventy-five years of age and has passed on the baton to us."

"So, what business are you into?"

"Crusher and Transport – we crush large rock chunks from the mines into smaller pieces and then transport it. I'll show you once you visit Birmirpur."

"Ok, and how many kids do you have?"

"I've four kids; two daughters and two sons – all are born at a two years' gap."

"Ok, sounds good. Do you have your daughter's *Kundali?* Please don't mind, but we would prefer to go ahead with the *Kundali* matching before taking this further."

"Mr Ghosh, it'll take a couple of more days to generate the *Kundali,* but I can provide you my daughter's birth details in the meantime, if you want."

"Oh yes, that will do."

"Mr Ghosh, what about you Sir? If you could tell me something about your family and son too, that would be great."

"Oh sure – we are a small family of four and you can classify us into an upper middle-class Bengali family. Both my son and daughter are convent educated. My son did his schooling here in Haldia, then went on to do his Mechanical Engineering from Bangalore University followed by an MBA from Rourkela. He is now employed in Mumbai, with an Indian conglomerate, which is also an MNC. He is residing in Mumbai for almost a decade now; his younger sister is also staying with him. She is employed with a bank for the last two years. My daughter is also an MBA, BTech. She couldn't fetch a job of her liking through campus placement and hence went on to hunt for a job in Mumbai and by God's grace, both my children are kind of settled in Mumbai. I am a Senior Production Manager with a public sector company, and have two more years before I retire, and my wife is a home maker."

"Sir, which company did you say your son is employed with?"

"Well, I didn't mention that. It is too early to reveal all details, please keep patience, you'll get to know everything that matters."

"Sorry Sir. So how do we take this forward?"

"Please note down my email id. Send me your daughter's complete biodata, along with her pictures. No passport photos please. Also, mention her date, time and place of birth. We'll check the horoscope compatibility and then if my son likes her, we'll proceed to the next level."

"*Thik achhey*, that sounds perfect. I'll wait for your revert…have a goodnight." Sanat's voice betrayed his elation as he put the phone down.

"Goodnight Mr Chell."

Sanat was satisfied with the telephonic chat with Mr Ghosh, which lasted almost 25 minutes. He liked the straightforwardness and sincere responses of Ghosh. Although it would be a long way to go from here, but then, *morning shows the day* – and then there's the boy and the girl's consent and above all, nothing can happen without any divine interventions. Whatever might be the outcome of this conversation, it had however not stopped Sanat from making some mental calculations which were very personal. The *city of dreams* could turn around his fate; he could regain some prestige in his social circle if this worked out. Mumbai is just 24 hours from Rourkela. With daily trains running between Howrah and Chatrapati Shivaji Terminus – the Chell couple could visit their daughter anytime of the year. His daughter would also be able to nurture her passion for music in the days to come, his younger daughter could also find something for herself in the *Maximum City*. And if everything went well, his elder son could also take a transfer from Faridabad and settle down in Mumbai. Sanat's opportunist mind gave an iniquitous smile. He felt enthralled and excited.

EIGHT
2014

Mumbai, Maharashtra, India

It had been over 48 hours since Sumit last spoke to Advocate Basant Panigrahi. His advance payment was done, which was acknowledged over WhatsApp and thereafter came no updates from the lawyer. Constant consternation made him restive and fidgety, as a sense of mixed feelings prevailed. He wanted to call Panigrahi, but didn't know if that would be appropriate. But then it was his case and he had every right to ask for an update. Sumit checked Panigrahi's WhatsApp profile – he was online a couple of hours back.

At around 9 pm, Sumit's phone rang. It was Panigrahi, "Sumit *Babu*, let me inform you, your petition has been filed. My juniors are fully on to it."

"Hello Sir, I was in fact just about to call you for the status."

"Well, I was out of town and had to attend the High Court for a murder case, and that's the reason I couldn't update you earlier. But you need not worry, the FIR copy and the 161 Statement of your case has also been generated," informed Panigrahi.

"161 Statement? What's that Sir?" asked Sumit.

"That's a report created by the IO, after examining some witnesses under CrPC 161," explained Panigrahi.

"Sir, what all allegations are being framed against us in the FIR?"

"Same old story, Sumit *Babu* – physical and mental torture, dowry demand blah, blah, blah. But some allegations are strong and have been corroborated in the 161 statement as well."

Physical and mental torture!! Sumit's blood froze. Did he imagine he heard those words? "Sir, can you please courier across a copy of all these documents? I would like to go through them and start creating a note countering the allegations."

"Sumit *Babu*, once the court grants bail, you have to appear here in the court and sign the bail bond. So, you anyway have to visit Rourkela soon. At that time, I'll handover all the documents to you. Will that do?"

"Okay Sir, as you say. But will we be able to succeed in getting the bail?"

"Surety of one hundred percent from my side," a confident Panigrahi replied. "Sumit *Babu*, let me also tell you, that in order to win a legal battle one cannot walk a straight path. At times, we'll have to take some crisscross routes and apply tactics – I hope you understood the analogy, can't reveal much over the phone."

"Sir, as I said, this case is now yours. Take full charge of it and do whatever you have to. All I can understand is that I am in deep trouble and you've got to get me out of it." Sumit knew he will have to butter up his words and serve them to Panigrahi.

"Well, tomorrow morning I'm heading to Birmirpur. I'll visit the police station, meet the concerned officer and see if something can be done, so that the court complexities can be avoided. Will try and win her over by some *sweeteners*. I'll keep you informed about the outcome of the meeting. For now, I've got to go."

Sumit felt relieved after hearing the status from the lawyer. Perhaps things were on the right track. Panigrahi had a strong police background and network; there was a high probability, he could convince the inspector about the fake allegations made against his family and the stratagem plotted against them.

But what if the Investigation Officer turns out to be a corrupt one and demands a monetary gratification? Till now police-lawyer-court were a part of TV serials and movies only; he couldn't believe that these were the kind of people he would be dealing with in practical life from now on. If those TV serials are to be believed, then characters like 'corrupt police officers', 'unfaithful lawyers' do exist – too many thoughts criss-crossed his minds. He decided to call his father in Haldia and inform him about the latest update he got from Panigrahi.

"*Dada*, what are you doing online? Come, let's have dinner. I cooked *khichdi* today," informed Sunita.

"That's awesome. You arrange the plates, let me quickly fry omelettes – *khichdi* with omelette and mango-pickle is simply heaven..." an ecstatic Sumit left behind his laptop and headed towards the kitchen.

"*Dada*, why don't you look up the tickets? We've to anyway visit Rourkela for the bail proceedings."

"Hmm...that's correct, I was thinking of *Tatkal* tickets, but then if I can book it in advance we can save on some money. Let me ask Panigrahi Sir for a probable date tomorrow. It's troublesome also, we've to reach Rourkela from here directly while *Baba* and *Maa* have to travel from Haldia."

"Any luck on your job-hunting spree?" Sunita asked as she served *khichdi* to her brother.

"That's what I was checking. It seems that the job market has no suitable offering for me, but I'll keep trying. I've got to get back to a regular job in order to finance all the legal expenses." Sumit's voice betrayed his sorrow.

Next day, Sumit woke up late, and headed towards the kitchen to make himself a cup of tea. Sunita, by then had left for the office. Generally, she would call her *Dada* after reaching office. But on this particular day, she purposely skipped it as she didn't want to disturb him. He not only went to bed late the previous night, but she also heard him squealing in the middle of his sleep. He had had a terrible nightmare.

Sumit could vaguely remember it; it was all about the ongoing imbroglio. The police force was at his door-step with an arrest warrant or something like that, which he didn't even want to recall on this bright sunny morning.

It was almost noon, Sumit glanced through his WhatsApp chat list – Panigrahi was last seen online at around 9:30 am. Sumit was anxious and extremely jittery about the meeting that might have taken place at Birmirpur PS. It would actually pave the path of this complicated case and help him decide the next course of action. In order to silence the questions running around in his mind, he messaged his lawyer, *"Sir, any updates?"* The WhatsApp chat box displayed just a single tick.

The criminal lawyer, on the contrary, had a rather unsuccessful day. The 6'2" tall, heavily built, pot-bellied advocate thought that this case would be an easy way out and some quick money could be made by settling the case out-of-court. He also thought of channelizing his wife's police network, but it turned out to be ineffective and hostile. He tried all sorts of professional tactics but failed. Panigrahi had left for Birmirpur around 9 am and didn't get time to have his breakfast. After spending more than an hour at the police station without any results, he was annoyed with the entire chain of events. Hopelessly, he drove back to Rourkela and checked into a roadside *Dhaba* for some *poori, sabzi* and *chai*.

"Sumit *Babu*, I tried my best to settle this case, but it seems that your father-in-law has fully swayed the entire police station and the IO at Birmirpur," informed Panigrahi while sipping his *chai*.

"Sir, what does that mean? Will they object to my bail application?" Sumit gulped in trepidation.

"When did I say that?" an irritated Panigrahi responded. "Please understand, today I was here to meet the IO and discuss your case. But the contemptuous, snotty officer didn't meet me. I've never come across such a disrespectful, rude and discourteous lady officer in my career spanning over two decades. Not only did she refuse to meet me, she asked her Havildar to convey the message that I should fight it out in the courtroom and not waste her time and mine in the police station like this." Panigrahi sounded furious. "How dare a freshly passed out policewoman misbehaves with me, unless she has some blessings from the upper rank officer!"

"But Sir, what exactly happened in the meeting?"

"Meeting! There was no meeting! I straightway went and met DSP Dash, who was my wife's ex-colleague a couple of years back. I told him about the false case being registered by Chell and his daughter. To which he just said – '*Calm down, why are you overreacting to this case? Your client is a culprit, and he has to face the consequences. Since he has hired you, you fight it out for him.*'"

"I objected and tried to convince him that Chell is out on a vendetta against my client. But he was least interested." Panigrahi sounded disappointed.

"Sir what do we do now?"

"Sumit *Babu*, don't panic. Listen to me carefully...I've assessed the situation here and I strongly believe that Mr Chell has highly influenced the police station. He has complete control over the DSP and the IO. The police driver is known to me, he will get me more information on this later. But for the time being, it seems that Inspector Shamita and her team will head to Mumbai, and has got a nod from the DSP. She'll be out of town for the whole of next week. Which I assume is the time when she is likely to visit Mumbai and take you in her custody. Again, this might not be true, but then it's always better to be safe than sorry."

Sumit felt a huge lump of shock trickle down his throat, he stood paralysed not knowing what to do next. Custody? Had he heard it right? In a convulsed, quivering voice he said, "Do you think I should leave Mumbai now?"

"Yes, and I am suggesting this from my experience and for your safety. In the name of investigation, they can put you behind the bars." Panigrahi finished his tea and rose to pay the bill.

"But Sir..."

"No ifs or buts, leave Mumbai as soon as possible. Go underground until I get the bail order for you and your family. And yes, wherever you go, take a new SIM card and a normal feature phone. Before leaving Mumbai, dump your existing SIM and smartphone. These days, police can track you easily through your mobile location. And don't forget to suspend all the SIM cards which were known to your wife," warned Panigrahi.

"Okay Sir, but how do I connect with you?" Sumit's mind started doing the calculations.

"Once you get your new SIM, message me the number and we'll be in touch.

Now don't waste time, please act fast. Good luck." Panigrahi disconnected the phone.

A stark, bewildered feeling, took over Sumit. Even in his befuddled state, he could sense a deleterious trouble. For a moment, he stood numb, with those words from Panigrahi echoing in his ears. He was losing grip over everything, falling deeper and deeper into an endless whirlpool.

NINE
2014

Birmirpur, Odisha, India

It was a breezy afternoon outside. A long spell of downpour had just ceased, leaving behind the Simdega Road waterlogged. Soon those carriers and heavy trucks would struggle to make their way through the potholes. The Simdega Road or NH-143 cuts through Birmirpur and connects the city of Rourkela with Ranchi. Birmirpur Police Station and the DSP's office stood face to face, separated by the serpentine highway at the *Chowk-Bazaar* area. And just 5 kilometres from *Chowk-Bazaar*, Odisha ends and Jharkhand begins.

The DSP's office premise was circumscribed by a four feet wall, within which Eucalyptus, Jamun, False-Ashoka and Banyan trees stood haphazardly. The drenched, heavy tree leaves swayed across in pace with the breeze. The red beacon Mahindra Scorpio parked near the iron grill gate seemed to be enjoying a quiet afternoon nap, while its driver was munching *ghutka* and was busy conversing over his mobile phone. A couple of officers were chatting in the front office as they waited for their respective files to be signed by DSP Ajay Dash.

The DSP planned to leave office early. There was a family function at his Civil Township residence for which he couldn't afford to be late. But then his morning meeting with Advocate Panigrahi was bothering him. Things just might go out of his control if not tackled now. In between signing those files, he sent out a text message *'Come in the next 20 minutes. It's URGENT.'*

3:45pm – A short, clean shaven quinquagenarian with dark ebony skin appeared on his bike with a jute carry bag. He parked his blue Bajaj bike right next to the Mahindra Scorpio, adjusted the rear-view mirror and combed his dyed black hair before asking the driver in thick Oriya accent "Sir *achhonti?*"

The driver nodded and directed him to the DSP's office.

"Dash *Babu, kaun hela!* You messaged me and see I am here leaving all my pending work aside, just to be at your service."

"Yes Chell, come in, I was waiting for you. There's something I wanted to discuss with you."

"Sir, before you start, here's something for your weekend." Sanat handed over the jute carry bag to the DSP.

"Which one is it?" asked the DSP without even looking into the bag.

"Sir, *Ballentine's fine blend Scotch,* especially for you." Chell responded with a grin.

"Ok, now listen. Your son-in-law has appointed a lawyer to counter your FIR..." Dash began.

"Sir, what to do now? This will now complicate the entire process. I thought you told me that nothing of this sort will happen." Sanat's voice betrayed his impatience and unrest.

"Don't panic Chell, I am here to handle this. The lawyer whom your son-in-law has appointed was here in the morning. Advocate Panigrahi is an experienced criminal lawyer with good connections. I suppose, the Ghosh family must have hired him to get them Anticipatory Bail against our FIR," a composed response came in from Dash.

"Why was the lawyer here?" asked Chell.

"Well, what I could gauge from his conversation is that, he was here to appraise the situation and wanted to have the IO in his confidence. I've sent him back, but we now need to manage him so that the situation remains within our control," the shrewd officer suggested.

"But how?"

"Leave this to me, Panigrahi's wife was my junior at Udit Nagar PS. So that can be taken care of. Over and above this, we need to influence the *Peshkars* and *Bench clerks* of the Rourkela court for some special treatment to their bail applications." Dash thought out aloud.

"Sir, you're simply a genius!" Chell seemed relieved.

"Chell, you arrange for some funds, I'll make sure that your machatunim doesn't get bail and is forced to visit Birmirpur PS as per the notice served," the DSP got up and signalled his driver to get the Scorpio ready.

In the month of March 2014, after a lot of persuasion from family members and well-wishers, when Moulina finally decided not to return to her husband in Mumbai, her father wanted to teach the Ghosh family a lesson for a lifetime, which they would never ever forget. Sanat was, in a way, euphoric with his daughter's decision to stay back in Birmirpur, something which he always wanted. He wanted his daughter to start working again, so that her income could be a few droplets of water in the barren land of the Chell household. Talks with St. Aloysius School in Fertilizer Township were on and that's when they realised that all the academic certificates of Moulina were with Sumit. Both father and daughter tried to convince Sumit and get those documents couriered from Mumbai. But every time Sumit insisted that it's risky to send those important documents via courier and they can visit Mumbai and get them from him anytime, not knowing the real intention behind the request. The father-daughter duo always bluffed that Moulina wanted to pursue her B.Ed. from Rourkela and hence needed those certificates. Sumit always maintained a clear stance – if at all she desired to do a B.Ed., she could very well do it from Mumbai University. He couldn't understand why Moulina had to go that far away to pursue her education.

By mid-March, Sanat approached the local *Thana* to file a complaint against his son-in-law, highlighting the fact that Sumit has forcefully possessed Moulina's certificates and was hindering her higher studies. The officer on duty refused to register a complaint and had sent him back, stating that it was a family matter and should be resolved internally. Adamant Sanat met Senior Inspector and tried convincing him, but all in vain, nothing materialised. He also sought help from a local politician, but then too it turned out to be a futile attempt. Almost all the options which Sanat tried, suggested that he should not take these drastic steps as they would hamper his daughter's future in the long run. Also, filing an FIR just because of academic certificates didn't make any sense. The police inspector instead suggested Sanat to re-apply for all the major certificates and for that he was ready to register a missing document diary.

Finally, in May 2014, luck favoured Sanat when Cuttack's Assistant SP Ajay Dash got promoted and transferred to Birmirpur area as a DSP. Dash, in his late 40s, was known to be a dynamic IPS Officer who had helped his department earn many laurels from the government in eliminating quite a few Maoist groups from the tribal areas of Odisha. Standing 5'10" tall, the handsome officer has a medium athletic build and was also known as a womaniser in his department. He preferred female officers in his team and directly supervised cases handled by them, whereas the male officers had to maintain the hierarchy to seek Dash's guidance.

Dash and Chell, go a long way back. The encounter of notorious wagon-breaker from Sambalpur area, which shaped up Dash's career eight years back, was only possible with some vital intelligence inputs from Chell, whose truck used to transport limestone then to the interior parts of Sambalpur. And now Sanat wanted to give a shape to his vengeance with the help of DSP Dash.

Sanat knew the officer's weakness towards some finest scotch and hence invited him at Brightfair Hotel's Caravan Bar on a Saturday evening. This treat was a quid pro quo for the DSP's commitment to help Sanat in fixing his son-in-law. After a few pegs, the perspicacious officer came up with a watertight plan which got Sanat's approbation.

The plan was fairly simple – by hook or by crook, pressurise and terrorize the Ghosh family to return all of Moulina's certificates and then later file for a judicial separation from her husband with a hefty maintenance. If the plan succeeded, Sanat's financial hardship would come to an end. His daughter would stay back in Birmirpur, and conveniently start earning as a school teacher. The much needed funds would help Sanat to restart his business, get his second daughter married off, and finance his wife's treatment. Knowing that his daughter was completely pissed-off with her in-laws, Sanat just wanted to ratify the plan with Moulina.

DSP Dash, however, warned Sanat that it would be a tight-rope walk. The plan would need to be executed as delicately as possible, so that nothing goes out of police control and lands up in a court battle. And in execution of such a mission, money should flow in. Though Sanat was hesitant with the monetary part, he realised that to catch a big fish, one has to bait a smaller fish. Whatever he would invest now, will pay him dividends later in the form of settlement amount from the Ghosh family. The deal was fabricated such that Dash would have a 25% share on the settlement value.

Dash got an FIR drafted from a final year law student, which made a case for dowry harassment against the Ghosh family. The FIR would enable the police to raid and seize Moulina's belongings from the Ghosh family, by virtue of which they would get hold of her certificates. It would also lead to an automatic arrest of the accused. And if any member got arrested, by default the other members would desperately beg for negotiation and settlement. At this point, the Ghosh family would obey any terms and conditions put forward by the Chells. And once a hefty amount has been extorted, the FIR could be withdrawn and later, through family court, both the parties could apply for a judicial separation followed by a divorce.

Voila! The DSP's plan seemed to be a flawless sixer, but little did he know that the opposition would bowl a googly by seeking a legal practitioner's intervention before the *Hajira*, and the Supreme Court would timely bowl a yorker by releasing an order of *no-automatic-arrest* in a dowry case.

❖ ❖ ❖

TEN

2011

Mumbai, Maharashtra, India

On his way to office, Sumit received an SMS from his Boss - *'Come to my cabin with the Brand Equity numbers as soon as u r in.'* Last quarter's figures were abysmal and that's the reason for this unplanned morning meeting.

And the day one would want to reach office early, is when one ends up being late…all because of weird Mumbai traffic where everybody is in a hurry to be on time. Sumit took a regular *kalipeeli* cab to his office at Lower Parel, which moved smoothly till Dadar but got stuck at Parel TT, followed by a chock-a-block Elphinstone Road that delayed him by 15 minutes.

Towards the end of the meeting, Sumit's phone vibrated thrice but he couldn't take the call. The meeting with the Boss stretched till lunch hour and by the time he finished off his lunch, a digital marketing agency was waiting for him at the reception. While the agency meeting was on, Sumit's phone again vibrated – this time he pulled out the mobile from his pocket only to find out four missed calls from his mother since morning.

Irked with so many calls, Sumit finally called back to find out the reason. Chitra wanted her son to upload a few latest snaps to his *Bengalimatrimony.com* account, which otherwise appeared ghoshtly with no profile pic. Without which she couldn't give away his profile id to the prospective bride's families who called to enquire. The silly reason behind so many missed calls, that too during office hours, drove Sumit mad and he disconnected immediately before committing that he would do the needful once back from office.

Both Sushil and Chitra were worried parents and why wouldn't they be! By the end of next year, Sushil would retire from his service and hence he aimed to get his son married before that. There had been several attempts made to find a suitable bride for him, but each time it ended in a rejection. They weren't sure what qualities their son wanted in his life partner. In between his busy office schedule, he often visited Kolkata and its vicinity, just to meet girls selected by his parents, but nothing transpired. Sumit had also met a few Bengali girls in Mumbai for the same purpose, sans any outcome.

⁘ ⁘ ⁘

The Ghoshs were a close knit family of four with a humble and modest background. Sushil belonged to a *zamindar* family but struggled a lot to reach where he was now. His grandfather had huge acres of farm lands by virtue of being a zamindar in some rural areas of Tamluk but had to give away most of it to his kith and kin during his last years, leaving Sushil's father with almost no share. With five children, life was difficult to manage and finally things worsened when Sushil lost his father at the age of 11. Being the eldest, Sushil took the entire responsibility of the family and continued his education despite all hardships. Parallel to his village schooling, he continued to do paltry jobs and slowly and steadily bought some more farming lands. From there on he went on to complete his graduation in physics and worked as a contractor, before joining Indian Oil's Haldia Refinery. Later, Sushil got all his sisters married and helped his only brother to settle down in his life.

Sushil had spent his entire service life in Haldia, which is just a few hours' drive from his native village in Tamluk and planned to settle down in the port city. All through his service life, the Ghosh family had been residing in company allotted quarters of the Haldia Township locality. Now that retirement was nearing, Sushil had booked a spacious 2BHK flat in Monalisa Apartment.

Sushil's life had always been a roller coaster and he had accepted life's challenges as they came along. He was hardworking and always believed in sincerity, honesty, integrity and accepted the fact that there were no short-cuts to success. The only thing that worried his wife was that he was too credulous and gullible, which could be dangerous in this complex social structure.

Chitra, on the other hand, came from a well to do family based out of Balichak, a semi-urban town, just 45 kilometres from Kharagpur. Her father worked with South Eastern Railways' Kharagpur and Chakradharpur divisions in various capacities, before retiring as a Station Master. She was the eldest daughter of five siblings; her two brothers were settled businessmen in Balichak, whereas her two sisters were married off in neighbouring towns.

Sushil was a complete family man – an introvert who rarely socialized. Every evening after he got back home from office, he would spend some time tending to his flourishing garden of herbs and vegetables, followed by watching political debates on news-channels and often played a game or two of cards on his computer before his dinner.

Like father, like son – Sumit was known to be a simple, generous, altruistic, benevolent and friendly guy among his circle of friends and colleagues. Though his father considered him to be a stubborn and disobedient son, Sumit was knowledgeable and multi-talented. Apart from his academic qualifications, he was a certified *tabla* player with keen interest in various forms of music; a national quizzer and a novice painter.

At the age of 33, Sumit's career trajectory was moving ahead at the right pace in the right direction. At this juncture, he needed a loving and caring life partner who would understand him and his family. And support him to achieve new heights and excel in his career goals and aspirations. At this age, while most of his school friends were happily married with kids, Sumit was waiting for the right person to enter his life as his better half. He wanted somebody who should be simple yet elegant, educated, talented, practical, responsible, down-to-earth and supportive. Someone who would be the centroid of his family and keep everybody in sync.

Little did he know that *"Homo proponit, sed Deus disponit"*

※ ※ ※

When every possible attempt comes to a dead end, man finds solace in astrology. Chitra wanted to end this ongoing search for a daughter-in-law, which had been on for almost four years. May be, astrology could help her understand how much longer they would have to wait or if there was any way out to speed up the process. She knew that her husband wouldn't support her in this matter, but she was also aware of the fact that there were many who had benefitted by using specific gemstones or by altering the spelling of their names or conducting some special *pujas.*

Chitra spoke to Dr Rajan Kandar, a Homeopathy practitioner in Balichak. Kandar was their family doctor who also knew astrology, and on Chitra's request agreed to analyse Sumit's horoscope in length and breadth. Astrology was not a profession but a passion for the doctor, so not many were aware of his skill. Kandar was known to Chitra's parental family since childhood. In fact, Chitra's father had financed some of those expensive medical books during his BHMS course.

"Rajan, we are really worried. It's been four years now and yet we are unable to find a suitable bride for our Sumit!" Chitra raised her concern.

"*Didi*, I've studied the horoscope thoroughly. Everything is going fine, you don't have to worry at all. Sumit will get a life partner this year. In fact, according to my calculations, I can see one match happening very soon."

"How soon?" Chitra's hopes shot up again.

"May be another couple of months. The reason for his late marriage is *Rahu's Antardasha,* something which happens because of the planetary movements and is unavoidable. I can see this *dasha* ending soon."

"Rajan, I'll also share some of the *Kundalis* that might come through. Now you have to find out the best match with Sumit's horoscope."

"*Thik achey Didi* that will be done. Don't brood over this now and keep the search on." Kandar reassured Chitra before disconnecting the call.

This time round, the elderly Ghoshs' stay at Mumbai was only for 45 days. They returned back to Haldia with the sole purpose of bride hunting and wanted to post another matrimonial ad for Sumit, before the wedding season kicked in. Based on Kandar's assurance, this time Chitra insisted on a coloured, featured advertisement for maximum visibility.

Sunday morning and Chitra was all busy with her household chores. She didn't even get time to glance through the newspaper. Sumit's matrimony Ad had appeared in the third column of the last page. As a result, Sushil remained busy attending calls that came through on his mobile phone. He carefully noted all the details in his notebook which he wanted to discuss with his wife later.

"Any interesting calls today? Or will this advertisement also go unnoticed like the previous ones?" asked Chitra while arranging the bed pillows.

"Bring me that notebook from my table, I've jotted them down. Two seem to be interesting…the rest are of no use."

"And where was the last one from? It seemed quite an illustrious call. You spent a long time brooding over it."

"The last one was from Rourkela and the first one from Jamshedpur. Others are from Navi Mumbai, Howrah and Siliguri." Sushil replied, flipping through the pages of his notebook.

❖ ❖ ❖

Chitra had some special attachment with Rourkela that transported her back to her childhood days. She still remembered those late night train journeys which used to speed through the dense forest and hilly terrains of the Chakradharpur-Manoharpur stretch, crossing tunnels and lesser known stations only to get down at a well-lit station named Rourkela. She used to hold her father's hand tightly whenever she saw those *RPF jawans* on the platform and then straightway used to head towards the station quarter. And for the next one month it used to be vacation time for Chitra and her sister. Memories of those days were still fresh in her mind, when their father used to take them for short trips in his white Ambassador. On weekends, they visited the *Steel Plant, Bondamunda railway workshop, Hirakud dam, Vaishno Devi temple and* other popular spots. She even recalled those black smoke emitting chimneys of the steel plant, never ending long trains of the workshop, lengthy blue stretch of water on one side of the dam and innumerable steps to climb up the hill to offer prayers to Vaishno Devi.

Her father had served the Indian Railways across Kharagpur-Chakradharpur-Jharsuguda divisions in different capacities. Five years ago, he left for the heavenly adobe, but those station names created nostalgic effects in her mind. A picturesque image lit up her memories – those countryside, green stretches had gorgeous hills and mountains in the backdrop of a small railway station, through which express trains used to pass at topmost speed, paying no heed to the livelihood of the local *santhals* – to whom a Stationmaster and a Postmaster were equivalent to God. The villagers used to bring in fresh vegetables, spices and fish to her father's residence. Life was so simple yet wonderful, all wrapped up in the warmth of nature's beauty.

Chitra was so attached to Rourkela that she insisted that her son take his MBA admission in RIMS, while other options were available to him as per his score in Orissa Entrance Test. Sumit too got to experience Rourkela during his two years' stay, and it almost matched with his mother's version of everything he had heard from her during his growing up years. And today, when Sushil informed her about the call from Rourkela, she soaked herself into those memories of her juvenescence.

Exactly 72 hours after his extended telephonic conversation with Sushil Ghosh, Sanat emailed his daughter's biodata along with two scanned photographs. Sushil forwarded the email to Sumit and simultaneously Chitra connected with Dr Kandar with the girl's date, time and place of birth. On rare turn of events, Sumit gave his approbation to proceed further while the doctor found a perfect horoscope match between the boy and the girl – it's a *Raj-jotak*.

"*Namaskar Mr Chell, kemon achen?* Have you gone through my email?" Sushil called up Sanat to enquire.

"*Na Sir,* we don't have any internet connection or a computer at home. On weekends, both my daughters visit the local cyber-café to check their mails. So, in between, on weekdays, there's no scope." Sanat responded. "But Sir, I'll ask my son to check, he has access to the internet."

"No worries, I've responded to your mail with my son's photograph and biodata. Go through it, show it to your daughter, discuss with your family members and then let me know."

"Oh! Thank you Sir, that's great. I hope your son liked our daughter."

"Well, too early to comment Mr Chell, let them meet face to face and then decide. This generation is smarter in all these aspects," tittered Sushil.

Sanat was all excited and jubilant – at 8:45 pm, he kickstarted his blue Bajaj and sped through the deserted roads of Birmirpur to reach Prestige Internet Café at Gole Bazaar. Luckily, there were two customers surfing the net, else the owner would've switched off the main computer in order to save his electricity bill. Around mid-November, shops in this locality generally pull down their shutters by 8:30 pm. Today the internet speed was decent enough to download the biodata and snaps in 9 minutes flat. Sanat also printed the documents for his wife and daughter back home.

Somehow, Sanat had an intuition that this *rishta* would work in his favour and if it has to be believed, then probably he would be able to silence all his critics and vilifiers. The Ghosh family's son was the perfect son-in-law he had been looking for – a highly qualified guy from India's commercial capital, working with an Indian conglomerate MNC. It would be the ultimate slap to all of his fault-finders. But then, what could be the salary of Ghosh's son? Something which Sanat couldn't figure out from the earlier conversations. But then with so many years of experience in MNCs, it had to be a seven-digit number yearly – Sanat's eyes brightened up.

Convincing Moulina was never an issue. Like an obedient daughter, she listened to her father narrate his conversation with Mr Ghosh and read out the biodata content of the prospect groom. All that enthusiasm and excitement in her father's voice didn't go unnoticed. Lina, who was helping her mother in the kitchen, came running into her sister's room followed by Maya.

"*Baba*, where is this Haldia? Never heard of this place," asked Lina.

"It's a port city in the southern part of West Bengal, I'd been there once. But the boy stays in Mumbai."

"Wow, *Didi* will shift to Mumbai!! That's amazing." Lina couldn't hide her zest.

"Show me that printout." Moulina pointed out to the snaps. "These pictures are so dark and unclear," she complained as she held them up.

"Yes, I brought them just to give you an idea. Tomorrow, we'll go to your Sarat uncle's place. They've broadband connection and there you can check the coloured picture and decide," responded Sanat.

Quite often, after dinner, Moulina spent time on the terrace, just wandering and staring at the starry sky. Almost every day, at this hour a blinking light appeared from the northern end of the sky and then disappeared in the dark – may be, some international flight. She had never boarded a flight nor even travelled in an AC compartment of a train. Her cousins enjoyed a sweet silent sleep in their air-conditioned bedrooms, while she had to pour buckets of water into the noisy cooler to have her good night's sleep. *Terrace Moments* were very personal to Moulina – she savoured these few minutes of peace and solitude, talking to her inner self under the vastness of an open sky. Only the fireflies played hide-n-seek among those dark mango tree leaves, without being bothered by her presence – wish she could also fly like them and enjoy the beauty of a night's darkness and calmness.

Mumbai - the city that never sleeps! How difficult it would be, to find the calmness of the night, this peaceful solitude, this "me" time. Moulina probably wouldn't be able to spend her *Terrace Moments* anymore. But above all, she desired to explore a lavish city life along the banks of the Arabian Sea, far away from this tribal inhabited town of Odisha.

Sumit Ghosh's profile eventually got a nod from Moulina.

"Good morning Mr Chell. I hope you've talked to your daughter. What's her opinion?" Sushil called up Sanat on a Sunday morning.

"Ghosh *Da*, I thought of calling you today evening only."

"That's okay. As a next step, I was planning to visit Rourkela along with my missus if only your daughter agrees to become our daughter-in-law."

"*Dada*, we all liked your son's profile, and my daughter also has given her consent to this *rishta*, so we can now look forward to building this into a successful marriage."

"Absolutely. My son will come and meet your daughter later next month, when he will be here on a short trip on the occasion of his birthday. But before that, we would like to come over and meet Moulina." Sushil politely replied.

"Sir, let me suggest one thing – Visiting Birmirpur twice will be hectic and tiresome for you. Instead, why don't you let me come over along with my daughter and wife to Haldia. And then if something positive transpires, you all can visit our place along with your son."

"That shouldn't be a problem. Still, let me discuss this with my wife."

To the Ghosh couple, Sanat's enthrallment seemed suspiciously weird. In all of their earlier interactions with girls' families, they had never come across such anomalous behaviour from the girl's side – they deliberated upon it, in order to shred all impediments. While Sushil made all efforts to come out of his cocooned traditional thought process, Chitra was still fretful and peevish about it. But finally, they agreed to Sanat's suggestion – as they could perhaps disagree and reject the match more easily, if anything wrong surfaced.

On the contrary, Sanat had always taken his daughter to the groom's house for initial talks, and he had a convincing explanation for the same. According to him, Birmirpur is an interior area with less public transport. Moreover, it is a tribal domiciled town, where the localites envied their neighbours and could go to any extent to paint a grim picture and spread rumours, thereby jeopardizing the groom's purpose of visit. This approach had also proved economical to Sanat, else the increasing cost of entertaining guests would've burned his pockets. Chitra deliberated upon it for hours, but couldn't pinpoint the exact reason why this whole deal seemed off. Nevertheless, she decided to keep it to herself.

Sanat and Maya Chell, along with their daughter Moulina, finally visited the Ghosh residence at Haldia. This meeting was very crucial for both the families. The company residence of Ghosh was all set to welcome the guests from Birmirpur – Chitra had made all arrangements to welcome the Chells.

The Chells were overwhelmed with the warm welcome extended by the Ghosh family. The meeting seemed like a rendezvous between two families who had known each other for ages – they talked, laughed, ate, and even went out for an evening stroll by the riverside. Like any other traditional Bengali household, *bhuribhoj and adda* remained the central theme of the meeting. The Ghosh family being great foodies, made all arrangements for the gastronomical pleasure of the Chells – breakfast followed by a scrumptious lunch and some roadside snacks during the evening walk followed by a delectable dinner left the Chells completely amazed. The visitors stayed overnight and left Haldia in the wee hours of the morning to catch the 8:30 am *Ispat Superfast Express* from Kharagpur Junction.

"I think she is the one, the perfect one for our Sumit," opined Chitra while sipping into her evening cup of tea.

"I quite liked her too. She seems like a sensible, mature girl" weened Sushil, while flipping through the pages of the newspaper.

"Did you notice – how hesitant she was initially, but didn't take much time to open up and gel along with us spontaneously." Chitra smiled as she pointed out.

"Yes, she even let go her trepidations and made us believe that she is very much a part of this family."

"She was with me for a while in the kitchen when I was preparing for the dinner and honestly confessed that she has no idea of cooking but is eager to learn." Chitra recollected.

"I think Sumit and Moulina will make a great couple. I can't think of anything wrong with the family either. Let's call Sumit and give him the news," proposed Sushil.

The Chell family's Haldia visit definitely made a positive impact; both Sushil and Chitra had synchronous views about Moulina. They had waited all this while to get a perfect partner for their only son and probably Moulina fit the bill. But again, Sumit would have his own opinions and that's what mattered the most. Moulina's nature, attitude and behaviour cleared Chitra's apprehensions and doubts. Mrs Ghosh wanted a homely, sweet, jovial, affable daughter-in-law which she started visualising in the form of Moulina. A girl who could mingle so easily with an unknown family, would never find it difficult to adjust to a new place, new surroundings, and new members. After all, Moulina was a well-educated, self-dependant, talented girl who had Bengali middle-class family values to her core. She was the eldest of all the siblings and hence responsible and authoritative. She was also a God-fearing, earnestly religious person, who believed in Shirdi Sai Baba. The Ghosh family saw no reason to say no to this match.

Now, if only Sumit approved, the Ghosh couple would be free from their moral obligations. The search for the right girl had lasted quite long, but it seems now that the wait was well worth. The Ghosh couple conveyed their opinions to Sumit and asked him to plan for his trip to Birmirpur.

On the other hand, an equanimous Sanat was assertive about his Haldia visit. His calculated moves were now paying off. Very soon, he will be out from the slump he had been in for decades, and would retrieve his lost glory in the Chell clan and society. Eagerly, he waited for the next call from Haldia.

ELEVEN
2014

Kolkata, West Bengal, India

Indigo flight 6E-319 made a shaky landing at 10:45 am, delayed by 25 minutes from its scheduled arrival. The Mumbai-Kolkata flight had to brave past some mid-air turbulence, just an hour after it took off from Chhatrapati Shivaji International Airport's 1B Terminal. It was drizzling in Mumbai and now a gloomy Kolkata welcomed the Ghosh siblings to the *City of Joy*. Though it wasn't at all a joyous moment for Sumit and Sunita, still they had to remain strong in the current situation.

The brother-sister duo booked a pre-paid cab from NSC Bose International Airport till College Street. Sunita instructed the Bihari taxi driver to drop them at the junction of MG Road and College Street. Throughout this thirty-minute's drive neither of them exchanged a single word with each other, as both were pre-occupied with the thought of *what-will-happen-next*. From the junction towards the Presidency College, there's a narrow lane on the right which makes its way through some crowded old book shops to a four storied white and blue building bearing a huge hoarding – 'Rajat Guest House'.

The road facing corner room on the third floor had already been booked over the phone by Sushil Ghosh earlier that morning. After making a resgistry entry, the hotel boy escorted Sumit and Sunita to room no 302. The non-AC, double room with an extra bedding came in for INR 750 per day. This hotel wasn't new to the Ghosh family; they had earlier stayed here on a couple of occasions. Most of the hotel staff were known to Sushil as the elderly couple often visited Kolkata for their medical check-ups.

"When will *Baba* and *Maa* be reaching here?" Sumit asked his sister while inserting the new SIM card in his new phone.

"Anytime soon, they left Haldia in the morning. Why don't you try calling *Baba*?" replied Sunita.

"I don't know the new number, and calling on the old number will be suicidal."

Before leaving Mumbai, Sunita bought a feature phone and two Vodafone SIM cards. She made sure that their regular smartphones were switched off and dismantled. Sushil also dumped his regular SIM card and handset for a new one. Sunita couldn't believe the fact that they had to actually get rid of their phones and make Rajat Guest House their temporary hideout.

After setting up the new handset, the very first thing which Sumit did was – texted Advocate Panigrahi his new number without revealing his current location. Around noon, the doorbell of the hotel room rang. Chitra and Sushil Ghosh entered looking distressed. They seemed to look much older than their actual age. Sunita went and hugged her *Maa* and whimpered, meanwhile Sushil rearranged all the bags and baggages in one corner of their 160 square foot hotel room.

"*Kandish na Sunita*, be strong. We all know that we've done no wrong, so nothing will happen to us." Sushil tried cheering up his daughter.

"*Baba*, everything is finished; don't know how long this litigation will drag!! *Dada's* future is spoiled forever." Sunita broke down and sobbed like a child.

"*Oye, kya ho gaya tereko* – all of a sudden, why are you being so worried and emotional?" Sumit mocked his sister.

"Okay, all of you freshen up, we'll go downstairs in next half an hour for lunch." Sushil declared.

There was a hotel downstairs adjacent to Rajat Guest House, which the Ghosh family referred to as *Odiya Hotel*. They made awesome fish curry which they rarely missed on their Kolkata visits. The owner of the eatery hailed from a village in Paralakhemundi in Odisha during the 1940s and had first set up a road side stall near College Street market. This old eatery is now being managed by his grandsons.

After a heavy lunch, a visibly tired and exhausted Ghosh family opted for an afternoon siesta, except Sumit, who tried to keep himself awake in order to catch hold of Advocate Panigrahi over the phone - but eventually dozed off.

At quarter past 4 pm, Sushil woke up to the *Azan* for *Namaz* from a nearby mosque. Next to him on the bed, he saw his wife and children, in deep sleep. And why wouldn't they be? The proceedings of these rueful days had clobbered the family's courage. With little mental and physical stamina remaining, they had all given in to sleep that afternoon.

He picked up the flask from above the cabinet against the wall and without waking anyone, strolled down the stairs and outside the hotel to fetch some evening tea for the family. Outside, the sky was still lit with traces of sunlight escaping behind the clouds.

"*Dada*, did you manage to speak to the lawyer?" asked Sunita, aware of the fact that her brother had been trying to reach the advocate's number since afternoon.

"No, twice his number was busy on some other call and the third time he didn't take my call."

"May be, he is busy with other cases. A lawyer handles so many cases. We aren't his only client," explained Sushil to his son.

"Ok, I'll call him around 9 pm then." Sumit toggled his mobile phone keypad and continued with some intermittent level of *Candy-Crush*. Sushil switched on the TV and flipped through the news channel, while the mother-daughter duo sat on the corner of the bed discussing about the adverse impact of this sudden unplanned leave, which Sunita took from her employer in the name of a family emergency.

At around quarter to 9 pm, Sumit's phone rang. Everybody in the hotel room stared at it in anticipation of Panigrahi's call.

"Sumit *Babu*, I was driving back from court to my residence, so couldn't take your call" the lawyer apologised.

"No problem Sir, just wanted an update from you and hence the call."

"Oh yes – the date for the hearing of our petition is day after tomorrow. You shall be a relieved man after that," assured the legal counsel.

"Thank you so much Sir, we all left our respective locations and are now together, just waiting for the bail. And Sir, here's my father who wants to have a word with you." Sumit handed over the phone to the senior Ghosh.

"*Namaste Sir,* you've been talking to my son and you know our current situation, *ektu dekhben*, so that everything gets over smoothly. I am growing old and my blood pressure spikes up thinking of this current chain of events." Sushil pleaded.

"I understand your pain Sir, *koi baat nahi*, I'll look into it. I just informed Sumit about the hearing dates. Once I bail out your family, we'll plan our next steps" the advocate assured.

"*Thik hai Sir,* as you say." Sushil thanked the advocate before hanging up the phone.

Slightly relieved from the ongoing angst, the Ghosh family headed for dinner at the *Odiya Hotel*.

⁜ ⁜ ⁜

The criminal lawyer on the other hand was under tremendous pressure. He had never anticipated that this dowry case was just the tip of the iceberg. Rather Panigrahi thought that he will have his way out in this case and will be able to get the Ghosh family out on bail, which would also create immense equity in the Rourkela court. Getting a Mumbai client out of a major family dispute would add to his repute. But DSP Dash was up with some dirty games of office politics. He was indirectly posing a threat to the lawyer's wife's departmental promotion to Assistant Deputy Superintendent of Police, which largely depended on recommendations from higher authorities. Dash also went a step ahead and straightaway offered some percentage to the advocate through his associates, which would be eventually squeezed from the Ghosh family by means of out-of-court settlement. The DSP knew that if he dragged Panigrahi's wife into the scene, Panigrahi would fold and forget his professional ethics. Mrs Panigrahi getting elevated to a higher post will have long run benefits and a different social standing. Dash's plan had little chances of failure.

While the Ghosh family kept counting days in the hope of getting justice, Panigrahi conveniently breached their faith, changed sides and procrastinated the proceedings, until one day Sumit discovered some inconsistency while conversing with the lawyer. In the past fifteen days, Panigrahi had made several excuses on why the bail petition didn't appear before the magistrate for hearing, but never revealed the truth. A suspicious Sumit finally requested his friend, Anup Bose, to visit the court and find out the case status. His speculations turned out to be true. Sumit was dumbstruck to hear that their bail petition got rejected on the first hearing itself. He started palpitating and gasping out of anxiety, shock and dismay. It hadn't occurred to him that Panigrahi would betray him like this.

Once the last date of *Hajira* got over, the Birmirpur police would come looking for them. With no more legal options available, Sumit felt absolutely vulnerable and impuissant – the fear of getting arrested gradually dawned upon their lives. As a precautionary measure, Sumit quickly disposed the SIM card he had used to connect with Panigrahi from Kolkata.

For an entire afternoon, room number 302 of Rajat Guest House turned into a planning room. Every member kept thinking about just one single agenda – *What next?* They just couldn't afford to waste any more time. Any further delays from their end would give the police enough reasons to issue an arrest warrant against the whole family.

The senior Ghosh couldn't get over the fact that a lawyer, whose advance fees was paid, who kept assuring all this while that he was on his toes to fight it out for them – had suddenly just backed off! Sumit couldn't even access his smartphone which lay dead somewhere in the corner of his backpack, else he could have Googled for another lawyer from Rourkela. That evening he visited a crowded Cyber Centre in the vicinity and thoroughly searched the internet for a Rourkela based lawyer but failed to get one; may be, because small towns still operated more offline than online. He didn't want to keep any kind of cyber trail on social media, hence avoided logging into his Facebook or Twitter – who knew, the Police might be silently tracking his moves!

Amidst all the apprehensions, Sushil suddenly remembered seeing a lawyer's signboard at the neighbouring lane, the day he went out for tea. The father-son duo visited Advocate Gautam Guha's chamber cum residence at Tamer Lane of North Kolkata, to discuss and explore legal options that could be availed at this juncture of the case. The young lawyer patiently heard their unfortunate tale and suggested them to approach the Orissa HC and move the bail petition from there. The HC of a state has special power to grant bail to the accused, if the same is being rejected at the lower court. A HC lawyer from Odisha only could get them out of the shambles.

Looking at the current chain of events, an empathetic Guha referred senior Advocate Pradip Panda from Bhubaneswar to the oppressed father and son. Advocate Panda, who simultaneously practiced in Orissa HC and Bhubaneswar's district court knew Guha through an interstate criminal case, which they had collaborated on half a decade back.

Meanwhile with 750 bucks daily plus lunch, dinner and snacks for the last twelve days; Ghosh family's stay at Rajat Guest House was turning out to be an expensive affair. Also, it wasn't safe to continue their stay at one particular location for such a long period. Hence, hunt for a new place commenced and finally they shifted to Alakapuri Lodge – located on the lane behind *Adi Mohini Mohan Kanjilal,* one of the oldest and most popular garment retail stores in north Kolkata. Rooms were smaller there, as compared to the earlier accommodation, but then at INR 400 per day, this was the best bet – considering the fact that they had no idea how many more such days they had to remain in disguise.

The senior lawyer from Bhubaneswar got a call from Sumit, heard him and agreed to take up his case. He strongly condemned the cowardly, unprofessional act of Advocate Basant Panigrahi and assured full legal assistance and support to the Ghosh family. He noted down the case number and asked Sumit to call him after two days; in the meantime, he asked the Ghosh family to remain underground and not to disclose their current location to anybody. Meanwhile, Advocate Panda applied for the True copy of the case papers from Rourkela court, through one of his local associates.

Uptil now, the Ghosh family remained aloof from their relatives so as to keep them away from unnecessary problems of the police, litigation, etc. Everybody remains busy with their day-to-day lives and it wasn't right to drag them into this ongoing crisis. However, Chitra sensed some upcoming running around to be done and thus came up with the suggestion of calling her brother to Kolkata from Balichak.

Next afternoon, Tapan Das arrived at Alakapuri Lodge and till evening listened to all the intense, spine-chilling and gripping instances which his sister's family had gone through in the past couple of weeks. He could very well gauge the extent of harassment the family must have undergone and surmised that it was far from over.

Though his nephew appeared normal, Tapan was sure that a whirlwind of thoughts preoccupied Sumit's mind. Tapan also felt pity for the current cramped up living condition of the entire Ghosh family – he insisted that they shift to Balichak, where his political connections with local party leaders would shield them from getting arrested. Sushil saw a merit in his brother-in-law's proposal and agreed to send his wife and daughter to Balichak, while he decided to visit Bhubaneswar along with his son.

At the end of July, the Rourkela's lawyer fraternity called for a strike, in demand of setting up a High Court bench at Rourkela. This strike further delayed Advocate Panda's case preparation for the Ghosh family. Procurement of the FIR copy and 161 Statement copies got pushed back by a few days. Finally, once the draft petition got prepared, Panda asked his client to visit Bhubaneswar and sign the *Vakalatnama* followed by the petition.

⊹ ⊹ ⊹

Early on a wet Wednesday morning, the minibus from College Street junction with just five passengers on-board, whizzed past the deserted Mahatma Gandhi Road followed by the iconic Howrah Bridge to reach the Howrah Station in flat 10 minutes. It continued drizzling as Sumit and his father waited for the *Dhauli Express* at the junction of platform number 19 and 18. By 5:45 am, when the empty rakes were allotted to platform number 19, movement of commuters gradually surged. Sumit finished his last sip of tea and was about to pick up his backpack and follow his father, who had already started advancing towards coach number D5. Just then somebody tapped his shoulder. Sumit turned back and even before he could realise what was happening, two heavily built plain clothed constables pushed him hard on the floor and handcuffed him. They started abusing him *"Abey sala, kahan bhaag raha tha? Humein chuthiya samajh ke rakkha hai kya?"*

Sumit cried in desperation *"Babaaa* you leave, I'll be fine. Go and meet Panda Sir."

Sushil looked at his son helplessly. Even before he attempted to alight from the coach, *Dhauli Express* steadily picked up its speed.

The policemen thrashed him, kicked him brutally. The crowd gathered but they were clueless. Sumit was bleeding profusely and kept on pleading "Please leave me, I am innocent. I've done nothing. Please Sir, please…"

One of the constables walked forward, shook him up and kept telling him, "Wake up Sumit, wake up. Everything is fine, we all are here. Don't worry, nothing is going to happen"

Sumit opened his eyes, just to find the ceiling fan rotating rigorously over him.

The entire family surrounded him around the bed, while his sister kept on giggling at this act of his. Sumit heaved a sigh of relief and tried to put up a brave face.

The next day *Dhauli Express* reached Bhubaneswar at 1:15 pm, delayed by 25 minutes. While Sushil and his son left for Bhubaneswar, his wife and daughter headed to Balichak with Tapan. The father and son were visiting the capital city of Odisha for the first time. Not sure which way to exit from, they stood for a minute on the crowded platform and immediately got surrounded by a couple of agents and taxi drivers, who started offering them a ride to the cheapest hotel nearby. Sumit ignored them all and walked out of the station, spotted a tea stall and decided to have a cup of tea before venturing out for an accommodation. Suddenly it started pouring heavily, the senior and junior Ghosh had no option but to wait till it stopped raining. Sushil took this opportunity to strike a conversation with the tea stall owner.

"Where can we get a budget hotel or lodge nearby?" asked Sushil.

"Babu epotey tikey sastaa miliba, sepotey taa mahanga" replied the tea stall owner with animated gesture.

Sushil had a puzzled look, as he couldn't make anything out of it. However, Sumit understood Oriya language and he continued to probe further. After having a thorough understanding, he explained all to his father, *"Baba,* actually there are two exit points here. The one we came out through leads to Puri-Cuttack Road. Along this road towards Kalpana Square there are innumerable budget hotels whereas, the opposite exit opens to a place called Master Canteen Chowk; hotel rates of that area are on the higher side."

Finally, after exploring a couple of places along the Puri-Cuttack Road, they checked into Hotel Gunjan, just 250 meters away from Kalpana Square. Room number 210 on the second floor of the four storied hotel building came at INR 400 per day. Sumit called up Advocate Panda to inform him about their arrival in the city. The senior lawyer sounded busy, asked Sumit to meet him at his chamber around 7:30 pm and texted him the address.

New city, new people, new lawyer – but Sumit was firm on achieving his intent of securing a bail. He didn't want to get arrested for an alleged crime which he never committed, he would never give into somebody's illegitimate demand, and swore to fight it out till the end. But in this battle of justice, he needed an honest, ethical, perspicacious, sagacious and obstinate lawyer with a cunning approach. After being ditched by Panigrahi, Sumit was slightly apprehensive about this Bhubaneswar lawyer *– what kind of a person is Panda, will he be able to get him and his family out from this obscurities and intricacies?!!!* A vortex of thoughts crossed Sumit's mind, while the autorickshaw made its way through the Rameswar Patna Road; a splash of downpour earlier in the evening caused some puddles along the narrow lane. The second last bungalow at the dead end of the lane bore a nameplate – Advocate Pradip Panda, LLM, High Court Lawyer.

The road facing room on the first floor, attached with the balcony is where the lawyer generally met his clients. One end of the rectangular room was occupied by two of his juniors, who were seated in front of their desktops, busy drafting petitions. The adjoining table had a laser printer cum scanner and stacks of files and folders. The other end of the room was where the advocate's desk was stationed, surrounded by racks full of legal journals, reference books, dictionary, files and manuals. A large oil painting of Lord Jagannath, Balaram and Subhadra hung on his right wall, whereas a sofa for the visitors was placed on his left.

A medium built guy in his late forties, with dyed curly hair and wheatish complexion having chevron moustache and dark framed glasses was busy signing some documents, when the visitors entered the room.

"Welcome to Bhubaneswar, Sumit." the lawyer extended his hand for a handshake after finishing off his signatures. "I hope you didn't face any difficulty in locating this place."

"Sir, I just took an autorickshaw from Kalpana Square till here" replied Sumit.

"Oh, that must have cost you a lot. These rickshaw guys can figure out the new comers and charge them inappropriately. I should've told you a cheaper way to reach my place."

"Yes Sir, the rickshaw charged me 150 bucks." Sumit replied with a puzzled look.

"There you see, it takes just INR 5 per person on a shared auto from Kalpana Square to Barik Sahi junction and from there it's walking distance to my place."

"*Mote sei file ta pass kariba,* please." Advocate Panda instructed one of his juniors.

After having some initial chitchat, the lawyer got straight into discussing the case with his client. He opened a blue coloured cover-file, which had hand written mention of *Sumit Ghosh vs Moulina Ghosh, GR Case no 989/2014, Birmirpur PS*. He took out a bunch of photocopied papers and handed them over to Sumit "These are your case papers – FIR copy and 161 Statements, this is your copy. I've got the true copies with me, which we've to file along with the bail application." Sumit carefully took the documents from Panda and kept them in his bag.

The lawyer continued, "I suggest, you later read through the FIR carefully and make a note of all the allegations made. Most of the 161 statements are written in Oriya, which you won't be able to follow. But for the time being, the FIR is the most important document, on which we should base our petition. He took off his glasses and ordered tea. Then he looked at Sumit and spoke, "I've gone through this FIR, but still want to hear it out from you, as to what all things have happened till date in a chronological order."

For the next forty minutes, Sumit detailed the series of incidents that had happened with him and his family. One of the juniors was also listening and quietly taking notes. All the while, the senior counsel cautiously listened to his client, closing his eyes and bending back on his brown swivel chair.

"You know what, these days filing a 498A is as easy as ordering a pizza. Walk up to a police station, talk some rubbish against a guy, and *prima facie* a complaint will be filed with a garland of IPCs. Even before you realise what's happening – the police, the neighbours, and the society will start judging you and tag you as a culprit. The beginning of your end commences soon after." Advocate Panda blasted in an irritated manner.

"Sir, we are helpless and incapable of handling this situation. We are roaming here and there like dreadful criminals to avoid an arrest. Nightmares are now a common phenomenon, we hardly go out in the open, and we seldom talk to unknown people. This created a consternation not to be easily allayed. And all these for some unknown reason," an upset Sushil replied. "Please help us, Sir" a frazzled Sushil added.

"Mr Ghosh, leave your worries to me. I'll get you all bailed out from the High Court. I know you had a bitter experience with your Rourkela lawyer, but trust me not all are like Panigrahi. I had been the President of Bar Council of Bhubaneswar court and I know that a bunch of miscreants create a bad patch to our profession." Panda replied sternly.

"Sumit, I've drafted your bail petition, would request you to go through the same and suggest changes. My junior, Shrikant will help you out with the same, you'll have to excuse me for some time as I'm expecting a family friend downstairs." The lawyer got up from his chair and made his way to the staircase.

Shrikant Mishra – the tall, fair, bald, tongue-tied junior of Panda had been the key person in his law firm, for the past twelve years. He hardly spoke, but wrote non-stop. He was the one who drafted almost all the petitions for the senior counsel without any narrations. For Sumit, he made two bail applications – one for his father, mother and sister which would be filed first, followed by the other which would be filed within a day's gap. After making some minor changes in the document, the printouts were taken, stapled and kept on the table for a final nod from Pradip Panda. Along with the petitions, a couple of *Vakalatnamas* were also arranged.

At around 9:00 pm, Panda glanced through the petitions, asked Sumit to sign his petition and imitate the signatures of his mother and sister on the other petitions. He also made Sumit sign the *Vakalatnama.*

It was getting late. Without any further delay Sushil asked, "Sir, how much do I pay you for all these?"

"3000 rupees for each petition, and then later on when the petition gets listed for hearing, you've to pay some more. Will let you know about it in advance, so that you can make the arrangements." The lawyer replied without any hesitance.

"How much would that be, Sir?" asked Sumit.

"Can't say it now, let's first file this tomorrow and then will discuss."

"What time do we come here tomorrow?" enquired Sumit.

"Same time, 7:30 pm should be fine. I'll be able to give you the case number as allotted by the HC."

Sushil and Sumit paid the lawyer his fees and signed off for the day. They walked the narrow lane and didn't pay much attention to their surroundings – the flickering streetlight, the playful slum kids, the Hindi number from Salman Khan's new release, and the gossiping shopkeepers; all seemed to be rejoicing after a hard day's work. The father and the son waited for an auto along the main road. They got down at Kalpana Square, walked into a restaurant, and had dinner before heading to Hotel Gunjan.

BLAPL-1090/2014 and 1985/2014, generated by Orissa HC's automated system, became the new identity for the Ghosh family which would last for the next couple of months to come. They went on to veil themselves at a semi-rural area of Balichak. The neighbouring people knew them all, and hence their presence as a whole family failed to raise any eyebrows. Their last Balichak visit was almost a year back, when Sumit had gotten married and brought his wife to meet his octogenarian granny.

Back from Bhubaneswar, Sushil and Sumit kept discussing about the lawyer. He appeared to be very professional and well connected. Like any other lawyer, he also boasted about his connections with political parties, news magazines, Bar Council members, big shots from the police fraternity and all. During their conversation, he kept on abusing the Chells and questioned Moulina's character, which generated mixed feelings in Sumit. At times, he felt that the advocate is empathetic about their situation and wanted to teach the Chells a lesson for their lifetime. Again, he never appreciated the advocate questioning the girl's character; as he still believed that something went wrong somewhere, and Moulina must have been brainwashed to write the FIR.

Life in Balichak wasn't the same as in Mumbai or Haldia. There was no tap water or overhead tank. The low voltage electricity made it impossible to run a television channel for long, and frequent power cuts in the middle of the night gave the mosquitoes a reason to celebrate. Limited number of mobile towers made it impossible to access 2G or 3G in full flow. Over and above this, lightning and thunder showers of the ongoing rainy season paralysed the normal functioning of electricity and mobile connectivity.

But a village had its own monsoon charm…the petrichor, the pitter-patter, the greenery all around, the pearls of water droplets on leaves, muddy roads, cacophony of the grigs and the frogs; were all fascinating. Not so long ago, Sumit used to often visit his granny during the monsoons. Half an acre of land was full of greenery with trees like mango, jamun, mahogany, teak, tamarind, false-ashoka, coconut, and eucalyptus. There were two ponds with varieties of fish in them. Vacations were fun…chasing the ducklings into the pond, running after the chickens, stone pelting the langurs, feeding the kittens and then playing muddy football with his *Mama*; were all exciting. And then gradually all of those childhood fun times faded. Sumit grew up as a man, got busy with his corporate life in a big city, visits to his granny's village turned out to be rare from being infrequent.

Mama's smartphone with 2G connection was the only way by which Sumit and Sunita kept a tab on the proceedings at the Orissa HC hearing through *cause-list* tracking. Frequent refreshing of the webpage was irritating due to slow connectivity.

Meanwhile, Sunita got an email from her office, which threatened to expel her, if she didn't report back in the next 10 days. Her office tried reaching her mobile number several times in the past and she remained incommunicado all this while. She hadn't revealed this litigation complexity to her Boss before leaving Mumbai. It was time to do it. She called up her HR Head and explained the situation. The HR agreed to a twenty days' extension of leave.

Uptil now Sumit had been consoling himself that his beloved wife just couldn't walk into the police station and register a fake complaint against him and his family. She must have been indoctrinated to do so, but with the FIR copy in his hand he felt completely shattered and wobbly. A deep sense of betrayal prevailed with anxiety, hopelessness, loneliness, restlessness and discontent – he gradually slipped into depression. Five pages of handwritten complaint; Sumit found it hard to imagine Moulina writing all of it. The last time he had seen her handwriting before this was on a yellow piece of paper, where she had listed the weekly grocery items that Sumit had to purchase while returning from his office. She had giggled and handed over the piece of paper to her husband saying, "If you forget these, then be prepared for today's *chai* without sugar and *daal* without salt." Sumit in reply had pecked her dimpled cheeks before leaving for office. He used to call his wife innumerable times from the office, just because his sweetie used to be all alone in their apartment. Not so long ago, every weekend was a special one with dinning out or mall hopping or night shows for the couple. They couldn't go for honeymoon for lack of leaves at Sumit's office, but he wanted to surprise her with a foreign trip, unfortunately that would never ever happen.

Sumit read through the FIR copy numerous times. Every allegation made was an asphyxia of his trust, each of those accusations were hypoxia to his blind faith. He felt ruined, cheated and devastated. Why the hell did she do this to him? He never harmed her, and always thought her to be his better half. He always cared for her, encouraged her, supported her – helped her choose a particular *Rabindrasangeet*, which she went on to sing and win her first prize at Navi Mumbai Bengali Association's cultural programme. Sumit still remembered how proud he was then as a husband, almost went tomtomming about his wife's achievement to every colleague on his office floor. And how conveniently, the FIR accused him of not letting her pursue her dreams and desires. How can she ever write that? Was she out of her senses when she complained about being kept in confinement! How could she forget those evening walks together, hand in hand, side by side – at times stealing a kiss in the public park, which embarrassed her so much that she vowed not to accompany Sumit next time, yet she would be the first one to be ready for the next day's walk. How could she ignore those discussions of having an adorable kid, whenever they spotted Dhabolkar's cute little daughter with curly hair and bubbly cheeks from the C-wing.

Moulina was also aware that her in-laws were financially helping her husband to own a flat in Mumbai. They wanted the newly married couple to settle down and get rid of the eleven months' rental agreement cycle permanently. She also at times, had accompanied her husband and father-in-law to check out the shortlisted flats in Chembur's vicinity. In spite of all these, how come her conscience didn't prick while she complained against her in-laws demanding and pressurising to get cash and jewellery from her paternal home? Sumit's father owned a WagonR, but Sumit was never a car enthusiast, he didn't even bother to learn driving. In fact, Sumit didn't even have a four wheeler driving license. But like any family man, he too dreamt of having a car once he got his next promotion…this was also known to his wife, but still that didn't stop her from blaming Sumit of demanding a car from the Chells. He just couldn't imagine this double-faced nature of Moulina – as a lovely, homely wife versus a 498A complainant. How delusional he must have been all throughout!

Every line written in the FIR hurt Sumit somewhere deep down enormously and made him wonder how the girl he knew for the last sixteen months suddenly changed colours like a chameleon – or was it his growing love which obstructed his ability to read between the lines and see through the illusion of events? Was it all pre-planned, fixed and he just became the victim of a deep-rooted nexus unknown to him and his family? The dichotomy and polarity of Moulina was beyond any realm of reasons. He gradually felt like a snail, muffled up in its own shell to stay away from social embarrassment and awkwardness – what would he answer to those ex-colleagues, who would enquire about his wife's musical aspirations? How would he avoid those faces who used to stare at them during their evening walks? How would he handle his neighbours' queries when they would find his wife missing from family functions? Tussle of mixed thoughts made him gloomy, he wanted to wail out his anguish somehow. Sumit could not express or explain to anyone what or how exactly he felt…it was as if everything that he was familiar with, or was a part of his life for the past year had either come crumbling down or suddenly ceased to exist overnight like magic! Talking to his parents about this wasn't an option. He didn't want them to see him weak and helpless.

Meanwhile, things didn't move as anticipated. The HC hearings went on at their own pace. Every night after dinner, Sumit and Sunita routinely checked the updated causelist. After refreshing multiple times, they would get lucky to download the causelist and scroll across the same to search BLAPL-1090/2014 and 1985/2014.

Luck never favoured the Ghosh family on this matter. Each day seemed almost like a month to them. And then suddenly one day, the Orissa HC lawyers went on to a strike over CBI's arrest of the former Advocate General for his alleged link up with a chit-fund scam, which rumpled the normal flow of case disposals per day.

In the meantime, the month of September bid adieu to August. Some minor depression at the Bay of Bengal caused heavy downpour with lightning and thunderstorm almost every single day and hence, the Ghosh family had to remain in confinement. And then, on one such moist, rainy evening; Sumit recieved a missed call from Advocate Panda. Almost instantly Sumit dialled back, Sushil and Chitra came running from the other room and sat next to him. Sushil instructed his son to keep the phone on speaker. Sumit horripilated, while the HC lawyer took some time to pick up the call.

"Haan Sumit, kaal BLAPL-1090 ki hearing hai, I've made all the arrangements. Don't worry, most probably after the lunch hour, I'll be able to give you the good news…" the lawyer spoke those words with frequent pause.

"That'll be of great relief, Sir." Sumit replied in a tottery voice.

"And as discussed, you now have to deposit 25,000 per person in my account. I shall be messaging you the account details, soon after the call."

"Twenty-five thousand per head! Sir what are you saying?" Sumit responded in utter shock, exchanging glances with his parents.

"Sumit, you've heard it right. HC matters aren't easy and hence expensive, didn't I tell you to be prepared?" the lawyer replied firmly.

"Um, yeah, but…"

"Getting bail isn't that easy and you must have realised it by now. The lower court has already rejected your bail and we are superseding it here, for which I've to make loads of setting for smooth functioning. Else if you follow normal procedure, the guarantee of obtaining a bail in dowry case diminishes. *Hazaro process hoti hai, tab jaake bail milta hai* – the Judge would call for the Case Dairy from the PS, the IO will appear, the government lawyer will object and then things will unnecessarily get into a complicated loop," narrated the lawyer.

Sumit was quiet all this while. He felt groggy while hearing it out from the senior counsel. Sushil however, signalled affirmative to his son on the amount.

"See Sumit, this amount isn't for me, this has to be distributed among the *Peshkars*, the Government advocates and their associates. There's a lot that happens behind the scene and we've to manage them well and keep them happy. The *Peshkars* will pass on our application to that particular judge, who isn't averse to dowry cases and will grant bail easily. Else if it appears before a strict judge who is antagonistic to these types of cases, then we are screwed. We've to make calculative moves." Panda explained it all.

"Ok Sir, so how much do I pay you now?"

"The first application has three petitioners, so INR 75,000 for now. But transfer it by day after tomorrow, once you get to know the good news. I hope you'll not make me follow up for the money."

"With which bank do you have your account?' asked Sumit.

"I'll message you all details, its AXIS Bank."

"But Sir, we only have an SBI branch here in this village. And I am sure due to extreme monsoon conditions here, there will definitely be link failure. I suggest you go ahead with your plan, we are coming to Bhubaneswar in the next couple of days – you will get your fees and we shall pick up the Order copy." Sumit responded with constant prompt from his father.

"Done, let me know once you book your tickets to Bhubaneswar." Panda uttered enthusiastically before disconnecting the call.

Sunita was quick to browse through her *Mama's* 2G phone and access IRCTC to book tickets for the entire family on Dhauli Express. While the brother-sister were busy booking tickets; Sushil laid back on the bed and took a deep breath, the lizard on the wall near the CFL bulb finally pounced on its prey and slowly started swallowing it. Outside, the frogs started croaking, while it stopped raining.

Money would come and go. But as a family head, as a father, as a husband, as a protector – his utmost duty was his family's safety.

TWELVE
2011

Birmirpur, Odisha, India

The display board at Rourkela station showed the arrival time of *Ispat Superfast Express* as 13:50 hours that was 25 minutes late than its scheduled arrival. Two gentlemen in their winter gear were getting agitated – one of them was frequently eyeing his wrist watch, and the other one had walked up to the enquiry counter thrice by now to understand the train's status.

Winters are extreme in the steel city, with an average temperature ranging from 7 – 9°C. Mid-December is characterized by chill in the air and northern cold breeze. Even at these early afternoon hours, there wasn't any trace of sunlight. Sanat Chell was getting worried, as it would take another one hour for them to reach Birmirpur from here. His younger brother Sarat waved at him and asked to follow him towards platform number 2, where the *Ispat Express* was expected in next 5 minutes.

Earlier that day, Sushil Ghosh had messaged Sanat their coach number. Accordingly, the Chell brothers took their position at the exit door of coach number C2. Most of the commuters from Kolkata, Kharagpur, Jamshedpur and Chakradharpur get down here at Rourkela, making the platform look like a crowded fish market. However, the section near the AC compartments was relatively less crowded. After a while, Sanat spotted Mr and Mrs Ghosh and raised his hand. Behind the Ghosh couple appeared a medium built, fair guy in denim jacket and jeans who was about 5'8" tall. He had a woollen muffler wrapped around his neck and sported a grey coloured woollen beanie cap – Sumit was stepping into this city, eight years after his post-graduation along with his parents. Chitra, loaded with childhood memories of this city was stepping in almost after three decades!

Done with the initial customary greetings, Sanat directed the guests to the parking lot "This unexpected delay by the train has ruined the entire plan. Let's quickly get into the car. Maya must be ready with the lunch."

"The train had some engine failure at Jhargram station, that's where it got delayed," informed Sushil.

"*Dada*, meet my younger brother Sarat. We came to the station in his car and have been waiting for the train for the past one hour or so."

While Sanat was doing most of the talking, he also had an asquint eye on his prospective son-in-law. The Chell brothers escorted the Ghosh family to a red Santro parked in front of the railway station, and without any further delay, Sarat raced his car out of the parking lot towards the Ring Road. Within the next eight minutes they crossed the 75 feet long statue of Lord Hanuman at Hanuman Vatika. Keeping the Civil Township to their right, the hatchback sped towards Panposh Chowk through Link Road.

Throughout this short city drive, a flash of remembrance crossed Chitra's mind. Her father was once posted at Panposh railway station. Back then, it was more of a semi-urban zone, which had now developed into a full-grown city suburb.

Sarat, while adjusting his rear view mirror, commented "Now we'll be crossing the Brahmani River, the second longest in Odisha after the Mahanadi."

"How far is Vedvyas then?" asked Chitra.

"Ten minutes from here. In fact, this Brahmani is formed by the confluence of the Sankh and Koel rivers at Vedvyas only," replied Sarat.

"I remember visiting the Vedvyas temple with my father during our school holidays," Chitra slipped into nostalgia.

"Mythology says that, this is the place where *Maharishi Parashara* fell in love with the fisherman's daughter *Satyavati*, who later gave birth to *Vedvyas*, the compiler of the Mahabharata." Sarat explained while applying the brakes behind a truck on the National Highway.

The father-son duo was tired and preferred taking a nap, while Mrs Ghosh enjoyed the ride and narrated snippets from her childhood days. The Santro swiftly made its way towards the Vedvyas Chowk along the NH 143. The road from Rourkela bifurcated at this very junction. One moved straight towards Sambalpur, whereas the other bent right towards Ranchi. Sarat slowed down the car and Sanat called up home to update their location and movement.

For the next forty-five minutes, Sarat drove smoothly without any halt. He switched on the car audio and tuned into Big 92.7FM, which played retro Bollywood numbers. Sumit opened his eyes to a soothing number of Kishore Kumar hit '*Aaj unse peheli mulaqat hogi*' – he could view ample greenery along the sides of the highway. Arjun, tamarind, eucalyptus, gulmohar and giant rain trees lined up on both sides of the asphalt highway. Distant mountains with varied shades of green cover along with the blue sky and candy floss clouds in the milieu gave a perfect visual ecstasy. Some unpaved, dusty, red soil country roads originating from the highway went past through the low lying green agricultural plots before disappearing into the distant woods. The white line marker on the highway, big boulders by the roadside, speeding trucks, highway touch Dhabas, the lone *adivasi* walking by the ridge of the farmland to an unknown destination, flocks of myna heading to the hills, cattle grazing in the fields – all created a hypnotic sense in Sumit's exhausted mind. Far from the concrete jungle of Mumbai high-rises, he wished to dissipate into these earthy elements of nature. Even though he had seen her pictures, Sumit was going to meet Moulina for the first time today. The curiosity and anticipation in his mind accentuated, at the sight of these equally interesting roads that led to Birmirpur.

After almost an hour's drive, the Santro finally slowed down and descended off the highway to a narrow tar road on the right. Another minute of a bumpy and dusty ride brought them in front of a two storeyed large mansion with rusted iron gates, just opposite to a deserted railway station. An old man in white *kurta-pajama* was standing at the gate to receive the Ghosh family.

"Meet my father Shri Rathin Chell, he is now seventy-five but quite young at heart." Sanat introduced the old man to the visitors.

"*Namaskar, apnader kono oshubidhe hoyni to?*" Rathin amiably welcomed the guests.

"*Na na*, its fine, just that we had never imagined Birmirpur to be so far from Rourkela," responded Sushil.

Rathin was a happy old man today. His house was all buoyant and lively with all his sons, daughters-in-law and grandchildren gathering here to meet the groom's family.

Meanwhile, Sumit's rumbling tummy sent out a signal of acute hunger, triggered by some awesome fragrance of delicacies emerging out of the kitchen. But unfortunately, he would have to wait till the conventional introduction and chitchat among all the family members of the Chell clan got over. Later that day, Sumit realised that not only the Chell family, but their tenants, neighbours and relatives had also flocked together to have a glance of a *Mumbaikar* groom. The mention of Mumbai itself was enough to invoke huge interest among the neighbours of the Chells. Some even enquired if Sumit had ever bumped into any celebrity there.

Lunch was heavy and scrummy. Sumit saw some of his favourite food items there, which meant his parents might have discussed about his taste and preference with the Chells on their Haldia visit. *Chingri-Malai curry, bhetki-r paturi, kosha-mangsho, vegetable fried rice, beguni, aamer chutney* followed by *misti doi* and *rosogolla* were all saporous and delightful. Throughout the lunch, it was Moulina's mother, aunt and sister who kept interacting with Sumit.

"How was the lunch, Sumit?" asked Maya.

"Oh, very nice, everything tasted perfectly awesome," Sumit replied politely.

Now that lunch was over, his eyes searched around for Moulina.

"Yes, that's because my *Didi* cooked it especially for you," teased Lina.

"Hmm, that's impressive."

"Now don't believe in Lina's words, she is simply joking. My Moulina just can't cook anything other than Maggi." Maya interjected and smiled.

"Lina, why don't you take this packet and keep it on the dining table." Maya instructed.

"What is it *Maa?*"

"Ghosh Aunty has brought home-made chocolate cake for us."

"Wow, that's so nice of her." Lina walked out of the room towards dining area.

Sumit was made to sit in Moulina and Lina's room. The showcase to his left had some stuffed toys on the upper rack, the middle rack was full of certificates and awards of both Moulina and Lina's achievements in music and dance respectively. Lower rack was full of books and some framed black and white photographs of the Chell family. Sumit picked up a Bengali magazine from the corner table of the room and flipped through the glossy pages. Sanat peeped into the room, but before Sumit could turn around, he left without uttering a word.

Meanwhile, Chitra kept interacting with Moulina in the living room. The spacious living room had some old furniture from Moulina's grandfather's era. The LG Flatron TV kept at one end of the room played some local news channel but was muted, so that it didn't interrupt the conversations.

"How is your college going, Moulina?" enquired Chitra.

"As usual, but winters are a pain. Waking up early to catch a bus to school is torturous," replied Moulina looking at his grandfather, who had dozed off sitting on the chair.

"And what about music, are you regularly practising it?"

"No Aunty, *shomoy hoye othey na je*, and now with the exam season over, there's additional responsibility of checking the answer sheets of my students," complained Moulina.

"If time permits, today also we would like to listen to your songs and if you have a *tabla*, Sumit can give you *Sangat* too." Chitra smiled at her prospective daughter-in-law.

"Oh, he plays *tabla*, is it?" responded Moulina with a look of awe.

"Yes, my son learned *tabla* for five years when he was in class 5. But rarely practices now, at times in his office events he plays the instrument," revealed Chitra

Lina entered the living room and without any hesitation asked Chitra "Aunty why don't you ask my *Didi* to go and talk to Sumit *Da*, he must be getting bored in the other room."

"Yes Lina, you're right. We should let the boy and girl talk as much as they can. By the way, where are your brothers?" enquired Chitra.

"*Dada* is in Faridabad and *Bhai* must be at his friend's house, he generally stays away from all social gatherings," responded Lina promptly.

Chitra didn't get time to mull over this strange fact. Lina just pulled Moulina away from her, and everyone's attention went to the fact, that Moulina was entering her room where Sumit was waiting for her.

✢ ✢ ✢

That day Sumit and Moulina conversed for nearly an hour. Somewhere both felt that they were made for each other and could complement each other. They talked candidly, with the flow, without any apprehensions. They chatted like good old friends meeting after ages, with no specific topic as such. They laughed and joked, questioned and answered; and somehow developed a sense of revere for each other.

Sumit was bowled over by her naïve beauty. Her brown almond eyes, silky straight hair, dimple cheeks, captivating smile, alluring lips, mellifluous soft voice incarcerated his attention. Her contagious smile and illimitable innocence startled him. She didn't wear any makeup except a small *bindi* on her forehead. She wore a maroon coloured woollen cardigan over a yellow *kameez*, and often played with her hair and cupped her hand to tuck them behind her ears while talking.

Moulina on the other hand, was impressed by his intellect and sense of practicality. The glow of his eyes, the depth of his gaze, his powerful and comforting voice, his sense of humour; his simplicity beguiled her. A multi-talented guy with overall knowledge, who had been tempered by maturity and experience. It was pleasant to hear him and she liked his hand gestures while he bitched about his office work and Boss. His bright eyes looked straight into hers as they talked, and she had to look away at times to calm her nerves. *He's the perfect soul mate*, she thought.

Their prolonged meeting was however interrupted by Lina, who brought in *adrak-wali-chai* with some *pakodas*. Even though Lina was younger to Moulina, her silent approval was a must in almost everything for the elder sister. So, Lina spent a good ten minutes interacting with her *Di* and future *Jiju*. She found all the qualities that she wanted her *Jiju* to possess – friendly, approachable, smart, ratiocinative and cool dude. Lina in her mid-twenties appeared to be equally attractive and beautiful as her sister. Sumit wouldn't mind having a sister-in-law who was bubbly, chirpy, congenial, mischievous and equally talented in *Bharatnatyam* and *Kathak*.

Out of all this, Sumit noticed one strange thing – while everybody from the bride's side interacted with him, right from Moulina's septuagenarian grandfather to her school going teenaged cousin brother, it was her father, Sanat, who maintained a distance from him. For some unknown weird reason, he avoided Sumit but kept a wonky eye on him. Sumit personally didn't like this bizarre behaviour and ignored him in return. He also would've liked to meet his would-be brothers–in–law, but they chose to be elsewhere while their sister made the most important decision of her life.

In the evening, before visiting the *Rani Sati Mandir,* on everybody's request Moulina sang a couple of songs, to which Sumit played *tabla* and Lina helped her *Di* on the harmonium. Sumit was spellbound and mesmerized by her sweet, crystalline, mezzo-soprano voice. *Now that's how an ex-All India Radio artist should sound like,* Sumit observed in awe.

The *Rani Sati Mandir* at Birmirpur is a well-known landmark and is located on the main road, bang opposite the SBI branch. Devotees mainly from the Marwari community in and around Rourkela and Birmirpur flock together to worship *Dadi ji.* Sprawling over two acres of land, the white marble temple structure is beautifully adorned with art and architecture that gives a look of a marvellous palace. The temple area has two well-maintained flower gardens with varieties of seasonal flowers. Besides *Rani Sati,* the premise also houses temples of Lord Shiva, Sita-Ram, Ganesh and Hanuman.

The Chells accompanied their guests to the mandir and spent almost half an hour there. The trustee members of the temple were known to the Chells, they offered them *Prasad* after *sandhya arati.* Moulina being religious and reverent, thanked the Almighty for getting her such a good *rishta* from a well cultured, closely knit family.

⁌ ⁌ ⁌

The Ghosh family returned to Haldia after their overnight stay at the Chell mansion in Birmirpur. Sumit had to catch the evening flight back to Mumbai on 27th December, just a day after his birthday. Christmas followed by her son's birthday had always encouraged Chitra to bake her own cake and she has been doing this for years now. In fact, her cakes were famous among her social circle. Sumit wanted to go back and celebrate his last 31st December as a bachelor with his group of friends in Mumbai, as he was quite sure that from next year Moulina would accompany him.

Sumit's birthday eve at Haldia was celebrated with a quiet dinner of home cooked chilli chicken and fried rice. For a change, all being cooked by Sushil, who happened to be an even better cook than his wife. At the dining table, Sunita was badly missed, as she had to stay back in Mumbai due to lack of leaves from her office.

"Ki re, kemon hoyechey ranna ta? Not as good as Chell's preparation the other day, huh?" Sushil teased his son.

"By the way, who had made all those preparations that day?" Sumit enquired.

"Moulina's *Kakima and Mami* did most of it. Her mother confessed that even she isn't a passionate cook," responded Chitra.

"So, what's your opinion on this *rishta*, Sumit? Shall we proceed further and fix an engagement date?" Sushil asked as he took bites of the delicious cake.

"Yes, we can go ahead. But there are a couple of concerns, *Baba*. I somehow don't get a positive vibe from Mr Chell…his behaviour towards me was weird," opined Sumit.

"May be, it's because he was busy that day, it's not easy to manage so many guests. Moreover, he has all your information from us. He just might not have wanted to ask you anything."

"Another thing, I forgot to mention and probably you can get a clarity from Moulina's parents. That afternoon, when we were busy chatting, an old lady suddenly entered in our room and repeatedly questioned Moulina – *"When did you get married? Why didn't you inform me, is this guy from Bhubaneswar?"* Mr Chell appeared from nowhere and whisked her off. He kept telling the woman – *"Chatterjee Di, calm down, I'll tell you everything, let's go from here now."*

"Oh God!! You should've told this to me earlier. Now that we've made up our minds, these things will disturb us." Chitra got worried.

"Wait, don't panic. I'll get clarity from Chell, I'll ask him directly about this. Also, when we all were en route to *Rani Sati* temple; Sarat was in a hurry to go back to Rourkela and when I asked him the reason, he told me that – his daughters had their exam and he needed to be there at home. Then on further probing, he told me that only Sanat stays at Birmirpur and all his three brothers had separated out and were staying together in Rourkela. I don't remember Chell talking about this," revealed Sushil to his son and wife.

"Could they be hiding something from us?" Chitra raised her suspicion.

"God knows. I tried to get information about the family from the localites, but Sanat stuck to me like a shadow and never left me alone to venture out. Anyway, I'll put forth these concerns to him and only if I'm satisfied with his responses, we'll go ahead with the engagement," proposed Sushil, to which his wife and son agreed too.

On the other hand, Sanat was quite confident about the show put up by his clan altogether. He had invested a lot on the arrangements for welcoming and entertaining his guests from Haldia. And he knew, if this *rishta* passed through, he should be able to overcome these expenditures in the long run. The only *bone in the throat*, was Chatterjee *Di* and he was damn sure that the Ghosh family would enquire about it in the coming days. However, the duplicitous and cunning side of Sanat was ready with a convincing response.

THIRTEEN
2012

Haldia, West Bengal, India

Haldia experiences around 10 – 12 °C in the month of January. Mornings are cold and foggy with low visibility, while the biting wind makes one feel dry and numb. Sanat and Maya braved the chilly winter morning and headed towards Monalisa Apartment. Both were equally excited and exultant, as they were going to take the first step towards fixing their elder daughter's marriage. They were on their way to the Ghosh residence to discuss and finalise the engagement dates. Though the Chell couple was confident of pulling it through, they were equally speculative about the Ghosh family's demands and expectations.

"I am a bit worried about today. What do you think? Will this match be fixed?" Maya asked her husband timidly, on their early morning bus ride to Haldia.

"Why not? Now for God's sake, please be positive," an irritated Sanat replied.

"You could have told them the truth at the beginning." Maya persisted.

"Maya, there's no value for honesty in today's world. To achieve your goal one has to bluff, else..."

"I've never seen such a manipulative person in my life...What have you achieved till date by being so deceitful? Your brothers are successfully running their business, while you're sitting home. They are enjoying a good lifestyle, while you're struggling. And now when our Moulina's marriage is at stake, you aren't being transparent with the groom's family. Why do you have to behave in such a deceptive manner?" exploded Maya.

"That's because I don't want my children to taste failure the way I have. I want them to lead a smooth, peaceful life. Had I revealed my unemployment and financial status to the Ghosh family earlier, reaching this stage would've been extremely difficult. Maya, think before you put all the blame on me. I'm only doing this for our children," revolted Sanat.

"And what if things fail to proceed from here on?"

"Ufff Maya, now please shut up. I'll manage it. Try and understand, there's a psychological difference between the two – the alliance getting called off before meeting the girl and after meeting the girl and spending an entire day with her family. Our Moulina is extremely beautiful and talented, I'm sure by now the groom's family is enamoured by her. Revealing those trifling bluffs won't have a significant impact on the decisions made," explained Sanat.

Maya chose not to respond any further. She always felt disgusted with her husband's shrewd, conniving approach towards life, and eventually would give in. In fact, she thought, it ran in the blood. That's exactly why, her father-in-law didn't think twice before adopting the surname of *Chell* from her father. Maya adjusted her *shawl* and took a deep breath, while the bus sped its way through the foggy highway.

Sanat loved to visit the Ghosh couple. On every occasion he got a royal treatment – it became a feast day characterised by mouth-watering, home cooked dishes to savour. The Ghosh couple surely knew how to treat their guests. This time around, Sanat carried a packet of traditional Bengali sweets and handed it over to Mrs Ghosh. *The discussion on engagement should start with a sweet note,* he thought.

Lunch was meticulously prepared by Chitra. Mr and Mrs Chell relished every bit of *muri-ghonto, potol-bhaja, bhetki macher kalia, mochar-ghonto, chutney, payesh and rosogollas*. And finally, some serious talks on the engagement commenced just after the lunch.

Sanat was quick to take the lead. Anticipating the Ghosh couple's grudge resulting from the Birmirpur visit, without any excuse, Sanat gave a thoughtful start to his conversation.

"Ghosh *Da*, I know there are some concerns revolving round your head and I would like to come clean on those aspects. I had purposely not spoken about it over the phone, as I thought it to be better to explain it upon our meeting."

"Okay, go ahead." Sushil was waiting for this moment.

"Let me first apologise for Chatterjee *Di's* behaviour. She is our neighbour and often visits us. Two years ago, she lost her husband. The incident affected her psychologically. She sometimes behaves weirdly. The other day, when Sumit was there at Birmirpur, she mistook him to be the Bhubaneswar boy with whom our daughter's engagement got cancelled earlier."

"What? Moulina was engaged before? Why didn't you tell us about this?" Chitra was so shocked she lashed out uncharacteristically.

"*Didi*, eight months back we were in talks with this young man for a probable alliance. Things were progressing smoothly. The boy's family from Bhubaneswar was of great repute, as they had a cinema background. His aunt is a well-known playback singer in the Odiya film industry. The smart looking man was well settled and was employed with Infosys. His family liked my daughter a lot, we went ahead with the engagement and then all of a sudden I got a call from an unknown number – the girl on the other side of the phone introduced herself as a long-time girlfriend of this man and requested me not to proceed with the alliance, as she could finally convince her parents and planned to marry him," Sanat narrated with a tone of disgust in his voice.

"Tarpor ki holo?" asked Sushil curiously.

"I decided not to go ahead anymore and finally called off the alliance." Sanat was thankful to note that atleast one of them was buying his story.

"Now this guy too had visited Birmirpur and that's how Chatterjee *Di* got confused between Sumit and the Bhubaneswar boy," explained Sanat before glancing at his wife, who was a mere spectator in this entire conversation. She didn't utter anything to support or negate her husband.

"Ok, now that you've given us the background, we'll convey the same to our son. He has been a bit sceptical and hesitant because of these questions running around in our head. Let me and my wife speak with him regarding this." Sushil soberly sat back onto the sofa.

"If you want, I can talk to Sumit and explain all this to him." Sanat suggested.

"No, that's fine. He liked your daughter and that's what matters the most. In fact, we all liked Moulina and want her to be a part of our family." Chitra expressed her desire.

"Yes *Didi*, my responsibility ends by handing over my daughter to you all."

"Well, there's one more thing Mr Chell. During our initial talks, I remember you told us that you all are a joint family. But your brother Sarat told me that, they all had separated from you a long time back and are staying together in Rourkela – why did you hide this from us?" questioned Sushil.

"*Dada*, what do I say about this? They're staying separately not due to any family feud. Their kids are in their growing years, whereas all my children are grown up and have atleast graduated. They feel that Rourkela has better schools and coaching classes to offer their kids and that's why they shifted. I would rather use the term *"shifted"* than separated. They still continue to have their well-furnished rooms in our Birmirpur house. On every family get-together, they make it a point to come down and we celebrate as a full unit; a big prosperous family." Sanat replied confidently.

"And before we discuss anything further, let me also reveal another truth – for the last ten months my business is down and I've almost no income. But I'm trying hard to set it up all again. Once I get my Moulina married, I can fully concentrate on my business front." Sanat carefully placed these words after taking a long pause.

"Oh, sorry to hear that. But I hope you don't have any debts in the market due to your business dealings?" enquired Sushil.

"No Sir, I am clear on that front." Sanat assured.

"Okay then, we've heard enough. We are glad we had this conversation and cleared it all up. I'm sure Sumit will be okay with these details too. I think the next big question left to answer is…how do we proceed with the engagement?" Sushil asked for a suggestion.

"*Dada*, I'll come to it. But I would like to ask you about your demands and expectations for the wedding first. Though I am financially broke, still as a girl's father, I'll try my best to fulfil them."

"Chell *Babu*, relax. We are a progressive family and don't support the dowry system, so we aren't negotiating on any such thing. We like your daughter and want her as a part of our family. Now its upto you, how you want to send her off to us. As far as we are concerned, by God's grace we've got everything. Your daughter will now come and complete our family." Chitra smiled at the tense-looking couple.

"Post engagement, let's just have a registry marriage followed by a reception. No need of any social marriage, as that'll be financially difficult for you." added Sushil

"Ghosh *Da*, of late my financial condition has deteriorated. But that doesn't mean that Chell family's legacy in Birmirpur will fade away. After all, it's my elder daughter's marriage. It should be a matter of discussion in my social circle. So, we'll definitely have a social function and I promise you that it would be a good one."

"Mr Chell, it's completely upto you. What we suggested was because of your financial inability. We are fine even if you usher your blessings through *dhan-durba* and keep the *Kanya Sampradan* ceremony simple, by giving away your daughter to us along with *kola-patay-chal*," Chitra commented.

"I plan to give my daughter eighty grams of gold jewellery and gift a golden chain and a finger ring to Sumit. Social marriage will be organised in Rourkela due to locational advantages of the guests. You just let me know the engagement dates, Ghosh *Da*." Chell said excitedly.

"We will discuss this with Sumit. He is the one who has to take leave from the office. Again, we are more eager to take your daughter and least bothered about what you gift her or your son-in-law." Chitra repeated.

⁙ ⁙ ⁙

*Half a truth is often a great lie…*and Sanat didn't hesitate to deliver those half-truths to the Ghosh couple. Probably as a middle-class father and a struggling businessman, who was over-burdened with the responsibility of a daughter's marriage; the only way out were those half-truths. Maya was stunned to see, how tactfully her husband converted fictions into facts and almost single-handedly steered the discussion without raising any suspicions.

Mr and Mrs Ghosh were perhaps the most gullible individuals, who didn't pay heed to the loopholes in Sanat's narrative. They were more concerned about getting their son married to a girl who could be his friend for life. They all unanimously liked Moulina and overlooked those small indicators which would play havoc in their lives in the months to come. Post the engagement meeting, Chitra quickly got in touch with Kandar and asked for an auspicious date for her son's engagement.

23rd January 2012 – was fixed as the engagement day for Sumit Ghosh and Moulina Chell. A small function was arranged at the Ghosh residence amidst family members, friends, colleagues and neighbours. Sushil fastidiously made all the arrangements for the visiting guests. Haldia's famous *Suruchi Caterers* were entrusted with the task of ensuring the visitors' culinary delights through their appetizing platters. Indian Oil's Guest House rooms were booked to accommodate the guests. The visitors from Rourkela included Moulina's parents, her sister, her paternal and maternal uncles and aunts, cousin brothers and sisters. They all came in as a picnic party and graced the occasion. Sumit's granny along with his maternal uncle and aunt, and paternal uncle, were all present. Some of Sushil's colleagues and neighbours were also a part of the ceremonial function.

Sumit and Moulina's engagement ceremony, which marked the beginning of their wedding concord, commenced with a brief *puja*, followed by an auspicious alliance of ring exchange ceremony amid conch shell blowing and frequent ululations. The elders showered blessing to the couple, while both the families exchanged gifts and sweets. Elegant gold necklace, classic golden dangle and drop earrings, stylish sleek yellow gold bangles were all specially crafted for Ghosh family's daughter-in-law from Kolkata's *PC Chandra Jewellers*. Moulina looked stupendously gorgeous in a magenta coloured *Chanderi silk* saree, which was handpicked by Sunita from Dadar's *Paneri* showroom.

The Chells blessed their son-in-law with a golden chain and a finger ring, which were ancestral and had quite a dated design. But the Yankee blue coloured, slim fit *Park Avenue* suit selected by Lina from Rourkela's *Indira Plaza* gave a stunning look to her *Jiju*.

The Marriage Officer, invited by Sushil, was also present at the venue. He took few signatures on a couple of forms for registering the event of marriage under Hindu Marriage Act. That's when Moulina first signed her name as *Moulina Ghosh*, a signature which she was silently practicing in those last pages of her diary for the last couple of weeks.

The day ended on a beaming note. Both the families were happy. The guests were impressed with the warm and welcoming hosts. Sumit posted some of those engagement snaps on his Facebook wall and congratulatory messages poured in instantly.

FOURTEEN
2012

Birmirpur, Odisha, India

Moulina's *terrace moments* these days aren't quiet and calm. Post engagement, things have changed...the vastness of the sky and the night's darkness now beckoned her and she was all set to explore the night's romanticism with her soulmate. She was all verbose over the mobile, busy and excited chatting with Sumit for long hours. The blinking light appearing from the northern end of the sky no longer bothered her, neither she was heedful to those frisky fireflies anymore and the distant barking dogs often irritated her.

Weekdays were limited to post-dinner gossips, whereas on weekends they were engaged in lengthy hours of phone chat. Both of them would end up sharing their workplace titbits and how their day was spent. They were already into that "husband-wife" mould. Like a caring wife, she would go on to ask about Sumit's lunch and dinner details, while he like a protective husband would give Moulina few tips to survive office politics. She would saunter on the terrace and hear him narrate his routine Mumbai life with a child's astonishment.

Moulina started visualising Mumbai's daily life through Sumit's detailed description. She already started feeling the pulse of the city – *vada pav, cutting chai*, local trains, *kali-peeli taxis, dabbawalas* were some of those iconic city elements which revolved around her. She had never been to the mega city but was raring to visit soon. In her early teens, she used to watch those long distance trains either speeding away or halting at Rourkela Station, and most of them had Mumbai's *Victoria Terminus* as their last destination. Back then, she felt a strange whim to visit that last station and used to bug her grandfather, who used to jokingly say *"Wait, we'll get you married to a Mumbai boy, so that you can visit that last station at ease."*

"Achha aame honeymoon re kuade jauchu" asked Moulina in impeccable Odiya.

"Why do you have to ask that in Odiya, all of a sudden?" Sumit asked confoundedly.

"Oh sorry!! Actually, this morning I was chatting with my friend Sonali. She got married last year and asked me about our honeymoon destination and I didn't have any clue. Since, we conversed in Odiya, I just asked you exactly what she asked me!" giggled Moulina.

"I can fully understand the language, but can't speak fluently," informed Sumit.

"Yes, I know that, your mother had once mentioned about it. Now please answer me – *kothay jachhi amra?*" Moulina enquired like a child.

"Well, even I've not given it a thought yet. But I have Bhutan in my mind, the Himalayan kingdom will be a perfect locale during the summers. By the way, do you have anything in your mind?"

"I am completely blank on this and will leave it to you," replied Moulina.

While Sumit-Moulina's lovey dovey coochie-cooing continued over the phone, almost every day for several hours; their respective family members were all gearing up for the final day. 16th May 2012 was fixed as the day when Moulina and Sumit would officially tie the knot. Excitement and jubilation gripped both the families as they prepared themselves for the auspicious day – wedding cards went for printing, guestlists were finalised, venue was booked, menu was decided and the never ending shopping commenced. For both the families, it was a special occassion, as it was the wedding of their eldest progeny.

However, in this special moment, Sanat seemed to be twitchy and worried. He always had a dream wedding in his mind, which he wanted to gift his coddled and most pampered daughter; but his present financial crisis kept him away from his proclivity. Many a times, Moulina suggested that her father embrace the current financial situation and plan accordingly and let go of those past glorious memories, when the business was in full swing; but it always led to a disagreement and ended in altercations. For Sanat, his daughter's nuptial ceremony wasn't just any ordinary family function, but a platform to send across the message to his social circle that *"he was back"* and hence he was desperate to accumulate funds. He approached all his old business associates, but nothing worked in his favour. His reputation had been ruptured and his separation from his brothers' business had also created enormous amounts of mistrust among a few of his earlier loyalists.

In such a situation, the only way out was to get financial aid from his own family members – his father and his brothers could easily contribute to make Moulina's wedding a grand success. Sanat also realized that, it's hard to extricate even a single penny out of them. And asking directly for monetary help from them would result into nothing but pure embarrassment. So, he let his machinated mind come up with some crafty ideas for fund accretion. For the next few days, Sanat made all efforts to convince his father about his lavish plans for Moulina's wedding. Being well aware of the fact that, if the old man is brought into confidence then everything else would fall in place.

"*Baba, tumi to jano amar* financial condition. I've been trying hard to setup my business all over again from scratch and I'm confident about it – it's just a matter of time, I'll bounce back for sure. But for the time being, Moulina's marriage is my priority. After putting lots of effort, we got a gem of a guy for your granddaughter and now I cannot step back and make ordinary arrangements for her wedding, just because I lack funds." Sanat puts across his honest views to his father, without any humbug.

After a pause, he continued "*Baba,* Moulina is the eldest daughter of this family. Chell family's prestige, social stature, recognition and honour are all inextricably linked with this sole event..."

Without even waiting for Sanat to complete, the Chell patriarch asked "So, what do you want me to do? How can I help you?"

"*Baba,* I don't want money. Whatever savings I have, I can manage with it. We are lucky enough to get the Ghosh family who doesn't even have any demands. But then there are other expenses like venue booking, entertaining the guests, gifting our family members as well as their's and then all *shaadi-ki-rasam, sangeet, baarat, bidaai* – it amounts to huge expenses. And if all my brothers can pool in some funds, then my burden reduces, and they will only listen to you on this – so, if you can convince them, then..."

"*Achha, ami bole dekhbo*...but I can't force them" assured Rathin Chell.

For Sanat, all his stars were in alignment, everything fell in place – his vocal tonic worked well on his father. Rathin pledged for a grand *send-off* of his adorable granddaughter, he also appealed to all his sons to contribute in whatever way they can, to make Moulina's wedding a magnificent one. Suddenly, everybody in the Chell family took up shared responsibilities in creating an impression in their social circle – they too saw this function as an opportunity to build networks among their old associates. Except Palash, both Sarat and Partha extended their support for their niece's wedding. Even Sanat's brother-in-law, promised to bear the entire catering and refreshment expense for the guests.

With assurance of help from his brothers and some relatives, Sanat felt relieved from his twitchiness. A great groom from a respectable family working in a reputed company from a mega city, can just do wonders – almost everyone from Chell family wanted to get a slice of Mumbai, now or in the near future, through this social amalgamation of the two families. Sanat's immediate younger brother, Sarat for instance had Mumbai in his mind, as his daughter when she graduated from NIFT could opt for Mumbai as her career destination in fashion domain. So, Sarat wanted to remain in his brother's good books and hence readily agreed to help, putting forward the logic *"Afterall Moulina is also like our own daughter."*

Sanat wanted a high-decibel, impactful wedding ceremony for Moulina. He chose Rourkela over Birmirpur as the venue. The famous Dipika Hotel along the Outer Ring Road was booked, both for accommodating the *Borjatri* and for the main marriage ceremony. Dipika Hotel's illustrious, air-conditioned banquet hall had witnessed some of the heavy-weight marriages of the steel city in the past. Guest-list for the mega event ran into few hundreds, and had names of bureaucrats, professors, officers from Rourkela Steel Plant, old business associates, suppliers, vendors and all those who mattered to Sanat's social image remoulding. Relatives from Chell's ancestral village in Bankura were all invited too. The *Mumbaikar* groom was endorsed so much, that people from Rourkela and Birmirpur actually started discussing, how lucky Sanat and his daughter might have been to make this alliance fructify.

Meanwhile, the Ghosh family kept it very simple. They left Haldia for Rourkela on the 15th of May 2012, a day in advance of the wedding day. Sumit's three cousin brothers were part of the *Borjatri*, who accompanied them to Rourkela. Sumit got only twenty days of leave from his office, on the condition of taking official calls during this period – something which he couldn't avoid, as the execution of an entire digital marketing campaign of an upcoming project, completely laid on his shoulders.

Every year, extreme summer engulfs the steel city with an average temperature of 45°C. The scorching sun is upto sucking every bit of water droplet available on the surface of the alleyways. The dry, broiling, sizzling afternoons compel even the poorest of poor of this city to invest in water-coolers, the only solace during the months of April-May-June. Intense heat waves often create highway mirages, giving it a wet shimmering effect on the distant hot asphalt surface of the Ring Road. College going girls prefer full sleeved tops along with arm gloves and face-scarfs to cover them up fully and avoid getting tanned. The autorickshaw drivers frequently use wet face-kerchiefs to cover themselves while driving through blazing noon. Heat strokes are common if proper precaution isn't taken.

Sumit was well aware of Rourkela's extreme summer conditions, he had had some tough time during his college days. He always preferred staying back indoors, while his hostel mates ventured out on bikes during summer mornings. And today, almost after eight years, he had no alternatives, but to brave the intense summer to tie the knot with his life partner.

The morning of 16th May was pleasant, the noisy window ACs of room number 202 and 203 were busy all night to keep the guests from Haldia comfortable indoors. The room service was instructed to act promptly on every call, so that there wasn't any scope of displeasure and complains. The Ghosh family was all busy the previous evening meeting relatives from the Chell family, who made conventional visits before the D-Day.

Since early morning, the supervisor of Rainbow Decorators along with his helpers, were there at the entrance gate of the Hotel with their tempo loaded. They had to quickly decorate the hotel entrance lobby, reception, banquet hall and cafeteria with flowers, garlands, frills, balloons and lights – all this had to be completed by 4 pm. The main function was late in the evening but guests would start walking in by 7-8 pm. The kitchen area of the Hotel remained engaged in preparing some great lip-smacking dishes for the attendees.

At 7:30 in the morning, Radhanath Adhikari, a quinquagenarian Brahmin priest was at the second floor of the Hotel, toggling between rooms to spot the groom's family. He was sent by the Chells, to assist the Ghoshs on performing various customary *pujas* and act as the *Pandit* from the groom's side. Ideally, the Ghosh family should've been accompanied by their own priest, but he pulled out at the last moment due to some family emergency. With no other options left, Sushil had to request Mr Chell to arrange for a local Bengali *Pandit*. Adhikari in his traditional attire of white *dhoti, Namaboli* along with *Rudraksh mala* and *sacred thread* was all geared up to perform the pre-wedding rituals. He also appeared to be visibly upset with the fact that, the requisite items which he had listed last evening were yet to arrive.

Room number 105 and 202 were separately occupied and used by the bride and groom's family to perform elaborate rituals on their respective part. Whereas the main function would take place at the banquet hall, late in the evening, between the auspicious timeslot of 9:30 to 11:00 pm for a series of observance like *Saat-Paak, Subhodrishti, Kanya-Sampradan, Sindoordaan, Mala-bodol and gnat-bandhan*. The *Nandi-mukh* ceremony which was supposed to commence by 8:00 am, got delayed by almost forty-five minutes and Pandit Adhikari got furious with the unnecessary dawdle.

"I've never seen such an irresponsible man ever. I had particularly asked Chell to get all the *puja samagri* beforehand, so that we could start on time. And look at him, he is busy socializing in the lobby but has no clue on the whereabouts of those items," an enraged Adhikari expressed his annoyance.

"Okay, let me see, if I can connect with Chell," Ghosh interfered and took out his mobile phone to call Sanat.

The *Gaye-Holud* ceremony that followed right after *Nandi-mukh* ceremony, happened well within the schedule, under constant and agile supervision of Adhikari. The experienced priest was very particular and punctual about all the rituals and got jittery on even a slightest deviation. On the other hand, a relatively inexperienced, young priest was representing the Chells.

For all the *bachchaa party,* which mainly consisted of Moulina's younger cousins – it was a combined treat of fun, celebrations and get-together. They kept running around the hotel premises, invading one room after another.

After a series of illustrious pre-ceremonies, just when Sumit was about to get ready in his *sherwani* and *kurta*, his sister walked into the room to give an update of the proceedings at the bride's end. An entire clan of ladies were all busy at the corner room of the first floor, giving final touches to Moulina's bridal make-up. Sunita described her sister-in-law to be looking drop-dead gorgeous in red *Banarasi silk*. Amidst all this, Chitra was busy looking for Pandit Adhikari, to discuss the evening's *Shubh-Muhurat* timings. And surprisingly he was nowhere to be found. Upon enquiring at the reception, she was told that the Pandit left the venue almost half an hour back. A flummoxed Chitra reported this to her husband, but it seemed that he had already been informed about it by Chell. In fact, Chell had texted Ghosh *"Adhikari Da has an emergency at home, he is leaving, and my priest will manage and take it from here on."*

About an hour ago, late in the afternoon, after completing the pre-ceremonial activities of the groom side, Adhikari was desperately looking for Sanat. He even tried calling, but the bride's father kept on disconnecting the call. He finally found him in the corridor of the second floor.

"Why aren't you picking up my calls?" the irritated priest complained.

"Adhikari *Da*, it's my daughter's marriage. There are thousands of things running in my head. Tell me now, what is it with you?"

"Sanat, if you require me to stay here for the full day, you'll have to confirm my service charges, else there's another client of mine, who needs my service at Sector-15 area. I'll not stay any longer, if I don't get an answer right now."

"Yes, I would need you to help the Ghosh family. But then, don't expect a single penny beyond two thousand rupees."

"But my full day charges are four-thousand-five-hundred, I already informed you." Adhikari lashed out impatiently.

"Two thousand. That's final. Take it or leave it."

"Sanat, remember one thing – not everything in this world can be bargained for. You are ditching a *Brahmin* on an auspicious day." Adhikari hurriedly left the venue after cursing Sanat.

By evening, the Hotel's banquet hall had perfected an ambience of a traditional Bengali wedding; pre-recorded *Shehnai* played in loop at the background in a mild volume. Cold drinks were being served to the guests on arrival, while six massive compressors were busy throwing cold air through the centralised AC vents. A dais with two decorative throne chairs were setup at the right corner of the hall, with focused spotlights. Whereas the left half of the hall got prepared for the main wedding function, with the *Havan-Kund* in the middle surrounded by plastic chairs for guests and relatives.

Geared up in groom's attire, Sumit looked all charming without being ostentatious. His cream coloured *Sherwani* embellished with hand embroidery along with stones and beads, shimmered in the spotlight. *Jodhpuri jutti* and maroon coloured *pagdi* gave him a magnificent, princely look. Moulina complemented him, with an equally ravishing bridal regalia – she looked like an angel in her heavy golden border red *Banarasi silk saree*. The big red, round *bindi* along with intricate design of sandalwood paste on her forehead gave her a divine look. Adorned with a white *mukut* along with *kundan* jewellery sets, the stunning bride looked no less than a beautiful goddess.

Standing side by side, Sumit and Moulina looked in amazement at everyone around them in the marriage hall, while guests walked up to the podium to congratulate them and pose for a photo with the couple; their families were beaming with joy and friends were happy to celebrate their matrimony. Moulina, however, kept looking at her father all the while. He was sitting next to the *Pandit*, quiet and content. Occasionally, someone from their distant family would come and congratulate him and his face would light up with all the pride. He always wanted this, and now he got it. She wondered what would happen next – *would he be able to bounce back in his business? Would he now concentrate on her other siblings for a better future?* Moulina's thoughts were interrupted by the flashlight from the photographer's camera, she smiled at it and then looked up to Sumit to meet his eyes. In that moment, she decided to consciously divert her attention to the promise of a beautiful future ahead.

At the dais, Moulina was all chirpy and loquacious, busy introducing her relatives, friends, ex-colleagues to her man. Sumit also met his brother-in-law, Lokesh, for the first time. Whereas Sumit just had his batchmate and his professor from RIMS to represent him.

Precisely at 9:15 pm, Lina and Lokesh escorted their sister and brother-in-law to the left half of the hall, where the main wedding ceremony was about to commence. Relatives and guests from both the families thronged round the *Havan* area. Without much delay, the young *Pandit* started chanting *Sanskrit mantras* and sprinkling holy *Ganga jal*. Sanat, who had to give away his daughter to Sumit, was asked to repeat some of those mantras. Even the bride and the groom weren't spared from those jaw-breaking *Sanskrit mantras* while taking their wedding vows in form of *saat-phere* or *shaat-paak* around *Agni Dev*. The *Pandit* was carrying a ready reference cheatsheet for those specific mantras and often glanced through in between. Rituals of *Mala-bodol* and *Subho-Drishti* was heavily accompanied by the traditional ululation and blowing of conch shells by female members from the attendees. These series of complex function and rituals however, didn't interrupt the kids present at the venue from running around and playing among themselves. To them it was one of those rare occasions when parents remained busy and they were all set loose to be on their own.

Amidst initial hiccups and some mismanagements, the jazzy and glitzy wedding function got over an hour past midnight. The newlywed couple finally sat beside each other for their dinner after several hours of fasting. Soon, the guests deserted the venue, and the caterer was busy winding up. The band party was seen counting and distributing notes among their members, while the lights around the decorative hoarding at the entrance bearing *"Moulina weds Sumit"* were switched off. The attendees were all impressed by the lavish arrangements. The Chell brothers finally pulled it off well, sending out a strong message of a *"comeback"* in their social circle.

FIFTEEN
2014

Bhubaneswar, Odisha, India

There was a brief power cut at the Barik Sahi locality. Advocate Pradip Panda's two storey residence wore a blanket of darkness in anticipation of resuming electricity supply. The day went hectic for the senior lawyer – apart from two cases at Bhubaneswar district court, he had to drive all the way to Orissa HC in Cuttack for the hearing of BLAPL-1090/2014.

Bail petitions are easy to defend, unless some heinous crime has been committed. And with the upward trend of 498A cases across states, the High Courts generally grant bail to the accused and their family. Advocate Panda was confident of getting bail for Mr and Mrs Ghosh along with their daughter – more so when a deal had already been struck with the Prosecutor.

Shrikant switched on his computer as soon as the power supply resumed. He knew his senior would come upstairs only after 9 pm, as he was busy talking to his daughter who had called up from Ahmedabad, where she recently got placed in a stock broking firm after completion of her MBA.

Shrikant updated his senior's diary entry for the next day's lined up cases, and then went up to Panda's table to fetch the case files placed in a haphazard manner.

"Inform Manohar to bring along the Order Copy of BLAPL-1090/2014 tomorrow, when he returns from Cuttack." Panda instructed Shrikant as he climbed up the stairs and entered the room.

"Bail granted?" asked Shrikant while he made a note of Panda's instruction.

"Yes, but the hearing started a bit late."

"Okay. Most probably Sumit was trying to reach you in the afternoon, but couldn't get through. He texted me to inform that he would be here in Bhubaneswar tomorrow with his family."

"I was in the courtroom then, saw his 5 missed calls later. However, I messaged him about bail being granted" informed the lawyer, while shifting his bag from the chair.

"He was asking me about the mode of payment, but then I asked him to discuss it with you."

"I had already informed him about the charges, why was he asking you the same again?" the irked lawyer responded.

"I think, he was mentioning about Cheque payment or something like that – But Sir, *apana ette tanka fees kahinki maguchanti bail pain?* Twenty-five thousand is a huge amount." Shrikant expressed his concern.

"Shrikant, do you remember watching the blockbuster movie *Sholay*?!! There was a beautiful dialogue which I want to quote here '*Ghoda agar ghas se dosti karega toh khayega kya?*'…you must remember that we are into the business of law. While we've to be empathetic to our clients' suffering and provide them legal aid, we should also not forget to exploit and capitalise the same for our profitability and existence. Else it would be difficult for me to run this law firm." The lawyer cautiously expressed his views and after taking a pause continued "Sumit's 498A case won't come to us. After this bail, the case would continue to run in the lower court and he might appoint another lawyer from Rourkela. In the given scenario, this is the only opportunity for us to get some money out of him."

Shrikant quietly listened to his senior's version and chose not to retaliate. After all, his monthly cheque depended on how much gets accumulated from various clients. There are no set rules, no transparency; unethical practices play large – but then when they are matters of self-income and hits one's own pocket, we human beings tend to turn a blind eye to these immoral approaches.

By now, the manager and his staff at Hotel Gunjan had become familiarized with senior and junior Ghosh, due to their earlier stays. A bigger room on the fourth floor was booked over the phone. The Ghosh family was greeted by August's heavy downpour in the *temple city* of Bhubaneswar. Delayed train, drenched state and heavy shower, left the Ghosh family with no option other than staying back in their hotel room. Sumit called up his lawyer to inform about their arrival and their inability to make it to his chamber due to extreme monsoon conditions. They then mutually decided to meet the next evening.

At 10 pm, it was still drizzling outside. Sumit called for room service and ordered dinner from the neighbouring eatery – *rotis, mixed vegetable, dalma, papad and salad* was heavy enough for the enervated family. Over dinner, Sunita expressed her disquiet over the approaching deadline of her office leaves – "*Dada*, now that we've been granted bail, when is your's expected? By any means, we have to wrap this up within this week. I've to then go back and join office, else I will be forced to sit back at home, jobless."

"Yes, I have that in my mind. Retaining your job is very important at this stage, without which it would be immensely difficult for us to carry on with the litigation expenses." Sumit took a sip of water as he acknowledged his sister's concern.

The senior Ghosh who was lost deep in his thoughts, finally spoke "Ideally, our lawyer should accompany us to the police station and handle the entire bail out process. But what if Panda denies to travel to Rourkela? Or charges a whopping fee for the same. Do we've a Plan-B?"

Sushil's sudden query made everybody uncomfortable and nervous. Pin-drop silence prevailed for a minute; their unpreparedness to handle the subsequent steps got exposed with that one question.

"Panda Sir should come with us, and even if he decides to skip – we can carry the Court Order and furnish the same at the police station. *Bass ho jayega,* big deal." Sumit spoke off-the-cuff.

"I don't think it's as easy as it sounds. We have never faced such a situation and hence have no idea about the chain of events that might unfold in reality. It's better to ask all these questions to the lawyer, when we meet him tomorrow." Responded Sushil in a composed manner and directed his son to somehow scout for another lawyer in Rourkela, as a precautionary measure.

Sumit thought of connecting with Anup once again for a competent lawyer contact in Rourkela, but refrained from it after he revived those vitriolic and malefic deeds of Advocate Panigrahi, that further complicated his case. Instead he called up his Marketing professor, briefly narrated his side of the story and implored him to find a local lawyer who would accompany them to Birmirpur PS and lead the bailout proceedings.

The prudent, down-to-earth, humble professor felt for his student and kept wondering where the institute of marriage is headed for the next generation. He recalled Sumit to be one of his intellectual, knowledgeable, smart students; who always had the aspiration of making it big in the corporate world. And today, that particular bright student had to let go all his career ambitions and gather all ammunitions to fight a court battle in order to recoup his dignity and prestige in the society. The professor was determined to help his student in whatever way he could and asked Sumit to call him in the afternoon…

"Good afternoon Sir, you had asked me to call you."

"Sumit, I know it's a hard time for you and your family. May God give you all the strength to fight this out. Remember if you're honest, no force can defeat you." An empathetic professor tried to boost up his student's morale.

"Sir, this world has changed. In fact, the honest gets screwed easily, whereas the dishonest celebrates."

"Please have faith in judiciary, you'll surely emerge as a winner. Now note down two contacts, which might help you to get out from this mire," the professor instructed.

"Yes Sir, please go ahead…" Sumit signalled his sister to get a pen and paper and jotted down the details being narrated by his professor.

"Try connecting with Mihir Ganguly. Being a Bengali, he can easily construe your case matter. This legal practitioner is a sharp criminal lawyer with almost twenty-five years of experience in Rourkela court. Also, being a union leader of lawyers' association, he is well connected to the fraternity compared to any other lawyer in the city. However, the irony is that Ganguly is very, very selective in taking up cases. In fact, he never picks up anonymous calls, unless the number is saved in his mobile phone."

"Sir, then what's the use?" interrupted Sumit.

"Give my reference. His wife is my ex-colleague. I suggest before calling, text him with a small intro and reference. Else he would never pick up your call," explained the professor.

"Thank you Sir, and if somehow this contact doesn't click? I mean if Advocate Ganguly shows no interest, then?"

"You first try, else I'll intervene," assured the professor. "Now take down the contact details of my brother-in-law – Gaurav Biswal. He is quite junior in this field, been practicing for the last four years. But for your bailout matter he can be handy."

Later that evening, at around 8 pm, Sumit visited Advocate Panda's chamber with his father. The senior lawyer and his associate greeted their client with a courteous smile. It looked, as if they were eagerly awaiting their arrival.

"Thanks a lot Sir, finally you got bail for my family" Sumit expressed his gratitude.

"It wasn't that easy. A lot of hard work has gone behind it, my boys had to work in a synchronous manner to get the results. And mind you, High Court matters aren't cake-walks. One should channelize all the resources and contacts to get a desired result," the senior counsel explained it to his young client.

"Panda Sir, the entire credit goes to you and your team. Thank you once again."

"Sumit, are you carrying my fees? I can't keep my affiliates waiting. Moreover, they're the ones who'll help me in getting your bail too," the lawyer said impatiently.

"Yes Sir, don't worry about the money," said Sumit calmly and signalled his father.

Sushil who was a mere spectator all this while spoke in broken Hindi and reached out to his folio bag and pulled out a bundle of five-hundred rupee notes "Sir, this is thirty thousand in cash. Request you to take the balance in form of a Cheque."

The lawyer was quick to grab the bundle with a cunning look in his eyes, which even his dark framed spectacles couldn't hide. He hastily counted those sixty notes, which was freshly withdrawn from the nearest ATM, a few minutes back. His machiavellianism gave bad vibes to both father and son.

"Cash payment ki baat hui thi na!! Now Cheque clearance will take time," responded the lawyer with a bit of annoyance.

"Sir please try and understand. We cannot carry that much cash with us all the time while travelling. Moreover, the ATM has its own limit of daily withdrawal. That's why I request you to accept the balance amount in cheque. I'm carrying AXIS bank's chequebook and since you also have an account with the same bank, the clearance will happen on the same day," assured Sumit.

"Hmmm…Okay, draw the cheque in favour of my wife then," the annoyed lawyer packed the notes in his brown satchel.

"As you say Sir, please spell out her name and I'll write the cheque right away."

Somehow, Sushil didn't like the way Panda reacted to the fees and the mode of payment. His unprofessional behaviour and money-grubbing mentality didn't go well with the senior Ghosh. But then in that situation, in an unknown city he didn't have many options. He quietly tolerated the *Janus faced* legal practitioner.

Once the cheque of rupees forty-five thousand was drawn, Sushil asked for the Order copy. The advocate in turn looked at Shrikant and asked *"Tanka Order Copy ta ready hei jaichi ki?"*

"We've applied for it and will get it by tomorrow for sure" confirmed Shrikant.

"Okay, in that case get them a print out of the bail confirmation from the High Court's webpage," directed Panda.

"Sumit, tomorrow when you come for the Order copy, you need to pay Shrikant 3000 bucks. Each Order copy comes with this amount."

Though Sushil was not too keen to initiate another conversation with the lawyer, he also couldn't resist himself from asking the various steps that needed to be followed once the Order copy was ready.

The lawyer yawned and while rubbing his eyes explained the steps that a bail applicant should follow "Ghosh Sir – the process at the police station is fairly simple, provided you have all the resources in place. Police now can't object to the HC order nor can take you in custody. You have to submit the Order copy, sign a bail bond, deposit a bail amount and it's done. Now the challenge is to get an assurer who is willing to sign the bail bond and guarantee the presence of the accused at the PS. Failing which his property can be seized and he too can be arrested. Oh yes, the assurer also needs to mortgage any of his immovable asset in this process."

"Panda Sir, how will I get an assurer?" Sumit interjected.

"Any local resident of Rourkela who knows you and your family can be a guarantor, but he should be ready to mortgage. Else the only way out is to engage professional bailers."

"What? Professional bailers!" Sushil exclaimed.

"Yes Sir, they charge you a commission to be your guarantor at the police station or court. But then they're only known to the lawyers' fraternity" replied Panda.

"Panda Sir, you're coming with us to Birmirpur PS – right?" asked Sumit.

"Else who'll manage all these complexities?" Sushil added.

"Well, as your appointed lawyer I should accompany you. But then, I'm too tied up here with High Court and session court cases, can't afford to waste time on travelling. And you know, it takes atleast sixteen hours to travel to and from between Bhubaneswar and Rourkela." Panda raised his concern.

"Sir in that case, would you mind referring a good lawyer in Rourkela? Who can take up the matter from here on?" Sumit quickly asked out of disquietude.

"I know a couple of them, but they're too junior to handle your case matter. Well, let me think over it. There are few more days to go, I'll let you know about my schedule in a day or two. Let's now concentrate on your bail petition."

"Sir we've full confidence in you. I know you can get my son out on bail too." Sushil expressed his views with conviction. He added, "And once both the Order copies are ready, please see if you can make it to the police station. Since you handled the bail matter, we would want you to continue the next course of legal action too."

The canny lawyer just nodded his head and responded "Hmmm...Okay, let's see. I'll update you on this."

The next day, just before lunch, instinctive Sushil instructed his son to connect with either of the lawyers from Rourkela. He somehow felt that Panda might ditch them at the last moment. They should better be ready now than being sorry later.

Sumit's several attempts to reach Advocate Mihir Ganguly went in vain. As instructed by his professor, before calling the senior lawyer he did sent out an SMS *'Hello Sir, got ur no. frm Prof. Sahoo of RIMS, wanted 2 discuss my case. Rgds Sumit'* but that didn't generate any revert or callback. Instead his calls simply got disconnected after innumerable rings. Bemused and baffled with the strange conduct,

Sumit sought an opinion from his father.

"If Ganguly isn't happening, try for Biswal. We can't afford to lose our time on contemplating," came a stern response from the father to his son. "Sunita, I did notice that you've got your smartphone back with you. But please note that your brother is yet to get his bail. And before that happens, refrain from activating your handset. We should avoid making mistakes, else it might cost us dearer."

"But *Baba*, I would just check for the ticket availability. I won't make any calls," explained Sunita.

"What if our numbers are still being tracked? What if the police locate us here and even before your brother gets bail, they take him into their custody? All our efforts so far will just be nugatory!" an irritated Sushil scolded his daughter.

"Let your brother fix a lawyer, then you two can go out to the cyber café and look for the tickets. Check for your Mumbai air tickets and our train tickets from Bhubaneswar to Rourkela," suggested Sushil.

After failed efforts to connect with Advocate Ganguly, Sumit finally dialled Gaurav Biswal. The junior lawyer from Rourkela session court was quick to grab the opportunity and agreed to accompany the Ghosh family and manage their bail matter. He would also arrange a vehicle for smooth commute between Rourkela and Birmirpur. Just as Sumit ended his conversation with Gaurav, an SMS from Ganguly arrived that read *'Sorry, I won't be able to help you. I'm out of town on a case matter for this entire week'*.

SIXTEEN
2014

Rourkela, Odisha, India

The *Intercity Express* reached Rourkela at 9:48 pm, delayed by almost 75 minutes. Unlike earlier visits to the steel city, this one was something that Sumit would never ever want to reminisce about in the years to come. The mother and son had to spend a brief period at the second class waiting hall, while Sushil and Sunita went out of the station premise to look for a suitable family accommodation.

Earlier that day – morning of mid-September; Sumit collected the Order copy of his bail from Advocate Panda and straightway headed towards Bhubaneswar station, where his family was waiting for him. As speculated by Sushil, their HC lawyer finally didn't turn up – his expectations were sky-high. The previous evening, when the father and son met Panda at his chamber to pay the final instalment of his fees, their conversation regarding PS visit turned out to be unconducive.

"Sir, tomorrow we are catching the *Intercity Express* to Rourkela. I hope you are accompanying us," asked Sumit while carefully sliding the Order copy into his folder.

"*Baap re*…tomorrow?! I suggest, if you can, postpone it to Saturday, that's 13th, then probably I can come" the lawyer advised. "If you can manage to do so, I would charge only INR 25,000 for the entire episode; of course you've to bear my boarding, lodging, food and local travel expenses. I also assume that you'll get me an AC chair car ticket on the intercity express" added the counsellor.

Sumit quickly did a mental maths and was sure that Panda didn't fit into the current scheme of things. He was prompt to respond, "No Sir, Saturday will be too late. We somehow have to get Sunita bailed out, so that she can go back to Mumbai and join her office. Else a termination order is inevitable."

The Ghosh family finally checked into Hotel Welburn, at a stone's throw from the Rourkela railway station. Even the train arrival and departure announcements were clearly audible from the hotel room, which penetrated the night's silence. Rooms were small, but a double bed with extra bedding at 650 bucks wasn't a bad deal.

Mixed emotions played large in their minds – while they all were relieved from being incognitos and could venture out freely, an equal sense of apprehension and disquietude prevailed, as they were unaware how things would mystify in this conflict for days to come. However, with bail orders from HC they felt like caged birds being set free and were ready to take on any challenges after months' captivity. Even a simple dinner consisting of *Roti, daal-tadka* along with onions and pickle, ordered from a roadside eatery, gave them all inner peace.

"Good morning Sumit. I came to know that the Intercity made a late entry yesterday and since I didn't want to disturb you all, I refrained from calling you last night," informed the energetic, young lawyer. "I already had a telephonic discussion with the IO – Ms Mohanty. She has asked us to be there at the PS after lunch hour."

"Did she ask anything else, Mr Biswal?"

"Nothing…but it seemed as if she was least expecting a bail order from the High Court. And please, call me Gaurav. I'm of the same age as you."

"Okay. So, when do we leave then?" Sumit felt like the lawyer would be good company. Under normal circumstances, he would've liked to befriend Gaurav.

"Hmmm…if we've to be there at Birmirpur by 2, then let's start at 1 pm. The Qualis will reach your hotel at quarter to one. I'll join you from *Chhend Colony*, however the vehicle will pick up Mathur Uncle from *Basanti Colony*." Informed Gaurav.

"Who is this Mathur Uncle?"

"Avinash Mathur is from my father's friends circle. He has some good hold in Birmirpur. I've asked him to accompany us and he agreed. You never know, what's there in store for us!"

"And what about the Bailer?" asked Sumit eagerly.

"*Woh meine set kar liya hai*…Bailer Iqbal Karim will directly reach the police station." Gaurav assured.

The Qualis ran at a speed of 80 kmph through a relatively traffic-less Simdega Road on a gloomy September afternoon. Before reaching Birmirpur, it made just a single halt at *Kuanrmunda* junction to fuel its 2.5 litre diesel engine. It was Sumit's third trip to Birmirpur. While the earlier two visits had their own charm, this one was full of suspense and apprehension. They hardly talked to each other – only Mathur was talking gibberish with the lawyer. Chitra kept chanting *Hanuman Chalisha* silently to herself, Sunita gazed out of the left window, and Sushil remained lost in his own thoughts. Around seventy minutes later, the Qualis honked its way to the right lane before the *Chowk-Bazaar* area and parked itself behind a police van preceded by a series of parked two-wheelers. The two storied, yellow building in front of the parking area read *Birmirpur Police Station, Odisha – 770099* both in dark blue English and Odiya fonts.

It was 2:15 pm – Gaurav asked everyone to stay back in the Qualis and slowly walked towards the entrance of the police station. Mathur followed him thereafter. The driver got out of his seat, leaned back on the bonnet and leisurely lighted a cigarette. The lawyer was seen to make some hand gestures while talking to the guard, before they were allowed to enter.

High humidity in the air and inner perturbation, made them perspire profusely – never ever in life, they had been to any police station. But now, due to these turns of events, they had to be there for their indemnity. Every minute seemed like an hour. Their driver who rightly sensed the issue, after having the last blow from the cigarette butt approached Sumit and in broken Hindi suggested *"Saab, yeah elaka thik nehi hai, yahan ke log bhi thik nehi.* It's better to settle these domestic *lafda* mutually out-of-court. *Nehi to poori zindegi nikal jayegi isi ke peeche."*

Everybody knows, how dowry laws are blatantly misused by a section to harass a husband and his family. It's a money minting game, where the husband is always at the receiving end. Nobody encouraged Sumit to fight it out, rather kept suggesting him to settle it mutually outside the courtroom – which made him more determined to fight it out in a legal manner and not give into the unscrupulous demands of his in-laws.

"We have to wait for sometime. The IO is out on a firearms confiscation case near Odisha-Jharkhand border area" informed Gaurav, who came out of the *Thana* after half an hour.

"Did you talk to her?" asked Sumit.

"I tried reaching her, but the IVR said *out of coverage area.* Her colleagues at the station informed me that she rushed to the crime spot a few minutes back."

"Okay, and where are the Bailers?"

"Iqbal is on his way, will be reaching anytime now. Let's have some tea. Are you coming with us?"

Sumit was hesitant, but on Gaurav's insistence and his parents' consent, walked out of the vehicle towards the roadside tea stall. The driver and Mathur along with a uniformed constable followed them too, while Mr and Mrs Ghosh along with their daughter preferred to wait in the Qualis.

It was a test of patience for the visitors. Even at 4:30 pm there wasn't any trace of Sub-Inspector Shamita Mohanty. Initially the Ghosh family waited outside in their Qualis and later, on Mathur's insistence a wooden bench was arranged inside, where the accused family continued to wait. The only relief was the revolving ceiling fan, which was at its maximum speed on a hot, sticky afternoon. Whosoever crossed the aisle would glance at each member of the family seated in front of Senior Inspector's cabin. The cabin was empty for the last eight months, waiting to be filled up by a new officer from Koraput district. The short aisle opened into a 150 square feet room to the right, meant as the workplace for the men and women in uniform. Piles and piles of dust coated files lay haphazardly on open shelves. A black desktop computer had an inkjet printer to accompany in the shabbily maintained police station. A dimly lit lockup of barely 20 square feet was on the left end of the aisle.

Mathur was seen proactively striking conversations with various staff member in the PS. To some he conversed in broken Odiya, and to the rest in flawless *Maithili*. He had a brief criminal past in Birmirpur area. Two and a half decades back when mines were active, Mathur once got involved in a gang war between the most dreaded limestone mafias of the locality. And that's why he was known to the police, politicians and administrations. Through those mini-conversations, he aimed to figure out the motive of the fake complaint registered by the Chells and tried to uncover any possible links for an *out-of-court* settlement. This task was assigned to him by Gaurav. In the meantime, the lawyer was busy interacting with two men who came on a red Hero Honda Splendor a few minutes back.

At around 5:10 pm, a porcelain white Tata Sumo honked its way into the police station through a widely opened rusty iron gate, and parked itself at the left corner of the building under a huge wood-apple tree. At dusk, flocks of sparrows and mynas engaged in a joyous chirpy cacophony before roosting for the night on treetops, were heedless to the rigid situation in the adjacent yellow building. The young lady SI swiftly alighted from the vehicle and straightway entered the building; followed by a team of ASI and Havildars who had accompanied her for the raid. While crossing the aisle, she reconnoitred a family of four that was persistently waiting for someone. Chitra instantly recognised the lady officer and gesticulated it to her son and daughter. Soon after, Gaurav walked in with Mathur while the other two fellows – Iqbal and Aqib were seen loitering outside in the parking lot.

After 5 minutes, Mathur came out and sat beside Sumit. The man with stoic expressions hardly spoke with the Ghosh family before, but this time whispered some words of caution into Sumit's ear. "Don't talk much in front of the officer…answer only in monosyllables. Also, don't give in to the provocation instigated by her. Just keep your cool. Remember, we are here to take the bail. Once done, the police won't have much role to play in this case."

He then got up and before excusing himself out for a smoke, looked at Mr Ghosh and said "Gaurav will manage the paper work, he is talking to the IO. We have to wait for some more time before we head back to Rourkela."

Before exiting the gate, Mathur instructed Iqbal and Aqib, following which the professional bailers entered the building, crossed the aisle and went straight inside.

At 5:35 pm, finally Gaurav came out along with Iqbal and Aqib. Sumit stood up in anxiety and asked "Is everything fine?"

"Yes, don't worry. Things will be done soon. The bail bond is of the amount 10,000 per person. Iqbal will stand guarantor for any two, and Aqib for the rest. Their charges would be 15% of the bail amount. So, you've to pay 6,000 in all to them" explained Gaurav. "But before signing on the dotted line, the IO and DSP would want to talk to you all."

"Why DSP? What are they going to talk about?" a visibly tensed Sumit questioned.

"About the case, I suppose. But try and understand one thing, whatever may come our way…they're bound to release us on bail. They just can't supersede a High Court order – *uska Baap bhi nehi rok sakta,*" winked the lawyer in excitement.

In the meantime, a lanky constable walked up to Sumit and his family and informed, *"Madam aap logo ko andar bula rahi hai."*

The young lady officer was seated at the centre table flanked by a constable who was busy getting some papers signed by her. The table to her right was empty, whereas the one on her left was occupied by another SI who was busy conversing over the phone. There was another room inside with few more staff members gossiping over a tea break. As soon as the Ghosh family walked in, Inspector Shamita grinned at the visitors and sarcastically passed a remark to Chitra, "Welcome Madam, welcome to Birmirpur. Sorry to keep you waiting, but as you can see, I was actually out on my duty, unlike *somebody,* who purposely kept us waiting outside her door."

Chitra was about to respond, but her daughter pulled her back and signalled to remain quiet. Meanwhile on Shamita's instruction, a constable pulled out four chairs from the inner room, for the visitors.

"Sumit *Babu,* finally we meet. Had been hearing a lot about you and your *karnama* from your in-laws. My Boss is also eager to meet you; he will be here shortly," informed the IO.

"Achha toh yeahi hai woh family? Kahan se aaye ho aap log? The entire Birmirpur now knows about your incident." The male officer next to Shamita asked, after finishing his call.

"We are from Haldia. My son and daughter are from Mumbai." Sushil turned towards his right and replied.

"So, they work in Mumbai?" continued the other officer.

"My daughter still works, but my son is no longer working. And because of this fake criminal case, he had to remain off from job hunting for some months now," informed Sushil.

Gaurav and Mathur silently entered and stood behind the Ghosh family just in front of the lockup area. The lady officer noticed it and asked them to wait outside until they finished off with the conversation.

"Hmm…now tell me, why your daughter-in-law fled from Mumbai?" the IO questioned directly to the elderly couple.

"We've no clue madam. Even we were in a shock when we saw her alleged complaint against us, there must have been some misunderstanding," Sushil tried explaining it to the officer.

"So, you mean to say, a thirty-year-old lady, woke up one fine morning, felt like going back to her parental home and without any reason, walked into our *Thana* to register a complaint against you all? Is that at all admissible?" the inspector frowned as she flipped the pages of the FIR.

"Madam, we seriously have no idea. We are still grappling with these questions – still wondering what made her write such a fictitious complaint against all of us!" Sunita chose to reply this time.

"Oh, stop all this nonsense now!" yelled the officer and then looked at Sumit and asked. "Yes *Mr Husband*, what's your version? Why do you think your wife left you? What exactly happened between you two, do you mind sharing it with us?"

"Isn't that your job to figure out through thorough investigation?" Sunita questioned the officer sternly, even before her brother could answer.

"Oh ho. Like mother, like daughter – huh! So now you will instruct me about my duties and responsibilities?" the annoyed officer responded.

Just when the conversation between the officer and the visitors were turning out to be a heated argument, the electricity supply snapped leaving the entire building pitch dark. A constable went running into the other room to get some candles. The irritated agonized lady officer got up from her chair to get herself a glass of water. Sumit started wiping his forehead with his handkerchief. Chitra asked Sunita to keep her cool. The bailers and the advocate were waiting outside to finish off their bit. It was 6:30 pm and the evening's dark sky was frequently lit up by flashes, a heavy downpour was just on the verge of making a plunge.

The semi-urban town of Birmirpur is often deprived of uninterrupted power supply. Evenings of summer and monsoon months are typically characterized by frequent load-shedding. Four heavily built figures promenaded along the lane in front of the police station, keeping a close eye on the Qualis and the activities of the visitors.

They kept updating it all to someone over the phone. They all looked like ghosts in the dark, their silver Indica was parked along the main road. They had been asked to be on standby mode and wait for further instructions. One of the four bumped into Mathur who was busy blowing smoke-rings from his cigarette right in front of the iron gate of the police station.

"Assalam walekum Mathur Saab!! Aap yahan kaise?"

"Akhtar! Tu kya kar raha hai yahan, police station ke aas pass?" Mathur was happy as well as inquisitive to see the henchman, who was once a distant member of a local wagon-breaker gang.

"Dhanda hai apna, Saab…kisi Mumbai walien ko uthana hai," informed Akhtar to Mathur, whom he used to look up to in his initial docile days.

Mathur quickly sensed something fishy, sneaked his arm around Akhtar's shoulder and proposed *"Chal chai peetey hai."* He also offered a stick from his *Gold Flake* packet to the 5' 11" tall monster figured Akhtar.

At the roadside tea stall, Mathur learned that – Akhtar and his associates had been hired to abduct any one member from the Ghosh family, slink across the Odisha-Jharkhand border and hold the kidnapped captive in a godown until further instructions. They also had the family's picture in their mobile phone to avoid any mess ups, a few extra bucks were on the offer if they succeeded in taking the family's son as a hostage. To any common man it could have been a spine-chilling tale, but to Mathur these incidents were normal.

"Mathur *saab* you didn't tell me, what made you visit Birmirpur PS at this hour? *Kuch lafda hai kya?"* asked Akhtar.

"What if I say, that I've come along with the *Ghosh family?"* Mathur stared at Akhtar.

"Anything for you Mathur *saab…"*

"Sun fir, chupchap wapis chala ja. I'll get your remuneration send to you in the next couple of days. By the way, *kitne mein deal hua tha?"*

"Jaane do na saab," Akhtar laughed it off at first. But on Mathur's insistence, Akhtar revealed that they would get 5000 for the job and additional 2000 if they got hold of Sumit. Mathur promised him 3000 plus a crate of *Kingfisher* and bid him adieu.

Meanwhile at the police station, Shamita was losing her nerves. Each and every member of the accused family denied charges. Her probes generated mundane responses resulting in her impatience towards the visitors. Immaturity and inexperience led her to frustration and discontent which was evident in her frequent howling at the Ghosh family. Had they not been shielded by the HC order, she would've surely detained them in the lockup. DSP Dash had strict instruction of keeping the visitors under tremendous mental pressure until he arrived to take it forward. The Ghosh family on the other hand were exhausted and completely drained out answering the same questions and denying all the allegations over and over again. They had never imagined that getting a bail would lead to such intricacies. Instead of being unbiased, independent and neutral – the IO seemed to have already assumed the husband's family as the offender.

By 7:10 pm, the lady officer was almost done with her round of questioning. Though annoyed with Moulina's in-laws, she didn't have any concrete and substantial ground to charge them and hence, had no option but to initiate the bail bond papers. The bailers were called in and asked to submit documents related to their identity and immovable property. Gaurav was quick to arrange all the papers and get it stamped.

Weary of excessive probing and cross-questioning, Sumit's tired soul gasped for some fresh air, his bladder exerted immense pressure for anxiety urination. The Havildar directed him to the toilet, where he almost ran to relieve himself. Electricity at the *Thana* resumed with a low voltage. On his way back from the toilet, Sumit could hear men and women quarrelling at the top of their voice. All these noises came in from the waiting room. As he advanced, he was shell-shocked to hear his father-in-law's voice – Sanat Chell was there with a group of locals who all demanded severe punishment for the Ghosh family for their heinous act of torture and attempted murder of Moulina. Tsunami of thoughts and speculations crossed his mind…*Who informed the Chells about their whereabouts? Why were they here? What else would unfold today?*

"The culprit family is finally here. We should all make sure that they're jailed for a day at least," demanded Sanat, which further got echoed among others.

"Because of them, my daughter had a miserable matrimonial life!" Sanat's wife pointed at the elderly Ghosh couple and screamed. She too got vocal support from another aged woman.

"*Madam tanku chadani* – they should get proper punishment," complained Sanat to the lady officer.

"Before fixing the alliance with us, these crooks sweet talked about their social status, well settled job in Mumbai, own flat, car and all. And once our daughter made an entry to that house – everyday and night they kept taunting her and demanded money." Sanat narrated all vociferously. And when he noticed Sumit entering the room, he added, "and this guy is spineless. For every little thing, he had to inform his parents. Bloody irresponsible kid, I now feel ashamed of my choice."

"What is this going on here? Is this a police station? I can't even believe that a gang just walked into the *Thana* and started abusing us in presence of senior officers?" Sunita revolted and yelled at the policewoman.

Realising the ugly turn of events, Sub-Inspector Shamita ordered the Chells to remain silent and voice their grievances to the DSP, who was expected anytime soon. Being highly humiliated and embarrassed, the Ghosh family preferred to remain silent and witness the high octane drama. Sumit tried to spot his wife in the group of men and women which had accompanied Sanat, but didn't find her. He knew nobody from the group except Mr and Mrs Chell, but noticed a young chap busy taking notes and scribbling. Sushil signalled his wife and children to come close, formed a huddle and whispered "Stay dull and quiet. Don't give into the provocations, be strong and have faith in God."

At around 7:35 pm, DSP Ajay Dash finally entered the police station. The on-duty staff greeted him with a firm salute. The DSP's office was on the other side of the road, but he was at the *Thana* to look into Sanat's daughter's case. As soon as he entered, Sanat and Maya started complaining like a kid – to which Dash made a hand gesture and asked them to calm down. A constable quickly slipped into the Senior Inspector's cabin and switched on the lights and AC, and arranged the chair and table for the DSP. Before entering the cabin, Dash commented with a smirk, "We called you all here to have a mutual discussion and the entire family is here with a bail order from the High Court! Isn't that strange? Unless you are guilty, why would you need a bail, huh?"

"Sir we also understand a bit of law. After charging us with half-a-dozen IPCs you expect us to come here without any protection? And you call this lawlessness as mutual discussion?" Sushil replied firmly.

"Any father whose daughter has been subjected to domestic violence and torture, would react like this. I don't blame him." Dash tried to justifying Chell's act.

"So, you are hundred percent sure that his daughter was subjected to torture; even before investigating and ascertaining facts, you've already come to a conclusion...is that how an independent investigating agency like police works? Or does it vary from case to case?" the senior Ghosh questioned.

Dash entered the cabin pretending not to hear Sushil. He called in Shamita and asked a constable to get all the case related files and documents. After a while, the same constable called in Sanat into the cabin.

Irked with the current chain of events, Sunita went towards the young lawyer and complained *"Yeah sab kya ho raha hai Mr Gaurav?* We've been waiting since afternoon and instead of initiating the bail proceedings, why are they harassing us? And why aren't you saying something? Every time I look around for you, you aren't visible."

"Please have some patience. These are tactics to frustrate you all. And my job is to argue for the case in court premises; not here in the police station." Gaurav calmly responded.

The trio – DSP, IO and Sanat; had a brief closed door discussion before Mr and Mrs Ghosh along with their daughter were called in at around 8 o'clock. Mathur and Gaurav too followed his client into the DSP's cabin. The police chief asked for the order copy from the lawyer and glanced through it.

"Sir there are two bail orders issued – first one has Sushil Ghosh, Chitra Ghosh and Sunita Ghosh as joint petitioner; while the second one has Sumit Ghosh as the sole applicant," informed the lawyer.

"Hmm…so you all approached High Court. Why? What happened with the lower court?" DSP asked the visitors, even though he was well aware of the past incidents. Further he added "It must have cost you a bomb to get a favourable order from HC, isn't it?"

The Ghosh family ducked the questions and preferred to maintain a silence. Sanat, who stood next to the lady officer, was antagonistic to the visitors and glared at them in hope of a reprisal for the 'ill-treatment' of his daughter. Dash looked at Gaurav and asked "Did you represent them at the High Court?"

"No, they have their lawyer in Bhubaneswar."

"Now since the state's highest body has ordered you all to be released on bail, what can we do but abide by the same? Sub-Inspector Shamita will do the needful…"

Even before the DSP could complete, Sanat interjected, "But Sir, how can you release them on bail? We'll protest, the *Mahila Commission* representative is here too. We want…"

"Chell *Babu, aap chup ho jao.* This is High Court's order; you cannot play with it. Else you will be booked for *contempt of court.* There are legal ways to object this – High Court *chale jao aur bail cancellation ki petition file kar do.* "

While Sanat was enraged and visibly frustrated, DSP's suggestion caused tremendous angst among the visitors. Sushil felt heavy palpitation, Sunita got a sweaty palm and they all turned diaphoretic even in the air-conditioned cabin. Only one thought was lurking in their minds *How will we defend this bail if Chell filed for cancellation?*

After signing the first bail order, the chief of Birmirpur police asked the Ghosh family *"Achha ab bataiye…hua kya?* What made Moulina leave your family? What did you all do to her?"

The proclivity of the question itself rarked-up Sunita. She asked in a vexatious tone "Isnt't it better to ask her? And what difference will it make if you hear our side of the story? You all have already considered us the prime suspects."

"Sunita *ji*, I've already heard their version. As an independent authority, I should also hear it out from you."

"Why is this man here? What is he doing in your cabin?" Sunita pointed out at Sanat and questioned. "When you heard them, were we invited? Then why should we let you know our version in front of him?"

Shamita immediately asked Sanat to leave and then tried asking Sunita the same question posed by her Boss.

"You should've asked us this question before registering the FIR. Now our version will have zero value. So instead of wasting our time, why don't you investigate and find it out yourself?" Sunita's anger was detectable in her voice. She also threatened to meet and inform the Magistrate about the ongoing anarchy in the police station.

It was getting late; the IO and her Boss were also fed up with the Chell-Ghosh domestic complexity. Solving a murder case instead would've been much more rewarding. After finishing off with the first bail order, the DSP wanted to wrap up the second one faster. He called in Sumit Ghosh, the husband, the prime accused. As Sumit walked in, the officers geared themselves to exert mental pressure on him, so that he would confess to any of the accusation made by Moulina in her FIR.

"Is this how you come to meet a DSP? Look at yourself – untucked shirt, rolled up sleeves, unbuttoned collar. Such a casual approach! Or is it *Mumbaiya* style! Huh?"

"Sorry Sir. It was hot outside, so…" Sumit hastily tucked in his shirt and buttoned the collar.

"These guys have no respect for others. And I'm sure, he didn't have any for his wife either," Dash looked at the lady officer and took a jibe at Sumit.

"Why did you torture Moulina?" Dash straightway asked in a fierce tone.

"Sir, I would've appreciated if your first question would've been an impartial one. You could have asked '*What happened between us?*' rather than assuming that I mistreated her. I swear to God, we've never ever ill-treated Moulina." Sumit answered politely.

"Again, the same stereotype answer, you all are in a denial mode today. And you don't teach me what to ask and what not to. Shamita, call Chell here. Let's hear it from him too," the DSP looked at his subordinate and ordered.

As soon as Chell entered the cabin, he started grumbling Odiya slangs angrily at Sumit. He indignantly rejected the claim of innocence made by the Ghosh family.

"Because of you all, my daughter's future is in jeopardy. Instead of giving her the status of a *'housewife'* you all have mistreated her like a *'housemaid'* – you never wanted a wife but a maid to get your household work done. And even after that, my poor girl was deprived of food and medicines. You all should rot in hell," he yelled.

He paused, sat next to the IO and continued "These imposters kept my daughter in confinement. She was beaten up black and blue. After fleeing from her in-laws, she couldn't sleep properly. Almost every night she used to get nightmares which made her shiver and crumble. You ask this man why did they do this to my Moulina!"

Sanat was in full swing. The presence of the DSP and IO encouraged him to reiterate the FIR version. All this while, Sumit maintained calmness of a sea. For the police officials, it was like unleashing a barking dog to a visitor.

"Okay, that's enough," the DSP signalled Sanat to stop.

"So…Mr *Husband*, what do you have to say in your defence?" mocked the lady officer.

"I am just wondering why this gentleman is wasting his time here. He should take up *'script writing'* seriously as a career. His loud voice is his only armour here. All I hear is random blabber. I would love to see how he proves these in court," Sumit smiled and leaned back into his chair.

The trio – DSP, IO and Chell, were infuriated with the *Mumbaikar's* composure. Their objective somehow wasn't being met. Chell couldn't stay quiet after this. He started roaring *"Haramkhor, gandu, saalien, tereko mein dekh lunga* – I'll drag you for ten years in this case, then you will realize whom you've locked horns with."

Sumit addressed the DSP directly "Sir, aren't you some kind of a top class government official? How can you allow this person to verbally abuse me like this in your presence that too at your workplace?"

"He is a traumatised father of a tortured girl. Of course, he isn't in his right mind." Dash defended Chell's action and asked him to remain silent.

Chell was trembling with anger. He took out his mobile phone and tried dialling some number "You wait right here. I'll teach you a lesson." He sneered at Sumit.

"Excuse me everyone, but I need to speak to my lawyer outside. This man is continuously threatening me, and the police isn't doing anything." Sumit rose from his chair.

"Wait mister, we aren't done yet." Shamita signalled him to sit. "We came to know that you've saved your father-in-law and mother-in-law's phone numbers as Mr Chell and Mrs Chell in the contact list. Please produce your phone right now."

"Yes, that's right; but how is that derogatory? This is how their numbers were saved in my mobile since the time the talks for our alliance had initiated. I didn't think of changing it thereafter."

"No Sumit, it speaks about your negative attitude towards your in-laws. Even the way you were responding to Chell now was shocking!" The DSP was obviously on a fault-finding mission.

"*Eei toka ra attitude problem achi…yaku aame chadibani bahare buliba pain.*" Dash whispered it to his subordinate and decided to rejig their decision. Thereafter he stood up and asked his driver to get ready, it was time for him to call it a day. Gaurav instantly entered the cabin and stood beside Sumit.

Chell on the other hand was desperately trying to reach somebody over the phone, and finally walked up to the DSP and spoke in a muted tone, "*Their* mobile is switched off, I had asked them to come prepared. *Their* silver Indica was also seen near the *Chowk-Bazaar* area few hours back."

"Did you pay some advance? If not, then forget that they will come." the DSP spoke in a hushed tone as he made his way out of the police station.

Finally, at around 9:15 pm, Sumit was released on *Conditional bail* – which meant that once in every fifteen days, he had to appear before the IO until the chargesheet was filed. The Ghosh family and their lawyer pleaded before the lady officer to relax the condition and make it once a month, but she was adamant. She even issued Sumit a letter for the *hajira*, sealed and signed with date.

The enervated, tired Ghosh family felt guilty for holding up the young lawyer, Mathur and the driver for the last seven hours. So, they decided to treat them to dinner on their way back to Rourkela. Being partially relieved, Sushil and Chitra kept wondering about their son's *hajira* timeline…How will he manage to get tickets from Mumbai once in every fortnight? *Tatkal* reservation is also subject to availability. And if he ever missed a date, the Chells would get a chance to file a bail cancellation petition.

"It's late. Let's move out of this area quickly," Mathur suggested.

After a ten minutes' drive, they all checked into a roadside *Dhaba* for dinner. Over dinner, Mathur revealed Chell's arrangement of having Sumit abducted and how he foiled it completely. Gaurav was ecstatic and ordered a bottle of *Imperial Blue*, all for his uncle. In between the conversation, Gaurav also slipped in a pair of *Vakalatnama* to Sumit and requested him to grant permission to represent his case. He also suggested filing a petition in the HC for waiving off the condition imposed by the IO. The Ghosh family didn't react to any of those stimuli as they were yet to recuperate from the after-effects of an eight hour long, extensive grilling session.

Around 11:30 pm that night, the Ghosh family remained busy planning their next steps. They were yet to get a competent lawyer. Gaurav was inexperienced and lacked voice – a pettifogger who didn't have any grip. Had he been uproarious, rollicking and authoritative at the *Thana;* they would've been convinced of his competency to defend them and wouldn't have had to face harassment for so long. Nobody was in favour of letting Gaurav take the reins of this case. At this stage, the lone option was to go back to Advocate Panda and get the condition removed. Without much delay, Sumit dialled him, only to find it engaged.

Meanwhile, Sunita quickly booked two tickets for next day's *Tapaswini Express* to Hatia from Rourkela, as she had a *GoAir ticket* to Mumbai from Ranchi that evening.

Sumit laid flat on the bed, closed his eyes and tried to recapitulate the day's proceedings. His engineering college ragging days taught him how not to react and give in to the provocations made by seniors; instead, remain placid until the opponents breakdown in frustration. He was interrupted by Panda's missed call…

"Sorry to bother you at this hour, Sir." Sumit called back his lawyer.

"No worries. Tell me how the bail proceedings went today?" the lawyer sounded weary.

"Sir tomorrow morning I am heading to Ranchi. My sister is taking a Mumbai flight from there. By evening I'll be back and will narrate each and every incident in detail. But for the time being, I need you to quickly file a petition at the High Court."

"Hmmm, Okay. But will you tell me some details at least, so I understand what is going on…"

"Sir, these buggers have granted me a conditional bail – *Hajira* at police station, once in every fifteen days."

"Whaattt? Don't they understand English? Your bail order clearly states that - *In the event of his arrest in the aforesaid case the petitioner shall be released on bail by the arresting officer on such terms and conditions as deemed just and proper by him.* Is this *'just'*? How are you going to get reserved train tickets from Mumbai? This is a clear case of harassment."

"Yes Sir, they kept us waiting and then mentally screwed us. Could you please draft and file the petition by tomorrow itself? Your fees will be deposited in your account soon." Sumit assured his lawyer.

"Okay Sumit. Don't worry, we'll get the condition removed in no time. Send me a scanned copy of the letter issued by the IO, I'll make sure that this officer gets a call from the High Court. She'll realise soon what the consequences of playing around with an HC order are."

"Sir, how fast can this condition be waived off? I don't want to visit that hell again."

"Let's first file your petition under CrPC 439(1)(b). It should happen before your next date."

Sumit thanked his attorney before disconnecting. His family was also happy to hear Pradip Panda's counter strike – they slowly started believing that for every wrong accusation targeted at them, there was some IPC they could use to defend themselves. Hence a brilliant, proficient lawyer would be the key. That night the family surrendered themselves to a quiet, relaxed, unperturbed sleep – something that was majorly missing for the last three months.

But the table lamp at Advocate Panda's bungalow on Rameswar Patna Road had to glow few more minutes before it called the night – the gluttonous, foxy lawyer was busy making a mental blue-print of minting money from his client. The client who he thought would never return, wanted his intervention – what more could he ask for. *Opportunity seldom knocks twice.*

SEVENTEEN
2012

Haldia, West Bengal, India

The morning of 18th May 2012 was all bright and sunny. Sushil and Chitra made an elaborate arrangement for welcoming the newlyweds. Three of Sushil's sisters, his nephews along with Chitra's younger sister and her octogenarian mother teamed up together to make a flawless ritualistic welcoming ceremony for their charming daughter-in-law. The very next day of their son's marriage, Mr and Mrs Ghosh returned from Rourkela and made all arrangements at lightning fast speed. The *Bou-Bhat* was scheduled for next day at Daffodil Banquets, near Haldia Township's Sector-13 market.

Chitra's cousin, Sudeep was at Kharagpur Railway Station with his Chevrolet Tavera to pick up the entire group that descended from *Gitanjali Express* at 10:15 am sharp. Sunita who stayed back with her brother, accompanied the newly married couple, along with Moulina's brother and sister – Lokesh and Lina. The Tavera loaded with huge trolley bags sped through NH-6. Lina and Lokesh preferred taking a catnap at the backseat, while Sunita put on her earphones and enjoyed the ride. Moulina, who was all excited about the new journey gazed through the windowpane and kept enquiring about the new places that went past their speeding vehicle. Finally, after an hour's exhilarating and voluble session, she leaned on her hubby's shoulder for a quiet snooze.

The Tavera honked its way into the Ghosh residence. The ladies of the house lined up to embrace their daughter-in-law. Moulina was overwhelmed with the simple, homely welcome by her in-laws with bouquet of flowers, garlands, ululation and conch blowing. Sumit's granny who was carrying the *Shagun-ki-Thali*, handed it over to Chitra for receiving the new member into her new home where she would begin her marital journey. Moulina was warmly received with a *tilak* of *kumkum* and rice, along with an *Aarti*. Females from neighbouring households also gathered to witness the alluring, gorgeous daughter-in-law. It was a joyous moment at the Ghosh residence.

19th May was an extremely memorable day for the Ghoshs – a rare occasion when all the relatives from Sushil as well as Chitra's side gathered to celebrate the

Bou-Bhat function. Sushil had been busy throughout the day managing the caterers, decorators, the florists, et al. Until some days back they had been attendees to various such reception functions and it was time for a role reversal for the Ghosh couple. Monalisa Apartment wore a festive look with LED lights hanging from the terrace, Daffodil Banquets too dazzled with various lightings and *Rabindrasangeet* played mildly at the background. Most of the invitees were present and past colleagues of Sushil – they all were greeted with *nimbu-paani*. Starters were served to the visitors, while they kept gossiping and giggling on the floor. The newlywed couple remained seated at the centre of the banquet hall and posed for pictures with the visitors and well-wishers. A grand dinner followed the evening's proceeding with *fish batter fry, hariyali-chicken, chicken-chaap, mutton-biryani, paneer tikka, chutney, raajbhog, rasmalai, ice-cream and meetha-paan* on the menu. The lip smacking, finger licking, delicious meal earned Sushil a lot of kudos from the visitors.

In this moment of celebration, Sushil was however displeased with a set of events that occurred that evening. He didn't express his disappointment but it was quite evident from his body language, which bothered Sumit as well…

Sanat had earlier conveyed that as many as thirty people would accompany him for the Reception function. But only three turned up – something which disgusted Sushil to the core. All those arrangements made, went in vain. Moreover, among others, it was Mrs Chell who gave the function a miss! How can someone miss out on her elder daughter's reception party?! Emotionally, Moulina felt gutted and dejected in absence of her mother, but did put up a smiling face.

Moulina's maternal and paternal uncle accompanied her father at the evening's grand function. But they walked in late, as they had missed the morning express train.

Over and above this, Lina along with her father and two of the uncles, went missing from the venue for a good one hour. Sushil desperately tried to reach Sanat on his mobile, when everybody wanted to pose for a family photo – somehow his calls were ignored. Sumit and Sushil thought this behaviour of Chell to be extremely inappropriate and untoward.

However, a day later – Lina revealed the real reason behind the disappearance act on the eve of her sister's Reception function. Though Lina had promised her father not to speak about it, but on Moulina's insistence she gave in…when Moulina's marriage to Sumit had gotten finalised, Sanat was determined to get Lina married off too and was desperately looking for an alliance. That's when he came across a Haldia based businessman; had preliminary talks with his family and on the evening of Reception function, stepped out of Daffodil Banquets for an hour to meet them at a nearby Café, so that the boy and girl could meet each other. Sanat successfully complotted it but at the same time exposed his opportunist side.

The evening's function was wrapped up well within 10:30 pm. Sushil and Chitra wanted the newly married couple to ease up and relax. Finally, it was an end to those tiresome rituals and ceremonies, hectic traveling, posing before the cameras, the make-ups, and the rigorous fasting, that had worn down Sumit and Moulina. The night belonged to them, the night of *Phul-Sojja*. The florist had earlier decorated their bed with lots of fresh flowers and petals. The sweet, natural fragrance of red and pink roses along with tuberoses, and jasmine created a hypnotic, aphrodisiac effect in their room.

A vortex of thoughts crossed Moulina's mind, as she sat at the corner of the bed waiting for Sumit…How many times had she imagined this night? Not many nights ago, she sat at the balcony of her terrace and thought bewildered whether she was prepared for these moments to finally arrive. *Life was so different until yesterday, and now time is running and I've had absolutely no time for myself, to sit and relax and make sense of anything. The wedding rituals stormed by one after the other. Between the mixed feelings of anticipation, happiness, sorrow, anxiety, even panic, I didn't even get time to say a proper goodbye. I wonder what Baba would be doing right now. Lina and Maa were crying uncontrollably during the Bidaai; but I could not clearly decipher my Baba's expressions. Was it pain? Was it relief? Was it grief?"*

The door knob clicked. Moulina's toes curled as she heard Sumit's footsteps. She still remembered their first meeting – how she got bowled over by his intellect, simplicity and sense of humour. They had come a long way since then – chatted long hours over the phone, shared some moments, planned for their future and what not. Eventually they went on to become good friends, felt comfortable and relieved in each other's presence. He was the music she needed for the lyrics of her dreams. Sushweta ma'am was right – he was a gem of a person, her prized possession.

They looked at each other and exchanged smiles. Sumit just couldn't take his eyes off her – those brown almond eyes and dimpled cheeks were worth dying for. Weren't they the first thing he noticed about her? Or was it her lovely, soft, sweet voice that he wanted to hear over and over again?

Inspite of being acquainted to each other, both were nervous and hesitant. It was their *wedding night* and they both had wanted it to be amazing and unforgettable. It was Sumit who decided to end the silence with some stupid comments. To him, Moulina was a friend more than anything else.

"You know, it feels so weird to think that I've to share my bed with you for the rest of my life!" Sumit took a pause, smiled at Moulina and continued "But at the same time, it feels exciting too."

With an animated scowling gesture and blown up cheeks, Moulina stared at her husband for a while. Sumit moved closer and pulled her cheeks before planting a kiss on the left cheek and in an apologetic tone said, "Aww…I was just kidding Mouli."

Moulina was quick to reciprocate with a tight hug followed by an instantaneous smooch. Sumit's arms circled her, gathering her against him as they rolled over the spongy bed, tangled together, and kissed each other crazily. He slipped his tongue gently inside her mouth, his sensual moves made her body melt into his. She gripped his hair and pulled him closer. Her veins thumped and heart pumped heavily. His intensity made her cling to him as the only solid thing in a dizzy swaying world. After several soft, passionate kisses she gave his bottom lip a playful bite, which exhilarated Sumit even more. He then slowly moved his lips over her jawline and then to her ears, and gently nibbled those soft earlobes.

Just when Moulina's hairpin pricked at his palm, Sumit realised she was still wearing her heavy bridal attire. He suggested that she change into a light saree, and helped her take off all those hairpins, tucked-pins and the heavy jewellery.

The junior Ghosh was playing with the AC remote adjusting the temperature, when Moulina walked in and sat beside him. She looked all exhausted and tired.

"*Ki holo tomar?* You look completely enervated."

"I've a back ache, the shoulders are paining too. Sitting for the entire evening, greeting the guests seems to have taken a toll on me."

"*Koi baat nehi*, I'll give you a wonderful massage and you'll feel better in no time."

Moulina prostrated herself on the bed of pink and red rose petals, while her husband gently stroked and kneaded her back. She was soft and delicate. The tender palpation, relieved her muscle tension, reduced stress and evoked some feeling of calmness. She closed her eyes and felt the soothing effect of his hands – the first memory that came to her mind was that of a seven or eight-year-old herself, running around happily in the cool, breezy October night on the terrace, trying to trap a firefly in a glass bottle. She couldn't remember where from she got the stained bottle, nor did she remember how long she had been chasing those fireflies. She just reminisced wearing her favourite frilly frock and at that moment, her desire had meant everything to her…just one firefly, she needed just one of them to make her lucky charm. Then, the bottle would be the perfect symbol of all the possibilities. Blinking intermittently inside, glowing with the secret that only she would know. That she was endless, she was invincible.

When Moulina opened her eyes, Sumit was looking straight at her. She turned around and hugged him. This was it – time to surrender, accept and belong. She wasn't going to wait for him to make the first move.

Sumit got the signal right, he kissed her again all over, slowly slipped off her saree, then the blouse followed by her petticoat. His strong, gentle hands began to stroke her. Slowly and gradually she undressed him, showered kisses all over while he caressed her back. To her complete astonishment, she felt herself becoming aroused. Knowing what he was doing, it startled her.

"Shhh," Sumit whispered. "Shhh…it's all right, don't worry, just relax and listen to your body."

Sumit was brushing her breasts with his fingertips, all the time shushing and stroking her. Moulina felt his hardness. She was dizzy with sensation and was ready to let him do anything to her. She wanted him to be deep inside her – he was slow, rhythmic, gentle, moving down her body. There was a brief sharp pain, a very brief one, and then a sweet spasm that went through her and seemed to lift her into the air like a gas balloon. And then no more pain, just sweetness, some incredible feeling that would be treasured. Both were all sweaty even in their AC bedroom. They cuddled each other as they lay side by side on the bed.

Every time he touched her, he fell more and more in love. Her skin was cold, may be because of the AC, and he felt the goosebumps on her arms, her waist. Her ivory bangles made intermittent noise, disturbing the sound of her short breaths that he cherished. Later, he tucked her hair away from her lovely face as she slept peacefully with her head on his chest. The moonlight streamed from the curtains onto her flushed face. Sumit could watch her sleep the whole night, it was simply overwhelming. Tender, loving thoughts ran through his mind as he told himself again and again…*I am no longer alone. She is here. My wife - My better half.*

EIGHTEEN
2012

Haldia, West Bengal, India

Even though Sumit took quotations from several Thimpu based tour-operators, he kept contemplating on the trip duration vis-à-vis his leave availability. Meanwhile, the airline and hotel rates skyrocketed during the peak summer season and he was left with no option but to drop the idea of Bhutan and settle for Darjeeling. Before he left for his marriage, Sumit had made a detailed itinerary of *Darjeeling–Kalimpong–Lava–Loleygaon–Rishap*. Advance payments for hotel bookings were done. However, due to huge summer vacation rush he got RAC train tickets, and was hopeful to get it confirmed, as the days advanced.

Every single day, Sumit would check their train-ticket position on the IRCTC webpage and get disappointed with absolutely no movement of the RAC status. Sushil encouraged his son and asked him to wait till the last day, as most of the cancellations happen then and their tickets would eventually get confirmed. Somehow, Chitra wasn't comfortable about his son and daughter-in-law visiting the hills for their honeymoon. The reason was the political unrest in demand of a separate state of *Gorkhaland*, which was pretty much unpredictable and the agitation could happen anytime without any prior notice. For a newly married couple, she thought it might not be a safe destination; but then her son had already made his plans.

Sumit and Moulina planned to leave for Darjeeling on the morning of 21st May; but then till the previous evening their tickets were yet to be confirmed. Chitra tried her best to hold them back by showing a piece of news on *Anandabazar Patrika's* fourth page that reported some clash between political parties and tea garden workers. But the newlyweds had already done their packing and were ready to leave.

However, even when by late night, the tickets failed to get confirmed. Sumit decided to drop the plan once and for all. Moulina got disheartened as she was eagerly waiting for the trip, it would have been her first trip to the mountains and tea gardens – Sumit promised his wife a bigger and larger vacation the following year and that too overseas.

For the next ten days, Sumit and Moulina had a great family time together at Haldia. Chitra was overwhelmed to have her daughter-in-law with her, she went on to teach her the basics of the Ghosh family etiquettes. And Moulina, like an obedient student followed her mother-in-law. She even went on to accompany her father-in-law for shopping trips to the local vegetable and fish market. Moulina's matrimonial journey started on a good note. Everything was new, yet exciting for her. She was slowly learning to operate the washing machine, the mixer-grinder, and the micro-oven. But couldn't get the right amount of sugar in a cup of tea. She was amazed by her mother-in-law's cooking skills and secretly noted down some of those recipes demonstrated by Chitra. In the evenings, Moulina accompanied her husband for a leisurely stroll along the banks of Haldi River. She had never witnessed those waves crashing onto the river banks with a splashing sound, nor had she experienced the saline river breeze that blew uninterruptedly – it defined freedom, serenity and relaxation. Far away from the claustrophobic Birmirpur, the river side of Haldia gave a fresh perspective of life. And with her husband's cosy company it made everything all the more special. On top of it, the roadside *phuchhkas and egg-rolls*, almost every evening was a bliss.

After a splendid holiday, Sunita left for Mumbai with some pleasant memories of her brother's wedding. She had to join office and couldn't afford to stretch her stay. A beautiful, adorable daughter-in-law brought tides of happiness to the Ghosh family. Moulina too embraced the change and started to feel as a long-lost daughter of a family, who showered all their love and affection on their new member.

"Beta...sab kuch thik hai na? How's it going at your in-laws, hope you're able to adjust to the new environment?" Sanat called up to enquire about his daughter, three days after the Reception.

"Yes *Baba*, they're all lovely people. My father-in-law treats me like his own daughter; mother-in-law is a bit strict, but she is very helpful and sweet. They all love me a lot," an overjoyed Moulina replied.

"And how is my son-in-law? You didn't say anything about him!" Sanat persisted.

"Baba, the entire life is now left to know him and be with him."

"Beta don't forget us, don't forget this small place of Birmirpur." Sanat's voice trembled as he couldn't hold back his tears and before handing the phone to his wife, he gained control over himself and said, *"ei ne tor Maa-r sathey kotha bol."*

Hearing her father sniffling with a shaky voice; Moulina's smiling, cheerful face turned gloomy. She gulped back her tears and complained, *"Maa* – why didn't you come for my *Bou-Bhat?* I missed you so much. Your absence was the cause of several murmurs here at my in-laws."

"I wasn't feeling well, Moulina. I regret not being there to be a part of your celebrations..."

Moulina interrupted her mother "don't bluff *Maa*, uncle hinted that you were annoyed with Sumit's decision to put up at the Guest House that evening. But *Maa*, if you were in his position, then you too would've acted likewise. I had witnessed how Sunita suffered a severe migraine attack in our basement room which was nothing less than a furnace. While we are habituated to the extreme summer conditions of Birmirpur, they weren't. We couldn't even arrange a cooler for your son-in-law. Sunita's health was deteriorating and he had no option but to move out and avail the air-conditioned room at the Guest House of *Rani Sati Mandir...*"

"*Achha achha*, forget all those. Now tell me, what all new things have you learned from your '*new Maa*'?" Maya tried to lighten up the conversation.

While Maya was about to ask something, Lina almost snatched the phone and enquired "*Di*...how is my *Jiju?* Isn't he annoying you? When are you guys going for the honeymoon?"

"Sshhhh...shut up, behave yourself. *Jiju* is fine, and we aren't going for honeymoon. Our tickets didn't get confirmed till the last moment, but yes a bigger vacation will happen next year."

"Then all the more reason for my *Jiju* to irritate you," giggled Lina. Moulina's face brightened up while she conversed with her sister.

Her facial expression was the canvas of her inner self. Sumit could figure out easily that she grew emotional over the conversation with her parents. It's not easy for a girl to leave behind her thirty years and not be weepy about it. As a responsible husband, he tried comforting her. That night he made sweet passionate love to her, thrice in a row, before they fell asleep canoodling each other.

With just three days left for Sumit and Moulina to fly off to Mumbai, the packing was on at full swing. Like any worried mother, Chitra wanted everything that a new couple would need to be packed off from Haldia. Though Sumit kept on iterating that every single item would be available in Mumbai – a mother's point of view would always be unique. That day, around 3 pm, just after lunch, the doorbell of the Ghosh residence rang twice. Sumit opened the door, and to his utter surprise found the Chell couple standing outside wearing a courteous smile. Even before he could react, he was agitated with a series of thoughts – *Why are they here again? It has hardly been a week, what will the neighbours and relatives think? Now it's time for some serious packing, who'll do mehmaan-nawazi with them? What do they want now?*

Even Sushil and Chitra were taken by complete surprise. Moulina was however elated to see her parents. She couldn't hide her emotions, she hugged her mother and started snivelling.

"How come you're here at this hour?" asked Sushil while helping Sanat with the luggage.

"Actually, Geetanjali Express got delayed, it stood still at Chakulia station for several hours." Sanat washed his face and made himself comfortable in the living room sofa chair.

"You could have informed us, we would've…"

"*Na na,* it's okay. The moment we got to know that their honeymoon got cancelled, we thought of giving them a surprise visit. Also, Maya wanted to see them before they left for Mumbai." Sanat explained.

The next two days were disgusting – Sumit was thoroughly irritated with certain acts of his in-laws, but he couldn't even express himself to anybody, not even to his newly wedded wife. The unwanted, uninvited Chell couple forced themselves into every activity of Sumit and Moulina – they became part of their evening stroll, would suggest unnecessary items for packing, and would even go on to exhibit their bond of affection for their daughter through certain eye soring activities.

Moulina, who made all her mental preparations to start a new journey with Sumit, was constantly being emotionally manipulated by her parents – as if to remind Moulina about their contribution in her upbringing, and that after marriage, it would be time for her to '*pay-back*'. This made Sumit rather uneasy and distant. The purpose of the Chells' visit was completely convoluted and it did raise a few eyebrows when Sanat and Maya came in *empty-handed* to meet their daughter – a pack of sweets or fruits was at least expected as per Bengali tradition on their first visit, post marriage.

Sumit wanted to openly discuss these concerns with his soulmate, but then left it for any other time when it would be appropriate…

Sunday afternoons are generally idle, when the streets of Kolkata preferred to skive. The deserted Belgharia Expressway only had a handful of Ola cabs running at their convenient pace. The iconic yellow Ambassador taxis didn't even bother to overtake the speeding WagonR of the Ghoshs. Sumit and Moulina reached NSC Bose Airport in flat two hours twenty minutes. In between, on Chitra's insistence, the car was diverted to *Dakshineswar Mandir* for a brief *darshan of Kali Mata,* but still they were well before time at the airport.

Throughout the Haldia – Kolkata stretch, Moulina gazed and rubbernecked at some of the city landmarks, its wide roads, high-rises, bridges and statues. She observed the city's intricacies in full amazement. To her, the centrally air-conditioned airport was a Wonderland. She observed the huge glass façade building with the wonder of a child. She was awed by the stylish, glamorous airhostesses and the hunky pilots who made their way through security check-ins. She thoroughly enjoyed the view of flight takeoffs and landing, the background departure announcements, the gossiping lady CISFs, the jazzy cafés and bookstores, playful kids, snoozing passengers and some foreign backpackers. In the midst of all, she felt solace in resting her head on Sumit's shoulder and sipping a hot cappuccino as they waited to board Jet Airways 9W-616 to Mumbai.

When the aircraft took off the runway with roaring engine and accelerated speed – Moulina flushed with excitement. A sense of freedom and sovereignty came in with the soaring altitude. She was all euphoric, grabbed her husband's arm and pointed out to those pink and white fairy-floss clouds of the dusk. She was even attentive to those inflight safety demonstrations and after her on-board meal, preferred listening to some music loaded in Sumit's mobile and fast slipped into a zizz – *I don't want to go back to my past, my present is sweet and flying high above those bumpy, potholed, dusty, muddy roads underneath. End of tracking those blinking light of flights from the terrace on a dark night sky, time to light up and look forward to my glowing future. My life is awesome, with a loving and caring husband by my side...*

NINETEEN
2014

Haldia, West Bengal, India

Left with just one week before re-appearing at Birmirpur PS, Sumit called up his lawyer to check the status of the petition filed for his bail's condition waiver at the High Court. He didn't want to get harassed and humiliated furthermore in the name of investigation. Advocate Panda asked him to keep calm, as his men were on it completely and trying to list the matter for a hearing soon – a favourable order would then debar the unnecessary *hajira* imposed on him. Panda also had an alternate suggestion…"Look Sumit, don't panic. Even if we don't get the order in time, you can still skip the summon. In that case, keep a medical certificate ready and then I'll contact the IO and your *hajira* can be deferred. Just don't worry, I'll handle it. Since you're on bail now, simply relax and look after your aged parents."

Unlike the bail application status, Sumit couldn't track the details of his condition waiver petition on Orissa HC's website and that exasperated him. Almost every alternate day, he would SMS or call either Panda or Shrikant. Rupees twenty-five thousand had already been deposited in Panda's wife's account to hasten the processing of the petition. Also, Sumit didn't want his lawyer to contact the lady officer, as any chances of foul play could cost him dearer. He even had the hunch that Panda had been overcharging them, but could do nothing about it.

As a *"Plan-B"* – Sushil however asked his son to book their train tickets to Rourkela for the first *hajira*. The appearance before the IO was crucial, as the complainant had asked for her educational certificates to be returned to her and if they failed, the chargesheet would bear some adverse report. Sushil had an intuition that probably Panda wouldn't be able to get the waiver in next seven days.

Back in Mumbai, Sunita commenced her office. She had to respond to an official *"show-cause"* notice issued by the HR for her prolonged absence from work. The Tilaknagar flat was in a shabby state when she entered after almost three months – electricity being snapped off, gas connection discontinued, dust coated floor and cobwebbed ceiling took off the shine from the apartment which was supposed to be the hub of happiness and mark a new beginning in her brother's matrimonial life.

"Sumit had called up this afternoon. We are left with just two days to list his petition and since I've no update on this, I asked him to wait till this evening." Shrikant informed his senior.

"Actually...we are in a bit of a soup. The bench clerk whom I know is on leave for a month, and I had already paid him some advance. But then he couldn't list the matter and had asked his subordinate to do so. Now this fellow wants some percentage as well" a worried Panda replied.

"So, what do we do now?"

"Somehow, we have to postpone this by a month; which means two appearances at the *Thana*. I've anyway informed Sumit to keep a medical certificate ready. If his opposition doesn't go for a bail cancelation spree, then this can be handled. Else it'll become a bit complicated." Panda kept thinking about alternate ways to address the bottleneck. After a pause he said, "Let me talk to him this evening."

Later in the evening, the senior lawyer gave two missed calls to his client. Sumit called back and could very well figure out the bluff from the lawyer's blabber. After dealing with so many lawyers in last couple of months, Sumit somehow could gauge from their tone when they were trying to pull one over on him. The moment *"they"* would want to hide facts or ask for fees, they would go on gibbering without any substance. Though Panda reiterated that he was trying his best to get the case listed and there was no need to visit the PS, Sumit decided to attend the summon and avoid further complications.

Sushil wasn't happy with the way their legal practitioner dealt with the latest petition. Even after paying the full amount, if they had to visit the police station and be subjected to embarrassments and harassments, then the merit in appointing a lawyer goes futile. He vowed to get rid of Panda once the bail condition was removed.

The morning of 26th September was pleasant outside but tense inside the hotel room. Fridays were supposed to be relaxed days in the steel city, but Sumit was getting cold feet. Within a few hours, he had to leave for Birmirpur from Hotel Welburn. A fortnight back when he was there for the bail matter, he had exchanged numbers with the Qualis driver and this time around, the same driver was hired for an entire day trip on a Tata Indica. They started from their hotel at 10:30 am, so as to reach early and finish off the formalities and return by afternoon; not knowing that a pair of eyes followed them on a Yamaha RX100 and kept informing about the Indica's co-ordinates to their handler.

The police station building stood tall facing the glaring sun, trying to get rid of the moisture on its surface caused by early morning showers. The drenched mynas enjoyed their sunbath on the neighbouring treetops. The father and son reached the police station at quarter to twelve, but were disappointed to find that the lady officer was out on highway patrolling with a few constables. They waited outside on a wooden bench. Sumit tried calling SI Shamita, but her number was out of reach. They kept waiting, waiting and waiting…few of the officers came up to them, inquisitively asked about their case and returned back without commenting; some showed solidarity by abusing the Chells and encouraged them to fight it out; others suggested to settle the matter mutually. Tired of waiting, the visitors walked up to the main road and sauntered along it towards the *Chowk-Bazaar* area. A Yamaha RX100 was seen parked near a local *paan shop*. They spotted a roadside eatery where most of the truck-drivers lined up for their lunch – *daal,* rice, soyabean-curry, pickle and sliced onions were available at twenty rupees per plate. The surrounding wasn't hygienic at all, and the food tasted horrible. Still, to keep the biological clock ticking, they had to re-fuel themselves. Just when they were about to leave, they met the driver of the police van. He was also there for his lunch…

"*Aap yahan pe lunch karte ho kya?*" asked Sumit to the stout driver.

"*Kabhi kabhaar kar leta hu…aap logo ka ho gaya kya?*" The driver guzzled and gargled the water as he finished his lunch.

"Did madam return from patrolling? We've been waiting for her since morning."

"Not yet, *chances kum lag raha hai aaj…DSP ke saath accha bana ke rakkhi hai, isi liye thaat se reheti hai.* And today DSP *Saab* is on leave," informed the driver while picking his teeth with a matchstick.

"Today I have my *hajira* before her…if she doesn't turn up, then what do I do?" Sumit asked indignantly.

"*Call kar lo unko,* she can assign somebody else from the *Thana* to take your attendance. But if today is your date, then try not to miss it. Else your opposition will get a solid ground to file a bail cancellation petition," suggested the man who had been driving a police vehicle for the last six years.

"*Waise dowry case hai na?* Why don't you talk to the DSP? He can mediate and have it resolved. He has done this before." The driver informed Sumit in a hushed tone.

"It's a fake case. The girl's side has cooked up a story against us and…"

"*Maalum hai Saab, jyada tar dowry cases fake hi hota hai.* Your *sasur* made multiple rounds at the *Thana* to lodge a complaint against you all. *Madam ke baaju wala jo officer baith te hai,* he refused to file an FIR as he sensed some foul play. That's when he approached the DSP," revealed the driver. "Why don't you do one thing…ask Mathur *Saab* to talk to our DSP and strike a deal. Last time Mathur *Saab jo aaye the aap logo ke saath,* is well connected to the police circle."

"Ohh, is it! Okay will explore that, but as of now let me first appear before the IO."

The driver gave away some valuable information, which would help Sumit to resolve the ongoing tussle. As a token of thanks, he paid for the driver's meal and sponsored a cigarette. Back at the police station, their wait for the IO continued. It was 3:30 pm, Sushil went on to take a short siesta on the wooden bench outside, while Sumit kept looking at his watch that ticked away blankly. He was fatigued by the unbearable long exhausting wait.

Soon after, a few officers and constables left the *Thana* and got replaced by their colleagues due to change in their shift. And the Ghosh duo still sat outside waiting for the IO to arrive. Though booked for the entire day, their driver got irritated and bored waiting inside the Indica.

As the evening progressed, Sumit's resilience succumbed to the mounting nervousness. He had been fighting out all the odds tooth-and-nail, and couldn't let loose just because the lady officer decided not to be there in office. He walked up straight into the Senior Inspector's cabin to voice his concern. The Senior Inspector who was relatively new in Birmirpur *Thana,* was in civvies and came in for the second shift. He briefly heard Sumit's grievance.

"Sir…my entire family has been framed in a false 498A case. Last time when we were here for bail, my father-in-law created a ruckus. He threatened and abused us in front of the IO and DSP. Today when we are here for the *hajira,* the IO is nowhere to be found." Sumit narrated all in one breath.

"I saw you waiting there at the wooden bench today morning. Who is that aged person with you?" The Senior Inspector was empathetic.

"That's my father. At this age, with high blood pressure and diabetes, he has been waiting with me the entire day."

"See…I am new here. I got transferred from Koraput last week. I don't even know my colleagues that well. But if Shamita is out or busy in some other assignment, her subordinate should deal with her case. Did you try to connect with her?"

"Yes Sir, every half an hour, I've been trying her mobile number. But no luck."

"Okay…wait, let me see what can be done. But if today is your appearance before the IO, then don't go away without attendance. It'll give a strong ground to her as well as your opposition to file a petition for your bail cancellation." The Senior Inspector warned.

"That's why we are here, Sir. It is now 6 pm, we've been waiting since 11 in the morning."

"Do you have anything to handover to the IO or to your opposition? Are you carrying it with you?"

"I was asked to handover all the educational certificates of my wife. I'm carrying them all." Sumit patted the leather bag on his shoulder, but didn't pull out the certificates just yet.

Though the Senior Inspector was barely a week old in his office, Shamita's equation with DSP Dash didn't go unnoticed. Her snobbish attitude towards her subordinates and her tendency to jump hierarchy had always been a part of corridor talks among the police officials. It was evident that the lady officer was on a spree to harass Sumit for some unknown reason. But as a responsible public servant, the Senior Inspector extended his help. He immediately called in ASI Chaurasia from Shamita's team and ordered him to get in touch with her and subsequently take Sumit's attendance and let them leave for the day. Chaurasia called up his Boss on her alternate number to inform about the latest happenings, to which the lady officer asked him to wait until she was back in office. With no alternatives other than waiting, Sumit preferred to walk upto the tea stall for another round of tea. His driver accompanied him too.

It was almost 7 pm, and the main road area was lively with haphazard movements of the localites. Some were out for shopping, while others were hanging around with friends. Sumit was about to sip into his glass of tea, when somebody lightly tapped on his shoulder.

"Assalam walekum Sumit Babu!! Achha hua aap mil gaye yahan..." Aqib, the bailer smiled.

"Aqib *Bhai,* how come you're here?"

"I stay nearby. And we keep visiting the *Thana* for various bail matters. So, this is our regular visit."

"Aur bolo, kya chal raha hai?" Sumit signalled the tea vendor to handover a glass to Aqib as well.

"Sumit *Babu, baat yeah hai ki...*accidentally I bumped into your *sasur* last week at the petrol pump. He took me to the nearest *paan-shop,* treated me with a grand *meetha paan* and politely said – *tu apna admi hai, yahin ka rehene wala. You know me well, fir bhi bahar walon ke liye bailer banne ka kya zaroorat tha. I suggest you visit the police station and withdraw yourself as a Guarantor to the Ghosh family. Woh log achhe nehi hai, meri Beti ko pareshan kiya, aur dekhna aagey ja ke tereko bhi faswayega. You pull yourself out from this matter, I promise to pay you INR 50,000/- once I win this case. That scoundrel family has to pay a hefty amount for all this."*

Sumit was traumatized to hear the narrative. He felt a tremor run down his knees, quickly gained control, and paused for a bit before he took a few calming breaths to get rid of the momentary consternation. He finished off his glass without saying much, but ultimately asked the bailer "So what was your reaction? What did you tell him?"

"Sumit *Babu*, I'm a professional bailer. This is my bread and butter. I told him that if he can pay me the bail amount then and there, probably then I might consider his suggestion." Aqib couldn't quite meet Sumit's eyes.

"Did he agree to pay you?"

"*Kahaan se dega paisa? Haraami hai saala, ek number ka nikamma…market mein udhari chalu hai uska.* He just kept promising me 50,000…*jiska koi guarantee nehi hai.* Like a mad man, he kept pompously announcing in the entire Birmirpur town last year when his daughter's alliance was fixed with you. And now see how he has changed his colours. You need not worry about this bail matter. It's all done and sealed. Just that next time when you come for bail at Rourkela court, you retain me as your bailer. *Gareeb ko thoda kamane ka mauka milega,* Sir."

"*Fir se* bail! What are you saying?" Sumit spat out his first sip from the second glass of tea.

"Hmmm…you need to take bail once more from the Magistrate. Consult your lawyer, he would be able to tell you better. Keep my number, give me a call. And I'll be there for you, at your service." Aqib kick started his Yamaha RX100 and disappeared into the traffic.

Back at the police station, Shamita finally arrived on her Honda Activa at around 8 pm. She wasn't in her police uniform, which suggested that she came from her residence directly. While entering, she looked at the Ghosh duo from the corner of her eyes. The fiendish pleasure she felt upon seeing the distressed and exhausted visitors was clear in her expressions…*Now they would've realised what it feels like to be kept waiting.*

"Did you bring your wife's education certificates?" asked the lady officer, while scribbling into a hard bound notebook.

"Yes madam, here it is." Sumit handed over a plastic folder.

"I believe all of them are intact and you've not misplaced any of the documents?" She curtly raised an eyebrow at him.

"You can check with Moulina."

"Yes, that I'll do. In case anything is missed out, you've to carry it with you in your next *hajira*. Now sign here." The Sub-Inspector pushed the notebook towards

Sumit and pointed at a section for signature.

"Well, next time when you come, carry the blue trolley bag. Chell told me that it's there at your Mumbai residence." Shamita spoke sternly while filling up the *seizure list.*

"But that's not mentioned anywhere, not even in the FIR," protested Sumit.

"Look mister, don't try to be oversmart. If you don't co-operate with us, then adding IPC 406 to your chargesheet won't take much of a time." The IO threatened.

Sushil immediately interjected and asked his son to do as the IO said. There was no scope in their lives for additional troubles.

At around 10 pm, Sumit and Sushil returned to their hotel room. Sumit called up his mother in Haldia and narrated the day's proceedings. He informed her about extending their stay at Rourkela for a couple of days in quest for a reliable, competent lawyer.

Next day, Saturday – Sushil and his son fixed up three appointments. To all the three, Sumit narrated his case like a programmed puppet, but then nothing materialised. The first one they met, discouraged them to pursue the case. The second one, who happened to be simultaneously practicing in Supreme Court gave all assurance of taking up their case, but avoided Sumit's follow-up calls to him later. The final one at Basanti Colony was a Bengali lawyer named Hrishikesh Basak. At the tea stall last evening, on Sumit's request bailer Aqib referred Advocate Basak as a shrewd Bengali lawyer who could be the best fit for his case. At Basak's residence cum chamber, while Sumit recounted his side of the story, the senior advocate was seen to be edgy and uncomfortable. Later he revealed that he had been already approached by Sanat Chell and assuming it to be the same case, he politely declined to hear any further.

TWENTY
2014

Rourkela, Odisha, India

After his first *hajira*, Sumit dialed Advocate Panda, who still couldn't list the last petition for hearing. Instead he insisted on keeping a medical certificate ready and repeated the same version *"trying my level best"*. Sumit also didn't divulge anything about his first apperance, and requested him to speed up the process.

Panda, however had something else playing on his mind. He was ecstatic about the fact that Sumit's absence for *hajira* would further complicate the case and allow him to play around with it at HC level that would result into some additional income for his law firm. Little did he know that the Ghoshs had already lost their faith in him and were in pursuit of an alternate legal counsellor. The foxy attorney even activated his contacts to get the mobile number of the IO and strike a deal with her.

With no time to spare before the second *hajira* on 11th of October, Sumit left for Mumbai to get his wife's trolley bag. He hardly remembered the contents of the bag, but had to spend almost ten grand to get it from his Mumbai residence. The one-way flight ticket and return *Tatkal* train ticket was expensive – there wasn't even an iota of doubt that the police had ganged up with his father-in-law to harass him unnecessarily. As a law abiding citizen, Sumit obeyed police orders to avoid any further snags.

Just days before, when Sumit was about to leave Mumbai with the blue trolley bag, cyclone *Hudhud* caused havoc in the states of Andhra Pradesh and Odisha. The coastal city of Vishakapatnam got severely affected, and major cities of Odisha were placed on high alert. Most trains were cancelled, routes of a few got diverted, while some remained stuck midway. Situations worsened. TV reports showed – torrential downpour, uprooted trees, flooded streets, loss of human life and disrupted civic life. Sumit decided to call the lady officer...

"Hello madam, this is Sumit. Can we talk for a moment?"

"Sumit? Who?"

"498A accused at your police station..."

"Oh yes yes...tell me, what made you call me now?"

"Well madam, as you know, cyclone *Hudhud* has hampered everyday life. Trains to Rourkela are running late by several hours, some are stuck in between. I've a *Tatkal* ticket, and am supposed to reach Rourkela on the evening of 10th October. By any chance if things get delayed, request you to consider a relaxed timeline for this *hajira*. Please madam."

"Hmmm…but *Hudhud* has had zero effect here. Mostly coastal Odisha has been affected. So why are you worried?"

"Agreed madam. But coastal area trains are getting diverted through this inner route and hence the anticipation of getting late." Sumit patiently tried to explain.

"See mister – 11th October, 11 am is when you have to appear before me, failing which will complicate things from here on. Now please cut the call, I've other things to do."

It was clear from Shamita's attitude that the Ghosh family had already been considered as offenders. There was no room for flexibility, and hence Sumit shouldn't provide any chance to the police or his opposition to have an upper hand in the case.

Fortunately, *Jnaneswari-Deluxe Superfast Express* reached Rourkela only one hour late on the evening of 10th October. Sushil, who reached Rourkela in the morning, was there at the station for his son. After a brief talk, they walked out of the station towards their hotel. Guided by his intuition Sushil avoided Hotel Welburn this time. Instead he booked a room in *Hotel Paulson* in the next lane. It was drizzling outside with frequent lightning and strong winds; Sumit called up their known driver for next day's travel to Birmirpur *Thana*.

Next day, their vehicle took almost one hour to reach Birmirpur. After a heavy night-long downpour, the morning was overcast with spasmodic drizzles. The waterlogged low lying areas along the highway became a temporary spot for water-football among the village kids, few *adivasis* were seen axing an uprooted tree along NH-143. Sumit showed absolutely no interest in these activities and outside sceneries. His frequent visits to Birmirpur had become chronic infirmity and his inability to get a stay on the condition tantalized him.

This time around, the father and son went mentally prepared for a long wait and redundant grilling by the officers – *Expect the worst and one would never be disappointed.* To their surprise, things happened faster, but not without humiliations.

Sumit got to know from a constable that Shamita was on leave. Without wasting any time, he immediately called her up to understand how the *hajira* would be taken!!

"Wait for ASI Chaurasia, I've already instructed him about your *hajira*," informed the lady officer. "Once you deposit the blue trolley bag, go and meet DSP Dash at his office. He wanted to see you."

Sumit had prepared a list which he wanted to approbate before submitting the trolley bag, and get it signed by the receiver. The bag had some of his wife's apparels, lingeries and cosmetics. While packing it off, he was so full of disgust and intense hatred that he didn't want to retain any of her belongings that would later trigger memories.

"Why don't you call your father-in-law here, so that he can check all the contents of this trolley bag," suggested ASI Chaurasia.

"I don't want to talk to those fraudsters. I would request you to call him here and take custody of this bag," replied Sumit.

"Okay…give me his number. And you two wait there, until Chell *Babu* arrives."

The ASI in his mid-thirty, with Bihari accent dialled Sanat Chell's number and soon stepped out of the police station. Sumit could see Chaurasia courteously addressing Sanat over the phone. He frequently let out a little laugh and chatted on jovially, as if they were known to each other for ages…something beyond a cop and complainant relationship.

Sumit and Sushil had to further wait for almost one hour before Sanat walked into the police station nonchalantly. He behaved like a remorseless perpetrator, ready to wreck vengeance on the Ghosh family. Most of the staff at the *Thana* knew him and addressed him as *"Chell Babu"* – as if the entire administration was taken into confidence or might have been coerced. With a disrespectful look, he shrugged off the presence of Sushil and Sumit, pulled a chair and sat across the table from Chaurasia.

In next fifteen minutes, the bag was handed over to Sanat via Chaurasia. It was then opened, checked, tallied with the list of items jotted by Sumit. A *seizure list* was then prepared, signed and filed along with the FIR papers. Before finally leaving the police station, Sanat murmured something to Chaurasia and then briskly walked away from his desk. Sumit was again asked to wait, before the attendance notebook got prepared.

"Sumit, abhi aap idhar aake sign kar do." Chaurasia called in the visitor after preparing the *hajira* write-up.

While Sumit was signing at the allocated column on the notebook, the ASI asked him, "Why do you have to bring in your father here for every appearance? He is an old man and is not needed for your *hajira*."

"He doesn't want to leave me alone. We've never ever faced police or judiciary in our life. And hence we move as a unit together," replied Sumit after completing the formalities.

"Chhote bachhe ho kya aap? Are you afraid that somebody will abduct you? Police station is the safest place here," mocked the junior officer.

"Are we done?" Sumit asked Chaurasia pretending not to hear him.

"Yes, for the time being. But I am afraid you've to now wait for the DSP. He wants to see you."

"When will he be here?"

"Oh! come on, I cannot go and ask my super-Boss when he will be here." Chaurasia replied with a wink.

Just when Sumit turned his back and was about to leave Chaurasia's desk; the curious officer enquired *"Kya hua tha aap logo ke beech mein?* Why did she leave you?"

"I've no clue. We all fail to answer this. But trust me, we've never mistreated her."

"Do you know – Chell *Babu's* daughters were all *numero uno* in our Birmirpur area! *Patakha thi, ladkon ki line lagi rehti thi...*and you couldn't handle her? *Size chhota hai kya?"* Chaurasia taunted the junior Ghosh and cracked up with laughter. He was further joined in by a couple of other officers who were silently listening to the conversation.

"Excuse me?" Sumit couldn't believe his ears. Without entertaining them any further, he preferred walking back to his father.

"I mean, were you incompatible in bed? She must have been unsatisfied all this while and then finally decided to leave." The ASI continued mocking and shared a good laugh with his colleagues.

Completely out of disbelief, Sumit was stunned to hear such rubbish from a junior officer. How dare he made such ignominious remarks? What instigated Chaurasia to ask such humiliating questions – the lady officer's absence or Chell's nasty trick? He was red faced, boiling with anger; yet could do nothing to soothe his temper in that hostile situation. He started sweating profusely and ignored all those babbles. He sat next to his father, plugged in the earphones and played some music.

It was already noon, but there wasn't any trace of the DSP. It was irritating to wait outside the police station even after the *hajira* was over. Suddenly a thought struck Sushil's mind, he walked up to Chaurasia and informed him about their train which was scheduled to depart from Rourkela station in next one hour and they had no options left but to leave immediately. The trick worked – the ASI dialled his super-Boss to seek permission. DSP Dash granted permission, but asked Sumit to call him on his mobile in next ten minutes.

Without any further delay, their Indica left Birmirpur behind and sped away. At a Dhaba near Kuanrmunda, they halted for lunch and that was when Sumit decided to call up DSP Dash.

"Sumit *Babu...aap miltey nehi ho humse?* And today you left even before I could reach. *Aise kaise chalega bhaiya?"* Dash mocked.

"Sir, we waited for you. But then we also had to catch the train and hence had to leave. *Next time mil lenge.*"

"Hmmm…how long will you continue to visit Birmirpur?? *Arey Bhaiya – aap Chell Babu ka saarey saamaan wapis kyun nehi kar detey ho!* I too don't intend to harass you, just co-operate with us and I promise to waive off your condition of fortnightly appearance."

"But Sir…I've already handed over his daughter's trolley bag to him." Sumit updated the cocky official with the day's events.

"*Achha suno…*for your next *hajira*, bring along the bag that Chell *Babu* had gifted to your sister."

Sumit slapped the dining table in disgust. "Sir, this was never communicated to me earlier. Every time I visit the police station, the opposition comes up with their demand for new things." He could hear somebody prompting the DSP with a list of items, Chell must have gone to meet Dash after leaving the PS.

"*Arey Bhaiya*…that's why you should've met me at the police station. Once and for all, I could have handed over the list of their demands to you. Anyway, next time you're here, carry the bag gifted to your sister Sunita along with other stuffs like makeup-kit, photo-frame, wrist watch a..and…the pen-stand. I believe these were all gifted to your sister."

"Okay Sir. I'll try and get it next time." Sumit gulped some water to control his anger.

"Don't *try*, you have to handover these items on your next visit. Else I'll make sure that your fortnightly *hajira* continues till the chargesheet is filed," threatened the police supremo before ending the call.

It was quite clear and evident that Birmirpur police was on a mission to harass Sumit. The thought of approaching Dash for mediating did cross his mind, but then it could be a well-planned trap. Mediation would anyway involve money, and the moment Ghoshs agreed to deliver on money, they could be booked with charges for bribing the chief-of-police, which might further complicate their case by several degrees. On the other hand, Advocate Panda's snail paced approach was even more frustrating. Every visit to Birmirpur ended in tremendous embarrassment.

The other day, an SMS from Panda at around 3 pm created a furore in Ghosh family. Sumit, who was still in Haldia, tried reaching the HC lawyer immediately, but his mobile remained switched off. The SMS read '*One Mr Basak frm Rkl was at OHC with bail cancel petition.*'

Failing to connect with Panda, Sumit dialled his junior and got to know that he had two back-to-back cases at the HC. The junior assured Sumit that he would ask Panda to call him soon after his return from Cuttack.

Shrikant Mishra sensed something wrong but didn't probe much, as he wasn't involved by his senior for Sumit's last petition on bail condition removal. Late in the evening when Panda was in his chamber, Shrikant informed him about Sumit's call – the nefarious counsel had some atrocious game planned in his mind. Purposely he gave two missed calls to Sumit at around 11 that night. He wanted the Ghosh family members to slowly bake in the oven of tension and habdabs.

"Panda Sir, what's happening? *Kya matlab tha us SMS ka?*" Sumit asked his lawyer while his heart pounded violently within his chest.

"Well…even I was dazed by this incident."

"But how did you come to know, Sir?" Sumit wanted to have a thorough understanding. He also turned on the phone speakers for his parents to hear the conversation.

"Remember I once told you that the bench clerks are my allies? So today afternoon between my case hearings, one of them informed me that somebody from Rourkela was there to file a bail cancel application. I didn't have much time to hear all the details then, so I just told them to manage it in whatever way possible." The advocate paused before continuing with the incident. "Later in the evening my men gave me all the details – Mr Basak, a criminal lawyer from Rourkela representing your in-laws, wanted to have a look at our bail application and started asking tough questions to the public prosecutor. He almost created a ruckus at the premise and then went ahead and filed a bail cancelation petition at Orissa HC."

"Now what do we do? Will the HC rule in their favour and cancel our bail?"

"What did I tell you just now?" an irritated Panda asked Sumit.

"Sir I'm unable to think straight right now, please pardon me in case I've missed out anything. Please just tell me…what are we going to do next?" Sumit asked impatiently.

"My men have managed the situation. The petition is now with them and has not yet been filed, *hum us petition ko daba denge humesha ke liye*…it'll be suppressed forever." The lawyer spoke confidently.

"What does it mean to us?"

"Nothing…just pay the price for this effort; then get into *forget and relax* mode."

"And how much would that cost?" Sumit looked at his father, who sat across him at the table, covering his eyes with his hands.

"They would've demanded more, but since they know me; it'll cost you just 1.5 lakhs."

"Sir…! We've just shelled out an equivalent amount to secure bail for us. And going ahead, the legal expenses will cumulatively soar high. Isn't there any other alternatives?"

"Don't you believe what I say? Next time when you're here, I'll take you to the bench clerks and then you can see those papers all for yourself." Panda raised his voice.

"No Sir, there's no question of disbelief. From my basic understanding of law, I know that if my opposition files anything against us, we can fight it out. Won't you be able to defend us in the court of law?"

"Yes, of course. I'm here to defend you, but then…"

"Then Sir, let it be that way. If you can defend us and if you're confident about it, then why take shortcuts that'll cost us a bomb?" Sumit took a pause and continued. "I would rather be comfortable paying your consultation fees than paying bribe to those bench clerks."

Sumit knew what Panda was doing, and he calmed down as he tried to manoeuvre the discussion in his favour.

"Okay. As you wish, then let the bench clerk go ahead with their normal way of functioning."

"Sir, what's the status of my last petition? It's been over a month now. Any further delay and the police will come up with an arrest warrant in my name."

"The try is on…will get it done soon." Panda disconnected the call in a hurry, and was upset that his trick failed. His attempt to hit the jackpot overnight fell flat on his face.

Sushil was proud of his lad. In a palm sweating moment, his son showed presence of mind and instead of giving in to the trap laid by the manipulative, unscrupulous attorney – Sumit asked some rudimentary queries, which stumbled the experienced lawyer.

Later at the dining table, Sushil and Sumit discussed about the flaws in their lawyer's narrative – last week when they visited Advocate Basak, nowhere did they notice *"Orissa High Court Lawyer"* being mentioned. A session court lawyer who practices in HC would certainly not forget to disclose it, as it's a matter of pride and prestige, and he would also get to demand a premium on his consultation fees. Even if the lawyer of the opposition party had to visit HC and file petition, why would he meet the bench clerks? He would rather submit the same at the submission counter and avail a tracking code. Panda's bluff got exposed and it was time to get rid of the demon and break free from his clamp. The Ghoshs figured that they couldn't trust their lawyer anymore. They even doubted his intention with their last petition. Sushil along with his son decided to pay a surprise visit to Panda.

TWENTY-ONE
2014

Bhubaneswar, Odisha, India

The Meteorological Department in Bhubaneswar had formally announced the exit of cyclone *Hudhud* from Odisha the previous day. But its effect was still visible – overcast weather accompanied by infrequent drizzles characterized the day. However, the atmosphere at Pradip Panda's chamber on the evening of 15th October was nothing less than a storm. The lawyer was completely taken off guard by his client's sudden visit – an awkward situation prevailed where neither could he avoid them nor he had any status to update. Sumit made it very clear that without a High Court order on his last petition, he wouldn't be leaving the city. Enough of assurances had been given in the past month, it was time for some real action. To tackle his client's rigidity, Panda asked the father and son to visit next evening.

With almost zero faith in their lawyer's assurance, Sumit looked up Google for an alternative and after scanning across half-a-dozen of lawyers from Bhubaneswar, he narrowed down on *Saxena & Associates* headed by Umesh Saxena. The law firm's website was professionally maintained and had details of the members' qualification, years of experience, area of specialization and practicing courts. Saxena was an L.L.M. with nineteen years of experience across session court, Orissa HC as well as the Supreme Court. Without wasting time, Sumit called up his office at Saheed Nagar and fixed up an appointment.

At the office of *Saxena & Associates*, a law intern took their basic details before Advocate Umesh Saxena attended to them. Sumit narrated his side of the story yet again, but this time maintained a balance – emphasised more on the current concern and gave an overview for rest of the events. The lawyer condemned the allegations levelled against the Ghosh family and agreed to help Sumit in waiving off the bail condition, provided Panda gave an NOC, without which it would be difficult for any lawyer to take up the case.

"I'll try my best, but I can't guarantee. I'm sure Panda will object to this," was Sumit's submission to the new lawyer.

"In the meantime, why don't you give me your case number? By today evening I'll let you know the exact status of the same." Saxena suggested as the visitors rose to leave.

"CRLMA 106/2014 – that's the case ID. What happens if Panda disagrees to sign the NOC?"

"In that case, you've to appear before the judge and give a declaration about appointing me as your lawyer for this specific case. We'll be able to carry on from there." Umesh smiled at Sumit.

Satisfied with Saxena's inputs, Sumit left his office and started preparing to drop the bomb of NOC on Panda when he would visit him in the evening. Meanwhile Panda was on a back foot and grappling runny waters. He hadn't utilized the fees paid to him in advance. Instead, he filched the entire amount and assumed that the petition would get listed automatically. He cooked up stories of the bench clerk being on leave and kept buying time from Sumit. In the process, he didn't realise that a month had already passed by. Sumit, who had had enough of Birmirpur police's mistreatment, decided it was time to talk tough.

"Sir, are you finding it difficult to list the case? What exactly is the problem?" asked Sumit with a grim expression.

"No problem at all, just that it's taking some time." Panda casually replied.

"I've waited for one month, yet nothing has progressed. Let me tell you that I ignored your advice and have appeared before the IO twice in last thirty days. Instead of helping me out, you're further complicating this case. I've been a matter of joke to those police officers at Birmirpur, and it's all because of you." Sumit took control over his temper, calmed down a bit and politely continued – 'I don't want to overburden you with this case anymore. You might be having other important cases to concentrate on, so you carry on with those. My only request to you is to sign an NOC, so that I can engage another lawyer for myself."

For a moment there was pin drop silence at Panda's chamber. The senior lawyer never expected his client to take such a drastic step. He was happily milking Sumit for funds and planned to continue the same. Signing the NOC would hurt his ego, his client deserting him mid-way would rupture his reputation…a swirl of thoughts crossed his mind. Slowly he removed his specs, kept it on the table, looked straight at Sumit and uttered rudely "I am not giving you any NOC, do whatever you can."

"Fair enough. If that's the stand you want to take, then tomorrow I'll plead before the honourable judge and seek a replacement." Sumit responded gently.

That drove the lawyer furious. Panda pushed his chair back, stood up and threatened Sumit "Do you know, whom you're dealing with? I can finish you. You won't be able to win this case ever. How dare you come to my place and ask for a NOC signature?"

"Don't raise your voice Mr Panda. You've been exploiting us since day one. Inspite of knowing this we kept mum. We weren't in a favourable condition to fight all these anomalies. We were completely distressed; we've never faced such crisis in our life. We came to you for legal aid and you kept squeezing us for money. Please have some professional ethics, you're a family man and have your children – God forbid, if you ever face such crisis, would you be appreciating somebody taking full advantage of the situation? And when your greed overtook your morality, you scripted a fiction in the name of Mr Basak. For your kind information, here's our call recording. Well, if I use these evidences and complain at the Bar Council, I'm sure your license will be seized. Even if that doesn't help, media houses are always news hungry and I am sure this piece is quite meaty for a primetime slot. Now let me ask your question to you – *do you know, whom you're dealing with?*"

The red-faced lawyer stormed out of the room leaving Sumit and Sushil waiting on the sofa below a revolving ceiling fan that witnessed the evening's dramatic turn of events. Quite expectedly Panda's junior walked into the room and pretended as if he knew nothing. Shrikant tried to understand the reason behind the fallout. Sumit was in no mood to repeat it all, so asked him to get a download from Panda himself. Soft spoken Shrikant tried to mend the differences and find a way out.

"I learned that you're unhappy with Panda Sir. But you should also understand the fact that in legal matters there are a few interdependencies…"

"Come on Shrikant *ji*, I see it as an incompetency for being unable to list a case in past thirty days! And that too after paying the entire amount in advance." Sumit interrupted even before Shrikant could complete. He then continued to corner Panda with information fed by Umesh Saxena. "Why didn't Panda Sir appear before the judge, when my petition was listed for hearing on the last week of September? And thereafter why didn't he push the bench clerk for listing it? What was he waiting for?"

"Where did you get this information from?" Shrikant asked in dismay.

"That's none of your headache. But we sensed something fishy going on here, and had to finally put my foot down. We just want Panda Sir to give us a NOC, that's it. And see how he started threatening us. Shrikant *ji*, remember one thing – never push an innocent person to the point where he no longer gives a damn." Sumit said with a flourish of finality.

"Look, I understand all that. But you people need to calm down. Here, check these news reports. There are so many cases where Panda Sir totally slayed the opposition. He is sincere, proficient and fights for his client's cause." Shrikant handed over a few paper cut-outs for the visitors to view. He was clearly on a damage-control mode.

"Shrikant *Ji*, this doesn't change my stand. Please convince your senior to give me an NOC, else tomorrow I'll head to HC with my new lawyer."

"Okay…so you've already appointed a new one?"

"Yes. I don't want to get exploited anymore." Sumit handed the cut-outs back to Shrikant without even glancing at them.

"May I request you to give me atleast a day's time? Let me have a word with Panda Sir."

It wasn't the first time Panda had rubbed his clients the wrong way, and Shrikant always came to his rescue. The junior practicing lawyer was a perfect firefighter. But this was challenging, with an obdurate Sumit deciding to move out, it would take some real mental jigsaw to derive an attractive scheme and retain him back.

Exactly after twenty-four hours, Shrikant called up Sumit and offered unconditional apology and requested his client to give them one last chance to defend the case. He went on to describe all the hard work that had gone in preparing the petition and lining up their contacts in the HC. It was also a matter of prestige for the senior lawyer. And it would be disheartening if credit goes to somebody else while the ground work was all done by Shrikant and Panda. And as an act of reparation – Shrikant offered that Panda won't charge a single penny for the next three court hearings. However, to line up the hearing in a day, he suggested Sumit to pay up another twenty-five thousand rupees.

Later that day, Panda called up Sumit for the first time, instead of giving a missed call and regretted on his unprofessional act towards them. He vowed to fight tooth-and-nail for a favourable order and stated that he would plead to initiate a disciplinary action against the lady officer for superseding HC's bail order.

After hours of discussion, the father and son finally decided to give Panda a last chance. However, Saxena was asked to shadow every activity of Panda related to Sumit's case. The case was subsequently listed for hearing and Panda kept his words – not only did he get a stay on Sumit's next visit to the PS but was also successful in issuing a HC summon to the IO.

The HC order meted a huge sigh of relief to the Ghosh family, their belief and confidence in justice grew in leaps and bounds. It also meant a huge setback to the Chell coterie. An HC summon would directly impact Sub-Inspector Shamita's next promotion. Slowly she started disassociating herself from the Chells and was eager to file the chargesheet within the stipulated timeline of ninty days.

Infused with enthusiasm, the Ghosh family's hunt for a competent, strong lawyer continued. A week later, Sumit visited Rourkela and met his Professor, who in turn took him to Advocate Mihir Ganguly. They met him at the court premise – Sumit's first visit to the Rourkela session court. Who knew how many more such visits would be needed to hit the final nail in the coffin of the fake case instituted against them.

TWENTY-TWO
2012

Mumbai, Maharashtra, India

Moulina's marital bliss began with lovely, cute, romantic moments – gossiping all night about almost everything on earth, cuddling and kissing each other, sweet love making, falling asleep on her hubby's chest and then finally waking up in his arms. She always woke up early and as a loving wife would prepare breakfast for her husband and sister-in-law. Though she insisted on cooking lunch for Sumit, which he could carry to his office – the caring husband never wanted to burden his wife and preferred ordering from the office pantry.

Alone in the flat, Moulina would often hum some of her favourite *Lata Mangeshkar* numbers and keep herself busy in the kitchen, and later in the bathroom doing laundry…these household errands were completely new to her and she wanted to have a hands-on experience before appointing a maid. Her husband wanted to keep a house-help, which she instantly rejected, citing the reason that the household chores would keep her occupied and would also give her an opportunity to perfect them. Above all, that would add on to their savings as well. In the absence of Sumit or Sunita, she had been strictly instructed not to open the door to any strangers – be it hawkers or newspaper-boy or watchman or cable-guy. Mumbai had just witnessed a gruesome crime in form of *Pallavi Purkayastha murder* and it was better to be safe than sorry. Moulina too ingrained the safety features and was in full liberty within the four walls of her 1BHK. Her husband would call her atleast thrice to chitchat over the phone in the middle of his working hours.

Sunita always left early and returned late as compared to her brother. But while returning from office, she would often carry something to munch at home. She knew Moulina's weakness for *kanda-bhaji* and her brother's love for *samosas* – together they would go on to have a great evening tea time at home. It was a sweet, happy home.

Moulina would spend the entire evening jabbering with her husband. She would either request him to play some of her favourite retro numbers from Youtube, or ask him to download a recipe. She would then prepare dinner and later go out on evening walks with her hubby. The young couple would walk several rounds along the periphery of the *Sahyadri Ground* before settling for a scoop of ice-cream or a *kulfi* stick, Moulina's favorite. It was during these evening walks that they would discuss about their future plans, dreams and aspirations. And often their past would also peep into their present and future.

"Do you know, never in my life I've spent a day all alone in a room? There was always Lina for company. But then I guess stages of life have variety to offer, soon I'll get used to this." Moulina candidly confessed.

"And do you know, there's a peculiar romanticism in being all alone?" joked Sumit.

"But not after you get married." Moulina pinched her husband and giggled.

"Okay, then let's gift you a junior. So that you can spend the entire day running after him or her." Sumit replied with a loud and hearty laugh, and continued, "Jokes apart, it's just been a month. Spend some time, get acquainted with Mumbai, keep scanning the newspaper classifieds for those teacher positions and then let's give it a try." Like an obedient kid, Moulina nodded her head in affirmation and grabbed Sumit's arm.

"In the meantime, I'll make a professional CV for you," assured Sumit.

"It is fine as of now because I remain engaged with household activities. But going forward, I think I'll get super bored."

"I understand Mouli, just don't let boredom overrule your inner self. I'm also at a vital juncture of my career. I plan to continue with this organisation for another year, and then might lookout for a massive jump. We've to buy our own house, our family will grow and then it would be difficult to toggle between rented accommodations every year."

"You're the captain of the ship, plan accordingly for a smooth sail. Now let's have some *kulfi*." Moulina dragged Sumit towards the *kulfi*-van stationed at one corner of the ground.

Slowly and steadily the Ghosh family's daughter-in-law was getting acclimatized to the new environment. She used to eagerly wait for the weekends, the only time when her hubby would assist her in the kitchen. She often accompanied him for grocery shopping. Some weekends were even more exciting as it was characterized with mall hopping and shopping followed by dinner or even a late-night show at the nearest multiplex. All of it was a first time for her. She would gaze in amazement, and get enthralled in excitement. Her staring at the window displays of large stores, hesitation to take the mall's escalator, awkwardness at the table of a restaurant, and her reactions to the theatre's dolby-digital surround sound didn't go unnoticed by Sumit.

He extended all support to make her comfortable in the new city life. Moulina too braved it all to make a transitional shift from the dull Birmirpur life to a vivid Mumbai life. Music was in her pulse and to keep it pulsating, Sumit often booked a Hindustani classical music show at NCPA or a Carnatic instrumental performance at Chembur's Fine Arts Society. To further encourage the same, he even asked her to enrol for a singing competition at Vashi's *Bengali Association*. Sumit was simultaneously channelizing his corporate contacts, so that Moulina could use her singing skills for advertising jingles. The small-town girl in Moulina was rather excited with the scope that the metro city had in store.

Everything was on track and moved in the right direction, except for Sanat, who wasn't a happy man. His grip over his daughter gradually loosened; she slowly got attuned to her in-laws and was focussing on her new role of building a happy family. Moulina's call frequencies to her parents dropped drastically. And all these were a matter of concern to her emulous, vitriolic father.

"*Ki re, kemon achis?* Have you forgotten us all here at Birmirpur? Seems like Mumbai has sprinkled some magic in your life...huh!" Sanat poked fun at his daughter over a phone call.

"Nothing like that *Baba*. I'm just trying to cope up with this new life here."

"And what about your responsibilities towards your parents and siblings? Your sister's admission to postgraduate course has to happen in next couple of months, followed by your brother's eye operation. And you know that I'm financially incapable of handling all these after your lavish wedding."

"What do you want me to do about that, *Baba*?" Moulina could very well gauge her father's intention.

"Nothing, you can shamelessly continue to lead a happy married life now while we struggle to make ends meet here," taunted Sanat.

"*Baba,* don't beat round the bush! Don't expect me to ask for financial help from my in-laws. It's just been two months that I've become a part of this family, and even if it was twelve months I couldn't have asked for the same. You can't always depend on others and cry for help. In the last few years, if you had tried to initiate some business, then probably things would've improved. But you chose otherwise." The irritated daughter responded sternly.

"I never asked for any monetary aid. But if Lina could have shifted to Mumbai along with you and pursued her post-graduation, then atleast some expenses could have been avoided. Or even if you had started working, then I could have asked for some financial support. I cannot ask for it from my son-in-law, but you're my own blood and I can rightfully claim it from you."

"We stay in a small 1BHK apartment here. How will Lina stay with us? As far as my joining work is concerned, I don't know when it'll happen. I suggest you stop expecting it from me and my family."

Sanat's calls would jumble up Moulina's thought process each time. He emotionally blackmailed her and made her feel guilty, completely forgetting that she had been supporting the Chell family all the while till she got married. Strangely, her father never asked for any financial help from Lokesh. Only when he visited Birmirpur once in twelve months, he would handover some cash in tune to twenty or thirty thousand to his mother. Arguing with her father didn't help either; it just would make her peevish for the rest of the day – something that clearly reflected in her body language and facial expressions.

Sumit would notice the uneasiness and hesitance in his wife's behaviour, but wouldn't prompt anything unless Moulina opened up while they were out on evening walks. And like a true partner she would belch out her frustration to her husband and relieve herself. However, she maintained a balance on what she spoke and always avoided loose talks that might invite trouble and rift in the family.

"I know that you must have felt odd when you learnt that my father was incapable of providing any sort of gifts to you or your family as a wedding custom." Moulina hesitantly said to Sumit one evening.

"Hmmm...so after spending these many days with me and my family, what made you feel that we would need gifts to run our family?" mocked Sumit.

"I meant, basic gifts given to the newlywed couple to start a new beginning."

"Look Mouli, I don't think we lack any such items that would hinder our journey. Just that I don't have a proper divan-bed here and that's not because I cannot afford it. It's purely because of the logistic issues I face while transferring. Don't worry, give me a few months – I'm planning to buy a 2BHK with financial help from Dad," assured Sumit.

"Wow, that's lovely!" Moulina's face lit up with a bright smile.

"Yes, I've already asked a few brokers to look out for places."

The other evening, Moulina revealed how it had seemed impossible for her father to pull out the marriage ceremony all those months ago, solely because of financial drawbacks; and how she had been supporting her father financially from her scanty monthly pay cheque all these years. Every time she wanted to open up and portray her father's failure in business and inability to support his family monetarily, the topic got lost in some other discussions between the couple.

In November 2012, Sushil and Chitra visited Mumbai, solely for the purpose of purchasing a new flat for their son and daughter-in-law. Mr and Mrs Ghosh were ecstatic to be with their children together under the same roof after a long time. Sushil's morning walks and Chitra's evening teas were incomplete without their daughter-in-law. Moulina too enjoyed the company of her *Papa* and *Mummy*, without whom weekdays were all dull and uneventful after Sumit left for office. Daily after lunch, when Chitra sat down to solve the newspaper crossword, a complaisant Moulina would sit next to her and help in solving the puzzle – life was awesome.

After a week long search, a magnificent, east facing 2BHK flat on the ninth floor of a two year old building got shortlisted with a consensus from all the Ghosh family members. Sushil prematurely broke some of his FDs and withdrew his Provident Fund in order to accumulate cash for the advance booking amount. Since it was a high value property, the senior Ghosh could convince the flat seller for a relaxed payment window. The financial part was never openly discussed in the Ghosh household, it was solely being managed by Sushil. But in one of those evening walks, Sumit told Moulina how expensive it is to acquire a house in Mumbai. He also gave her a rough estimate of the ongoing prices and various modes of payment prevalent in Mumbai real estate market…advance-payment, black-component, EMIs, loans and all. As a new member she never bothered much about it, but was aware of her *Papa's* several trips to the bank branches and a cash accumulation made in tune of three lakhs.

The year of 2012 was left with just one more week before it slipped the baton to 2013. It was a restless day for Moulina. She was ambivalent about her roles and responsibilities in life. Her insoluble dilemma of relationship liabilities between a wife and a daughter kept her on tenterhooks. Earlier that day, on a quiet Wednesday afternoon when Moulina stayed back home and didn't accompany her in-laws for a shopping trip to Phoenix Market City at Kurla; she discovered a grey duffle-bag tucked in between *Mummy* and *Papa's* luggage. Out of curiosity, she unzipped the bag and was gobsmacked to see numerous stacked currency notes of 500 and 1000. She picked up a couple of bundles and inhaled the sweet smell of neat, crispy notes. The unusual glimpse of hard cash stunned her. Mixed feelings of joy and inability raided her mind. She was proud to have her in-laws helping her husband to finance a flat and felt equally grim to imagine how a portion of the same could have ended the struggling life of her parents back in Birmirpur. She felt a void of helplessness and was suddenly desperate to speak to her parents.

Sanat was waiting to grab an opportunity to manipulate his daughter against her in-laws so that he could take control over his son-in-law. Once Sumit was beguiled by his daughter, then it would be a cake walk – he would shift his base to Mumbai. The very first step of his plan was to create friction within the Ghosh family members and gradualy side-track Sumit and take him into confidence. The task was tricky but wasn't impossible with his daughter's enticing beauty and impeccable innocence.

The father-daughter connected over an hour long telephonic conversation. Sanat's eyes brightened up with greed as he learned about the bag full of cash. He tried to provoke anger and sow seeds of hatred in his daughter's mind. He tried instigating her in every possible way through vocal tonics and waited for the day when there would be a fall-out with her in-laws.

TWENTY-THREE
2013

Mumbai, Maharashtra, India

The New Year didn't quite take off as was expected for Sumit. Frequent cannonading of unfortunate incidents made life hell. The most disheartening was the deal cancellation of their shortlisted flat. Brokers involved in between betrayed them and dumped the Bengali family even after being paid a token amount. The senior Ghosh couple lost all hopes and with a heavy heart, went back to Haldia.

Meanwhile, office was getting tough for Sumit – a change in company strategy, brought in alteration to his reporting structure. Earlier life was easy when he reported directly to the Marketing VP of the company, who had clear objectives and spelt out tasks explicitly without any ambiguity. With introduction of a GM as his Boss, life changed for the worst. The new superior was clueless about many things and as a result often got bashed up by the MD at several meetings and forums; the repercussion of which mostly trickled down to the team members. Moreover, the new guy was insecure and resorted to filthy office politics. Sumit started suffocating and as an alternative measure initiated a job hunt through his network of friends and ex-colleagues.

Back home things slowly turned sour – Sumit's disturbed office life cast negativity in his family life. Though he tried his best to keep his personal life away from his professional life, somehow irritation and impatience crept into his natural behaviour. Moulina on the other hand got piqued by the mundane life; and boredom started grasping her steadily. This resulted in frequent conversation with her father every week. Thus, Sanat got ample opportunities to manipulate his daughter. Her fragile emotions gave in to her father's wicked ideas – all of a sudden Moulina felt like she was being treated unfairly at her in-laws'.

"Hey Mouli, I plan to invite some of my Bengali colleagues for dinner. They've been pestering me for a while now. My last promotion as well as my wedding treat is due. I could have taken them out, but then by inviting them our social circle will unfurl. You'll get to know some new people too. What do you say?"

"Sounds great. But what about Sunita?"

Sumit wasn't expecting such a reaction from his wife. "What kind of question was that? Isn't Sunita a part of this house? Everybody knows that my sister stays with me. So her presence in the get-together, is quite obvious. Now tell me, will you be able to manage the kitchen or do we order from outside and cook some basic stuff at home?"

"If you don't have any confidence in your wife, then get it from outside." Moulina snapped and raised the TV volume, as if to end the conversation.

"Well, I didn't mean that. But the fact that you're not an expert cook is known universally."

Moulina preferred not to respond to her husband's mockery on her cooking skills. She was thoroughly pissed off since afternoon after having a prolonged conversation with her *Baba*. Sanat had compared Moulina with Sunita and pointed out how she was being underplayed in the family. And that was the reason why she had made such a loose comment against Sunita. She also knew that Sumit won't tolerate any rubbish against his sister and hence pretended to remain busy surfing TV channels for the next couple of hours.

The evening of 10th February could be termed as the beginning of an end in Sumit-Moulina relationship. Though Sumit tried his level best to pacify the situation, somehow things went out of control and the friction surfaced. It was a completely changed Moulina – atleast not the simple, submissive, naïve, innocent one whom Sumit had known when he married her.

On Moulina's insistence, the dinner items were all home-cooked. Sunita and Sumit also helped her in the kitchen. Sunita cooked couple of dishes and helped her sister-in-law with a few.

The dinner, all in all, was not much of a success. The *Doi-Rui* went completely abysmal with disproportionate *masalas* along with salt deficiency; the *Rotis* turned out to be like pieces of leather. The guests were modest enough to continue eating what was being served without any complaints – they laughed, giggled, joked and bitched about their Bosses. Sumit however was embarrassed with the situation, and preferred to remain silent. He knew that in office, this dinner episode would be discussed in high decibel and would be the focal point of all gossips for the next few days. At a critical juncture when office life was anyway becoming miserable and unbearable, these gossips would further fuel things up. It was Sunita who could analyse the situation and felt really bad for her brother. Moulina however, was clueless about the inefficacies.

"*Dada*, we could have simply ordered food. It would've been less of a hassle and this awkward situation could have been avoided," suggested Sunita in a hushed-up tone, feeling bad for her brother.

"*Jaane de na...jo ho gaya, so ho gaya* – anyway my days in this organisation have come to an end. Just waiting for an opportunity to make my move," a dejected Sumit replied.

Moulina overheard the brother-sister conversation and taking a tangential meaning out of it, almost burst out in frustration. At the top of her voice she yelled...

"I know what you guys are up to. Now I'll become the main culprit of the evening. Because it was my suggestion to prepare it all at home and I'm the one who screwed it up. Okay, I admit that I'm not good at cooking. Then is that my fault? Mr Sumit, why did you marry me, if you wanted to have a cook to manage your kitchen? You send your sister out for a job and ask me to remain indoors and manage your kitchen, what kind of justice is this? And now you shamelessly blame me for all this mess. This is unendurable, unjust and unexpected from you all." She sobbed out her exasperations to her husband.

Pin drop silence prevailed...the Ghosh siblings were taken completely by surprise with Moulina's bizarre behaviour. While Sumit kept pondering as to what might have led to the outburst, Sunita was clueless why she was being dragged into it and being subjected to comparison? For the first time they witnessed a different Moulina – her aggression, stubbornness, retaliation and vexation, reflected clearly in those fiery eyes. But why did she overreact? Or was it a manifestation of a deep-rooted conspiracy that was being hatched but couldn't be achieved. Sunita was about to respond, but Sumit signalled her to remain quiet.

After a day's monosyllabic conversation, Sumit made the move to iron out the disputes and offered to take Moulina for an evening visit to the *Gateway of India*. And like an overjoyed kid, Moulina agreed. They strolled hand-in-hand along the promenade, clicked pictures, sat and watched the ferries navigate while Sumit narrated the infamous 26/11 terror attack at the *Taj Mahal Hotel* that has its majestic presence along the sea front. Before returning back home, they crossed lanes and walked along the alleyways of Colaba to have dinner at *Bade Miya*. It was like any other normal day for the couple – they chatted, tittered and joked. Before calling it a night, Moulina apologised for her arrogance, smooched and cuddled up to her husband.

An idle mind is devil's workshop – Sumit pretty much realised it after Moulina's sudden paroxysm the previous week. He tried his best to find something that would keep her engaged throughout the day and generate some additional income too. Meanwhile, the school teacher vacancies which Moulina circled in the newspaper classifieds were all located at far off places like Vasai, Kalyan, Panvel – which could only be accessed through local trains. And that was precisely what Sumit didn't want his wife to do – board an overcrowded train, travel for hours and return home completely drained.

Instead, he tried other alternatives. Handbills and newspaper inserts for home tuitions were sent out, and a few online transcription jobs were applied for.

It had been a few weeks after that queer behaviour of Moulina. While Sumit was assured that it was just a one-off case and things had normalised thereafter, Sunita was suspicious and vigilant. She was of the view that someone might have been instigating her sister-in-law to create a nuisance in their family.

Mid-March of 2013, just when Mumbai started getting hotter, situation at Sumit's Tilaknagar flat worsened. The digital marketer had to visit Ahmedabad for a project launch on a long weekend, leaving the two ladies in each other's company. Sumit was glad that his sister's bank also observed Friday-Saturday-Sunday as off and that wouldn't give his wife a chance to complain of being lonely at home. Little did he know that his prolonged absence from home would not be all that merry.

In those three days, Sunita witnessed the other side of her *bhabi*, which was beyond her imagination. Moulina's insolent and rude behaviour made Sunita feel guilty and unwanted in her own brother's home. In a family where Sunita had been pampered all throughout for being the youngest member, Moulina made her feel like a liability who had been burdening her brother. Initially, Sunita was a little broken and dejected by her sister-in-law's comments, but later gained some strength and didn't pay any heed to it at all. Instead, she reported those conversations to her mother, just to divulge the real face of Chell's daughter.

Moulina constantly probed Sunita to find out if she had any boyfriend or not. She even advised to find someone in her office and get hooked up. Sunita was also suggested to find a soul mate online and get married as soon as possible to lessen the burden on her aged parents. Further, she was body shamed and given beauty tips to look attractive. Sunita was stunned and at the same time hurt. She couldn't even imagine that her own sister-in-law would stoop so low. *But what was she trying to prove?*

Earlier on Saturday morning, Sunita woke up to a high volume from a TV channel operated by Moulina. She was further puzzled to find an insufficient number of *Chapatis* for lunch along with an oversalted curry. Sunita preferred not to complain and later made herself a bowl of Maggi as her lunch. Moulina often remained busy conversing over the phone and Sunita was damn sure it wasn't Sumit she was talking to, as he would hardly talk to anybody in the family while touring for work. In the evening, when both the ladies sat together for the TV serials, Moulina took control over the remote and kept changing the channels frequently and unnecessarily tried testing Sunita's patience.

Sunita's revelations made Chitra look wishy-washy; a daughter-in-law who was supposed to bind the family together was instead using cheap, dirty tricks to divide it!! It was on her insistence that the alliance had materialised and just nine months after her son's wedding, things were on shaky ground. *How could I have misjudged Moulina?* She kept asking herself. Sushil however had a different take – he felt that probably their daughter-in-law wanted some personal space to enhance the bonding with her husband and lead a happy, conjugal life; which might be getting occluded by Sunita's presence. The father-mother-daughter discussed various possibilities and finally decided to separate out Sunita from the couple and let them lead a harmonious life. Meanwhile Sunita kept enquiring at several Working Women's Hostels in and around Chembur and Ghatkopar area.

Just before signing on the dotted lines and depositing a security amount at Chembur's Working Women's Hostel, when Sumit was informed about his sister's decision to shift, he just couldn't control his annoyance…"You all have taken such a drastic decision and never bothered to consult me for the same? First of all, you tell me what pushed you to make such a choice?" a furious Sumit questioned his sister.

"*Tera bhai mar gaya hai kya?* that you've to leave this house and stay separately in the same city? Let me be very clear, as long as I'm here, such nonsense won't be tolerated." Sumit whisked out of the room after tearing the application form into innumerable pieces.

He was terribly upset with the incident and could gauge what might have happened in the background before his parents and sister were compelled to take such a step. Moulina, on the other hand, was disheartened to find her husband playing the spoilsport in Sunita's exit from the house. However, she maintained her innocence and ignorance towards the whole episode. Back in Birmirpur, Sanat was somehow happy to hear about the incident – at least some rift had been initiated in the family.

Though Sunita stayed back, she maintained safe distance from her *bhabi*. The cordial relationship between the two females turned hostile within a span of few weeks and Sumit could feel the friction and mutiny in the air. Yet he believed that with passing time things would automatically smoothen up.

One Friday, just when Sumit was leaving for office, Moulina pulled him into a quick hug. Her hands around his neck, she smiled up at him and asked him to come back home soon. Sumit removed his bag off his shoulder and held her waist, "May be, I should take a leave today." He giggled and took the day off to spend time with his wife. The couple spent the entire day at home lazing around in each other's company. Moulina gave a nice, relaxing, warm oil body massage to her husband before they made intense love under the cold shower. Udupi lunch was called in from *Hotel Krishna,* after which they sat on the sofa canoodling each other and watched a Spanish romantic movie on the laptop. Tired of reading the English sub-titles, Moulina quietly slipped into a nap while Sumit passionately watched her and pecked her cheeks. In bewilderment, he kept wondering how could his lovely innocent wife turn bitchy unless being whipped up by someone!! And who could that *someone* be?

Later that evening, Sumit received an unexpected call from his brother-in-law from Faridabad, probably for the first time since his marriage, to seek some guidance.

"*Jiju* – How are you doing? How is *Didi*?" Lokesh sounded all excited.

"Hey Lokesh, we are doing great. I thought you've forgotten us completely. Your new job must be keeping you all occupied, huh?"

"That's correct, *Jiju*. The management keeps us on our toes. I returned from Hyderabad just last week. My office had sent us for a month-long training there and prior to that I got my eye operated at AIIMS. So, all this really kept me busy," explained Lokesh.

"Oh, I see; how did the operation go? Did anybody from Birmirpur visit you? Eye operations are quite delicate," Sumit showed his concern.

"Doctors have intimated that it'll take time for the eyelid to open fully. As of now it is better than what you had seen earlier. I might have to undergo another operation next year." Lokesh sounded a bit sad and added "*Baba* and *Ma* were supposed to be here, but their train tickets didn't get confirmed. An office friend accompanied me to the hospital.

"Now *Jiju*, I want some inputs from you and that's precisely why I called you." Without wasting much of time, Lokesh wanted to clarify his concern.

"Okay, go ahead…" Sumit set his tea aside.

"At our Hyderabad training centre, they've given me an option of relocating to Mumbai. I've heard that Mumbai has better opportunities. So, if I shift now, then my next jump will be easier. *Aap kya boltey ho?*"

"Where is your office in Mumbai?" asked Sumit after a brief pause.

"Goregaon East."

"Well…Mumbai's only issue is its high rental accomodation. A major chunk of your salary will go out in paying rent, unless one decides to stay a little on the outskirt and take the pains of daily local train travel. For you, places like Mira Road, Bhayandar, etc. will be ideal. Or else share a flat with a couple of friends and stay closer to office. PG accommodations can also be explored." Sumit indirectly made it clear that his rented flat wasn't open for his brother-in-law to stay in.

"Thanks *Jiju*, for your inputs, never thought in that direction. Where's *Didi*? Please pass on the phone to her."

"*Eii Mouli phone ta niye jao,* your brother wants to speak to you…"

TWENTY-FOUR
2014

Rourkela, Odisha, India

Advocate Mihir Ganguly came across as a strange character. He had some peculiar professional practices – he never attended any anonymous calls nor undertook any case that had been previously handled by other lawyers. He wouldn't hesitate to quit a case midway, if his client supressed a fact here or there. Yet he offered free legal services to the backward tribal classes of Rourkela.

Sumit and his father were asked to wait at the drawing room of Ganguly's residence. The two storeyed beige coloured building at Koel Nagar wasn't difficult to spot as it was well known among the locals. Ganguly's wife operated a vocational training institute for housewives on the building's ground floor, which served as a prominent landmark to that area. Earlier that day, Sumit met the criminal lawyer at Rourkela court premises along with his Professor and gave him a brief overview of his case. Initially he was reluctant to represent Sumit, but on the Professor's insistence he kind of agreed.

After a ten minutes' wait, the Ghoshs were called in to the other room and asked to wait further. The room was in a complete mess – two wooden shelves stood along the wall perpendicular to each other. It had a variety of books ranging from encyclopaedias to legal journals, criminal law manual to secondary maths and geography, Bengali film magazines to family law manual – all stacked up in a haphazard manner, as if somebody was comfortable with and quite used to such kind of arrangements. A framed family photo of Ganguly with his wife and two daughters hung on the wall just above the computer table.

A guy in mid-thirties entered the room with a tray in his hand and handed over two cups of tea to the visitors and then went ahead towards the shelf, pulled out a file and started reading something. Thereafter entered Advocate Mihir Ganguly – a medium built man in early fifties. He was wearing an orange T-Shirt and sported a cotton flat cap to cover his bald head. He too was holding his cup of black tea; pulled a chair in the room and sat in front of his visitors.

"Sorry to keep you waiting. I was on a client call. And by the way, due to my high blood sugar, only black tea is served here at my house. So, while you at least have the privilege of having it with sugar, mine is just a cup of mildly flavoured hot water!" The advocate joked and smiled.

"Good evening Sir, this is my father." Sumit pointed out at Sushil, who stood up with folded hands *"Nomoshkar Sir…"* and even before he could utter anything else, the lawyer's phone rang. Visibly irritated, he picked up the call and blasted *"Joshi ji, aap bar bar kyun phone kar rahe ho?* I'm your lawyer, leave all your worries to me. I'll do the needful and will keep you posted."

After disconnecting the call, he set his mobile on silent mode and continued *"Nomoshkar Sir, apnar cheler sathey kotha hoyechey amar.* Don't worry I'll see what best can be done." And then turning towards Sumit, asked him to narrate the entire case in detail. Meanwhile the other guy sat next to Ganguly and took short notes in his diary. The criminal lawyer listened carefully, asked queries, scratched his head, closed his eyes, scribbled on the writing-pad, wore his specs and again asked some questions to clear his doubts. The entire narrative went on for almost forty minutes with Sushil plugging some facts in between and heaving a long sigh of despair to express his anguish.

Ganguly then asked for the FIR copy and went through it twice before jotting down the set of IPCs slapped. He then handed over the copy to his junior who also glanced through it once.

"The content of this FIR is very superficial without any factual information. It is more qualitative in nature," observed Ganguly.

"Sir, is it good or bad?"

"If you have the right evidences to counter their allegations, then this FIR can be crushed in no time." Ganguly smiled at Sushil.

"Yes Sir, we do have some documentary proofs to counter the FIR statements."

"That's awesome. I suggest you make a list of all the proofs that you have – either in form of documents or audio recordings or video clips. Keep them ready, we would need them later when our case starts."

"Okay Sir. But now what? I mean what would be our next steps?"

"Nothing. Simply relax and lead a normal life. We'll wait until the Chargesheet is filed. Oh, by the way – do you have any kids out of this wedlock?"

"No Sir…"

"Okay. Then we'll give them a tough fight. I'll make sure that not a single penny is paid to those fraudsters. If there was a kid, I would've suggested you to pay a lumpsum for the child's upkeep on humanitarian ground."

Sushil spoke with moist eyes and a broken voice, "Sir believe us, we are completely innocent and have been framed. The allegations of dowry and torture are absolutely false. The last few months have been utterly nightmarish. Two accomplished lawyers we hired earlier cheated on us. We've lost hope and don't know what's there in store for us next!"

"Ghosh Sir, please don't worry. This FIR says it all. But then that's how the judiciary functions. 498A which has been devised to shield women is now being grossly misused to settle scores. Moreover, by default the police takes the women's side and does a shoddy, arm-chair investigation and submits a Chargesheet which becomes a carbon-copy of the FIR. I suggest let's wait for the Chargesheet to spot further loopholes in the investigation. We'll also closely observe our opposition and devise strategies accordingly. The thumb rule of handling 498A is fairly simple – if the girl is in a hurry, we'll use delaying tactics; and if they move slow, we will speed up the proceedings. Meanwhile, if they approach us to settle the case out-of-court, we will see to it. Be assured, as your attorney I'll provide you maximum possible relief. I won't even call you here to Rourkela frequently, unless there's some urgent requirement."

"By the way, do you know who the girl's legal counsellor is?" Ganguly enquired.

"As far as I am aware, Advocate Basak is handling…"

"*Arrey wah...fir to mazaa ayega...*" the lawyer interrupted. "Basak *Da* is a shrewd professional and is senior to me." Ganguly informed his clients from Mumbai. He then asked his junior to get a *Vakalatnama* signed by Sumit, so that *Ganguly & Associates* can represent Ghosh family in the case.

"Sir, what would be our next step now. Have you thought of any strategies?" Sumit still wasn't completely sure.

"What did I tell you all this while then?" an irritated Ganguly responded. "We'll wait for the Chargesheet and meanwhile you lead a normal life, but report to me if any unusual activity related to this case occurs. And last but not the least, at any point in time, if you feel that I'm unable to handle your case, feel free to ask for an NOC." Ganguly said with finality.

By the time the Ghoshs left Ganguly's residence, it was already 10 pm. There was a slight chill in the air and the streets bore a deserted look. First week of November and the steel city was already gripped by early winter.

Ganguly appeared to be honest, outspoken and a little erratic and kooky. He was attentive and didn't recommend any clichéd solution, instead preferred to wait and watch. He didn't charge any exorbitant fees in the name of consultation, but asked for the bare minimum expenses that he would incur to apply for the true copy of the case related documents. Sumit's Professor repeatedly promulgated Mihir Ganguly as an experienced criminal lawyer best fit to fight a fake 498A case – and the Ghosh family was grateful to believe the same.

Meanwhile at Chell's residence in Birmirpur a lot of incidents happened after the case was registered. The father-daughter realised that it wasn't a cakewalk as was being potrayed by DSP Dash all this while. Slowly they were also being dragged into the quicksand of court matters. Almost every alternate day, Moulina quarrelled with her father for such a blunt decision. In pursuit of making some quick money, they now had to shell out funds to incur legal expenses. Meanwhile, Dash had got transferred to Balasore a few weeks back, and as a result, his interest in helping Chell died down naturally, leaving Sanat frustrated and restless. Sub-Inspector Shamita too started avoiding them. Whenever they met at the *Chowk-Bazaar* area, she would cite some excuse or the other and evade Chell's queries. She was keen on completing the Chargesheet and relieving herself from the case. The previous month, Sanat lost his father who couldn't survive the severity of prostate cancer. His brothers too maintained a safe distance from them. Until a few months ago, the neighbours who sympathized with Moulina's fate, kept enquiring about the progress of the case. They were eager to know when would her in-laws be jailed for their wrongdoings. That too started diminishing as people eventually began to lose interest in the matter. Somehow, Sanat's evil plan fell flat and boomeranged. He was extremely upset and disgusted with the Ghosh family, whom he had expected would approach with a lumpsum money to get the matter settled out-of-court. Sanat kept consulting his lawyer and wanted him to pressurize his daughter's in-laws until they succumbed. Over and above the regular legal fees, Chell even offered Basak a flat 15% commission on the amount that he could extort from the Ghosh family through this case.

Advocate Basak was often kept in the dark. Everytime he asked some tricky questions to Moulina, she would snivel and claim her innocence. However, the lawyer was experienced enough to understand that the Chells were lying to him, yet used all his tricks to defend them. Sanat made weekly visits to the lawyer's chamber to take stock of things and pushed him to fast pace everything. With not many options available in hand, Basak suggested Chells to file a maintenance petition at the family court, atleast that would ensure some bit of regular cash flow every month till the case got resolved.

December of 2014 had just started. Sumit was planning to leave for Mumbai, when a missile in form of a registered post struck his Haldia residence. The postman categorically wanted to handover the envelope to the person it was addressed to. Panic clasped the Ghosh family in no time. Multiple attempts to get in touch with their lawyer failed and finally ended with an SMS from Advocate Ganguly *'Will talk to u in the evening, busy at court now.'*

"Sir, this afternoon I received a family court summon. I guess my in-laws have filed a maintenance petition and I'm asked to appear before the court on 8th January 2015." A worried Sumit uttered it all in the same breath.

"Oh, I see. Can you read out the IPC section applied by them in the petition?" Ganguly calmly asked.

"Ummm…wait a minute. It says – *Petition u/s 18 of Hindu Adoption and Maintenance Act, read with section 7 of Family court act for Maintenance.*" Sumit read quickly.

"Okay. Look at the top of the petition, you'll find a case number. Give me that number, I'll pull it out from the court tomorrow."

"It mentions CP No. 244/2014."

"Okay Sumit. Don't panic, I'll take care of it. By filing this petition, they're indicating the fact that they are in a hurry. So, let's play the delaying tactics. Most probably you don't have to come to the court on the mentioned date. I'll manage it and let you know the status." The senior counsel assured his client.

"But Sir, I'm worried about the amount they've claimed as monthly maintenance…"

"How much is it?"

"She wants eighty thousand per month. In the petition, they mentioned that I'm still employed and 50% of the monthly salary is what I should shell out as a statutory obligation towards my wife. The truth is that I am unemployed and Moulina knows this full well. In fact, she knew that I had resigned. But still…"

"Relax…*thik hai na*…let them claim whatever they want. Didn't I tell you that we won't give a single penny to those assholes? For them the institute of marriage is a matter of joke."

"Sir, how would you manage those dates?" Ganguly's mere assurances weren't enough to pacify Sumit. After all he had believed in the words of his earlier lawyers and suffered.

"*Ufff*…leave that to me. Every trade has its own secrets and tricks. Why do you have to bother with all these when you entrusted me with the task of defending you? Let me pull out those papers and go through it all. I'll call you back next week, to discuss the matter. Also, I might need some money to manage those dates. Not much, but will inform you about that too. Let me repeat – don't get tensed up. It'll have an adverse effect on your aged parents too. Truth will always prevail. Good night!"

Sumit held the phone tight for a few minutes even after he heard Ganguly disconnect the line. The helplessness and lack of options stifled him, but Ganguly's confidence in his ability to tackle the case comforted him.

TWENTY-FIVE
2015

Mumbai, Maharashtra, India

It was a quiet New Year celebration for the Ghosh siblings, with just a dinner on the 1st of January at *Singh Saab* near Chembur's Basant Park. Sumit was a bit relaxed as his first ever court appearance had been efficiently managed and postponed by his lawyer. The next appearance would happen only after ninty days, as Ganguly made all arrangements of placing long dates before the family court.

Finance was crucial and this kept bothering Sumit. Since he didn't want to get into any fulltime employment at this juncture, he started looking out for freelance opportunities. That would give him flexibility, and on any urgent court summon, his mobility wouldn't get affected. Mumbai, being the archetypal *City of Opportunities*, it was a testing time to explore some of them. Everyday, after Sunita left for office, Sumit would thoroughly search the internet for a suitable opportunity and then end up watching Youtube videos of upcoming movie trailers or short-films. He also enjoyed videos from food vloggers *Mark Wiens* and *Trevor James* – not only did it showcase varieties of food across the globe, but also had glimpses of the destinations they visited. It was from these videos Sumit drew inspiration and launched his own educational channel on Youtube. He taught subjects like Operation Research, Digital Marketing, and Statistics through Powerpoint presentations with his own voice narrative in the background. However, he operated the channel under a pseudonym, so that Google couldn't identify him when searched for. He was very particular about not leaving any cyber trails behind for his opponents to pick it up and use against him in family court matters. Within a few weeks of its launch, his channel flourished with good number of likes and shares. He was posting atleast two videos weekly, and with good traffic, Google Adsense generated a decent revenue for him. One of his channel subscribers even approached him with a proposal to teach at his private coaching class in Ghatkopar, to which he agreed. On weekends, he took classroom sessions and on weekdays he edited and posted videos online.

The summer of 2015 not only carried excessive heat wave to the commercial capital but also brought in some hardships to the Ghosh siblings. By mid-March, they were asked to vacate their rented flat immediately, which otherwise had a contract signed for three years. Some anonymous caller informed the owner about the ongoing court cases, which was spiced up with stories of Moulina being subjected to physical torture and confinement at the flat when she was living there. Moving into a new house at this juncture was quite expensive – with all those brokerage charges, along with increased rental value and shifting expenses. Few days later, luck ran out when somebody claimed copyrights over one of the videos posted by Sumit, for which monetization got stalled. He was left with only weekend classes and thus, his search for new means of income resumed.

The month of April was full of anxiety, uncertainty, and additional expenses. The consternation of family court dates kept haunting Sumit. He had never been in such a situation, where he would be asked to stand in the witness-box and defend himself and his family! However, Ganguly informed Sumit about the postponement of his date yet again by another month, as the judge was on leave. Somewhat relieved from the ongoing turmoil, Sumit concentrated on his freelancing career. The owner of the Ghatkopar based coaching centre once tried his hands on social media, but failed miserably, yet he wanted to market his classes through Facebook and Instagram. One day, over a casual discussion, when he expressed his desire to Sumit – the digital marketer in him leapt at the opportunity. He took a contract of three months, within which he promised to increase the page likes and get admissions done through social media campaigns. His Youtube activities slowly got replaced by Facebook page activities.

For the next 5 – 6 months; he got busy with two more classes from Kurla and Andheri, bagged contracts of managing Facebook pages of a local restaurant, Zumba classes and a fashion boutique store. Besides work, he thoroughly researched and studied various family court cases across the country where maintenance had been denied to the estranged wife. He even did his best to keep a tab on Moulina's whereabouts.

May 2015 was a bit of a double whammy for Sumit. Just when they were busy taming the maintenance case by all possible tricks, another registry letter from Rourkela court rocked their confidence. This time it was a summon from the Criminal Court. The police had finally submitted the Chargesheet for *GR Case no 989/2014*. From here on, the case needed cautious approach to maintain a balance between the proceedings of family court and criminal court. If not tackled carefully, things could go haywire leading to an enormous amount of frustration.

As a true saviour, Sumit's legal counsellor had his plans ready. He called up Sumit proactively.

"Sumit, I called you to inform that your case has been Chargesheeted. You might get a court notice soon."

"S...Sir, we got the notice today and I...I was about to ca...call you." A visibly tensed Sumit stammered.

"Okay. First things first – don't get worried, stay calm. I've my strategy in place..."

"S...Sir, what does the Chargesheet say?" Sumit wanted to be clear.

"It's the exact same as the FIR copy, just that the police have added another IPC 406 to it. That's for claiming *Stridhan.*"

"*Stridhan?* Oh! Sir, did you manage to get a copy of the Chargesheet? Can you please courier me a copy of the same?"

"Yes, I have a copy and I've already gone through it. Why do you need a copy, when I'm telling you that it's an exact replica of the FIR? Next time when you come for the family court *hajira*, I'll give it to you." Ganguly asserted.

"Sir, do I've to come for the family court appearance this month?"

"*Ufff* Sumit...you ask too many questions! Okay, let me clear your doubts one by one. For the family court appearance, get me a medical certificate. I'll be able to postpone it further by a month. And now for this criminal court summon, I've decided to get a stay order from the High Court and then challenge the cognizance." Ganguly further explained, "If we don't put a stay on this, then your entire family will have to come down here, surrender at the court and then take bail. After that, the criminal court will issue you dates. It'll be difficult to manage criminal and family courts simultaneously. Instead, my plan is that we put a stay for a year or so and frustrate the opponent."

"Alright Sir, do as you please. But who is going to represent us at the HC?" Sumit wanted to know all the details.

"Well...I'm associated with Advocate Mohapatra. Most of my HC cases are handled by him. He is a super senior lawyer and an ex-judge. Post-retirement, he and his son manage their law firm in Cuttack. Now if you'll excuse me, it is time for me to wrap up for the day. I'll be in touch. And I repeat, don't worry yourself over this."

Hrishikesh Basak and Mihir Ganguly were the only two Bengali lawyers practicing in Rourkela court. In the past, there had been several face-offs between them, of which Ganguly maintained an upper hand over most of the cases. However, professional rivalry never interfered with their personal life. Outside court, they were courteous, friendly and fellow Bengalis. For the case of Sumit vs Moulina, inspite of Basak trying to create pressure on Ganguly, the latter played tactfully using all his resources. Ganguly easily influenced the bench clerks and managed those dates; whereas Basak kept struggling to even get his last month's fees from Chell. Fighting court cases is an expensive affair. Without money it becomes extremely difficult to steer it as per one's own wish; and Basak had been having trouble with his client. Everytime he sought financial support, he got to hear the same rhetoric from Chell *"Basak Da, manage kar lo please...case jeetney ke baad 15% to aap hi ka hai na."*

Basak's dual attack on the Ghosh family fell flat when they managed to get a stay order on the criminal proceedings from Orissa HC. Basak knew full well that his colleague Ganguly would put all his efforts into keeping the stay order active for the next one year. For the Ghosh family, it was a huge relief that came in at a humongous cost. HC matters are way expensive than that of session court charges.

At this juncture, Sanat got desperate to end it all as soon as possible. His lawyer seemed to be helpless and insisted on sticking to theoretical approaches, while the opposition played delaying tactics effectively. Since Ghosh dragged it to the HC, Chell too had to defend the same – something which couldn't be afforded for a longer period of time. Sanat went ahead and tried unscrupulous methods to create pressure on his daughter's in-laws.

"Sumit Babu...humein pehechana kya?" a grating voice of an unknown caller kept Sumit guessing for a while.

"Naam nehi bataoge to kaise pehechanunga?" replied Sumit.

"Iqbal Karim – aap ka Bailer bol raha hu."

*"Arrey Iqbal Bhai...*how are you? Didn't expect your call. And this number isn't even saved in my mobile." Sumit was somehow pleased to receive this call from an old acquaintance.

"Koi baat nehi, save it now." The bailer joked while somebody else's voice could be heard in the background, who might have been prompting Iqbal.

*"Chalo kar lenge save, ab bolo...*what made you call me this afternoon?"

"Aajkal kya kar rahe ho? Kahin job pe ho kya?"

"Usse aapko kya matlab? Whether I am into a job or not, what has that to do with you?" replied Sumit with much displeasure. He didn't want to reveal anything to some random person he had only met once in his life.

*"Nahi aise hi poocha...*got to know that your case has been Chargesheeted, so you all have to visit the court and avail bail. Incase you're in a job, then you probably will have to plan your leave accordingly..."

"How nice of you to call me and express all this concern all of a sudden!" Sumit failed to hide the sarcasm and displeasure in his voice.

"Haha...aap to bura maan gaye, Sumit Babu. I had called you to check if I can

be of any help in being a bail guarantor to your family again. *Mujhey bhi do char paise mil jaatey.*" Iqbal covered it up nervously. The whispers in the background continued.

"Okay. Fair enough. I suggest you meet my lawyer and then he will decide the next course of action."

"*Hmmm…woh to thik hai, lekin ek baat bataun, bura to nehi manoge na?*"

"Go ahead…" Sumit was getting impatient. He didn't trust this man, but wanted to hear him out nonetheless.

"*Aapka Sasur bahut harami kisam ka admi hai…*he plans to drag this case for the next ten years. He is a jobless, old shrivel. Everyday, he visits the court and meets the Judge *Sahab*. Now, you belong to a respectable family. Why get into these unnecessary troubles and hassles? *Aapko settlement kar lena chahiye*, give him a few bucks and end this once and for all." Iqbal tried to sound like a genuine well-wisher.

"Thanks for your suggestion, Iqbal. From now onwards, whatever you have to say regarding the ongoing case, please meet my lawyer and tell him. He will take steps accordingly. Is that understood?" Sumit said sternly.

"*Woh baat to thik hai*, but these lawyers are such thugs, Sumit *Babu. Case ko kheenchte hai aur apne client ko chooste hai…*still, let me know in case you want to discuss on the settlement. Your in-laws and I are from the same locality, so I can contact them easily."

"I can see that. Thanks again, Iqbal. I've to go now. Please don't bother to call me again." Sumit disconnected with deliberation.

In the meantime, Sushil too got a couple of anonymous calls. Both the callers gave some random identity and introduced themselves as well-wishers who didn't want the Ghosh to engage into a dirty legal battle with the Chells. Instead, they suggested to get rid of the Birmirpur's scoundrel by paying him money which they believed could be negotiated once they decided to proceed. Instead of giving in to the pressure, all those calls were meticulously reported to Advocate Ganguly. The calls were even recorded as a part of collective evidences against the Chells.

After strategic delaying for almost two months, Sumit finally had to attend family court on 22nd July. It was just a customary marking of attendance only. Though Sumit reached early, he had to wait for Advocate Ganguly who arrived at around 11 o'clock. He was further made to wait at Ganguly's desk for another hour before heading towards the family court. The delay was deliberated to frustrate the opposition. Ganguly asked three of his juniors to accompany them. At the courtroom, Ganguly read out the case number to the *Peshkar* who was busy managing piles of files; yet within next five minutes he pulled out the requisite file containing the maintenance petition. The *Peshkar* flipped through the petition and asked Sumit to sign at the last page with proper date. Just when he was busy signing, Ganguly asked the *Peshkar* to keep the next date in the month of September – October in a hushed tone. And by the time he finished signing, Advocate Basak stormed into the room accompanied by Sanat and Moulina. While Moulina avoided making an eye contact, her father gave an ugly vengeful look to Sumit. Basak spoke to the *Peshkar* in Odiya and then asked Moulina to sign right below Sumit's signature.

Sumit stared darkly at the petite woman who appeared from behind her father and picked up the pen he had just signed the petition with. He saw her struggling to figure out where exactly to sign as she put the cap of the ball pen at its butt. It was her habit. She never let the cap of the pen stay astray, and always capped it from behind when she used it – whether it was signing their marriage certificate, or correcting her music notes in the battered old notebook she kept near the bedside table. *A familiar stranger – that's what she was,* Sumit mused as he leaned back in the chair.

Soon as she finished signing, she coldly pulled the papers from the table and handed them directly to her lawyer, "Here, I have signed them. I hope this case now appears before the Judge soon. My father is bearing all my expenses here and that gentleman there continues to enjoy his singlehood lavishly." She said it with such spite and malice in her voice that Sumit was jolted out of his reverie. He watched her grab hold of her father's arm and sit on the wooden bench nearby. Sanat bemusedly looked at his daughter's eyes, knotted together in angry determination. And just like that, Sumit's train of thought took a different route. In rushed the flashes, of his beloved wife turning into the misbegotten betrayer, who brought doom to his family. He turned his face away in absolute hatred.

After the day's smooth proceeding; Sumit met Ganguly at his newly opened chamber near City Hospital at around 7:30 pm, to discuss the next steps. Ganguly's chamber was relatively easy to access as compared to his residence. The 200 square feet room housed within Sector-18's marketplace, sandwiched between a stationery store and a photo studio appeared messy even though it had just been a week since its inaugural.

"Didn't I tell you that nothing will happen beyond your attendance?" Ganguly gleefully commented as he leaned back in his chair.

"But Sir, how long will this dilly-dallying work?" asked Sumit. He trusted his lawyer, partly because of lack of options, but zero visibility into the future of the case worried him.

"Let's see. We'll keep ourselves ready with our ammunitions and will hit them hard when time comes. Anyway, they've started showing signs of frustration."

"Why do you say so?"

"Your dear father-in-law made a couple of attempts to influence my juniors. He offered them some money, not knowing that I'll get to know about it," said Ganguly with a wide grin.

"What the fuck! That bastard has now got into these dirty tricks as well!" Sumit burst out unable to control himself any longer.

"Cool down Sumit. We lawyers can be very nasty, more than he can ever imagine. For the time being, let him do whatever he wants to…"

Sumit wasn't convinced. "Sir…this means that someday or the other, he will approach you too!"

"Yes. He can and I'm sure he definitely will. I'll create such pressure on him that he won't have any other option but to meet me. And when he does, I'll put forward my condition." Ganguly said blithely. He seemed to be enjoying the situation. "Don't worry. There's time for that moment to come," he added.

"But Sir, let me warn you – he is a dangerous man…"

"You need not tell a lawyer that. We can sniff the character of a person we meet!"

For a change, the criminal lawyer was in a relaxed jovial mood. That evening, he didn't keep any other appointments. He knew that his Mumbai client won't be able to visit Rourkela often and hence allotted an entire evening to him. At his new chamber, he had all the liberty, unlike at his residence where he had time restrictions, sound modulations and black tea limitations – all chalked out by Mrs Ganguly, so that their daughters' studies weren't hampered. Ganguly's elder daughter would be appearing for matric board exams and was preparing hard for the same.

It was the first time that Ganguly wanted to hear out every detail of Sumit's matrimonial life. He even briefly asked about Sumit's sex life. Later, he narrated his version to his junior, who took notes elaborately. The entire fourteen months of the Sumit-Moulina episode was penned down in a twenty pager note, with Ganguly's hypothesis and analysis appearing in red between some of the paragraphs. After an extensive session of discussion, the legal practitioner and his client went out for a brief stroll. It was 9:15 pm and most of the shops in the marketplace had downed their shutters. In the next one hour, Ganguly drafted a detailed Written Statement (WS) in response to the opposition's maintenance petition and kept it ready for future submission.

Next day, when Sumit was returning to Mumbai by *Hatia-LTT Superfast Express*, Ganguly called up to inform him that 7th October had been allotted as the next hearing date. He also insisted that Sumit should surveil his estranged wife and start collecting information about her working status, relationship status and other whereabouts. And only after providing some leads, would Ganguly deploy his men to churn out meaty evidences that would help them stay ahead of the opposition.

Back in Mumbai, one thing that kept bothering Sumit was gathering latest, relevant information on Moulina. At one point, he thought of appointing a detective agency to shadow her. But their exorbitant charges restricted him to further explore the same. Hence, the only option left was to scout for someone in the known circle. He called up his college friend Anup several times, but he seemed to have distanced himself from Sumit and his legal turmoils. Just when he gave up all hopes, he recalled a guest from his wedding function who had shared his visiting card then and had introduced himself as an LIC Agent. Sumit vaguely remembered him as the financial advisor to Moulina's uncle, Sarat Chell. Immediately an idea clicked – an LIC policy would cost lesser than any detective agency. Luckily, the bait of purchasing a policy worked and in came those vital bits of information, straight from the Chell family, uninterrupted.

The month of October raced in pretty fast. Luckily, Sumit's hearing date got postponed yet again. This time, thanks to his opposition lawyer Hrishikesh Basak who survived a severe road accident and was suggested complete bed rest upto three months by the orthopaedic surgeons of Jeevan-Jyoti Hospital.

Sushil being cryophobic, generally preferred Mumbai during the winters. End of October and the elderly couple left Haldia for Mumbai. This time round they wanted to stay with their children for a longer period of time and be their support system. They always kept talking to their son and had instructed their daughter to do the same. By no way did they want their son to feel lonely and slip into depression. They did notice a gradual change in Sumit's behaviour but they ignored it, and never made him feel guilty of his acts. At the slightest of disagreement these days, Sumit who used to be a calm and level-headed guy, got irritated and often ended up in a quarrelsome situation with his parents. Socially, he withdrew himself from his friends' circle and was hardly seen chatting with them. He rarely went out during the day time, his daily evening walks reduced to once in a week on Saturdays. Sushil and Chitra knew that these are the stages when an individual becomes vulnerable to negative thoughts towards life and turn suicidal. They didn't want to lose their only son, just because a girl had betrayed him and decided to walk out of his life. They wanted their son to believe that life is beautiful and has much more to offer, bad phases don't stay forever and this too shall pass.

Mid-December, when the rest of India was shivering in cold, Mumbai was comfortably at an average temperature of 18-19 °C with much dryness in the air. With semester holidays on, it was a relaxed week for Sumit as the B-Schools where he took up visiting faculty role through Sunita's reference, were shut until the new semester commenced the following year. After a simple home cooked lunch, when he was busy editing his client's Facebook page and his mother was busy solving an intricate crossword puzzle, Sushil woke up from a nap to a sudden phone call on his son's mobile.

"Sumit there's a registered post from Rourkela Family court addressed to you. I wasn't at home; your Aunty has received it. Come and collect it in the evening," informed the previous landlord whose premises Sumit had vacated a couple of months back.

*"Thik hai Uncle...*I'll be there in the evening."

"The postman ideally shouldn't have given it to us. But since he knows us, he was comfortable handing the parcel to us. We are aware of your litigation and hence received it."

"Thanks a lot Uncle..." Sumit cut the call. A sense of foreboding prevailed in the afternoon.

Just when the Ghoshs were recovering from the dual attack of maintenance petition and criminal court summons under 498A; the new envelope brought in much of eagerness, curiosity, apprehension and discomposure. Finally, it turned out to be another summon – this time for a divorce petition filed under *Section 27 (1) (d) of Special Marriage Act* for dissolution of marriage. The five-pager petition was a reiteration of the same shit that was mentioned in the FIR along with a prayer to pass an order and decree dissolving the marriage and fix an alimony in the interest of justice and equity.

Sumit's pensive emotions took him through a brief flashback – the same month of December four years ago was when he was all excited to start a new chapter with Moulina...who would've thought what the forthcoming Decembers would be, full of pain and misery! If divorce was the main objective, then she could have openly talked about it. If she was really suffocated in the matrimony, then she could have asked for a mutual separation. It was an arranged marriage after all. With a melancholic mood, Sumit dialled up Ganguly that evening.

"Are you sure that the envelope wasn't received by you?" the shrewd lawyer asked Sumit twice to confirm while his cerebral activity was up to some further tricks.

"None from us received it. The registered post was handed over to my previous landlord." A despondent Sumit answered.

*"Ab ayega maza, tum sirf dekhte jao...*I suggest you go out and enjoy, take your parents for a nice dinner. And leave your worries to me." Ganguly sounded all excited.

"Sir they've asked for alimony. What do we do now?" Sumit couldn't shake the wretched feeling in his stomach.

"Let them dream big...*thenga milega...*I'll pull out those papers from the court tomorrow, till then, goodnight!" Ganguly signed off.

TWENTY-SIX
2013

Mumbai, Maharashtra, India

Things at the office worsened. The convoluted office politics got to his nerves. Sumit's GM had become nasty towards him. In order to save his own arse, he started blaming Sumit for every failure of his. Sumit was even traduced at various meetings, mostly in his absence. The backbiting phenomenon crossed all limits of tolerance and forced him to desperately look out for an opportunity.

16th May, Thursday, was Sumit's first wedding anniversary. He wanted to spend some quality time with his beloved wife at a beach resort in Ratnagiri's Dapoli. Accordingly, he applied for a short leave covering the entire weekend and planned to resume office the next Monday. Till 14th things looked positive, but the very next day his leave failed to get an approval. Instead he was asked to travel to Bangalore on that weekend for a project launch. Sumit got thoroughly pissed-off and confronted his manager, who instead made a poker face and passed on the blame to the top management.

A disappointed Sumit had no choice but to alter his plan. The couple celebrated the anniversary evening with a lavish dinner at *Hotel Taj Land's End* followed by a long stroll along the Bandra's Bandstand promenade. For the first time ever, Moulina experienced a five-star hotel treatment and enjoyed every bit of the evening in her husband's company.

Moulina was aware of her husband's ongoing office tension and was rather worried. The thought of running a family without a steady job in a megacity gave her cold shivers. She had already experienced such bitterness in life – when her father was thrown out of their family business. He didn't have a proper source of income for several years, and it became extremely difficult to run a family of six without any savings then. Moulina often raised her concern with Sumit and suggested him to stay calm and compromise with his Boss till he bagged another job.

Meanwhile office workload doubled for Sumit. As a result, he often carried work home. He would work late on pending presentations as his wife slept next to him. On one such occasion in July, at around midnight when Sumit was busy finalising the Executive Summary of his presentation, Moulina's mobile phone beeped once. Without paying heed to that alert tone, he continued with his work. The fact that marketers kept sending promotional messages past midnight irked him. After almost thirty minutes at quarter to one, just when Moulina changed sides in her sleep and Sumit was about to switch off his laptop; the mobile phone beeped yet again. This time with much annoyance, Sumit picked up the handset to put it on silent mode only to realize that both the messages were sent by none other than his father-in-law. Initially he thought of ignoring it, but sensing some exigency, opened up the message box – only to get a rude shock.

The first message read *'I am taking Temazepam daily'* followed by an apologetic second message *'Sorry Beta…Goodnight.'*

He was gobsmacked reading those messages. He didn't know how to react. *What were the father-daughter duo upto? Were they cooking something up?* Sumit stood baffled not knowing what to make of those texts. He switched off the table lamp before going to bed. With mixed thoughts swirling in his head, he tried to settle his nerves. For long, he tossed and turned on the bed before falling asleep.

The next day was quite crucial for Sumit – first, because he needed to understand the mystery behind those text messages and second, to present an effective Digital Marketing plan to the CMO. The office meeting was slotted for the second half and hence, he decided to reach office late. Probably for the first time, Sumit woke up before Moulina with his sleep deprived puffy eyes.

Unaware of what had happened late night, Moulina was taken by surprise to find her hubby awake at as early as 6 in the morning. She was mindful of the important meeting that Sumit had to spearhead at the office that day, and linked the same with his early rise.

"You slept late, yet woke up early!! Don't worry dear, today's meeting will go absolutely fine." Moulina uttered in a slumberous voice, smiled and pecked his cheek.

Not knowing how to react, Sumit asked sternly "Did you check your mobile phone?"

"*Naah…*what's there to check? It must be lying somewhere on the table." Moulina responded casually. She yawned and continued "You go freshen up; I'll make tea."

This further confused Sumit, he grabbed Moulina's hand, pulled her towards him and asked indignantly "What's going on Mouli? Your father sends contentious messages late at night and then you pretend not to have any idea of it?"

"Why would I pretend? And what messages are you talking about?" Moulina revolted and picked up her phone to check. She was stunned to see those texts from her father. Now she understood why Sumit was so furious. Without even thinking twice, she dialled back and started scolding her father. Then she went silent all of a sudden, attentively heard the person on the other side of the phone and finally disconnected the call saying "Okay, let's discuss this in the afternoon."

Moulina turned to her hubby and said "Leave this to me. I'll handle it, will talk to my father in the afternoon…seems he was feeling depressed yesterday, but now is absolutely fine. He even wanted to talk to you. I refused since you've an important meeting today. Its better you concentrate on it. Now go and get ready soon, I'm off to the kitchen to prepare breakfast."

She stormed out the bedroom, leaving Sumit in a confused state. He wasn't convinced, but was also getting late for office. He parked his thoughts pertaining to this matter and rose to go brush his teeth.

In the evening, Sumit returned home fully drenched after struggling through Mumbai's monsoon traffic over two hours. He came home a defeated warrior. His presentation was frequently challenged and his Boss remained a silent spectator. Ongoing market slowdown added more spice to the meeting, and his annual budget was stripped off drastically. With no support from the top and frequent backbiting; he made up his mind to quit.

Earlier that afternoon – Sanat explained his daughter the motive behind those provocative messages. He encouraged Moulina to perjure herself, use innocence to her defence and pose some tough questions to her husband. Once emotionally sabotaged Sumit would give into his manipulations easily.

At the dinner table, a dejected Sumit narrated his unsuccessful day at office and his subsequent plan to quit his job and go for a *Durga Puja* vacation before he returned back to the grind. He was so ruffled with the day's proceedings that he decided to skip office the next day. With his energy completely drained, he didn't show any interest in demystifying last night's SMS episode and left it for the next day's topic of discussion.

As the next day unfolded, the husband-wife got involved in an ugly spat. Moulina came down heavily on Sumit accusing him for all the mess. A well-crafted script was successfully delivered by a daughter; ignoring a wife's obligations and responsibilities. At the time when a husband needed his wife's support the most, he had to face her seemingly misplaced and pointless wrath instead.

"How is your father? What exactly happened the night before, that compelled him to take sleeping pills?" Sumit wanted to get to the bottom of it.

"You know what – my *Baba* is right. I've never paid attention to his detailed observations about you. And probably these are some of the concerns which led him to depression." Moulina defended her father's act quite convincingly.

"*Arre*...but what did I do? What are you even accusing me of?" a visibly shocked Sumit questioned.

"It's been a year that we are married and yet you've never addressed him as *Baba* or *Papa*. And you maintained the same stance for my mother as well. Remember the day we got engaged? I started addressing your parents as *Mummy* and *Papa*. This means you've not accepted my parents as your own until now." Moulina snivelled.

"Oh God, why are you making a mountain out of a molehill? If this is the only reason for which your father is depressed, then I question his mental stability." Sumit tried mocking and continued explaining. "Well, to be honest, the observation made by him is valid and I won't deny that. Every individual is different. I'm an introvert and take time to open up. For me, it will take some more time to address your father as *Baba*. Trust me, it'll happen over a period of time..."

Before Sumit could complete, his wife interjected "You should understand that my father is very sensitive to these behaviours. He doesn't have any steady source of income and his emotional support system is now married off; he is all alone there. Throughout his life, he has been betrayed and taunted for his deeds. Before my marriage, he used to get heckled by our relatives for his inability to find me a worthy groom and now, he doesn't even get the due respect from his son-in-law..."

"Wait a second Moulina. I'm shocked at the way you are putting me on the centre stage of everything. How come he is all alone? What about Lina, Lokesh and Lalit? What about your mother, isn't she there for him? Doesn't he have any responsibility towards them as well? And if he is unemployed today, that's all because of his authoritative nature. Else it's impossible for an elder brother to be kicked out by his younger siblings from the family business. And yes, we came to know all these facts later from your uncles. So, if you blame me for your father's depression, then you are utterly wrong. Moreover, one cannot demand respect, it has to be earned. So, tell him not to be a cry-baby and instead, do something substantial to portray a better image. The way you are pointing fingers at me, I too have many things to say which I personally didn't like about him. But I refrained from getting into the muck, I know that his daughter is my better half now and in our journey of life, we'll slowly overcome all these minor differences." Sumit was pretty much aggressive in putting forward his point of views. For the first time in a year, he was able to voice his opinion about his father-in-law directly to Moulina.

Caught off guard, Moulina steered the discussion quite tactfully. She continued whining "It has been a year and I've not visited my parents. Nor do we have an option of calling them here. And the reason you would give is known – *we have a small place, we cannot accommodate guests, blah blah blah.* But still your sister finds a place in this 1BHK, your parents already visited twice. Isn't this a differential treatment? You indirectly discouraged my brother's desire to shift to Mumbai. You are just so selfish."

"Now that's enough. You've been accusing me irrationally. Let me remind you, you are married to a family in a different city. It's not in the same city that you can visit your parents whenever you want." Sumit was furious, but still maintained his composure and negated his wife's baseless assertions. He continued – "Imagine you're out of town admitted in a college and leading a hostel life. How many times yearly would you get permission to visit your home? Doesn't this mean that you've not yet accepted this house and its members as your family and Birmirpur keeps pulling you back every time? Yes, we genuinely have a cramped-up space and hence I'm making all these efforts to buy a bigger house. Aren't you aware of this? Now imagine, your father started hue and cry just because he has not been called *Baba*. I won't be surprised if this very person starts mocking me for accommodating him in this small 1BHK. And why do you have to target Sunita every single time? Today she is with us, tomorrow she'll get married and will definitely move out. What is it about Sunita that irks you so much? Please tell me how has my family failed you!"

Moulina had no answers to this. She turned away and started sobbing.

Sumit calmed down and tried to pacify his wife. "Mouli please don't get carried away by baseless speculations, instead I urge you to be practical. We've just started this journey and whatever I'm doing is for the betterment of our future. I know you share a special bond with your father. But now, you're also my wife. Please try to balance the two relationships in your life."

Moulina was however adamant. She demanded "Whatever it is, I wish to visit my parents this time. Please make the necessary arrangements."

"Okay. Let me end the ongoing squabble at my office. I'll put down my papers next month and serve a notice period of two months. By October first week we'll visit Haldia and from there we'll go to Birmirpur. We will plan the *Durga Puja* accordingly, so that we can spend time both at Haldia and Birmirpur equally. Happy now?"

Moulina wiped her eyes. "And what about your job? Do you have anything in hand as yet?"

"Don't worry on that front. I'll come back and search. Also, I'll make efforts to open a music school for you, so you don't have to spend your days in this cramped 1BHK. Now, can we please put this behind us and have a good cup of tea together?"

Sumit never considered these tiffs to be a serious matter and always thought it to be a normal couple thing. However, Moulina was of a different view – fuelled by her *Baba's* inputs, she was determined to requite. She wasn't a sport, and couldn't take her father's criticism lightly – that's where Sanat played his trump card through emotional manipulations.

Sumit's office notice period passed in the blink of an eye. By the end of September, the couple was all busy packing. Lately, Moulina didn't show any emotions about her husband's last week at work. She was all soaked in to the excitement of visiting Birmirpur after almost an entire year – the first time after her marriage. She was all chirpy and chatty with Lina over the phone, making plans of visiting places and relatives together.

"I'm carrying my woollen sweater as it generally gets cold by October end," Moulina chimed as she zipped her trolley bag.

"Hmmm…don't stuff your bag with too many things, else it'll get difficult to carry," suggested Sumit.

"*Achha*…shall I carry my gold jewellery?"

"Wear a few of them and use those imitations. Carrying it all the way in a train journey isn't safe."

"Well, shall I carry my original marksheets and certificates too? They're of no use now, you've the photocopies anyway."

"Wait, w…what? Are you leaving Mumbai permanently? Won't you ever come back and fetch a job for yourself? What happens when the interviewer asks for those original documents?"

"Okay okay. I'm sorry, let these be here then." Moulina returned the folder into the almirah.

"You know what Mouli – somehow I feel you won't come back to Mumbai with me after this festive season." Sumit stared at his wife before bursting into laughter.

Moulina didn't reply. She was facing the almirah, so he couldn't even read her expressions. Just then, his phone rang and Sumit left the room to attend to it. His words hung in the air, carrying different meanings for the couple in that moment.

The puja vacation got over abruptly. But it didn't go as it was planned – Sumit and Moulina celebrated *Durga Puja* at their respective parental homes of Haldia and Birmirpur separately. Just the day after they reached Haldia, Sanat paid a surprise visit and took away his daughter for the holidays and invited Sumit to Chell house in Birmirpur for the Diwali celebrations. The Ghoshs allowed it to happen, as they too felt that their daughter-in-law should breathe some fresh air of her parental home. Little did they know that indirectly it would aid Sanat to perpetrate such an act of perfidy…

During the festive celebrations, Sumit felt the absence of his wife and missed her terribly. He would end up calling her multiple times in a day. Moulina often remained unavailable as she would either be at her relative's place or out with her friends. At Birmirpur, Moulina got a star treatment – everybody wanted to have a descriptive slice of Mumbai, the *Mayanagri*. For her first Diwali after marriage, she got umpteen invitations from all her relatives and friends. Those who taunted her when she was struggling to get married, were the ones who showered invitations the most. Moulina didn't have time to analyse it all, she was enjoying all the attention. She took pride in calling herself as a *Mumbaikar*. In the glitz of all pomp and glory, at times she ignored her husband's messages or forgot to return her in-laws' call. She enjoyed every moment of her grandeur in the small town. Visiting her home town after a year made her realise the strong emotional attachment with the semi-urban simplistic life of Birmirpur. It was almost like a reunion with her lost love. Honestly, she didn't miss her husband as much as she missed her Birmirpur days. She was back to a place where she belonged.

The subsequent months of November and December didn't quite favour Sumit. Situations worsened with each passing day before it went out of his hands. Some form of food poisoning restricted his Diwali visit to Birmirpur and then his mother-in-law's chronic arthritis forced his wife to stay back with her parents. Sumit returned to Mumbai sans Moulina by mid-December to attend an interview. The call frequency between the couple declined drastically with reduced talking time. Sumit slowly and steadily fell prey to circumstances. On his 36th birthday, his phone had to be submitted at the service centre after an inflated battery was detected. Moulina made several attempts to reach him, but couldn't. This drove her crazy resulting into a brief brawl followed by a weeklong silence from both ends. It came to a point where the mothers had to intervene and get the couple to talk to each other again.

Sumit expected a positive outcome from the interview he had attended a fortnight back, but unfortunately, he couldn't make it to the final round. His career seemed to be doomed. Emotionally, he was shattered and due to the ongoing tiff with his wife, he didn't want to portray himself as a loser. On the other hand, Moulina gave cold responses to Sumit's emotions. Instead of empathizing with her husband, she continued to be within a halo of enhanced self-worth feeling. The rift in their relationship was quite evident and with each passing day, frequent disagreement over infrequent conversations confiscated the sweet, loving relationship between the couple.

TWENTY-SEVEN
2014

Mumbai, Maharashtra, India

It was a saturnine start to another New Year for Sumit. His woebegone look couldn't hide his depressed state of mind. Things seemed to be moving away from his grip. Meanwhile, Moulina celebrated New Year's Eve in company of her cousins and Lina. Strangely, for the first time, Sumit and Moulina exchanged New Year wishes through SMS only. The void between them was taking shape with each passing day; and someone was definitely benefitting from this disastrous situation. Sumit insisted that his wife return back to Mumbai, but Sanat kept encouraging his daughter to prolong her stay in Birmirpur on the pretext of her mother's ill-health.

It was nearly four months that Moulina stayed back in Birmirpur and Sumit intuited something dubious. Even though they conversed every alternate day, the spark in those conversation was amiss. Moulina's mood and tonality rendered her lack of eagerness to chat with her husband. Sumit was in two minds whether or not to be uncompromisingly forthright and ask his wife about her intentions. However, he wanted to have some concrete info before confronting her. On the occasion of his brother-in-law's birthday he called him up only to realise that something was terribly wrong somewhere.

"Hey Lokesh, many many happy returns of the day. May God bless you and fulfil all your wishes." Sumit greeted his brother-in-law with all cheers.

"Thank you *Jiju,* it means a lot" an ecstatic Lokesh replied.

"*Hmmm…kya plan hai aaj?* Where are you partying today?"

"No time for celebrations. Office schedule is tight, I'm taking my colleagues out for a lunch and may be in the evening will have a small get-together with my friends."

"Yes, just go and have fun. *Office mein kaam to rahega hamesha.*"

"*Jiju,* what about your job? Did you get one anywhere?"

"Not yet, but will soon give you some good news on that front. By the way, how is your mother recovering from arthritis pain?"

"*Maa* is fit and fine. She never had any arthritis! Who gave you this stupid information, *Jiju?*"

"Are you sure, Lokesh?" asked Sumit with much disbelief.

"Yes *Jiju,* day before yesterday I had a long chat with her and again today morning, she called up to wish me. She never uttered anything about arthritis and she has no reason to keep me in the dark about her health issues…" replied Lokesh with strong conviction.

"Oh, never mind Lokesh, it might have been some minor pain which I wrongly termed as arthritis. You enjoy your day." Sumit tactfully evaded Lokesh's query before ending the call.

Sumit was indignant at his own stupidity. He blindly believed his wife, while she bamboozled him and kept faking about her mother's health. *But why was she behaving in such a bizarre manner? What were her intentions?* Instead of keeping these questions to himself, he decided to confront his wife. After all, as a wife she owed an explanation to him. That evening Sumit decided to talk tough.

"Today I won't ask you much. Let's keep it straight and simple – When are you returning? I want a specific date." Sumit asked stiffly and held his breath.

"Listen, you can't talk to me like this. I am not your house-maid," retorted Moulina.

"Look, I've been extremely patient all this while. You left in October and now January is nearly at an end, yet you don't intend to return. What are your plans? Why are you playing this hide-and-seek? Are there any concerns? Try and put yourself in my position Moulina, and then you'll realise, what made me behave like this. I've never ever raised my voice at you. I also don't remember being rude to you. But still I fail to understand why on earth you are behaving like this!"

"I never said that I won't come…" Moulina lowered her tone.

"Yes, but you also never confirmed any return dates. Isn't that true?" countered Sumit.

"What do I do if suddenly *Maa* falls ill…"

"Bull shit. Cut the crap now, how long will you keep bluffing? I know your mother is perfectly fine. In fact, she never had any artheritis problem…" Sumit lost his cool and almost shouted over the phone, but immediately controlled his temper and continued in a calmer tone. "This cannot go on for any longer, if you have any issues please speak up. Let's resolve it through a discussion."

Absolute silence prevailed for a second, while Sumit could hear somebody prompt his wife from the background. And all of a sudden before handing over the phone to her father Moulina hesitantly said, "Why don't you speak to my *Baba* on this."

"Hello Sumit *beta, kemon acho?* We are connecting after ages. I think you're a bit upset right now. Let's do one thing – we'll talk tomorrow, you go and relax. Cool heads are always preferred for a meaningful discussion," suggested Sanat in a composed tone before disconnecting.

Sumit was all bemused and couldn't decipher anything from what just happened. He felt horrible, as for the first time, he had shouted at his wife. The entire Ghosh family was baffled not knowing how to handle the situation. Chitra sensed something fishy and suggested her son to keep his eyes open and be polite to his wife. She dialled Birmirpur to cobble the gap between the two families. Sanat was very courteous and at the same time apologetic about his daughter's inability to convey a prominent return schedule. However, he reassured Chitra that their daughter-in-law would soon be with them. But the fact that Moulina didn't converse properly with her, gave Chitra enough reasons to be apprehensive about Sanat's words.

Meanwhile at the Chell residence, an impermeable plot was being concocted to entrap Sumit. It was all spearheaded by Sanat who didn't get any support initially but eventually after sessions of indoctrination could convince his daughter to go against her in-laws. Moulina was finally cajoled to act against her husband.

Sanat always wanted to utilize Sumit to his own benefit – be it for monetary gains or for societal status. His every attempt was successfully steered away by the Ghosh scion. His whole idea to start a new business funded by his son-in-law's high salaried job failed to take off as Sumit maintained a safe distance from him. Sanat's jobless status prevailed and was often needled by his brothers and friends. He gave away his daughter to a *Mumbaikar*, yet never got a chance to visit the city in last one year, which again was often discussed among his social circle. He would've ignored these insults, if Lina was allowed to stay in Mumbai and pursue her masters or Lokesh could take a transfer to Mumbai, but even that didn't happen. Sanat firmly believed that it was Sumit who foiled his every move; and waited for the right opportunity to take reprisal of his son-in-law's actions – to him Sumit's unemployed status turned out to be a boon in disguise.

For next few weeks, the husband and wife conversed over the phone quite normally. But every time Moulina tactfully avoided Sumit's query on her return dates. She also rescinded Sumit's proposal to visit Birmirpur in order to bring her back citing one excuse or the other. Then finally one evening Moulina let the cat out of the bag and told her hubby about her plans, which had her father's approval and shocked Sumit to the core…

In one of those habitual conversation Moulina probed about Sumit's job hunting status and came up with a surprising proposition "You must be finding it difficult to fetch a job, isn't it? I wonder if I could be of any help and contribute to the financial well-being of our family…"

"Oh, come on Mouli, this is a temporary phase. You don't have to bother, just be by my side and I'll take care of the rest. And that's why I insist you to come back soon."

"I need to be more specific about it, I need to tell you my plan…" Moulina replied in excitement.

"Okay, go ahead…"

"When I was in Mumbai, I saw a huge opportunity of school teachers there. Almost every alternate Ad was about teacher recruitment. And the salary they offer is also good. But the only issue is that – they all want a candidate with a B.Ed degree. So, I've decided to pursue it this year. What's your view on the matter?" asked Moulina quite candidly.

Not knowing where the conversation was leading, Sumit replied diplomatically "I think that's a good idea, but you're already Masters in English. Is it necessary to do B.Ed again? I mean, am not discouraging you. But a school teacher with MA in English should've greater weightage – isn't it? Apart from that you're a well-qualified vocalist, you can try for the post of a music teacher in various schools. Still if you insist, let me Google out some information on the B.Ed courses offered by Mumbai University."

"No no, you don't have to worry on that front. *Baba* has already got few application forms here. I've to appear for an entrance test and am preparing for that right now." Moulina sounded all excited and at the same time anticipated her husband's reluctance.

Sumit was completely taken aback. Those words from Moulina came as a bolt from the blue. His fear of losing his beloved wife was turning out to be true. Closing his eyes, he took a deep breath and tried to elucidate the pros and cons – "Look Moulina. I hope you understand the efficacies. If you want to pursue B.Ed, then you can do it from here. Why do you have to do it from Birmirpur or Rourkela? It's a two-year course, so for this entire period you're going to stay away from me?! *Why* are you doing this? And if B.Ed was so important to you, *why* did you agree to marry me? You could have completed all your studies and then opted for marriage. Besides, what do I tell to my friends, peers and neighbours? Is it at all justifiable?"

Even though Sumit tried to control himself, his voice rose to a higher pitch to express his annoyance over the whole issue. Not allowing his wife to speak, he continued questioning her "You've taken a decision and I am the last person to know about it. Didn't we vow to be friends for life? Then how come I wasn't a part of this decision. Do you at all consider me as your husband?"

Sanat pretty much expected Sumit's reaction and accordingly penned down his script carefully. Moulina just parroted it impeccably. Maintaining her composure, she added "Please don't get me wrong. I completely understand your viewpoint, but here I am just extending my support. Once I start earning, I'll be able to aid you financially. In future even if you're out of job, you can take your time to fetch another one."

"Moulina please try and understand. I'm not against your B.Ed. I want you to do it from here in Mumbai. I still fail to understand why you want to stay back there for the course!"

"Simple – while I study, I will take tuitions simultaneously and fund my father to run this family." Moulina answered casually not knowing Sumit's next set of questions.

"Are you the only child of your father? Lokesh too is employed in an MNC with an awesome salary, where does all his money go? And even if you want to contribute, can't that be done form here? You can take up home tuitions here in Mumbai and send back money to your Dad. I still struggle to find a logic behind your strange decision!"

Rattled with so many straight forward questions, Moulina didn't have any ammunitions to defend her lies. She stood perplexed and perspired profusely. Guilty of her own wrongdoing she didn't want to succumb to Sumit's honesty and sincerity. She was just helping her father, who promised her to keep things under control and create some pressure on his son-in-law and teach him a lesson. However, with no definitive response to please Sumit's suspicion, she simply disconnected the phone in the middle of the conversation and switched it off. Simultaneously grabbed her father's mobile and texted her husband *'battery dead…mobile getting charged, let's talk tomorrow.'*

Caught in a cuff, she turned ferociously at her father and questioned him. "*Baba* where will this lead to? Don't you think our lies will get exposed? I guess we are heading towards an abstruse situation. Let's stop here before it gets ugly."

"Ohh…just shut up and do as I say, before it goes out of our control." Sanat scolded his daughter and asked her to keep the conversation crisp. "Who asked you to blabber so much? In spite of several attempts, you can't even put across those points properly and trap him. Why can't you understand that in the name of college fees, we can extract some amount of money every month from him?" Sanat turned a bit hyper.

"*Baba,* this is enough. I can't bluff anymore. Unnecessarily we are…"

Even before Moulina could complete Sanat retorted. He got upset with her and reminded that whatever he had done so far was only for the betterment of his family. He was extremely patient for last one year and waited for an opportunity to strike hard. He tried his luck through all means, but then a cat in gloves catches no mice –

hence he had to take up this manipulative step. Sanat emotionally steered Moulina into her childhood days when her every childish whim was duly appeased and it was all possible due to a steady income then. Money is always important, no matter how it is achieved.

Despite all efforts to conciliate, Sumit was left baffled and bewildered. He kept aside his job hunting spell, and aimed to end this crisis. He connected with his brother-in-law to understand the pulse of seriousness back in Birmirpur, but Lokesh seemed to have no idea about his *Didi's* new obsession for B.Ed. Sumit also called up his sister-in-law, but Lina refused to comment citing it as her *Didi's* personal choice. And mysteriously enough his mother-in-law didn't even have a whit of knowledge about her daughter's decision. Further to quench his suspicious mind, Sumit called up his wife's college friend Rupali and conversed in general. And that very telephonic chat made him feel like the rug had been swept off from under his feet...

After those initial exchange of pleasantries, Rupali congratulated Sumit for his upcoming official trip to Europe, which she had got to know about from her friend. She also expressed her disappointment of being a government employee's wife, where the scopes of foreign visits are almost nil. Though Sumit was completely taken by surprise, he wanted to get to the depth of it. On further probing, he got to know that, Moulina had even informed Rupali that, once her visa papers were ready, she would join her husband in Copenhagen in a month's time.

Just to avoid further embarrassing questions, Sumit excused himself for an 'urgent incoming call' and abruptly disconnected Rupali. His ears turned hot and red as he stood fuddled. He could slowly understand the conspiracy that had engulfed him. The series of incidents which he ignored earlier as petty domestic issues were the plots built to entrap him. Those feigning and snivelling seemed to be all cover-up acts to trick him emotionally...beneath all those crocodile tears, love and show-offs of affection, lay a well-orchestrated ploy which he had thus far failed to identify. As he pondered the future, questions about the past began to bubble up in his mind. Somewhere deep inside, Sumit felt a sense of betrayal from his beloved partner. The reason of which off course wasn't known to him. With strong resilience he decided to dial up his father-in-law and demand a clarification.

After a tiresome day with much irritation Sumit dialled up Sanat Chell for an elucidation of the entire saga. He firmly believed that his father-in-law was behind all of it and had been a killjoy shitbag to ruin his blissful married life.

"Now everything is crystal clear to me. It's you who inculcated hatred in my wife's mind, you always wanted to have a control over me through your daughter and when you failed, you started this dirty game..." Sumit charged his father-in-law directly without even greeting him.

"Hey, hey Sumit, now mind your language. Just because I treat you like my son, doesn't mean that you'll test my patience. If your wife isn't willing to join you, speak to her and sort it out rather than blaming me for your failures." Sanat retorted rudely.

"Never in my life have I come across such a mean-minded, contemptible, conniving person like you – who could stoop to any low to fulfil his ill motives! How can a father ruin his daughter's future? I just fail to understand this!" Sumit continued his vicious attack on Sanat.

"Hey you shut up, shut your bloody mouth. One more word and you'll see the worst in me!" Sanat lost his cool and shouted. He continued with a threatening tone, "Do you know who I am? Don't you dare mess with me, else you'll have to pay a hefty price for it."

"Mr Chell, honestly, I don't care who you are. Just be informed that this conversation is being recorded, and if the need arises, I can drag you to the police station with a charge of abducting my wife and threatening me with dire consequences." Sumit warned and made his intentions clear.

Sanat controlled his temper, calmed down and tried to convince Sumit. "Look *Beta* there must have been some misunderstanding. I suggest, you talk to Moulina and hopefully a solution can be found…"

"That's exactly what I've been doing since last couple of months. Whenever she grapples to answer me, she either hands the phone over to you, or disconnects the call. And then again you refresh and revive her with your vocal tonic and make her ready for the next conversation with a bunch of lies…*aakhir kab tak chalega yeh?*"

"Okay, give me another week. Let me speak to her and see what best can be done. In the meantime, I request you to courier all her marksheets and certificates. She would need them for her B.Ed admission." Sanat lowered his tone and requested politely.

Sumit contemplated on the request and with indomitable attitude continued, "Mr Chell, I'm not falling into your trap anymore. I won't be sending any such documents, if she needs them let her come over here and collect the same."

Sanat's sinusoidal temper finally reached its peak and broke all the boundaries of soberness. He suddenly turned abusive and made derogatory remarks on his own son-in-law. "*Abey madarchod…*I've been trying to be good to you and you aren't in a mood to listen. *Tu to maha chutiya hai yaar! Ab tu dekhtey ja mein kya kya karta hu tere saath…*"

For a second Sumit couldn't believe his ears. Instead of freaking out he maintained his calm and sternly responded "What did you just say? Mr Chell, finally you showed your true colours! Never expected such low class behaviour from you.

Luckily, I haven't been addressing you as '*Baba*', which would've been an insult to such a Godly figure as mine. Fair enough, let me just make a few clarifications – from now onwards neither will I call you nor will you do the same. Your daughter is my legally wedded wife, so I continue to talk to her and refuse to entertain any kind of communication from your side. Goodnight..."

In order to unmask the real face of his father-in-law, Sumit called up his wife's grandfather, one of her uncles, aunt and cousins and played the recorded conversation. Sanat's father and brother felt ashamed and sorry for the incident and promised to arbitrate and end the tussle on a sweeter note. Meanwhile Sanat was in a fix...just one wrong move and things seemed to be moving out of his hand. Immediately he instructed his daughter to call up Sumit and apologise on his behalf. Simultaneously to gain sympathy and support from his relatives, he weaved a fictitious tale of his daughter's ill-fated, torturous stay at her in-laws; where she was repeatedly heckled, harassed and kept in captivity for demand of dowry.

After much deliberation, Moulina called up her husband to apologise for all that had happened earlier. Meanwhile Sanat too had sent a regretful SMS so that things weren't blown out of proportion. Strangely enough Moulina started defending her father's action and blamed his hypertension which preceded the circumstances, that was exactly when Sumit couldn't take any more and yelled at his wife. Moulina sobbed out her concerns to him and made her intentions clear...

"Mr Sumit, in last three months you've changed a lot. From a sweet loving husband to a frustrated jobless jack, your transformation worries me. I doubt if you still care for me, else you wouldn't have shouted at me. It has now become almost impossible to go back to a family where I'm not valued anymore. I just can't bear those lonely, suffocating moments within the four walls of your flat. I am unable to adjust with your fast-paced city life, where the neighbours maintain a strange distance. I feel insecure to sit back at home whereas your sister goes out every day to work. Every now and then I felt like a housemaid, who is there to serve tea and cook lunch and dinner. I'm fed up. I can't go back to that hell anymore."

Sighing wearily, Sumit came down heavily. "So, my current status of being 'jobless' is what disturbs you more than anything else, huh! How come all these things that suddenly started worrying you appeared all rosy before our marriage? Didn't we inform you about our family structure, about our lifestyle and everything else – how come everything appealed to you so much then and suddenly after just one year, those very things started asphyxiating you? After engagement you desperately wanted to leave Birmirpur for a better city life and today Mumbai has become an agony? You are such a double-faced traitor. For the last one year you just pretended to be a good wife and an obedient daughter-in-law. Moulina you just played with our emotions and simply betrayed us, something which I will never be able to forgive. Now without mincing any more words, please let me know your intent."

An awkward silence prevailed for a moment – while Sumit felt guilty of being harsh, Moulina didn't expect such an ugly turn of events. For Sumit the dam of forbearance had overflown, as he couldn't dangle with his situation anymore. Whereas Moulina unwillingly got into an uncomfortable zone and went completely blank. Realising the clumsiness of the current situation, Sumit volunteered to offer a solution and asked for his wife's reaction – "Well, listen Moulina I think we need to firmly decide and move ahead accordingly. A marriage succeeds on the fundamentals of mutual respect and understanding. And if that is missing, then no point in continuing with this social binding. You've known both the families now and there will always be some good and bad in each of them; take your time and let me know your decision – whether we should continue, or mutually part our ways."

Moulina was taken completely unawares by Sumit's sudden pronouncement. She least expected such an extreme step but managed to control her emotions and steadily reverted "Ours was an arranged marriage, so we just cannot take any such random decision without our parents' consent. Hence, I suggest you talk to my father on this matter before finalising anything."

"No, I am sorry, but I would never ever talk to such riffraff. I've clearly communicated it to him yesterday. Aren't you a full grown adult capable of taking your own decisions? Why the hell do you have to ask his opinion on every bloody thing? Let me know your decision in a week's time." An infuriated Sumit blasted over the phone before disconnecting.

The father-daughter were pretty much in a pickle. Their game-plan nosedived into troubled waters even before it could take off. On the other hand, sympathy poured in from all quarters and everybody supported Moulina's decision to stay back home and not give into her in-law's dowry demands. Suddenly the Ghoshs turned villainous to Chell's neighbours and relatives; whereas, the father-daughter got a new twist in their narrative to the outside world. Sanat's dogged determination would not let him quit the game yet, even at this unpropitious situation he kept pumping hatred in his daughter's mind.

"Did you observe that guy's audacity? Even after apologising he isn't ready to talk to me! And that too without a job in hand. Tomorrow if he gets a job, I wonder how will he treat your father." Sanat continued to play mind games with his daughter.

"But *Baba*, you're at fault. Even I'm shocked as to how can you use such cusswords…"

"Now forget that, I admit that it was a mistake made in the heat of the moment. But just imagine how unwanted you've become at your in-laws' and how Sumit hates you. He didn't make any effort to come down to quell the situation. Never mind my darling daughter. Even if he isn't willing to take you back, I'm here…*tera Baap abhi bhi zinda hai*, keep this in mind always."

"But *Baba*, your son-in-law never said that he is abandoning me. He just wants to know my opinion and I find it quite logical!" Moulina showed some courage to support her husband.

Sensing some sort of revolt from his daughter, Sanat ingeniously steered the conversation. In a situation where a father should've buried all the differences and moved forward to make his daughter's marriage work, Sanat chose to be a wrecker. He continued from where his daughter stopped…"Neither should you dump your husband. Marriages are made in heaven and we should make all efforts to keep them intact. But then I cannot allow my beautiful talented daughter to be treated unfairly. I think you should put forward a few conditions in case you decide to join him back in Mumbai."

"What are those conditions? And what if he doesn't agree to them? *Baba*, once again, I'm not sure what are you trying to achieve."

"Stop questioning. You continue to converse with Sumit normally and somehow get those certificates. Those are vital documents for further studies and future employments. I'll let you know those conditions in a day or two."

Sanat was miffed with his son-in-law's undaunted act of exposing his ugly side that besmirched his image among his nephews and nieces. He wanted to fix him and teach him a lesson. And with his daughter by his side, he would go to any extent to wreck vengeance on the Ghosh scion. But Sumit's possession of those certificates stood as a major hindrance to his vicious plans. As a matter of fact, he decided to meet DSP Ajay Dash who recently got posted to Birmirpur and discuss his concerns and give shape to a fitting retribution. The sultry late summer evening of May 2014, when DSP Dash and Sanat met at Caravan Bar over a drink, Moulina dialled her husband to put forward a few conditions that would save their marriage and ensure a quick reunion.

"You know what – I'm fortunate enough to have you as my husband. You have always taken good care of me, shielded my shortcomings and covered my mistakes. I really enjoy your company. Even though you had busy office schedules, you made it a point to go out with me for our daily evening walks. You make me laugh when I feel low and most importantly when I was with you, you rarely complained when I messed up with your morning cup of tea…" Moulina sounded emotional while narrating her stay at Mumbai and often giggled recalling few awkward moments.

"But more than a loving and caring husband, you've been a protective brother and an obedient son and that's what imbalances your responsibility towards your wife." Moulina took a long pause before uttering those lines.

From the manner in which his wife initiated the telephonic conversation, Sumit knew something harsh was coming his way. He was anyway ready for the worst, hence with a poker face and normal tone, he said, "Hmmm…so what is it now? Please come to the point."

"Well, please don't get me wrong, but we can't stay together unless your sister gets married and your parents stop visiting Mumbai. We have a life and I don't want your parents' interference every now and then. I can't stand Sunita's tantrums, it becomes difficult for me to adjust there." Moulina hesitantly unfolded her decision.

After an initial jolt, Sumit regained his composure. He didn't want to get emotionally exploited and hence firmly responded to his wife. "Okay…so these are your conditions? I wonder who fed you with these stupid ideas!"

He chuckled to himself and continued "So, basically, to save this marriage, I should get Sunita married off immediately and abandon my aged parents. And you actually thought I would value our one-year old relationship more than anything else that has been a part of my entire life? Blood is thicker than water to me. I'm afraid that in last one year you just couldn't read me, else you wouldn't, or rather shouldn't have uttered these words. Moulina, I am not justifying anything here, but for a second, just put yourself in my shoes and then you'll know what's what."

"I knew this is how you would react! As a son and a brother…that's obvious. Anyway, I'm not calling it off now – you have a couple of years to get Sunita married off and in the meantime, I can finish off my B.Ed. Therefore, please send me my certificates so that I can initiate my admission procedure." Moulina relaxed her stand with the prime objective of obtaining those documents from her husband.

Sumit however understood the underlying game that was wrapped with certain terms and conditions. He promptly responded "Two years' separation is too long a period. I don't think it's viable, and what if we fail to find a suitable guy for Sunita in next 700 days? Will you still comeback or extend your tenure?"

Moulina was completely flummoxed with such an unexpected question. She always knew Sumit to be sharp and intelligent and such a logical query caught her completely off-guard. Not knowing what to say, she mumbled hastily "Will see to it then, as for now – please arrange for my certificates."

Sumit smiled insidiously and sighed before responding "Let's see…will let you know."

TWENTY-EIGHT
2015

Rourkela, Odisha, India

Capitalising all his resources, Advocate Ganguly successfully tricked his opposition and triumphed in misplacing the divorce petition filed by the Chells. As a result, no hearing dates appeared before the family court in last four months, leaving the petitioner infuriated and baffled. Meanwhile, the senior counsellor carried out his own independent investigations for the interest of justice being meted out to his framed client. Ganguly deployed his close acquaintances in Birmirpur and Rourkela, who shadowed Sanat's daughter for a month and gathered vital information from Chell's neighbourhood as well as from the *adivasi* maid employed at their residence. Though the advocate was fascinated with the outcome, it was quite heart-breaking for his client.

When Ganguly shared the findings with Sumit, first came disbelief...He almost laughed at the lawyer's words hurled at him. It just couldn't be, he thought.

But just as Sumit was about to completely dismiss the allegations against Moulina, Ganguly produced a folder containing proofs of depositions held with the Dasgupta family from Bhubaneswar, whom Moulina was claimed to be living with for a month after her engagement with their younger son, early in 2009 – something which the Chells conveniently kept away from the Ghosh family. The engagement video and few family pictures from the Dasguptas featuring Moulina spoke volumes. It was Sanat who suggested Moulina to stay put at the Dasguptas, so that she could feel at home after her marriage – a suggestion unheard of and completely weird. However, since Moulina gelled well along with Dasgupta's daughter, they never resisted the proposal. It was after a month's stay that Moulina went back to her parents and never returned. Later to their surprise the engagement was called off and Sanat started blackmailing the Dasguptas.

Since the Bengali family had a reputation in the Odiya film industry, they feared vulnerability of besmirched reputation, societal gossips and filmy muck. Mr Dasgupta's daughter's fame as a playback singer was at stake – so, finally they gave in to Sanat's unreasonable demands. They hushed up the matter with an undisclosed amount and had to part with the gold jewellery that was gifted to Moulina by the Dasguptas as a token of love and affection for her.

Sumit stared at those documents as he leaned forward to hold them. At once, he felt a tightness in his throat and he couldn't utter a word. He looked up at his lawyer, whose face suddenly read pity for Sumit.

Sumit felt a hot rush of embarrassment in his cheeks. Everything to him was out of focus. The words he read were suddenly too much to comprehend. They seemed to be dancing in front of his eyes, making fun of him and ridiculing his trust in his better half. He struggled as he read on, with his mind losing battles and his heart wrenching at the immense betrayal he had silently, unknowingly been suffering all this while.

Sumit's hurt had already crossed the stage where it made him weak and feeble. Instead, he felt like he could destroy everything he had ever laid eyes on. His teeth gnashed in anger and he felt the heat rise up to his ears –*She ruined me. She ruined my whole life by lying to me again, and again, and again. All the promises of a blessed matrimony were bullshit. She never cared for me nor my family. Never. How could I not see all this while, that the person I'm sharing my life with, is such a con? How did it get past me?*

Further Ganguly also collected employment details of Moulina. He was slowly piling up those evidences against the opposition. With uncertainty over the divorce petition, only the maintenance petition was effectively left for the Chells to pursue at the court. Whilst Sumit tactfully avoided most of the hearing dates, Sanat and his daughter made it a point to remain present for each and every date – they would patiently wait for the entire first half and then walk up to the Judge's cabin and complain against the Ghosh descendant's absence for the hearing. However, Ganguly kept a tab on every activity of the Chells at the court and preferred striking back at the right time.

On one such hearing date, when Sumit failed to appear, Sanat and his daughter tirelessly waited outside the Magistrate's cabin and finally at around 4:30 pm when there weren't any more cases left for the day, they silently tucked into the room. After initial greetings, Sanat suddenly fell on his knees and with folded hands to the Magistrate, implored humbly. With teary eyes he begged justice for his daughter – "Sir for every hearing we eagerly wait for the respondent but he succeeds in dodging the dates. If you check for the last three dates, he never turned up. This is delaying the entire proceeding. That scoundrel has ruined my daughter's life. My Lord, please do something about it, even their lawyer is playing with the loopholes of the system. In fact, he has misplaced our petition too with the help of the clerks. Sir only you can help us…"

"Just a minute. I've often seen you sitting there in the corridor. What's your name? Which lawyer is representing you? Is that *Bombay walla party* respondent of your petition?" The sixty-year-old Magistrate who was due for his retirement in next couple of months asked few details after he heard Sanat's grievances.

"My Lord, I am Sanat Chell from Birmirpur and this is my daughter. Hrishikesh Basak is our lawyer. And my son-in-law is the main culprit and yes, he is from Mumbai." Sanat quickly delivered those lines and signalled his daughter to speak up.

Moulina who was standing next to her father, suddenly burst into tears while narrating her ill-fated story at her torturous in-laws'. The entire act was instantly orchestrated by Sanat who frequently whimpered in between to draw some sympathy from the Judge. After a while, just before the *Peshkars,* typist and the clerks could reach the spot to shoo away the father-daughter; the sexagenarian Magistrate sternly responded, "Stop all this nonsense. Remember this is family court and not your living room. I've witnessed all these for my entire career, those tears won't move me. Go and ask your lawyer to maintain a proper protocol and file relevant petitions to move this case further."

Ganguly reported each of those developments to his client back in Mumbai. The fact, that Sanat gave a written complaint to the Bar Association, made it difficult for the *Peshkars* to keep the divorce petition under wraps any longer. Hence it might come up anytime sooner or later. The opposition was also lobbying it hard to get a favourable judgement on the maintenance petition before the current Magistrate retired. All in all, it wasn't a conducive environment for the Ghosh family.

2015 was about to end and Ganguly could only stretch it a little further for the next appearing date, citing his inability to remain present on medical grounds. But early next year, Sumit would be left with no option but to visit Rourkela and appear before the Magistrate. Ganguly wanted the Magistrate to change before he could rearrange all the pieces and attack his opponent afresh. For the time being he continued to provide mental dope to his client, who was all nervous about facing the Judge from the witness-box and brave those tough questions. Sumit needed to tame his emotions and be practical in the battlefield where he would have a faceoff with someone, who once vowed to be his partner for life.

Three months later on a hot summer afternoon of March 2016, Ganguly called Sumit…

"Sumit, please don't get me wrong. Listen to me carefully, discuss it with your father and then let me know the decision." Ganguly sounded a bit serious when he called up his client this time. "We would then proceed accordingly," added the lawyer.

"What is it Sir?" Sumit who was anyway fidgety, got intrigued with his lawyer's sudden call.

"Well, last year went dawdling with the case. But this year seems to be full of actions. Look there has been few developments here, and on the basis of that I want to ask you something." The lawyer hesitantly informed. He reluctantly continued "I'm not only your lawyer, but also a well-wisher and hence from that perspective, I'll always suggest to you a path that will give you instant relief."

"Sir now don't create any more suspense and please let me know about those developments."

"Well…do you have a capacity to shell out two to three lakhs? Once and for all we could then settle the matter. The opposition has got some demands, which is in tune to around ten lakhs. We'll negotiate hard and bring it down to a bare minimum…" Just when Ganguly tried to explain the mathematics behind the opposition's demand, he was interrupted by his client.

With much annoyance and disappointment, Sumit stated "But Sir if we had to settle it out with money, then we could have done it much earlier. Just imagine the amount of time and money we've spent in the last two years – it's enormous. We knew the financial repercussion that we would face in the coming years, still we decided to fight for justice and stand up against the fake case. And now if such kind of suggestion comes from your end, then the entire purpose of this fight becomes futile."

"Hang on. Let me explain this to you – at this juncture the Chells are completely frustrated to see you come out unscathed. Their toothless attack and leaky defence have fallen flat to our strategies. The opposition lawyer has given us a hint of monetary settlement and this is the right time to negotiate and close the matter. Else just imagine – this case will run into several years and you've to bear all those expenses. In the process a lot of your precious time and energy will get wasted. Rather isn't it a smart idea to get rid of it by paying some amount?"

"But are you sure about all this? As far as I know, my father-in-law is hell-bent to wreak retribution on me. I still remember those police station days, where he openly threatened me to inextricably trap me with various sections of the law, so that it takes me more than a decade to come out clean." Sumit spelled out his apprehension to Ganguly.

"Look Sumit, that's exactly the pattern in which a fake 498A petitioner behaves. They remain all pumped up in the initial years and when you give them a tough fight, they soften their stance. Chell's lawyer even asked the Judge informally to allow you and your wife to meet at the court premises and amicably resolve the matter. So, your presence in next hearing date is compulsory. Hopefully we'll be able to close this case in the next couple of months."

End of April 2016, when the sweltering summer afternoons made life impossible under the blazing sun, the Sumit-Moulina case had set the courtroom temperature to soar even higher. For the first time in the last two years, the estranged couple met face to face, to fight for their honour and dignity. While Moulina was bubbling with confidence, Sumit was full of apprehensions. It was the first time that he would face the ultimate authority of a family court and feared aggressive grilling. But for Moulina, certain aspects like being well-versed in the local language, earlier interaction with the Judge, regular attendance at the court, all played to her advantage.

Whilst Sumit waited in the corridor for his turn, back in Haldia, his mother sought divine intervention through prayers and observances. While waiting, he caught a glimpse of Moulina, who was accompanied by her father and seated next to her lawyer. She looked ravishing in a cyan outfit. She looked different though – the simplicity gave away to some heavy makeup with light foundation, eyeliner, a deep red lipstick and a new hairdo. It was definitely not the girl Sumit knew, things had really changed in last couple of years.

After a brief wait, when the peon was heard shouting Sumit's name for the hearing, the junior Ghosh stood up firmly, closed his eyes and took a deep breath before he moved quickly towards the Judge's cabin. One of Ganguly's juniors accompanied him as well. At the entrance, the peon asked Sumit to remove his shoes and switch off his mobile.

An old gentleman was seated at the centre of the air-conditioned room facing a sofa captured by Advocate Basak, who was busy flipping the pages of the maintenance petition of his client. Moulina along with her father stood on the right hand side of the Judge and kept whispering among themselves. As soon as Sumit entered the room, he was asked to stand next to Moulina.

"Good afternoon Sir." Sumit greeted the Judge ignoring the presence of Sanat and his daughter beside him.

The *about-to-retire* Judge nodded his head in response and asked Sumit "Where is your lawyer? Let's start the proceeding soon." He then looked at his right and asked Sanat to leave and wait outside. Advocate Ganguly entered the cabin thereafter and apologised for being late. He too opened up a file and pulled out the petition copy. Meanwhile the aged Judge picked up the remote control to adjust the temperature and looked straight at Sumit and asked "Is she your wife? What happened between you two? Are you willing to take her back?"

"Yes Sir, she is my wife. We got married in 2012 and after a year she left me for some unknown reason and didn't return back. Instead initiated a false case against my family. Even though she is wrong, I'm ready to forgive her and take her back." Sumit replied promptly and then looked at his lawyer.

"Sir…this is a clear case of desertion." Ganguly paraphrased in support of his client.

Basak chuckled at his colleague's comment and was about to retort when the Judge signalled him to keep quiet, turned towards Moulina and quizzed her. "Well, your husband wants to take you back, what do you have to say on that?"

"No Sir. I won't go back to Mumbai. I don't want to return to that rotten hell anymore. I too have the right to live with dignity. They've ruined my life." A teary eyed Moulina complained and made her stance loud and clear.

The sexagenarian Judge heard the young couple, picked up the AC remote yet again to adjust the temperature and in his slow croaky voice continued "Look, you're a young couple. There are so many years left in your life. I suggest don't spoil this precious time in fighting a complex legal battle that probably can be solved by just talking to each other. I advise both of you to sit across the table, discuss it among yourselves and sort it out amicably. Go to the next room, have a one-to-one discussion and then come back to me. What do you think Mr Ganguly and Mr Basak?"

Both the lawyers nodded in affirmation and signalled their respective clients to meet them after their discussion was over. Moulina and Sumit were guided by the peon to a room next to the Judge's cabin.

With Sumit and Moulina seated face to face, an awkward silence prevailed in the room. Hesitation and consternation ruled both the individuals for initial few minutes. It was a mixed moment of angst and emotions for the Ghosh scion; whereas Chell's elder daughter grew alethophobic, avoided eye contact and perspired mildly. Sumit stood up, walked a few steps to his left and opened the windows – fresh air and bright sunlight engulfed the otherwise damp, dark and dusty room.

"*Kemon achho Moulina*…How are you? How is everybody at home?" Sumit finally broke the ice with those gentle questions.

"We're all doing fine. And you?" Moulina replied reluctantly.

"Oh yes, we are having a rocking time – just that we got a bit tired playing hide-n-seek with police administration; in the process *Baba's* blood pressure and sugar levels are at an all-time high and *Maa* has become insomniac. But gradually we are getting used to it. And well, I'm still jobless. We are certainly having some good times." Sumit replied sarcastically, and then bending towards his wife he politely continued, "I'm ready to take you back, Moulina. Let's forget all this and start with a new beginning. Please speak out your concerns and let's see how we can resolve them. I won't even ever ask you a single question about this entire ordeal. You're still a part of our family – your absence is acutely felt and you've been frequently remembered by *Baba, Maa* and Sunita at many instances in the last couple of years. Now please end this and come with me."

Her husband's constant supplication made Moulina emotional. She was on the verge of tears and almost choked up, but regained her consciousness about the situation and replied, "I don't think that option is open anymore. There's a difference in our mentality and I cannot adjust in that megacity life. It's better that we part ways…"

"But Moulina, please give it a thought before discarding it completely."

"No, it's impossible. Let's not waste our time anymore. And since Judge *Saheb* asked us to settle the matter through discussion…let me know, how much you can pay; accordingly, I'll withdraw all the ongoing court cases against you and your family." Moulina replied unrelentingly avoiding any eye contact with her husband.

Those words from Moulina, struck him like a thunderbolt. Irony just died a painful death. With clenched jaws and tight lips, he intensely stared at her for a moment before losing his cool. "Whatttt! W…What did you just say?"

"You heard it right. Give me thirty-five lakhs and you're a free man. After all you've some spousal obligations to fulfil." Moulina parroted those words casually, driving her husband crazy.

"Just get the hell out of here. I'm not going to give you a single penny. And if you think that we are going to succumb to your preposterous demands, then please be informed that I've enough evidences to prove this case a false one." Sumit almost shouted at his partner.

"Relax Mr Sumit. Think logically and then act accordingly. We can negotiate the amount anyway. But burdening yourself with a criminal case for the rest of your life isn't a smart choice at all. Let me know, by how much you can come down! See I've my expenses and that's what I'm asking for. I can't go back to my father for the same. I've enrolled for a B.Ed course and that's going to cost me huge…"

"A B.Ed course for 35 lakhs? Come on Moulina, even MBBS or Engineering courses aren't that expensive. Your imposter father now wants to build his bank balance out of this deal, huh? Go and tell him that it's not going to work." Sumit challenged his opponent before he stood up and stormed out of the room. Sanat who was waiting in the aisle outside with Basak, immediately entered the room to console his daughter.

After that hostile meeting and failed attempt to reach a settlement, both the parties ultimately decided to lock horns in a fierce legal battle. They walked away with their respective counsels while the next hearing date was fixed for June 2016. However, Ganguly wanted the matter to adjourn till the Magistrate retired. Accordingly, he dodged the system and succeeded in proroguing dates under the pretext of being unwell. Finally, by the year end, in the chilly month of December, the Judge hung up his boots leaving the Chells stranded in their pursuit of making some quick bucks.

Meanwhile with lot of efforts, Basak finally pulled out his client's divorce petition that went missing since the very month it was filed. But the timing wasn't conducive as the lower court generally experiences prolonged wait before another Judge was allotted. Meantime, Basak concentrated on the HC matter to lift the stay order on criminal proceedings against the Ghosh kin. This time with some financial support from the Chells, Basak had put all his resources to work in order to succeed at the HC.

Back in Mumbai, life wasn't easy for Sumit. Few of his income sources gradually dried up. Visiting faculty was never a steady option, once the semester got over it was a yearlong wait. Incidentally he met a *Bihari* who stayed with his brother at a nearby construction site and was looking for a job, and he happened to be an amazing cook. Struck by an idea to start a tiffin service for the office-goers, Sumit was quick to connect with some of his ex-colleagues and managed to get few clients to start with. Home-cooked food from his kitchen got delivered to nearby offices through *Dabbawallahs.* For further enhancement of his small setup, he created a Facebook page and shared it among his networks.

Amidst all odds, Mr and Mrs Ghosh led their routine life in Haldia. Just that, too many blank calls made to their landline number was worrisome, forcing them to suspend the BSNL connection permanently. But then that triggered innumerable missed-calls made to their mobile phone from unknown numbers, strangely nobody dialled them to talk. Finally, Sunita suggested that her parents get new SIM cards. She even gifted her Dad a smartphone specifically loaded with an automatic Call Recording App.

Every evening they went out for long walks along the bank of Haldi River. On one such Sunday when Chitra couldn't accompany her husband due to ill-health, Sushil was heading back home after a light session of freehand exercises. At the junction of Sector 4 and 5, he was stopped by a middle-aged anonymous person who sought directions to the *Mohana Market.* And just when the senior Ghosh was about to explain the route, two more guys appeared from nowhere and encompassed him. One of them pushed him while the other forcibly inserted a folded piece of paper in his shirt pocket. Sushil lost balance and tripped over a boulder on the footpath, hurting himself with a bruised knee. Even before he could raise an alarm, the trio immediately fled the spot on a bike.

The first of its kind incident left the family in utter shock. Sushil wanted to file a complaint at local *Thana,* but his wife opposed. Chitra didn't want to complicate things any further, instead she reported the assault to their lawyer. The folded piece of paper had a message typed on it in *Garamond* font, which stated *"Settle the case out-of-court. That will be good for you, else face consequences."*

After that attack on her husband – Chitra mostly accompanied him and never let Sushil venture out alone, they also avoided secluded areas. But things got slightly creepy when Ghosh's WagonR tyres were found deflated at the basement of their building and a piece of paper with the same message was tucked in between the car's wipers.

In Mumbai, Sumit wasn't spared from those anonymous calls either. For him the calls originated mostly from Delhi NCR that often ended up in abusive languages – so much so that he stopped receiving calls from unknown numbers. He also noticed a sudden rise in friend requests on his Facebook profile, mostly from unknown females with revealing pics as their DP.

On a lazy November afternoon of 2016, when Sumit was lackadaisically browsing his Facebook profile, he came across a few messages from someone named *Animesh Chowdhury;* who had no connection in common with him. As a result, all those messages landed up in the *"Others"* folder. This unknown guy from Jamshedpur was desperate to get in touch with the junior Ghosh. The messages sent consecutively in last three months provided new twists and turns to the ongoing court battle. It read…

'Hello Mr Sumit, I would like to talk to you regarding your ex in-laws – the Chells. My brother has received a marriage proposal from them for your sister-in-law, Lina. Can you please help us with some info? Thanks in advance.'

'Hi Mr Sumit, pls reply. We need to take a call based on your inputs. If you don't mind, can you pls provide me with your mobile no?'

'Pls respond. It would be of great help.'

After consulting with his lawyer, Sumit finally shared his contact number for further discussion. On a weekend the two gentlemen spoke for almost an hour and exchanged few vital information; which helped both in their pursuit of truth. Sumit recorded the entire conversation so that he could draw references during trial court sessions.

Animesh Chowdhury introduced himself as a Professor of Thermodynamics in a Jamshedpur based private Engineering College. Their family hailed from North Kolkata and his younger brother was a practicing doctor in a private Medical College in Ludhiana. Through some family acquaintances, the doctor received a marriage proposal from the Chells. All these were happening since the month of September 2016 – initial talks and meetings had already happened between Chowdhurys and the Chells. The boy and the girl liked each other and their families were in the process of finalizing the alliance. But it was during one of those casual conversations, that the Chowdhurys spotted some inconsistencies and kept the engagement ceremony on hold. They often noticed that whenever Chells were asked about their elder daughter's marital status, a cloud of uneasiness dampened the mood of discussion. However, after a lot of probing, the Chowdhurys could get the name of Chell's son-in-law and then after a series of Google and Facebook searches, ended up messaging Sumit.

"Mr Ghosh, on behalf of Chowdhury family I would like to thank you for agreeing to speak to us. I won't take much of your time but would need some information to clear a few of our doubts before we proceed with this alliance." A courteous husky voice on the other side of the phone sounded all gracious to Sumit.

"So did Sanat Chell voluntarily give out my name and details to you?" Sumit chuckled.

"No, he didn't. In fact, he was hesitant and often avoided discussing you. But in one of the conversations between my brother and Lina, your name featured along with the company where you worked for. And then on further enquiry, Lina briefly revealed that her elder sister had a bad marriage and got divorced. Later when we asked Mr Chell, he too told us the same. As a result of which we further asked him the specific reasons that led to the separation and that clearly made him uncomfortable..."

"Hmmm...so what did he say?" Sumit eagerly asked that and at the same time was expecting to hear something weird.

"Well Mr Ghosh, I know it's very personal, but before I answer that, why don't you tell me what led to your separation."

Displeased with the manner an unknown person started asking him random queries, Sumit had to be brutal and take full control over the conversation. Quite annoyingly he said, "Boss! Let me be very clear, technically we are not yet divorced and the matter is sub-judice. Hence expect limited information from my end on this matter. Rather, I would appreciate if you let me know what all stories that asshole has cooked up and fed you guys in order to make the alliance work. Well, apologies for using such slang. But believe me, no better word comes to my mind when I think of that bastard."

Gauging the tone of the conversation, the Professor was quick to apologise and continued "I'm extremely sorry if I've irked you unknowingly. I wasn't comfortable discussing what Chell told us and hence wanted it to hear from you."

"Are you cross-checking with me on what has been told to you? Or is it that you don't believe in Chell's version and have your own hypothesis? Look Animesh, I could have easily ignored your Facebook message and we wouldn't have had this conversation. But then I didn't want others to fall prey to somebody's greed and wrongdoings. My life is already spoiled and I don't even know how long it'll take me to come out of this imbroglio. So, I request you to shed all your inhibitions and talk straight."

"Okay…so we were told that the son-in-law was impotent. Though the family was aware of their son's inability, Sanat's daughter was always blamed. She was constantly taunted and tortured for not being able to conceive. Life became miserable for her and she wanted to end the marriage amicably, but her in-laws resisted and that's why Sanat had to take legal step and get his daughter divorced from her worthless husband."

"Wow! Such a lovely piece he has crafted for you all. This guy simply amazes me with his immense potential to narrate incredible stories. And his confidence in lying is just laudable." Though Sumit's blood boiled with rage, he kept his composure and with sarcasm in his voice continued to converse with the Professor. "And what made you realise that Chell might be faking it to you guys?"

"Honestly we believed him initially. But then the calculation didn't match and that's when we thought there must be something more to his version."

"Calculation? What's that?" Sumit asked in amazement.

"Let me explain – my brother while conversing with Lina, dug out tentative dates of your wedding followed by separation dates, etc. And we could figure out that Chell's version had loopholes. He mentioned that his daughter was subjected to physical and mental torture at in-laws for over three months. Now if I start reverse counting, then ideally by fourth month the families realised the medical problem. Which means between fourth-fifth month the girl would have to be expecting, add nine months to it…so fourteen months would have been the entire tenure. But your wife stayed with you for around a year and am sure modern-day couples don't start family planning on the day they exchange vows, atleast not in arranged marriages."

"Ummm…interesting! I guess it's a matter of common sense and some bit of logical thinking that can expose the falsity of any claims…"

"Okay, now that you have heard Mr Chell's version, would you mind sharing the actual reason for the separation?"

"Well, to be honest, even we are clueless as to why she chose to leave. However, in her FIR complaint she mentioned dowry demands, physical and mental torture being the ground for moving out. Needless to mention, those allegations were completely untrue, yet she slapped 498A, 323, 294, 506, 34 of IPC on us and wants to extort money. The last time I met her at family court, she demanded a hefty sum of money to settle the case out-of-court." Sumit gave an overview without divulging much details.

"Did the police arrest you? Section 498A is deadly and prima facie detains the husband and his family." The professor expressed shock over the fatal IPC that had shattered families.

"Luckily, we weren't arrested, but had to undergo a huge trauma. We are yet to recover from it. I would suggest you stay away from that family and save your brother's life. For further details of my ongoing case, you can visit Rourkela court any day and meet my lawyer to access the FIR copy and other relevant papers."

"Well Mr Sumit, I had one more query – do you have any knowledge of your sister-in-law's affair with any guy?"

"Look professor, when I got married, Lina had just completed her graduation and took admission in some college in Raipur. So even if she had some affair then, I wouldn't be knowing. But then the way you guys have started digging out information, what does your investigation say?"

"We were told by her ex-roomie that she was seeing a guy and it seems they had an intimate relationship too. And now that the 498A has come into light, we know what to do next."

"Completely upto you Sir. But let me remind you again, my matter is sub-judice, hence please don't drag me into your mess." Sumit warned the professor before ending the call.

The next day evening an elderly lady called up from Kolkata to thank Sumit for all those vital inputs and blessed him for saving her younger son's life and career. Sumit in turn requested her to be a witness and aid the trial proceedings that would attain new dimensions and help him to nail the culprits forever. The old lady agreed in principle and vowed to extend every possible help from the Chowdhury family in the future.

TWENTY-NINE
2017

Rourkela, Odisha, India

Another year went by, yet Sanat couldn't make any significant progress with those petitions. He was also clueless as to why Lina's alliance with the Chowdhurys didn't work out – just that all of a sudden, they went completely incommunicado. Frustrations mounted large, funds started shrivelling up and their neighbours' unwanted curiosity with the case made life a complete hell. Previous month the Chells weren't invited to a marriage function of a fellow Bengali family in their locality. From receiving sympathy to being ignored and isolated – clearly the public perception about the ongoing case had changed over the years. Moulina's matrimonial dispute had become the fuel for every gossip in Birmirpur's local neighbourhood. Those silent, curious stares and cold shoulder responses began to haunt her. At times she felt that these unnecessary hassles were all unwarranted for, life could have been smooth sailing had she chosen Mumbai over Birmirpur. Now that the arrow had already been released from the bow, there wasn't any better alternative left with her, but to team up with her father. To get rid of the growing discomfort and uneasiness around, Moulina had to avoid Birmirpur and stay at her aunt's place in Rourkela.

Sanat strongly believed that Advocate Mihir Ganguly had dampened all his efforts to catch upon the hip of his opponent. The cunning lawyer stood strong in between, safeguarding the interest of his client. Had he not been around, Sanat would've easily entrapped Sumit and coerced them into his demands. Though his earlier attempt to influence Ganguly's associates failed miserably; Sanat dared to try out his luck again. This time he met Ganguly directly at his desk in the court.

*"Ganguly Sir kettebela asibe...*When is he expected?" Sanat enquired with the associate who was busy setting up the table on a pleasant morning of January 2017.

"Sir is coming late today, will be here around 11 am." The intern who joined Ganguly just a month ago, responded with much apathy.

"Seems these days your Boss has lot of spare time, huh!! Anyway, inform him that Sanat Chell was here to see him and I'll be back after an hour."

For Ganguly it was relatively a relaxed day at work and hence decided to accompany Vidhi, his younger daughter, to school and thereafter reach court a bit late. It wasn't often that he got time to be with his daughters, but as a doting father, never missed any opportunity to be by their side whenever required. His elder daughter, Veena, would be appearing for the twelfth standard exam and aspired to be a Professor. Whilst Veena was close to her mother, Vidhi was an apple of her father's eye. At a tender age of thirteen, Vidhi closely observed her father tackle complicated cases and aimed to be a successful lawyer. She always liked the fact that policemen never meddle with lawyers.

At around noon that day, when Ganguly was about to dictate petitions to his associates, Sanat resurfaced from nowhere wearing a fake smile that annoyed the lawyer to the core. With folded hands he greeted the senior advocate *"Namaste* Sir *ji…*if you've few minutes, then can we go out for a cup of tea?"

"Chell *Babu* – how are you, *yahan kaise ana hua?* Unfortunately, a bloodsugar patient like me can't go out and have tea anytime. Plus, I came late today, so I've lots of work pending now. You can tell me here."

"But I wanted to discuss something one-on-one." Sanat hesitantly uttered after glancing at the other legal practitioners surrounding Ganguly's table.

"Don't dither, they're all my associates. We work as a unit. Carry on please…"

"Well, we don't get to see your client appearing before the court these days! It seems they aren't interested in pursuing the case further…"

"If my clients have to be here on every date, then what am I appointed for? How do I justify my fees?" Ganguly interjected with sarcasm even before Sanat could complete.

"Oh yes, absolutely. You're paramount to the progress of this case. But let me warn you, we are going to win this case, come what may. I won't hesitate to drag this to the HC followed by Supreme Court. Delhi *mein sab pehechan ka hai mera*, some of the SC lawyers were my batchmates. That's why I suggest, let's not further complicate this and come to a settlement. Why don't you convince your *Mumbaikar* client and end this hassle once and for all? Even we don't want Mr and Mrs Ghosh to deal with legal intricacies at this age. And for Sumit – there's a bright future left for him ahead, let him get out of this so that he can re-marry and settle down." Sanat's fake concern was quite evident in his tone and facial expressions.

"Wow, your noble thoughts for my client are really praiseworthy. But who is stopping you? Even my client is ready and that's why they were here last time."

"But Ganguly Sir, nothing comes free." Sanat uttered with a wicked grin and continued "You initiate the talks, we are ready to negotiate on the amount and most importantly if you succeed in closing the deal, I promise not to disappoint you and your team either."

The seasoned lawyer got absolutely cheesed off with Sanat's reckless and indomitable attitude, yet he stayed cool, ridiculed and purposely insulted the visitor "Hmmm…so basically you're here to put up a price for your daughter's service to my client, huh? You are such a pimp and you expect my client to shell out thirty, thirty-five lakhs for sleeping with your daughter for a year or so? Sanat *Babu,* at this price he could have afforded bespoke services from high profile callgirls in Mumbai quite easily. And unlike you, atleast they wouldn't have blackmailed him with fake cases. Now I request you to leave this place immediately before I lose my patience and charge you IPC 506 for criminal intimidation. And all these gentlemen here who had been witnessing your nonsense for the last ten minutes wouldn't hesitate to testify against you!"

Completely taken aback by Ganguly's offensive stance, Sanat was made to feel humiliated amidst the junior lawyers and associates who guffawed at those remarks. The slanderous statement from Ganguly didn't go well with him and he vowed to retaliate when time would be on his side. Before leaving the lawyer's desk, with clenched jaws and grinding teeths he uttered in disgust, "Ganguly Sir, I didn't expect this from you atleast. I was here to offer a solution and you…"

"Just leave! Your audacity to offer me a bribe is so appalling. We do maintain some professional ethics and it would be better if you respect the same. Let's meet on the next hearing date, till then *sayonara.* "

Meanwhile an elderly *Marwari* trustee of *Rani Sati Mandir* who had been hearing of Moulina's ill-fated marital discord and her struggle with court cases, offered help. Sanat was quick to grab the opportunity and with his daughter's consent they went ahead with it. A private school in Jaipur, sponsored by the *Marwari* community was looking for an English language teacher and Moulina bagged the offer with due recommendation from her hometown. Life was becoming difficult for her in Rourkela-Birmirpur and she realised that changing her location might freshen things up a bit. She was anyway getting drained and hemmed in by the ongoing legal battle, it wasn't what she expected. It definitely did not go as was persuaded by her father. Somewhere she felt a huge blunder has been done that led to these uncertainties. By now she could easily have started a family back in Mumbai had she been around with her husband. Sumit always adored kids and often desired to have a cute, naughty little one with chubby cheeks, just like his darling wifey. With shattered dreams, strangled hopes and bleak future; Moulina shifted to the *Pink City* in pursuit of a new beginning.

Thoroughly repulsed with Sanat's behaviour the previous month, Ganguly tweaked his strategy and decided to take the opposition head on. He adopted an aggressive stance through dual attack of family court and criminal court. Ganguly made necessary arrangements to lift the HC stay and pursue criminal proceedings at the lower court. Through criminal trail he would cross-examine the petitioner and her witnesses and beat the shit out of them.

On the contrary, Basak took all the credits of dismantling the stay order. He even charged a hefty fee from the Chells for the same. The otherwise dejected Sanat was all rhapsodic with the developments, it was a morale booster that enthused his dying hopes. Together they conspired to object the bail plea that the Ghoshs would require to submit at the session court for further proceedings. Ganguly was well aware of the opposition's probable move and briefed his client appropriately…

As instructed by his lawyer, Sumit gave an SOS call to bailer Iqbal Karim and pleaded for help. *"Iqbal Bhai, Sumit bol raha hoon…*I'm in need of your urgent help again. All this while our criminal proceedings at lower court was stayed by HC, but few days back, Chell's lawyer managed to lift the stay order. Now we've no option but to visit the court and take bail from the Magistrate. Since you bailed us out earlier, I thought of approaching you at this hour of crisis." Sumit narrated all in one breath and made it sound realistic.

*"Sumit Babu fikar mat karo…*I'll definitely help you, that's what I do for my living. You just tell me the dates and I'll arrange everything."

"Thank you so much Iqbal *Bhai.* Well, the session court has summoned us by middle of next month, that's 20th March, a Monday. So, may be by 15th we all will be there at Rourkela and within a day or two let's wrap it up. We must move swiftly without our opponent having an iota of our plan. I would also request you to be in touch with Ganguly Sir for further instructions."

"Haan ji, mein baat kar lunga Ganguly Sir se…apka kaam ho jayega," assured the bailer who was also double crossing the Ghosh family.

As expected, information got leaked out and Basak was asked to put all his resources at work, so that the bail petition hearing gets deferred and the entire family could be taken into custody for a day or two. Sanat this time was confident of getting the best deal out of his daughter's in-laws. Until now he wasn't able to get a grip on them, but putting Sumit and his family behind bars for atleast a day, would make things easier for him.

Contrarily Ganguly was tight lipped about his plan. None of his juniors were involved in this episode. He scrutinized every movement of Basak and meticulously planned an escape route…booked one of his known bailers with a hefty advance and took the Public Prosecutor in full confidence. Basak is widely known to take Wednesdays in a relaxed, lethargic manner…he often skipped the hump-day and allowed his junior associates to take control of things. And for other Wednesdays he generally turned up late after lunch hour.

Ganguly took full advantage of this lacunae – fixed the morning hour of a Wednesday, called in the entire Ghosh family at 9 am sharp on 8th March, took them to the Magistrate, got a couple of papers signed and bail was granted in a matter of thirty minutes flat without any hiccups. The known bailer of Ganguly was a Good Samaritan, he reached the court premises early and cooperated with the visitors throughout. For the entire thirty-forty minutes, around seven-eight associates of Ganguly escorted the Ghosh family to the Magistrate's chamber.

Yet again, Chell and his squad failed miserably to clamp their opposition. Ganguly's sharp presence of mind, vast experience and ability to think on his feet outwitted the Chells and left them in despondency.

THIRTY
2017

Mumbai, Maharashtra, India

Amidst tough circumstances, pushed to the brink and grasping for few shreds of joy, the natural ebb and flow of life had some good news for the Ghosh family. The news of Sunita's promotion came in as a gust of cool breeze in a parched desert. However, she was worried about her brother, whose smooth sailing career experienced shipwreck shudders and ceased to take off thereafter.

Though not a firm believer in astrology; Sunita still suggested her brother to consult somebody and get a clarity on the future scheme of things related to litigations and his career revival. With much reluctance, he met a couple of them but nobody gave him immediate remedy to his problems. The shadow-reader from Charni Road, the gemologist from Powai and the palmist from Vashi had one prediction in common – *"your opposition will be compelled to withdraw cases on you and your family, sooner or later."*

However, none could foretell a specific time frame nor could cite reasons for the withdrawal. On further probing he was suggested either to perform special *puja* and *havan*, or wear a specific gemstone to speed up things. Owing to the high cost of those astrological recommendations, Sumit decided not to pursue them and left it all to destiny.

Inspite of friendly and courteous colleagues, Moulina was completely alone in Jaipur. Her PG accommodation at Indra Nagar was almost 12 kilometres from the school at Gautam Vihar. Once in a fortnight she would visit her cousin, uncle Sarat's younger daughter, at her Engineering college hostel near Ajmer Highway. Else it was those four walls of her PG stay which she kept herself confined into. She rarely went out or spoke to anybody apart from her parents back in Birmirpur. Lokesh from Faridabad often visited her on alternate weekends. Life for Chell's elder daughter pretty much went back to the same loop as it was before her marriage. She always disliked extreme summers and Jaipur's blistering temperature wasn't any less than that of Birmirpur's blazing heat. She hated those long bus journey to Rourkela then and now she equally disfavoured the long travel to work every morning via school bus. More than anything she missed her husband's cosy cuddle that often took away the day's stress from her – Sumit actually used to care for her. He was sweet and supportive. Many a time, he would motivate her to pursue her dreams and took away all her frustrations during those evening walks. She missed embarrassing him in crowded local trains by hugging openly and stealing a kiss or two. Unknowingly things changed for the worst and there wasn't any scope of reconciliation. But those memories of togetherness kept haunting her, no matter how much she ignored them. Just when she was lost in those thoughts, her phone rang…

"*Kemon achis re…*dinner over?" enquired Sanat.

"Yes *Baba.* Had dinner almost an hour back, was just fiddling with the phone Apps."

"Be careful with your phone, *Beta.* And stay away from social media. Even if you intend to open a profile, take help from your brother and get a fake one. By no means should our opposition know your whereabouts. Incase they discover your employment details then it'll be a strong ground for them to object our maintenance plea. And you know, Sumit is a sharp guy. He can find out every detail from the internet through various permutations and combinations." Sanat warned his daughter, who wasn't tech savvy at all.

"*Achha aur ek baat* – a new Judge has joined the family court last week. Basak has fixed the next date in the first week of June. Apply for leaves citing your mother's illness, I'll book your tickets in the meantime. Basak is confident to close the family court matter in the next few months and get us a hefty maintenance amount." With the thought of bulk money, Sanat sounded all excited.

"*Baba,* was all this really necessary? We still have time to mend it. Let's quit this dangerous game and call for peace. This will ruin us all and lead nowhere…"

"Shut up! This is not the time to get emotional and cut off your nose to spite the face. Whatever I've been doing is for the betterment of our future. Forget all that has happened in the past; stay strong and focussed to fight it out."

Infuriated and embittered with her father, Moulina abruptly disconnected the call and banged the phone on her bed before switching off the light of her room.

Ganguly was eagerly waiting at the lobby of Hotel Rudra. It was 10 pm and yet his client had not checked in. He reached the hotel directly from his chamber and wanted to ratify the final version of the WS, which he would submit at the court next day. He made a few changes to the earlier draft and wanted Sumit's approval.

"Sorry to keep you waiting, Sir. My train stood still for over an hour at Jharsuguda station before getting a green signal. Right time at Rourkela was 8:45 pm and now see how late it eventually got."

"I thought so. Never mind, now that you're here we've the entire night to brief you on tomorrow's hearing," guffawed the lawyer.

Just to save time, Sumit ordered dinner at his hotel room and requested Ganguly to join in as well. The lawyer was hesitant at first, but finally gave in to his client's repeated request. Over the dinner they discussed about the changes made in the WS and how to face the new Judge, who according to Ganguly was sensible and pragmatic. This time around Sumit didn't have any inhibitions about facing the Judge or court proceedings, primarily because he had already experienced it in his last appearance. Contrarily Ganguly provided enough dope to survive a cross-examination and also conducted a mock-up session with Sumit. End of all, his only suggestion to Sumit was to analyse each question practically and not emotionally. Simultaneously he should also map the body language of his opponent to assess the situation and accordingly place his next question or answer. The mind game should be played fiercely, with due diligence.

It rained late that night leaving the road slick and the puddles quite still. The morning of 6th June was characterised by a pleasant breeze, bright blue sky with wonderful puffs of white radiating the heat back to the space. Sumit started his day quite normally without worrying much about how it would unfold. He went out for a morning stroll and while returning back to the hotel had his breakfast with piping hot *poori*, *sabzi* and a cup of cardamom tea. The roadside stalls near Rourkela station served lip-smacking breakfast items early in the morning.

Before leaving for the court, Sumit called up his parents back in Haldia, comforted them and asked them to have faith in Almighty. Chitra was edgy and kept chanting *Hanuman Chalisha* to get rid of daunting thoughts and gain inner strength.

At Ganguly's desk everybody was busy giving final touches to Sumit's WS before he signed on every page of the document that vehemently denied the allegations made by his wife. At around 11:30 am Ganguly asked his associates to escort Sumit straight to the record section, where he signed for his attendance. And then entered the Chell squad along with their lawyer Basak, who straight away asked for the sheet where Sumit signed and extended it to Moulina for her countersignature. Meanwhile Basak cracked some joke in Odiya which made the clerk cackle with laughter. The opposition camp was relatively in a lighter mood and their confident body language gave away vibes as if they had already won the battle. Sanat sported a casual look with a striped red Tee which looked weird against his dark complexion. Surprisingly this time around, Moulina who appeared in a magenta *kurti* and white leggings, didn't wear any makeup except thin *kajal* eyeliner and sported her simple look which Sumit always adored. However, the sight of his wife didn't evoke any emotions in him anymore. Instead, as advised by Ganguly, he kept analysing every sequence in the milieu. He also noticed his brother-in-law for the first time in the court. Something just clicked in his mind – hastily he pulled out his mobile phone, activated the 3G connection and tapped on the Facebook App. Next, he typed *"Lokesh Chell"* on the search bar, selected his profile and glanced through the details of his recent check-ins. Bingo!! He could connect the dots easily. Quickly he logged out and kept his phone on silent mode and proceeded towards the corridor.

The Judge's cabin bore a new nameplate *"Dr Subhendu Kumar Nayak"*, else every setup remained exactly the same as it was, a year back when Sumit last visited. The fifty-seven-year old hunchbacked, dyed hair gentleman with thick glasses carefully read those petitions while complete silence prevailed in the room. Ganguly and Basak were seated in the sofa whereas the petitioner and the defendant stood quietly by the side of the table. The other corner of the room was captured by a typist who awaited the Judge's dictation on the case.

Justice Nayak took a while to glance over the maintenance as well as the divorce petition and then looked at the solicitors and suggested "Let's hear the maintenance case first and then later we'll take up the divorce case, what say?"

"Yes, my Lord." Ganguly nodded in agreement.

"Yes, my Lord…but let me add here that this case is being dragged beyond imagination. My client, who is also a female, takes all the pain to come down from Delhi for each date. So, if we could also take up the divorce matter simultaneously then it would benefit us all." Basak tried to have an upper hand through his submission. However, Justice Nayak peered over his glasses, looked at Basak and said sternly, "Then go and file a transfer petition for Delhi to facilitate your client. Provision is already there in the books of law. Now let's continue with the maintenance plea please."

The experienced Judge pulled out a few papers, scribbled something on it and looked at Sumit. Politely he asked, "Now give me a few details about yourself before we commence the cross-examination…your name, father's name, your age, occupation and residential address."

Before answering those details Sumit looked at his counsel, who asked him to carry on with a nod. He gulped, took a pause and answered, "Sumit Ghosh, S/O Sushil Ghosh, 38 years, unemployed, and I am from Haldia."

As soon as Sumit completed, Moulina objected and complained "Sir, he is lying. He stays in Mumbai and not in Haldia."

Vexed with such unexpected revolt from the petitioner, Justice Nayak looked at Moulina and said, "Please keep calm, you'll get your chance to cross question him. Till then hold your horses." The Judge then looked at Sumit and questioned "Is she correct about your current residential details?"

"Sir, let me clarify…I shuttle between Mumbai and Haldia quite often. But after she had lodged a false case against us and with no job in hand, I currently stay in Haldia to look after my aged parents. And then again, I've to visit Mumbai sometimes, where my unmarried sister stays all alone. She is the sole breadwinner of our family and stays there on rent. That's all, your honour."

Not convinced with the response, Moulina was about to rebut but Basak signalled her to hold on. Contrarily Ganguly got impressed with his client's composure and the way he conveyed those key points to the Judge who presided over the case.

Keeping his spectacles aside, the Judge continued to probe Sumit. "I believe the earlier Judge tried for a reconciliation but failed and now your wife wants maintenance from you. What do you have to say? You can start cross-examining her, while I take a note of the proceedings. Go ahead."

"My Lord. I am incapable of providing any maintenance to her as I'm unemployed for the last three years, the main reason being those fake IPCs against me. Every time I tried cracking an interview, the company HR would find out these criminal charges against me through background verification and cancel my appointment. My career is ruined because of her. It was her father who called up my past employer and bad-mouthed me. My reputation in the professional circle was ruptured badly. And…"

"Oh, I see. In that case Mr Sumit, you can file a petition and claim maintenance from your wife, only if she is earning. Our law has that provision too, I'm just informing you," Justice Nayak intervened the narration of the defendant.

"Thank you, Sir. I'll consult with my counsel about it. And yes, let me inform this court that she is currently employed. She is an able-bodied, highly qualified individual; why would she need maintenance from me?" Sumit gambled here by declaring Moulina's employment without having proper evidence and simultaneously mapped her body language.

With such revelations by her husband, Moulina grew fidgety and conscious. She turned red, stuttered and revolted. Rubbishing her employment status, she said, "Sir, this is utter nonsense. I'm pursuing my B.Ed from Delhi and here this guy is assertive about my job. Ridiculous!" Moulina was perspiring in the AC room, yet was on top of her voice to prove her husband wrong.

Undeterred with his wife's claim, Sumit aggressively questioned, "So can you show some kind of proof to this court? Any document that can prove that you're pursuing your B.Ed from Delhi? Why don't you show your journey ticket from Delhi to Rourkela? Huh! How far will you defend these falsehoods?"

Without even expecting any answer from Moulina, Sumit lowered his tone and politely addressed the Judge again. "Sir…let me tell you, from the very beginning this lady has been faking. Everything she wrote in the FIR is fictitious. And I've enough evidences to prove those allegations wrong. She and her father are trying to extort huge money from us. In fact, when the earlier Judge asked us to resolve the matter amicably, she asked for thirty-five lakhs to settle this matter!"

Even before Sumit could utter anything more, Moulina looked at the Judge and said, "Sir, I think he is talking all trash. This gentleman is just trying to develop a convincing story and mislead this court, in order to avoid the maintenance. He is conveniently employed with his earlier employer and drawing a handsome salary. He is also enjoying a lavish life in Mumbai."

Looking at his wife, Sumit said politely, "Please don't have this misconception. I've each and every documentary evidence to prove you wrong. And I'll bring it up when the right time comes." He then looked at the Judge and continued…"Sir as far as her allegations of my employment status is concerned, I can furnish my resignation letter and relieving letter from the employer she mentioned in her FIR."

"Now Sir, let me disclose few more facts about this lady…she is a qualified and talented vocalist, an ex-AIR artist. Before our marriage she was employed with Municipal College and even now she is working in Jaipur. She doesn't even live in Delhi, it's her brother who stays in the NCR. And I'm also sure that this time round, her brother travelled from Delhi to Jaipur and accompanied her to Rourkela. She has created all this fake drama just to harass us and squeeze money from us. I am not in a position to pay any maintenance. However, I'm ready to forgive her and take her back as my wife with full dignity. That's all I have to say, my Lord."

Justice Nayak was listening to Sumit carefully and paraphrasing it for the typist at certain intervals of the entire narrative. He then turned at Moulina and with a grin said, "Look he is willing to take you back…"

Moulina who suffered a jolt from the fact that her husband knew every details of her whereabouts, quickly regained her senses and implored "No Sir. That's something impossible for me to do. I've left that place and would never go back again."

"Okay. So, you left your in-laws voluntarily? Or were you asked to leave?" enquired the Judge.

"I left out of my own will."

"Sir, this is a clear case of abandonment and hence non-maintainable. Moreover, my client is ready to take the petitioner back in his family and lead a harmonious life."

Ganguly filled in to conclude the day's hearing session. Surprisingly Basak chose to remain quiet and didn't attempt to invalidate his colleague.

After an exhaustive session that went on for an hour, the court was adjourned for lunch. The next and last date of hearing for the maintenance plea was fixed for mid-July, after consulting both the parties. Ganguly was visibly elated with the day's proceeding. His young client came through as a surprise package in maintaining constant pressure on the opposition and left them striving hard. On the other hand, Moulina emerged completely perplexed and tensed at the same time. Things didn't quite go as they thought it would, and now some of her bluffs were even recorded as well, which couldn't be retracted.

Ganguly had his plans in place for the next hearing. Moulina's confessions at the family court would be highly beneficial to him when he would take charge of the criminal trial proceedings later. For the July date, he asked Sumit to get some specific evidences to prove the opposition wrong. He aimed to file a deposition in the shape of an affidavit under *order 18, rule 4 CPC* with all the documentary evidences annexed to it. By doing this Ganguly planned to corner his opposition and get a favourable judgement for his client.

The next thirty days just whizzed past. Ganguly decided to file twelve evidences altogether for the final leg of the hearing. Photographs, transcripts, certificates, call-recordings, CCTV footages and audio recordings were all stacked up for a fervid attack on the Chell squad. Out of all – the voice recording of Moulina demanding money to settle the case was most vital. Sumit's presence of mind prompted him to record the entire conversation when they met to discuss amiable settlement at the behest of the earlier Judge. Few photographs of the couple together at Mumbai's restaurant, musical concerts and key landmarks would be appended to prove that they indeed led a harmonious conjugal life. Transcripts of SMSes sent by Sanat to threaten the Ghosh family would also act in their favour. CCTV footages of the Mumbai flat would clearly prove the fact that the couple frequented outside and Moulina was never kept in confinement as being claimed in the FIR. Abusive calls from Sanat that were earlier recorded, were cut into a CD for court submission. Ganguly, equiped with all his ammunitions was raring to go.

Conversely, Basak took it easy for the final hearing date. He literally did nothing apart from instructing Moulina how to cross-examine her husband. He knew that if the opposition furnished employment termination letter, then they won't have any strong ground to claim maintenance from the Ghosh scion. Basak envisaged a bleak future of this case until a sudden Google search result brought in fresh level of ebullience into the case. He planned a scathing attack with the new found information and briefed Moulina accordingly.

THIRTY-ONE
2017

Rourkela, Odisha, India

CP No. 244/2014 was listed third for hearing before Justice Nayak on 14th July. Sumit visited the Oath Commissioner, signed the affidavit in the officer's presence and submitted his deposition. A copy was then handed over to the opposition's lawyer for reference. It sent shivers down the spine, when Moulina discovered twelve documents enlisted in form of evidences.

Worried and gasping for air, with a feeble voice she asked her lawyer, "Now what? They've furnished a dozen documents to counter our statements. Do something Basak Sir, else this will go completely out of our grip."

"Let them present thousands of those documents. What we possess is a *BrahMos*…just one is enough to create a havoc. You relax and rehearse for the cross. It's a make or break situation now." Basak lent some encouragement to his visibly terrified client.

Sumit was relaxed yet cautious. He could see the petitioner gang stirred up a bit, but never underestimated them. He intensely watched every movement of his rivals in the court premise and pretended to remain engrossed in the game of *Candy-Crush.*

Finally, around noon, they were called in. The Judge might have had a tough day with the previous two hearings, which almost took the first half of the day. With ruffled hair exposing mild baldness, Justice Nayak quickly glanced through the papers as he welcomed the lawyers of the petitioner and defendant with a courteous smile. Ganguly took the lead, opened his file and promptly handed over his client's deposition, flipped onto the last page, read through the evidences and handed over each document to the Magistrate.

"Your Lordship, here goes the proof that supports all claims made by my client. This is the original relieving letter from his previous employer. Here goes the CD with all requisite call recordings and CCTV footages. And these are some of the photographs that captures beautiful moments of a husband-wife relationship, wife and mother-in-law bonding during the petitioner's tenure at her in-laws."

The utilitarian, proficient Judge heard Ganguly's verse patiently and took some time to tally those evidences along with various paras of the affidavit. The entire bunch of documents was then handed over to the clerk for court submission. All this while Moulina stood still, staring blankly at the Judge. Her lips trembled and ears turned red, yet she could do nothing. Even though the room was chilly, sweat stood at the roots of her hair and ran down behind her ears. She looked at Basak in despair, who in turn nodded his head and signalled her to keep calm. The silent communication between them didn't go unnoticed by Sumit. He also managed to get a peekaboo of a printout that was stacked within the file that Basak possessed…the logo emblem at the corner of the page seemed to be quite familiar to him. He was vigilant enough to understand on what lines he possibly could be attacked by the petitioner.

Slowly and steadily Moulina regained confidence and geared up for a fierce attack on her husband. After receiving a go ahead from Justice Nayak, she initiated cross-questioning. With a harsh tone and aggressive stance, she asked "Can you tell this court – how do you maintain yourself in such an expensive city of Mumbai without any source of income?"

"I'm completely dependent on my sister. She is now the sole earning member in our family." Sumit answered calmly without even looking at Moulina.

"But as far as I know, her entry level income won't suffice to lead a basic life in Mumbai. By the way, how much is her monthly take home?"

"Why should I tell you that? I'm not bound to disclose Sunita's salary details here." Sumit replied with much annoyance and then looked at the Judge and continued "Your Honour, she is asking irrelevant questions which has no connection to this case."

The Judge peered over his glasses, looked at Moulina and remarked "Request you to ask questions pertaining to your maintenance and not on how he maintains himself." With that comment, Ganguly gave a scornful smile and exchanged glances with his colleague. Meanwhile the typist took a quick break and chugged down half a bottle of water before engaging his fingers on the keyboard.

Indomitably Moulina continued with her cross-questioning, looked at the Judge and continued "Sir, I am asking all this because this guy is trying to mislead all of us. Here I want to bring into your notice that Mr Sumit is currently working as a Visiting Faculty with *Pernod Institute of Management* and I can prove the same." With that startling revelation she signalled Basak to bring forth the documents and show it to the Magistrate.

While Basak firmly pulled up few printouts from his file and advanced towards the Judge's desk, Ganguly suffered an unanticipated jolt of disbelief. He avoided eye contact with Sumit and kept thinking hard about his next course of action. Sumit however maintained his composure and let his opponent present those documents.

"My Lord, the defendant earlier today deposited the relieving letter from his employer but somehow supressed his current employment status with this management institute. Please have a look at these printouts – this is the homepage which talks about the college in detail and this one displays faculty profiles with their respective photos. I would now like to draw your attention to those details enlisted at number four with the name '*Prof. Sumit Ghosh*'. That's all your Honour." Basak made a strong comeback with those solid evidences and was confident about the icing on the cake.

A sense of accomplishment prevailed among the petitioner gang until Sumit opened up to explain the discrepancies. He politely asked the Judge to provide him a chance to elucidate the matter and Justice Nayak nodded in affirmation.

"Sir, I won't deny my involvement with this college. But the way it has been put across, is completely incorrect. If you look at the second printout – there's a section for permanent faculty and my profile isn't listed there, which means I'm not an employee of this institute. Now let me explain how I got featured here. MBA colleges generally have industry-academics interface and I was invited to take a module on Digital Marketing, when I was holding a position of Digital Marketer with my previous organisation. And if you carefully note the descriptor of my profile – it mentions my name, qualification, my designation along with the company's name. Which makes it clear that the college and the company were in an agreement to share resources to impart industry knowledge to the budding managers. This happened way back in early 2014, but the college hasn't updated their webpage since then."

"Yes Sir, these days, colleges are selective in sharing information on their webpage to attract new admissions. My client is no way employed with them and the petitioner's claim here is completely baseless." Ganguly ascertained after listening to Sumit's explanation.

"Hmm…being a plaintiff do you have anything else to ask?" the Justice asked Moulina while he kept those printouts aside and prepared himself to dictate the summary of the day's hearing to the typist.

"No Sir…" a dejected Moulina replied in bewilderment.

"Okay. Please wait outside and sign the papers before you leave." Justice Nayak informed both the parties, then looked at their lawyers and instructed, "Next date, come prepared for the argument of this case, judgment will follow thereafter. Hopefully we'll be able to close this soon."

Ganguly was exultant, he patted Sumit's back for putting up a brave show, appreciated his sangfroid throughout and applauded his logical, convincing responses.

Contrarily Basak failed to guard his fort due to lack of evidences. For some unknown reason, the Chells never shared full information with him which was a major roadblock in defending the complainant. Basak could prognosticate an inevitable defeat in the hands of the opposition. He even opted to quit and was ready to sign an NOC, but on Sanat's insistence he retracted on his decision.

"We are in a fix now and don't see a great judgment coming our way." Basak warned his client.

"Please do something about it, Basak *Babu*. A lot depends on the verdict of this particular case. My social standing, prestige, honour and Moulina's future; everything is at stake. It'll be devastating to see them win," pleaded Sanat knowing the difficulty in defending all the bluffs and idiosyncratic beliefs.

"Now the only way out is to keep lingering with this case until Justice Nayak is out of the system. But let me apprise you that the Ghoshs are sitting on enormous evidences and the ones they presented are just a trailer of a bigger show. I am sure they've retained a larger chunk to corner us during the criminal trials. Ganguly is a rogue when it comes to defending his client. Also, I wonder how could you miss out on two key IPCs in your FIR – 377 and 497! The offence of unnatural sex and adultery could have bamboozled them."

"Basak *Babu*, we never thought that this will get dragged into such complicated litigation..."

"Two non-bailable IPCs of 377 and 498A could have tightened the noose around your opposition. Anyway, now it's too late to even think of including any such sections. Let me see what I can do to delay the proceedings." Basak sunk in deep thought to get rid of the current situation, while assuring the best to his client.

After fighting tooth-and-nail, and almost taming the bull by the horns; the Ghosh squad had to give into Advocate Basak's treacherous moves, who threw all his weight behind delaying the argument session. And just days before the argument date in the month of August; Moulina filed another petition on behest of her counsel – this time seeking court permission to call in the accused for another round of cross-examination as the earlier one was inconclusive. Ganguly was quick to sense the anomaly and advised Sumit to stay away while he managed those dates.

Finally, in November the news of Justice Nayak's transfer brought in some respite to the Chells. They awaited the next Judge to resume office and then would strategize accordingly. Meanwhile frustration swamped Ganguly; he was so close yet had to let go off his grip. Just one victory could have destroyed the house of cards created by the Chells. However, he kept his cool and swiftly went on with his next tactical move. He made all arrangements to initiate the criminal court proceedings.

Ganguly started preparing for a thorough questionnaire after going through the entire case history of his client along with relevant case studies and judgements from several HCs and the SC. He also channelized his resources to get subtle support from the Public Prosecutor. Just when Ganguly was gradually organizing his arsenals for the ultimate combat, the criminal court Judge got transferred...shattering all his hopes and ruining his plans.

With no more court dates to attend in the next few months, Sumit started looking for a job in Mumbai. He was interviewed by a couple of top notch firms; however, his gap in service wasn't accepted, and he had to face harsh rejections. His frequency of interaction with his counsel dropped drastically, but the duration increased. In one such interaction Ganguly predicted the future behaviour of the litigant based on the present circumstances.

"Good evening Sir. Any update on the next date? When are the Judges expected to join?"

"*Ruko yaar, abhi kahan?* Replacements don't happen so fast...these bureaucratic procedures take months to materialise. But we are fully prepared, it's just a matter of time before we burst the bubble of their misconception."

"Okay Sir. But do you see the father-daughter at the court premises these days?"

"Sanat is often seen. He even tried to befriend my juniors in a couple of occasions. But I've never seen your wife since that last cross session. And if my accomplice is to be believed, she is nowhere in the vicinity of Birmirpur or Rourkela. She has skedaddled. Mark my word, when the court sends out summons through registered post it'll have no receivers and this will further delay the general proceedings of criminal court..."

"But Sir, isn't it the state's responsibility to get her before the court and make her face the trial?"

"Absolutely. The court would order the IO to produce her and the police would conveniently report her absconding. That's why I request you to locate her. If possible, get her new coordinates, so that we can send the court letter directly to her."

"Sir, it's almost impossible for me to get that info. Through a little bit of cyber stalking on her brother and cousins, I know for sure that she is somewhere in North India. Beyond this I've no clue. And the fact that Moulina isn't present on social media makes it further tough to map her moves."

"Hmm...keep trying. And finally, if you don't succeed, we've to get a non-bailable warrant issued in her name. Only worry is that it would take time."

"Is that possible Sir?"

"Yes, initially we'll send out summons, if she fails to appear, we get a bailable warrant against her and finally a non-bailable warrant."

THIRTY-TWO
2018

Mumbai, Maharashtra, India

Sumit's case entered into its fourth consecutive year. Just one tragic incident had taken away all of life's shine and glitter. He lived one day at a time, with no plans for the future which appeared bleak and uncertain. Often those railway tracks, highriser terraces, ceiling fans, and sleeping pills enticed him to end all the sufferings which he had been silently tolerating all these months and years. Time and again circumstances made him weak and feeble, pushing him to think the ultimatum. But then self-immolation would mean gifting away victory to the opposition, it would also bring in excessive trauma to his aged parents. Atleast they deserved much better. Amidst all these melancholic thoughts, he would finally get an inner kick and tell himself –*There are many who had undergone much worse than this. These are phases of life and this too shall pass. Let's now beat them at their own game.*

His visits to *Siddhivinayak and Babulnath temple, Haji Ali and Mahim dargah, Mahim church* had one prayer in common – an earnest request to the Almighty to draw an end to the ongoing legal tussle, so that he could start living again.

The fact that his wife suddenly went incognito and couldn't be traced was bothering Sumit for a while. He tried all his sources in Rourkela without any success. He got in touch with a couple of private detective agencies too, but their lack of astuteness discouraged him to go further. He feared some new game plan of the opposition through this disappearance act.

In last four years Sumit had often experienced empyrean support in various avatars that pulled him out of deepest troubles at the last moment. And this time around it wasn't any different either – Dhruv Rathore, one of his engineering buddies, who had last called up from Jaipur in 2012 to congratulate him on his wedding, jokingly sent him a snapshot of a sari clad lady surrounded by kids in school uniform. The WhatsApp message accompanying the picture read *'Look what I've found…ur wife's clone. Or are u guys here in my city n I'm just unaware of it! Scene kya hai bro?'*

Sumit was dumbstruck to find the picture having close resemblance to Moulina and the fact that Dhruv might have clicked it somewhere in Jaipur drove him mad with excitement. With trembling fingers, he immediately dialled Dhruv for a detailed discussion.

Way back in their mechanical engineering days, Sumit and Dhruv along with a couple of Malyali guys were a part of the backbenchers' gang who were always upto annoying their Aerodynamics lecturer. College life was all rocking and boisterous. And then after graduation Sumit went on to pursue his MBA, while Dhruv got into their family business in Gurgaon. In fact, when Sumit got his first job and had to shift to Gurgaon, Dhruv helped him find an accommodation in that unknown city. Life advanced and so did their career; Sumit later relocated to Mumbai and almost after four-five years Dhruv left for Jaipur. He had to quit and shutdown his business due to some issues with his Japanese supplier. Back in Jaipur, Dhruv made good use of huge acres of ancestral land and got into farming and agriculture. Today he was among the largest producers of Aloe Vera in Rajasthan and doing pretty well. Four years back he was blessed with a baby boy and remained busy with his kid apart from managing business. Even in the busiest phase of each other's life, Dhruv and Sumit had been in contact and often exchanged jokes and memes over WhatsApp. The latest message from Dhruv was a complete shocker…either a pure coincidence or some kind of divine miracle!!!

After the initial hi-hello which eventually ended up in abusive college lingo and exchanging few info on their old acquaintances and reliving nostalgia, Sumit had to open up and let his batch-mate know about his troubled marriage. Dhruv felt sorry for his friend and vowed to help him in every possible manner.

"Tell me something, how did you happen to click this photo? More than that, how the hell did you recognise this very female as my wife?" Sumit eagerly asked.

"Well…the lady in this picture is a newly appointed English teacher in my son's school. I often visit his school to pick him up. That particular day in the corridor this lady was surrounded by few kids and when she turned around, I was surprised to find her looks so identical to that of your wife…" even before Dhruv could finish, Sumit interjected to clarify his doubt.

"*Abey…kyun mazak kar raha hai?* How do you even know about Moulina's looks? You were not even there during my wedding! This is so bloody confusing."

"Relax dude. Let me explain…I wasn't sure about this teacher and that's why I immediately clicked her photo and later compared it with the cover photo of your Facebook which you had uploaded way back during your wedding days. And that's when I figured out that this one might be a look alike or she herself…"

"But why would you retain my wedding pics? They aren't even there in my Facebook album anymore. *Tharki saale, doosro ke biwi ko stalk karta hai?*" Sumit cracked up laughing at Dhruv.

"*Nahi yaar…*It so happened that, I started collecting photos of our old gang members from their Facebook profiles to create a collage. I've everybody's snap from their college days, followed by their wedding picture and meanwhile if they've become parents, I've that too. So that's why I had your wedding picture stored in my laptop folder."

In next few weeks with Dhruv's help, Sumit got all the crucial information about the English teacher who turned out to be none other than *Mrs Moulina Ghosh*. Details about her appointment date, salary breakup, mobile number and PG address were all dredged up without any shadow of doubt. Back in Rourkela, Ganguly was completely thrilled to learn the whereabouts of the opposition. He was equally amazed to find out how an average Bengali guy in Sumit pulled out a *James Bond* act in order to locate the subject and get all the requisite details. Only an immaculate soul strives to prove his innocence unlike the corrupts who have no qualms about their misdeeds.

In last couple of months, Ganguly altered his work schedule completely to fit in his younger daughter's study timetable. With CBSE exams round the corner, the legal practitioner preferred spending few hours daily with his daughter. Though Vidhi went for private tuitions, she would eagerly wait for her father to clear a few doubts regarding Mathematics, Geography and English. She also enjoyed those courtroom stories in between studies, which her dad often narrated.

Except retaining few complicated ones, Ganguly assigned most of the ongoing cases to his subordinates. Only on weekends he was available at his chamber, and through the rest of the weekdays, he worked from home. This rejig in his work itinerary also made him a rare figure in the court for a month or so. However, he kept a close tab on the cases he retained so that it remained well within his control.

Finally, in the month of April 2018, when a lady Judge joined the criminal court of Rourkela; Ganguly didn't hesitate to push for court summons to the petitioner in order to initiate criminal trial proceedings.

On a sweltering summer afternoon, when the postman from local Post Office reached Chell's Birmirpur address to deliver a registered letter, he met Sanat's bewildered gaze who was reluctant to receive it on his daughter's behalf. Instead, with a dry smile on his face, Sanat tucked a folded hundred rupee note into the postman's chest pocket and asked him to mention *"House locked, family out of station."*

That very evening Sanat went and met Basak to understand the next course of action. He was very upset with the court summons and felt that they might be slowly losing all control over the case.

"Basak *Babu,* what's happening? Why a court summons to my daughter all of a sudden? And how is it that you're not aware of it? What are your sources doing?" Sanat bombarded his lawyer with questions in a pretty annoying tone.

"Well, Ganguly must have initiated trial proceedings. With no progress in the family court they now aim to expedite the criminal matter. And that's why Moulina has been summoned…it's a normal practice."

"So, what's your rescue plan? It seems you're unable to keep up with the pace of your colleague. Ganguly has his game-plan chalked out well in advance whereas you are just struggling here." Sanat deliberately dragged the opposition's counsel into the discussion and took a jibe at his own lawyer.

"Isn't that obvious Mr Chell? Ganguly's client shares every detail with him which helps him to thoroughly prepare for the fight. Unlike me, who is kept in the dark on most of the past incidents related to this case," Basak too voiced his concern.

"Anyway, I suggest that you do not to get bogged down with the court notices. There will be a couple of them on its way in next few weeks, before they approach the Magistrate and get bailable warrant issued against your daughter. But I'll make sure that this gets delayed to the maximum. Meanwhile, why don't you channelize some of your resources, reach out to the Ghosh family and settle the case once and for all? Even I can initiate the process, if you want." Basak reached out for the water bottle kept alongside his working table and then after wiping his sweating forehead with a towel he continued "Look, you only had mentioned earlier that this litigation happened by chance and wasn't intentional. If the objective is to pressurise your opposition and get a monetary settlement, then this is the right time to negotiate. If the trial begins and they succeed, then you won't get a penny from them."

Basak's unexpected suggestion struck him dumb, with a discombobulated look Sanat expressed himself, "I'm shocked to see you talk like a lost soldier. When I was looking for a lawyer, Dash referred to you as a ferocious warrior. But it seems you've lost all the fizz. It's really disheartening to see that a senior counsel of your stature is in no mood to concoct a counter-attack."

"Chell *Babu*, court cases are won by citing evidences and not through emotional storytelling. If my sources are to be believed, Ganguly possesses a few solid evidences which when brought up during trial will wreak havoc. And what do you have to back your claims? Just a bunch of 161 statements given by your close acquaintances…huh! Half of them will mumble and fumble, while rest will talk gibberish when exposed to rigorous cross-questioning. Game over…that's it." Basak let out his frustration by pointing out the inadequacies in Sanat's planning.

Realising the trial proceedings to be a ticking bomb, Sanat swallowed his attitude and softened his stance towards Basak. He solicited his lawyer in an unassertive tone…"Can't we do anything about it? Isn't there a way out?"

"Well, we are professional lawyers and our fraternity is always up with Plan-B for every situation. We can manufacture absolutely anything and go to any extent to defend our client's interest. To get you out of this situation I've a blueprint that would help you achieve your sole objective of implicating your rivals. But the question is, will you be willing to take that risk?"

With a bemused expression on his face Sanat hesitantly asked, "Unless I get to know the plan, how can I commit?"

"Are your sure, Chell *Babu*? This isn't easy but if well executed then you'll have an upper hand on this case."

"Don't hesitate to share your plan. Please go ahead."

Basak looked at his assistant and signalled him. The junior associate adjusted the fan regulator to maximum before leaving the room. Revolving sound of the ceiling fan would prevent their conversation to penetrate the walls of the room. After much deliberation the senior counsel finally opened up with his lethal plan to thwart his nemesis…

"Okay…for next few weeks let Moulina pretend as if she has realised her mistakes and wants to go back to Mumbai and join her husband. She should make them believe that she is truly remorseful for her naivety and stupidity. Let her initiate talks with her husband and in-laws in an apologetic manner. If the Ghosh family gets convinced, they might propose to meet you all. But before that, make sure Moulina meets only Sumit on the pretext of reconciliation. Let him travel to Rourkela, arrange for his stay in a hotel of my choice. Then let your daughter go and meet him in phases – first day her sister might accompany, next day you may escort and finally let Moulina meet Sumit all alone. That's the day when she has to enact perfectly and make Sumit realise that all these years she missed him so much and in this entire legal turmoil how much she desired and missed making love to him. Let those small talks be full of sweet memories, then let her seduce him so that he indulges in her curvaceous beauty, luscious lips and finally gets involved into some steamy action. Don't let the session run too long, abruptly let her withdraw and hurriedly make her way out of the hotel room and complain at the reception desk about Sumit's misconduct and his act of forcing himself on her. Since the hotel staff are known to me, we'll lock the boy in the room and call police. And then let's initiate a new episode of rape case; section 375 which is also non-bailable will do wonders. Just that we've to prepare a water tight FIR and those hotel staffs and CCTV footages will be our evidences."

After narrating the entire plan Basak looked at Sanat with a sparkle in his eyes and eagerly waited for an approval. Contrarily Sanat listened to the chronicle carefully and gave no reaction to it. He was thoroughly disgusted with the so called *blueprint*. Enraged at Basak's insensitivity, he got up from his chair and yelled at the lawyer, "To hell with your blueprint. I'm a father, not a pimp. Enough of your moronic ideas which only you think are a class apart. You can't even control the ongoing case, yet want to add-on few more to it. Do you even realise how this could impact my daughter's future? How do we face this society? Already we are under tremendous pressure. Every now and then we are bombarded with queries from neighbours, friends and families. Those inquisitive eyes silently follow us everywhere. Moulina couldn't face the ordeal and had to leave Birmirpur."

"Anyway, I don't expect any kind of legal remedies from you. From hereon I'll have to do something to get rid of the opposition's movement." Sanat grumbled before storming out of the chamber, banging the door behind him.

THIRTY-THREE
2018

Rourkela, Odisha, India

It was a lovely Friday morning of mid-June with pleasant weather outside. The day was characterized by overcast skies accompanied by cool monsoon breeze. The gulmohar tree top next to the window rhythmically swayed in zephyr. Ganguly had a relaxed day at court and was enjoying the window view from his seat; when a tall, well-built man with military haircut appeared along with one of his associates. The man in mid-fifties had a gym toned physic and sported a Ray-Ban aviator along with a white collar T-shirt and regular fit Wrangler jeans.

"Sir, this gentleman was looking for you downstairs. So, I brought him here." The associate informed his Boss.

"*Saale...phone kyun nahi uthata hai?* I've been trying to reach you since last week!" The man was all smiles while informally addressing the senior lawyer, whose associates gave a perplexed look.

Ganguly was puzzled too, as he couldn't recognise the visitor. Though he extended his hand for a handshake he tried reminiscing the face that looked familiar. And the guest chortled at the fuddled expression of the lawyer. He then volunteered to introduce himself and kill the suspense. "Am sure you didn't recognise me. It has been over two decades since we last met. But then, how can you forget your bosom friend?"

"Mallesh Naidu – right? What a pleasant surprise! And look at you, what a transformation. From a guy-next-door look to fitness aficionado. But what brings you here at Rourkela court?" Ganguly finally identified his old college friend and was euphoric about the visit.

"To meet you, what else it could be?" joked Naidu.

"And all the way from Ranchi? You must be kidding!"

"Ranchi is passé. My last posting was in Raipur and now here in Rourkela since last month. But I'm still wondering – what prompted you not to take my calls!"

"Oh, don't take that seriously. I generally don't pick up calls from unknown numbers. *Ab yeah bata, tu kya kar raha hai court mein?"*

"Well, was passing by and thought of meeting the Public Prosecutor in connection to a recent drug peddling case. And once the meeting got over, I enquired about you and here I am. *Waise aaj evening ko free hai kya?* Let's catch up and revive those old memories."

DSP Mallesh Naidu, IPS officer of Andhra Pradesh cadre – batch of 1990, was born and brought up in Rourkela. His family hailed from Rajahmundry and his father's job with Indian Railways brought them to the steel city way back in the 1960s. After his graduation when his father retired, they went back to their hometown. In his illustrious career, DSP Naidu had many feathers in his cap. He had been elevated to the Anti-Narcotics Cell (ANC), before being posted to Ranchi. After a series of achievements and successfully controlling the drug menace in Ranchi he was later posted to Raipur to curb the mounting cases of drug trafficking. And now with increasing number of drug peddlers dodging the enforcement in Rourkela, Naidu was given a freehand by the state of Odisha to deal with the drug Lords, who often played hide-'n'-seek with the jurisdiction of Odisha and Jharkhand.

In the last five years, Rourkela and its neighbourhood emerged as a safe haven for drug dealers. With a host of Engineering and Management colleges attracting students from the adjacent states, psychotropic drugs gained popularity among the youths. Even the high school students weren't spared from its grip. Drug Lords with the help of local handlers were doing brisk business and were on a mission to rampage the social fabric and spoil the future of the youngsters.

Naidu implemented a few basic protocols as soon as he joined office. Apart from forming a core team of brave officers he created a strong network of local informants among various party circles in the city. The hangout zones for college students were heavily patrolled. The inter-college fests were also brought under ANC's radar while the entry and exit points of the city were closely monitored too. Earlier cases of cannabis and analgesic consumption were widely reported but with passing days, usage of blots, meth and meow-meow caught up with the teens of the metropolis.

Meanwhile the third summon sent to the Chell residence drove Sanat absolutely crazy. His face turned red with suppressed rage. Burning wrath hissed through his body like deathly venom, screeching a demanded release in form of unwanted violence. He spent the entire day thinking of various ways that can keep his daughter away from facing the criminal trial. Finally, in the evening he impetuously called for a meeting with their *adivasi* maid's brother at a local country liquor bar. The dingy bar behind

Birmirpur bus stop typified with fetid, pungent smell of *Mahuli, Handia, Taadi and Tharra*, being frequented by the local tribals to unwind themselves after a laborious day's work, played *Bhojpuri* number in the background to set the mood. The meeting lasted for one hour with some intense discussion between the two men. Later Sanat paid the bills for the liquor, cigarettes and *chakna* before disappearing into the dark.

Meanwhile, Ganguly was all set to file a petition for the issuance of a bailable warrant against Moulina. But a minor accident kept him away from action for a while. The draft remained in the file as it is, since the lawyer was advised complete bed-rest for a week. The pre-monsoon showers in the month of July left the asphalt roads slippery. Ganguly lost control of his bike at Koel Nagar junction and skidded off the road. With bruised knee and twisted ankle, he struggled his way home that evening. As if this wasn't enough, his wife too went down with viral fever that very week. There was something sinister about Ganguly family being hit with this double whammy and little did he know that another gruesome incident was waiting to send shivers down the spine.

It was a gloomy Friday evening. The rain God probably was enjoying a recess after a heavy afternoon downpour. Puffs of grey clouds swirled like spilled black ink in water covering the twilight sky. The blanketed, dark sky gave away claustrophobic tension and waited for yet another rainstorm. Broken branches lying in the puddle were victims of windy breeze that preceded the previous night's heavy shower.

Ganguly siblings, Vidhi and Veena braved the afternoon rain to reach their respective tuition classes at Koel Nagar's D-block. After the classes got over, they waited at their tutor's residence for the heavy downpour to recede and by evening when it temporarily halted, they were quick to leave for home. Though just 5 pm, it was already dark outside. D-block main road wore a deserted look with just a few men gathering around the corner tea stall to grab a cup of tea. There wasn't a single autorickshaw seen plying along the alleyways, and shops had downed their shutters early. It seemed that everybody anticipated another session of heavy downpour and prefered to stay indoors for rest of the evening.

Veena asked her sister to wait along the footpath while she hurried towards the xerox shop to get her notes photocopied. Like an obedient kid Vidhi loitered around while tinkering with her umbrella. All of a sudden, a speeding bike whizzed past her and the pillion rider flung some kind of liquid at her and disappeared in the dark. A terrified Vidhi cried for help hearing which, her sister came running down from the shop. Few shopkeepers who found the young girl snivel inconsolably gathered at the spot. It happened so fast that none could catch a glimpse of those masked goons. Vidhi complained of a strange itchy sensation along with cooling effects on her right arm and neck area, where the liquid was hurled. A passer-by who suspected an acid attack suggested Veena to immediately take her sister to the nearest hospital and simultaneously inform her parents.

At City Hospital's OPD, daddy's little girl was surrounded by friends, families, neighbours and policemen. Everybody was worried about the ghastly incident that shook Koel Nagar locality. Only the attending doctor's verdict brought solace to the visitors. He carefully examined young Vidhi and finally declared her safe.

"Nothing to worry about. It wasn't any kind of acid though the modus operandi was made to look like one of them. The attackers used isopropyl alcohol to instil fear in the child's mind. Isopropyl alcohol, often referred as rubbing alcohol is non-toxic and has no harmful effect on our human skin. However, it might leave sensitive skins dry and flaky." The doctor made his observations and suggested few counselling sessions for Vidhi so that she could smoothly overcome the trauma. He signed few papers and finally discharged his patient.

Back from the hospital, Ganguly's younger daughter became the centroid of all discussions. She enjoyed all the attention showered to her. Those hugs, kisses and chocolates from the visitors made her feel very special. However, she knew for sure that her father's awkward silence towards the whole incident spoke volumes and was just a mere calmness before the storm.

Ganguly limped heavily and rushed to the hospital when he heard about the incident. He called in his associates too, who informed the police immediately. Until the doctor gave his verdict, the father wore a faded look with anxiety and apprehension overpowering his brain. Flashback of some adorable moments with his daughter played at the back of his mind, while he managed to put up a courageous, strong appearance. Questions like, *Who could have done it? Why did they do it?* never crossed his mind. In spite of being an atheist he didn't shy away from praying to the Almighty for his kid's recuperation. Contrarily Mrs Ganguly kept howling like a child and blamed her destiny. The junior associates however got in touch with a few acquaintances in the police department to track the perpetrators. And finally, when Vidhi was declared 'out of danger', everybody heaved a sigh of relief.

Later that evening – dark clouds raced across the sky, thrumming with the charged energy they were desperate to release. Winds shrieked as rain battered the windows in the dead of the night. The cracking sound of the thunder was omnipresent while the streak of lightning ripped apart the dark canvass repeatedly in irregular intervals.

Koel Nagar police remained completely clueless and couldn't nab the culprits even after a week of that horrendous incident. Ganguly escalated the matter to the highest authority of police. Along with his friend Naidu, he went and met the Police Superintendent to apprise him about the heinous crime that was attempted on his daughter. The head of police assured him thorough investigation and detention of the crooks at the earliest. Even Naidu, in his individual capacity, extended support to his friend. Since his men patrolled the periphery of the city; he instructed them to keep a tight vigil on every passing vehicle, mainly two wheelers.

Into the month of August, and the police was yet to make any arrest in the mock acid-attack case. For the past one month the investigators had tried hard to gather evidences – they questioned Vidhi's close friends, tuition teacher, school authorities; analysed CCTV footages from railway station and bus stop, but nothing eventuated. Local newspapers ran stories highlighting police inefficiency, while administration tried their best in handling the reprehensible crime – a first of its kind in Rourkela municipality area.

Meantime Ganguly recovered from his injury and continued with his routine work of handling court cases. But every now and then, he kept wondering – *Who could have masterminded this harrowing act!! What message did he or she want to convey? What was the motive behind this?*

For a criminal lawyer of his stature who handled a diverse spectrum of cases, ranging from murder, abduction, rape, theft, embezzlement and frauds; there had been innumerable enemies that sprouted in his career span. They did try to terrorise him by various means – from threatening calls to mowing down his bike; from stabbing him to hockey stick attack. Whatever happened never got spilled over to any of his family members. And for the first time ever in his career, somebody tried to infuse fear in him by targeting his innocent, naïve, daughter. As a father, he would never be able to forgive this offender in disguise.

THIRTY-FOUR
2018

Rourkela, Odisha, India

On the personal front, Ganguly went through a rough patch, yet he didn't let his professional commitments dampen in midst of all tensions. His clients were unaware of the grievous incident and like any other day, kept pestering him over the phone. The senior lawyer entertained most of the calls and updated them on their respective cases with equal zeal.

On an early September evening just when Ganguly was about to leave for home after a hectic day's work at the court, he received an unexpected call from Naidu. His friend had got some lead in connection to the acid-attack case and wanted to meet him at Kumjharia police outpost.

Kumjharia is a rural neighbourhood along the Simdega Road, 22 kilometres from Rourkela city centre. Just 6 kilometres from Kumjharia village is Birmirpur, beyond which the jurisdiction of Odisha ends and that of Jharkhand begins. This little sleepy village is sparsely populated with tribals. While the elders traditionally engaged themselves in farming and agriculture, the youths mostly migrated to either Rourkela or Ranchi in search of a better living. With low literacy level and lack of proper development in and around the village; many juvenescences indulged into various illegal, anti-social activities to earn some quick bucks. They mostly ended up as drug peddlers, wagon-breakers or petty offenders.

Recently a gruesome murder at a local country liquor bar followed by the arrest of the murderer revealed a few facts that had possible linkups with the mock acid-attack, staged a couple of months back, on Ganguly's daughter. After questioning the killer at the police lockup, it was divulged that in the month of June-July, the deceased, Sohag Murmu, had engaged Khokon Soren for a "simple" operation. However, after successful execution of the operation, Khokon's payment was withheld and instead he was immediately asked to go underground for a while in order to avoid any kind of police interception. Khokon had to sleek past the border area in the middle of the night and stay put at his cousin's place in Jharkhand's Dongapani village for next few weeks. Being a neighbour, Sohag was known to Khokon since childhood. So, when he was approached to drive the bike with Sohag on the pillion, he readily agreed and the deal was sealed at INR 6,000. They even recced the streets of Koel Nagar a day before the operation was held.

Khokon who hailed from a family that struggled to put together two square meals a day, agreed to aid Sohag, just because the money could fund his father's thalassemia treatment, who many a times had to buy several units of blood for regular transfusion and treatment.

Dispute cropped up when Khokon failed to get his dues from Sohag after repeated reminders. With extension of every promised payment dates, Khokon's disappointment grew multi-fold. And finally, one evening, hell broke loose when after a couple of drinks Khokon stabbed Sohag to death during an altercation over the pending money at a local bar. The caustic combination of weeds and *Handia* transformed Khokon into a treacherous monster that evening; he kept demanding for his money while stabbing Sohag several times until the 5'7" lanky body laid motionless in a pool of blood.

It took nearly forty-five minutes for Ganguly to reach Kumjharia. Hurricane-lanterns and candle lights came to their rescue in a load-shedding hit police outpost. Naidu in his civvies was eagerly waiting for his friend. Straight away, they headed to a small cabin meant for the station head.

"The guy in the lockup has confessed his crime and is repenting for his action. We didn't even pressurise him, instead he voluntarily narrated everything sequentially." Naidu briefed his friend on the arrested offender.

"Hmmm…but why did they carry out such a barbaric operation? And most importantly who is behind all this?" Ganguly raised a few valid questions.

"Well, our questioning revealed that the mastermind behind this act was known to the deceased only. And the arrested guy knows nothing about him. In fact, the murderer lodged in the lockup never had a criminal past, whereas the murdered was a history-sheeter. In 2016 he was detained for supplying marijuana to sleeper cells of local Maoist groups, later he was released on bail. However, we'll continue to question this man and get more clues."

"Being a lawyer can I see him now? Will just ask a few questions before you take charge."

With due permission from Naidu, Ganguly walked into the dark, dingy, suffocating lockup where a man aged around twenty-five years with bushy eyebrows, ruffled hairs and light stubble was seen weeping. A constable brought in a candle light and a bottle of water and left it on the corner table. There were bruises across his left arm and right leg, probably due to police thrashing. Ganguly pulled in a chair and introduced himself in a relaxed tone. He also promised him to fight his case free of charge if he answered him correctly and revealed all details related to the acid-attack incident.

In his twenty minutes' interaction, Ganguly couldn't extract any extra bit of information from Khokon. It was almost a repeat version of Naidu's narration. Instead Khokon was worried about his ailing father, he repeatedly pleaded guilty and wanted to confess his crime before the Magistrate so as to avoid harsher punishment. According to him, the action was completely impromptu and he couldn't even believe that he ended up stabbing Sohag fifteen times.

After bidding goodbye to Naidu and his colleagues that evening, Ganguly decided to meet the bereaved family of Sohag Murmu in pursuit of some clues. Sohag was survived by his sister and mother in a small thatched house along the backstreet of the village market in Kumjharia. His menial job to support his mother's income often landed him in various disquiets in the past. But they never imagined that Sohag would be hacked to death in such a brutal manner. The lawyer tried consoling the ladies and tactfully attempted to extract info on Sohag's confederates. Out of the few names that emerged – a short, fubsy, dark man surnamed Kisku used to frequent the Murmu residence a couple of months back. The sister even recalled the thumping sound of Kisku's Enfield Bullet that woke her up in the middle of the night, when he dropped her brother back home on a few occasions.

That night Ganguly struggled to fall asleep – a thumping sound hovered around his head, and a fuzzy figure rode an Enfield Bullet along the back alleys of his locality. He tossed and turned on his bed restlessly, trying hard to sleep. Meanwhile his subconscious mind was rattled with a series of unanswered questions – *Who was this Kisku? How could he get hold of him? How would he locate the Enfield Bullet rider? What was his motive in targeting young Vidhi?*

The family court finally got their Judge after a long hiatus of nearly ten months. Inspite of his ongoing personal crisis Ganguly geared up for a dual attack on the Chells. Impregnable petitions were prepared with lot of iterations and valuable inputs from Ganguly himself in consultation with his senior associates from HC. Few landmark judgements from the SC and various other HCs were referred and cited to make a strong plea against the maintenance demand. While the family court case was well underway, the petition for issuance of bailable warrant against Moulina was filed at the criminal court. The Chells were eventually being cornered by their opposition.

Weeks after Ganguly's visit to Kumjharia, info on the Enfield Bullet owner brought in some cheer to the legal practitioner. One of his aides got him accurate information after several days of shadowing the motorcycle with a Jharkhand registration number. Ludicrously when the local police couldn't see anything unusual beyond the Khokon-Sohag scuffle leading to a vitriolic murder; Ganguly's quest for the mastermind got him to the root of the crime resulting in fishing out Kisku from the dark underbelly of a ghetto. With only four petrol pumps operating along the highway between the stretches of Vedvyas Chowk to Birmirpur, it was easy for Ganguly's aide to locate the suspected vehicle. The used motorbike was bought from a garage in Jharkhand by Dulal Kisku, a resident of Hatimpara village in the periphery of Birmirpur.

Hatimpara traditionally has been infamous for being home to few notorious wagon-breakers. Few decades back when mines were active and goods trains frequented the area, the wagon-breakers made a fortune out of it. With progressing time, the village lost its glory as the wagon-breakers gradually got involved in other syndicates.

Dulal Kisku, a school dropout always believed that he was destined for great things and his job at the local highway side *Dhaba* as a cashier was just a starting point. His family of four largely depended on his sister's income, who worked hard as a housemaid in Birmirpur. His alcoholic father died of kidney failure a few years back forcing his younger brother to quit studies and join a local grocery store as a helper.

After gathering detailed information on Kisku, Ganguly decided to meet and confront the delinquent youth, who didn't have any criminal record, yet acted as a middleman to various unorganised crimes in and around the city. He operated as an enabler who undertook contracts and executed them seamlessly. Being well connected with the youths of his neighbouring villages, he exploited their abject poverty to his advantage and lured them with lumpsum money. And being a *Dhaba* cashier, he was known to truck drivers, transporters and fleet owners – this in turn helped him to deal with multiple illegal cross-border activities like adulterated fuel supply, stolen two-wheeler trafficking and drug peddling. It would've been impossible for Ganguly to dig out such comprehensive information on Kisku, had there not been a wagon-breaker client from the same area, whom the criminal lawyer defended a decade back and won his case. He was now engaged in diverse philanthropic activities and widely known for his work in empowering the tribal youths.

End of October, and the whole of Rourkela was yet to come out from the festive hangover. Lower courts were still enjoying the long *Durga Puja* vacation while Ganguly reached *Ranjit da Dhaba* on Simdega Road. The lazy Friday afternoon failed to anticipate the day's proceeding at the *charpai* set along the left corner of the *Dhaba*. Ganguly concealed his real identity and introduced himself as a businessman from the steel city. Before entering the *Dhaba* he took a gander at the black shiny Royal Enfield parked in the front yard – the 350 cc beast stood majestically without paying any heed to its surroundings.

The lawyer ordered lunch and silently kept an eye on Kisku who was managing the cash counter. Since there weren't any customers around, Kisku was seen glancing through a glossy filmy magazine while listening to retro Hindi songs on some FM radio station. Since lunch was just an excuse, Ganguly quickly finished off his *rajma-chawal, sabzi* followed by a glass of buttermilk. He proceeded towards the cash counter and on pretext of paying his bill, struck up a conversation with the dubious cashier.

"Mera kitna hua...kette hela?"

"Hundred and ten." Kisku extended a bowl full of sugar-coated fennel seeds with a hand written slip mentioning *Rs 110/-* tucked into it.

"And how much do you charge for organising a kidnapping act?" the lawyer firmly looked at Kisku and asked him in a suppressed tone.

The unexpected query from an unknown gentleman caught Dulal Kisku completely off-guard. But he was quick to control his body language and remained composed. Looked straight into the lawyer's eyes and replied in a flat, expressionless tone "Did you just say something to me, *Sahab?*"

"Yes, you heard it right. I want my business rival's son to be kidnapped for a ransom on his way to school. This is my number, give me a call to discuss in details." Ganguly passed on a chit after carefully looking sideways.

Without getting stirred up Kisku maintained a poker face and said *"Sahab,* it seems there has been a mistaken identity. I am not the person you're looking for...*kisi ne aap ko galat information di hai.* I'm just an ordinary cashier at this *Dhaba.* Here's your change *Sahab.* Have a good day and thanks for visiting."

Completely baffled by Kisku's unflappability, Ganguly undoubtedly was on the back foot. Even the cashier's reluctance to take the bait disappointed him hugely. Without wasting much time, the legal practitioner grabbed a few mouth-fresheners, and started to walk out of the *Dhaba.* Just when he was near the parked two-wheeler, he turned around and asked Kisku "Is this yours?"

*"Haan ji…*my *Didi* financed it two years back. I'm now working hard to repay the loan." The cashier informed with pride.

"But I never asked you about your bike's financing!"

"That's okay. Generally, people keep asking me about this prized possession and then they wonder where I got all the money from! Some unwaveringly quiz while others cook up their imagination," Kisku replied with a smile.

On his way back home, Ganguly just couldn't put two and two together. Kisku was shrewd enough to speculate the lawyer's motive behind the visit and managed to keep him guessing by those ambiguous responses. Startled by Kisku's lack of interest in carrying out the abduction; the senior counsel blamed himself for such lame approach. Probably he should've taken Naidu's help in squeezing out particulars from Kisku. However, as a highly experienced lawyer with wordsmith capabilities, Ganguly recollected and analysed few of those afternoon talks to retrieve possible hints that could connect him to the mastermind of his daughter's attack.

Meanwhile at Monalisa Apartment in Haldia, the Ghosh couple had a visitor who introduced himself as a local businessman. The thirty something man with his grating voice, owned a travel and tourism agency and shared his visiting card with senior Ghosh. Apart from owning a fleet of mid-sized vehicles, he also provided *Tatkal* booking of rail tickets to his clients. Though the elderly couple was meeting him for the first time, it was clear that the man knew almost everything about them and their ongoing court battle with the Chells. After those initial formalities, he straight away got into the point and made his intentions very clear.

"Uncle it's been four long years and I know the tremendous amount of hassle you all are going through. Is this how you intend to spend rest of your retired life?" The visitor pretended to be concerned about the Ghosh family's incessant problem.

"Who has sent you here? Look, if you are here to intimidate us then I must say that you're wasting your time. Let the law take its course and you may leave now." Chitra was quick to take control over the situation and came down heavily on the visitor.

Without getting stirred up the visitor politely continued, "Aunty, this isn't the time to be hyper. Being a fellow citizen and well-wisher, it's my responsibility to suggest to you, the right path in your time of distress. After all you're like my aged parents…"

"And how much did Chell offer you for this arbitration?" Sushil who was listening to the gentleman all the while finally spoke. He continued, "Since you visited us for the first time I request you to finish off your cup of tea and leave immediately; don't compel me to dial 100. You've a business to look after and it wouldn't do any good if you get involved in police complaints."

"Uncle, this is where the problem lies. Try and look at the bigger picture. Being stringent in your approach and holding on to it doesn't always help. Remember that your son and daughter stay away from you in a big city, anything can happen to them at any point in time. Even for you, God forbid, at this age anything can happen. And that might leave the entire family devastated…"

"Are you here to threaten us?"

"Nooooo, not at all! Am just trying to say that there are bigger worries in life. Why keep the legal tussle alive when you can settle it among yourselves?"

"Okay…and how do we do that?" Sushil calmed down and gave the visitor a chance to present his side.

"Well, your opposition has certain monetary demands. On fulfilling the same they promise to withdraw all the cases and free you from the cuffs of litigation."

"And what is the MRP of this settlement?"

"If you agree, only then I can talk to Mr Chell and get the figures from him. For the time being even I'm unaware of their demands."

Sushil chuckled at the excitement in the visitor's face and politely thanked him for the information which eventually got captured in the wireless micro-spycam hidden in the wall clock of the living room. The audio-video recording could be utilized as a piece of evidence during the criminal trial proceeding. The unsuspecting visitor didn't have an iota of idea of the recording act, and went back happily, in the hope of earning 3% of the settlement amount as his intermediation commission.

Next day, Ganguly received two consecutive calls divulging new facts that were equally exciting and thrilling. His client from Haldia called to brief him about the visit of a 'well-wisher' and informed him on how ingeniously they captured the audio-video clip of the entire conversation. The elderly Ghosh's presence of mind was praise worthy – over a period of time they had probably learnt to live with their predicaments and overcome all anxieties, regain composure and deal smartly with hostile situations.

Ganguly's aide who was assigned to shadow Kisku's sister called later in the afternoon with some meaty information. After a week's meticulous tailing, the revelations were pretty much in line with the lawyer's expectation – the sister who worked as a housemaid never financially helped Kisku to obtain his shiny, black Enfield. The bike was in fact a part of a refurbished vehicles' consignment that was bootlegged across the border. Being a domestic help to three families, the sister's day commenced as early as 6 am and went on till 6 pm in the evening. In these twelve hours, she would engage in sweeping, mopping, vacuuming, doing laundry and cleaning dishes. She even cooked meals for one of the family who in turn provided her with daily lunch. By end of every month she would make around a scanty 1200 in all. A brief detail of each family where Kisku's sister worked was also collected – out of which one name stunned Ganguly to his core. It compelled him to think various possibilities that matched his calculations and hypothesis. In high probability things got clearer to him. He got the hang of things as to why his daughter was attacked on that tragic evening. Meanwhile he vowed to teach an appropriate lesson to the perpetrator by giving him the taste of his own medicine – a loving father's soul sought an abstruse revenge.

A distraught Ganguly called up Naidu to seek his advice and find a way forward. The two gentlemen met over a weekend and discussed various possibilities in depth. The criminal lawyer shared his findings and linked several incidents together to put up a theory behind his daughter's attack. It was loud and clear – Ganguly was not going to spare the criminal mastermind at any cost. The ANC supremo assured all help to his friend in his pursuit of an elusive nemesis. . Together they chalked out a flawless plan to enmesh the suspect and kept it all cryptic for others to understand.

THIRTY-FIVE
2018

Rourkela, Odisha, India

Early November and there was already a chill in the air. A sudden drop in temperature along with misty mornings had created a perfect precursor to winter in the steel city. While it was mildly cold outside, warm wishes kept pouring into DSP Naidu's office. His office land number remained busy for the entire day and was flooded with congratulatory messages. Bureaucrats, ministers, activists, journalists, ex-colleagues, friends and families were all ecstatic about Naidu's latest and undoubtedly the biggest achievement in northern Odisha. Naidu's mobile ran out of charge due to innumerable incoming calls and messages. The remarkable feat of Anti-Narcotics Cell under the able leadership of DSP Mallesh Naidu got featured as a front page article in most of the vernacular dailies. A couple of news channel stationed their OB van just outside the DSP's office in order to interview the swashbuckling officer.

"Congratulations Sir! This certainly is an amazing accomplishment. Never before there has been a drug seizure worth rupees ten crore from this city and its suburbs. What do you have to say?" A TV journalist with an English news channel posed questions to Naidu while the cameraman kept rolling.

"Thanks! Yes, our department really worked hard to achieve this. For the past one-week, various hot spots were kept under surveillance by plainclothed officers and finally we succeeded in seizing a huge amount of Ketamine that was set to change hands." Naidu briefly answered the young TV reporter.

"Sir, you arrested three and managed to lay hands on a total of around 100 kilograms of Ketamine. Could you tell us something about this operation? Something on the entire trail of narcotics?"

"Well…there you've got all the info. At this stage I can't disclose much. But as per our intelligence there are a few more consignments which are waiting to cross the Odisha border and we'll try our best to nab the culprits and foil their plan." The DSP kept it short and ended the interview immediately.

The daredevil officer might have kept his interview short without revealing much. But only he and his department knew the tremendous effort that went behind this successful seizure. The force completely relied on local intelligence and heavy input from the informers. The circumjacent villages of Lathikata, Kansbahal, Kuanrmunda, Bondamunda and Bangurkela were put on high alert as soon as the team got to know the modus operandi of the peddlers. Packets of synthetic hallucinogen were stuffed in pumpkins, bottle-gourds, ash-gourds, green papayas, chili peppers and other plump vegetables; which were then camouflaged with fresh vegetables and smuggled into Rourkela through roadways. Vegetable vendors then carried it forward and home delivered it to their respective clients. The distribution network operated in a discreet loop and a new entrant could only procure this psychogenic drug through known acquaintances, unlocking their familiar code languages.

After receiving a tip-off, ANC officials accompanied by the local police force raided several vegetable trucks en route to Rourkela and seized the dissociative anaesthetic powder. On questioning the truck drivers, it was revealed that majority of the consignment was meant to be transported to the coastal Odisha's port area, wherefrom possibly it could have taken a sea route to South East Asian countries – undoubtedly Naidu's team made a dent in the international drug cartel's logistics plan.

In the midst of his hectic schedule, Ganguly somehow missed out on the success story of his friend that was making news across Odisha. It was Mrs Ganguly who brought it up and briefed her husband on the recent raids and seizures of huge quantity of contraband across various location of suburban Rourkela. She also insisted on inviting Mr and Mrs Naidu for dinner at their residence, to which the lawyer readily agreed.

Naidu's love for Bengali and Punjabi food was widely known among his friend's circle. Hence he was euphoric to receive a dinner invitation from his college buddy and was equally delighted at the idea of digging into some home cooked Bengali delicacies.

It was feasting time at the Ganguly residence on a mid-November evening. The Naidus arrived early to avoid the evening traffic. Mrs Naidu, who was fond of kids, carried a teddy bear for Vidhi and gifted handmade chocolates to Veena. Since her first miscarriage and subsequent complications to conceive, the Naidus remained childless. With Naidu uncle and aunty in company, Veena and Vidhi were happy and excited.

After a scrumptious dinner involving prawns, chicken and mutton dishes; it was time for some sweet dishes to savour – something which Ganguly craved for but had to stay away from because of his diabetes. Surprisingly this time around, Mrs Ganguly didn't pose a hindrance to the lawyer's desire to gulp down a few *rasgullas and gulab-jamuns* followed by a scoop of butterscotch ice-cream.

While the ladies and the kids were busy downstairs, gossiping and playing among themselves; the two friends preferred enjoying their ice-cream on the terrace, below the vastness of the sky. Ganguly congratulated Naidu for his attainment and discussed about the city's deteriorating law and order. Both the gentlemen shared few of their professional challenges that they overcame in the recent past and some future concerns. Naidu who had already lit a cigarette after finishing off his ice-cream seemed to be worried…

"*Yaar*…next couple of months would be really tough for me and my department. Expectations are sky-high and challenges are humongous." Naidu shared his concern as smoke gushed out of his mouth and nostrils.

"Why? What's bothering you, when you've full government support? In fact, they've given you a free hand to run the department, haven't they?"

"That's right. But the intelligence input coming in is very scary."

"Can you be more specific, if you don't mind?"

"*Vakil Babu, yeah tera courtroom nahi hai*…that you'll start cross-examining me!" The ANC chief joked at his friend's remark as both the men guffawed. After taking a puff, Naidu continued "*Yaar,* the issue is with the kind of drug that's entering Rourkela these days. Peddlers have now grown smarter and have started implementing newer ways to dispose the psychotropic when confronted. Had it been natural drug, we could have deployed the sniffer dogs to work for us efficiently. But tracking synthetic drug becomes trickier."

"Why is that so?"

"Generally, dogs are trained on cocaine, heroin and opium – the common natural drugs. Whereas, LSD in pure form is odourless and almost goes undetected by the canines. Unfortunately, Rourkela youths' new found love for LSD blots and mephedrone are giving us sleepless nights." Naidu explained.

"Hmm…and why is it that only the next two months are crucial? Any specific reason?"

"Well as per departmental archive, December and January sees a spike in transaction as well as consumption of drugs in this city; primarily because of a series of events that are scheduled in winter. Firstly, there's a week long inter-college fest at the zonal Engineering College, followed by the national B-school meet at the university campus. Then comes Christmas followed by New Year. This mega amalgamation of students from various corner of the country calls for a grand celebration, and these hallucinogen helps them to get high and dance away the nights of the rock concerts."

Ganguly who was attentively listening to Naidu all this while had a plan running in his head. He wanted to sound it off to his friend but was sceptical, until, the

DSP enquired about it upfront. The two friends revisited their earlier strategy, tweaked it to make it impermeable and get rid of the suspected acid-attack mastermind...

On an early morning of mid-December, a short while after dawn, when the mild, subdued sunlight was about to make its way for a misty winter forenoon; the Anti-Narcotics team raided the warehouse of Hornbill Courier Services Pvt. Ltd. in Birmirpur outpost area. The plan of this incursion was made beforehand after receiving specific inputs of huge shipments waiting to be diffused among drug higglers across the city. The supervisor and security guard were nabbed immediately while another employee managed to escape through the backdoor. Questioning the two didn't result in any substantial output, hence ANC officials swung into action and initiated a massive combing operation across the warehouse premise. Two sniffer dogs were brought in to assist the officers. After an hour-long search when the undeterred officers were about to call off the rummage, it was one of Naidu's deputies who went up to look into the piles of corrugated cardboard sheets meant for packaging. And to his surprise, discovered A4 sized blots concealed in those layered cardboards. The entire premise was sealed and the acid blots were immediately seized.

Following a few more tip-offs, Naidu's team busted several stationery stores across the city who were selling the blotters disguised in geographical maps and stickers of Disney characters. Another team at Lathikata detained few fishermen who were caught with two kilograms of mephedrone concealed in several clams, all of which had been glued shut.

After a week's rigorous vigil, ANC was able to collar contrabands worth 2 crores in the illicit market. Media elaborately covered each of the operations and made a hero out of Mallesh Naidu overnight. Yet, his duty wasn't over...there were a few more domestic raids to be completed before he embarked on his week-long vacation to his native place in Rajahmundry.

As a part of their continued effort to end the drug menace, Anti-Narcotics team made two more arrests – one from Bondamunda and the other from Birmirpur. This time round the alleged peddlers were picked up from their residence after significant amount of forbidden substances were found in their possession. They were immediately booked under relevant sections of the Narcotic Drugs and Psychotropic Substances (NDPS) Act, even though they cried foul at the police action.

In the wee hours of a chilly winter morning, when it gets absolutely difficult to pull out from the comfort of a bed laden with layers of quilts and blankets; the owner of the house had to wake up to the sound of frequent doorbell. Morning's serenity was disturbed by haphazard banging on the front door of the two storied building opposite to Birmirpur railway station which stood secluded in the midst of a heavy smog.

With half-closed eyes, the householder put on his sweater and staggered through the corridor to open the door, only to find a few uniformed men waiting outside to take him into their custody. Even before he could utter anything, two officers headed towards the living room and ransacked the shelves. They stumbled upon a sealed envelope containing several printed sheets that were perforated into tiny squares. Apart from few white blank sheets, most of them had Hindu Gods and Goddesses printed on them. The helpless housewife came running in, but two lady constables debarred her from interfering in the police procedurals. Things happened so fast that even before the family could realise what caused such action, ANC officers took away the landlord in their van leaving behind a smoky exhaust, probably due to clogged carburettor.

THIRTY-SIX
2018

Rourkela, Odisha, India

Since morning Ganguly was in a cheerful mood; whistling and humming few of his favourite *Mohammad Rafi* songs – a very rare instance that symbolised some kind of accomplishment which was known only to him. Even Mrs Ganguly was taken aback by her husband's buoyant state of mind. Surprisingly, the senior lawyer decided to take the day off from his work and spend quality time with his daughters. An impromptu family lunch at *Madhuban Restaurant* was decided.

While breakfast was ready, Ganguly remained busy fiddling with his phone. He clicked a specific report from the morning newspaper and WhatsApped it to his client in Mumbai. And just when he was about to finish his bread toast, in came a call from Mumbai.

"Sir, what did I just read! Did it really happen or are you celebrating April fool's day in the month of December?" An over excited Sumit called back his lawyer in disbelief.

"It's all over the news here in Rourkela and its suburbs," confirmed Ganguly.

"But that's unbelievable. The entire family is now ravaged. How did all this happen?" Sumit still couldn't believe the news piece he just read from the WhatsApp forward.

"May be some form of karmic payback. Karma mostly boomerangs." Suddenly Ganguly sounded all spiritual to Sumit.

"Sir, isn't this the right time to tighten the noose around our opposition? I suggest you start with the criminal trial immediately."

"Are you sure? Don't you have any emotions left for that innocent beauty? How can you be so ruthless?" the lawyer joked and cackled with laughter.

Meanwhile at a local nursing home, Maya was recovering from a terrible anxiety attack. Moments after the police picked up her husband from their residence, she collapsed. She sat in bewilderment gasping for air. Her heart thudded in her chest, hands shivered, feet tingled and vision blurred before she fell unconscious. Neighbours came to her rescue, who also informed her relatives in Rourkela. Moulina and Lokesh, who took a week off from their respective workplaces in Jaipur and Faridabad were informed about their mom's deteriorating health while nothing was revealed about their father's arrest. Hell broke loose, when the siblings heard the narration of that fateful morning from one of the neighbours. Along with uncle Sarat, Lokesh visited the local *Thana* to get some clarity. Surprisingly, none of the constables or sub-inspectors were ready to open up. Most of them refrained from commenting, since the arrest was done by Anti-Narcotics officers which was under the purview of the state government and monitored centrally from the Police Commissionerate's office. Being disheartened, just when the uncle-nephew duo was about to leave Birmirpur PS, a lady officer spotted Lokesh and intervened.

"Aren't you Sanat's son? What are you doing here?" The lady Sub-Inspector asked Lokesh while parking her Honda Activa.

"Madam, we wanted to meet the officer-in-charge who made the arrest. There must have been a mistaken identity. My father is completely innocent." Lokesh pleaded with teary eyes.

"I am not the right person to validate your statement. I was the IO for your sister's matrimonial discord and as far as I remember from my interaction with Chell *Babu* then, I don't think he could do any such illegal activities. But then ANC has got strong evidences and have pressed section 22 and 29 of NDPS Act, which are stringent and non-bailable. I suggest you quickly consult a lawyer and provide legal aid to your father. Hope things work in your favour." Sub-Inspector Shamita signed off after extending few pieces of advice to Lokesh.

Maya was brought back home from the nursing home and since then, not many relatives visited Birmirpur. Lokesh's attempt to find a competent lawyer failed. Suddenly all the near and dear ones of Chell family seemed to be extremely busy with their respective work. Even uncle Sarat excused himself every time he was asked to accompany Lokesh in search of an expert legal practitioner. Unexpectedly the neighbours maintained a safe distance from them as well. The changes in people's behaviour towards the Chell family was quite visible. Behind their back, a few also started criticising the alleged role of Sanat that resulted in his arrest.

Just when the devastated family required more of Lokesh, his employer back in Faridabad was in no mood to extend his leave and asked him to resume office immediately. Left with no option, he headed back to his workplace while his *Didi* took charge of the current situation. She had to split her time looking after her ailing mother and consult lawyers to get bail for her jailed father. Life for Moulina seemed to be getting worse with each passing day. A chain of unforeseen events tended to entrap and sink her deeper into the pit.

Fed up with the ongoing search of a specialist attorney, Moulina finally approached her existing counsellor Hrishikesh Basak, so that her father could atleast be out on bail. The Bengali lawyer however wasn't keen on representing Sanat. Initially he avoided Moulina, but finally vented out his frustration with the ongoing matrimony case and vowed not to take up any further case of the Chells.

"Sir, since the last few weeks my father has been languishing in jail for no reason. Whereas I've been running from pillar to post, trying to get him out on bail. And now that I want you to handle this matter, you're acting nonchalantly! But why Sir? What wrong have we done?" Moulina implored her lawyer to change his mind.

"Look, we lawyers have certain work ethics and principles. They say '*never lie to your doctor or lawyer*'; but while defending your case I learned otherwise. Till today I'm unaware of the truth. I was always kept in dark till the very last moment of drafting my petition. Let me tell you, NDPS Acts are tough and makes it more difficult to fight without any transparency from the client's end. Unlike domestic dispute cases, where you can shed a few tears in front of the Magistrate to gain his sympathy, the narcotics cases are dealt with severity and the consequences are far stricter." Basak voiced the challenges he had experienced and justified his stand.

"So, you won't take up this case because it's complicated, huh! And then you brag about being a top criminal lawyer in Rourkela?" taunted Moulina before she decided to leave.

"You're free to think whatever you wish to. But remember, a professional lawyer won't fight your case with his fees pending for months. And your father still owes me a lot. Every time I asked him to clear my dues, he kept offering me a percentage of the alimony that I should get him from your in-laws. Well, we have certain court related obligatory expenses that can't be availed on credit..." Basak asserted his displeasure and continued in a pitched up voice so that Moulina could hear him even though she was on her way out of his chamber – "don't get me started; there are some nefarious activities which your father indulged in, in the past and you probably aren't aware of it. The ANC this time might have got their hands on the right guy. I suggest that you look for someone else to fight your case and excuse me. Also, if you want your ongoing case to be handled by some other lawyer, feel free to approach me for the NOC. I won't mind letting it off."

Frustrations mounted large on Moulina. Never in her life had she gone through this situation, where a maze of regulations and indictment was restricting her to get her *Baba* out from the legal entwine. Even for the last four years of her ongoing matrimonial case, she had never faced such hardships – she just marionetted the acts suggested by her father, DSP, IO and lawyer at various stages of the case. None of the members from their extended family paid any heed to this crisis – it was as if they already considered her father as a transgressor.

Had something similar happened to her in Mumbai, her husband and in-laws would've acted as a shock-absorber and never let her suffer. The thought of dropping all charges against her husband and patching up with in-laws did strike her, but then it was too late. Probably her in-laws were far more supportive and helpful than her uncles and aunts whose insincere display of emotions and superficial sympathies now stood exposed.

Just when Moulina had given up all hopes, Sub-Inspector Shamita came to her rescue. The lady officer referred her to one Advocate Nitin Chandrakar – a talented *Chattisgarhi* who graduated from Rourkela Law College six years back. A novice lawyer with indomitable spirit, enormous energy and never-say-die attitude might probably get Sanat out on bail from the clamps of NDPS Act. A quick meeting was arranged and the young lawyer swung into action after hearing it out from his beautiful client. He was ready with an unassailable petition and as a part of Plan-B, hired a localite who would act as an alibi for that morning's incident.

The thirty-year-old legal practitioner empathized with his client who broke down twice while narrating that morning's unfortunate event. He couldn't take his eyes off her, and gazed at her in astonishment, while Moulina snivelled to describe how helpless her mother was, when police barged into their house and arrested her father. The young lawyer was bowled over by her euphoniously tranquilizing voice complemented with sheer innocence and felt sorry for her. He swore to take the prosecutor head on and provide some relief to the Chells.

"Madam, for my understanding could you please tell me exactly what happened that evening? When did Mr Chell return home? Who all visited him?...and other details that will possibly help me draft this petition better." Chandrakar asked Moulina while rebooting his laptop.

"Well…I was in Jaipur then. *Maa* told me that, like every evening *Baba* returned from *Superior Petrol Pump* at around 8 pm and watched TV for an hour before having dinner. It was at the dining table that he received a call and asked somebody to come over. Then at around 10 pm, *Maa* heard the thumping sound of a motorbike that waited outside the gate and honked twice before *Baba* went downstairs to meet somebody and collect a packet from him…"

"And next morning police raided the house and discovered a packet full of blots. Isn't that too much of a coincidence? This seems to be a clear-cut conspiracy to frame your father. Somebody meticulously planned everything to trap Mr Chell. But don't worry I am confident of securing a bail for your dad. I can guarantee you that he will be a free man in a couple of days." The overexcited lawyer also read out a few similar cases from an HC journal in order to boost the morale of his client.

However, the question of *Why did her father accept the packet without knowing its content* hovered in her mind and failed to fetch an explanation. Even Chandrakar was left baffled with an uncomfortable silence to his client's valid query.

The young lawyer was smart enough to avoid the question, and with a smile replied, "Our first and foremost job is to get your father out on bail and then we'll throw this particular question to him for an answer."

THIRTY-SEVEN
2019

Birmirpur, Odisha, India

February almost edged out and early spring embraced the quiet neighbourhood of Birmirpur. Surrounding's tranquillity was often broken by a distant cuckoo's enchanting notes among those verdant eucalypti. Few squirrels played heedless with little unripe guavas here and there, while a swarm of fluttering dragonflies crisscrossed each other's flight path exuberantly. In midst of such lyrical beauty of a spring morning; stood a devastated, impassive figure on the terrace. With rumpled hair and thick greying stubble, he appeared like a zombie. Drastic loss of weight made him look pale and drawn, almost haggard. He stared blankly at the leaves sprouting from the tree trunks which would eventually turn into healthy green foliage in coming weeks, but his future looked bleak. Two months' incarceration was unbearable, as his lawyer struggled to get him out on bail.

Not so long ago, this two-storied house used to bustle with the presence of near and dear ones, and had often been referred to as a landmark by the localite. Today people avoided talking about it. Losing all its past glory, the worn-out mansion stood like a ghost with a grave's silence around it. The last sixty days seemed like years to Sanat in the confinement of *Rourkela Central Jail* and unexpectedly, nobody visited him except his daughter, brother-in-law and a lawyer; while his wife remained bedridden. Even his own brother, Sarat, disassociated himself from all this and remained busy in his daughter's engagement ceremony with her long-time boyfriend. The Chells were almost ostracized by their immediate family members much before the localite could do it.

Loneliness grasped Sanat. There wasn't anyone to accompany him. No, not even the wind as he closed his eyes and sank into oblivion leaving himself to mourn over his recent loss – the untimely demise of his dear wife. Maya was his support system and silently reinforced all his decisions, no matter how fallacious they were. She often complained, but eventually compromised. Henceforth, there won't be anybody to nag him, nor criticise him over his actions – a deafening silence prevailed, that frightened him to the core. Hopes for a better tomorrow diminished into the darkening distance.

Just when the fiery beast of grief was about to vanquish him, Sanat heard his daughter call him downstairs.

The bereaved family was preparing for the last rites of Maya Chell, who suffered a severe stroke and finally succumbed. Just few days back, when news of Sanat's bail rejection came in, bedridden Maya behaved in an unusual manner. There was a sudden numbness on her right side while she struggled to speak with a droopy face. She felt dizzy and everything around her appeared blurred. Moulina was in the patio speaking to the lawyer over the phone – it was the second instance in last two months that her father's bail plea got rejected. But on hearing a terrific thud she rushed into her mother's room to find her lying paralysed on the floor. With the help of neighbours, Maya was rushed to the nursing home where she was earlier admitted, but absence of a *tPA* injection compelled the management to transfer the patient to Rourkela General Hospital. It was on the way that she slipped into a coma and didn't respond thereafter – Mrs Chell was declared brought dead.

Chandrakar who miserably failed to secure the crucial bail for his client in spite of all his assiduous effort, filed a prayer seeking parole for Sanat. The local court granted a week's leave to Sanat for attending his wife's last rites. Meanwhile the young counsel made all arrangements to approach the HC in pursuit of a bail for Mr Chell.

Immediate family members and a few distant relatives gathered at the Chell residence where the mortal remains of Maya was kept and being prepared for cremation. Dressed in red with a streak of vermillion on her forehead and light makeup, she looked resplendent like a Goddess in deep slumber. Adorned with sprinkled flowers, holy basil and garlands; the deceased appeared pious and saintly. Friends and relatives paid their last respect while the priest officiated the final rituals through prayer and hymns. The grieving family members sat in one corner of the room with Sanat's heart-wrenching stare at the cadaver and Lina's inconsolable wail. Though Lokesh succeeded in putting up a brave face in greeting the guests, teary eyed Moulina often broke down. The fact that there won't be anybody to be called *"Maa"* anymore, gave an acute emptiness among the siblings.

As an elder daughter-in-law, Maya had always been a strong foundation to Chell's extended family. She stepped into this family forty years back when she was barely seventeen. At a tender age when she was supposed to attend college and enjoy her youth, she took up the responsibility of this family with all smiles. Those initial days at Chell residence weren't smooth enough when she frequently had tiffs with her mother-in-law. But out of respect she never disobeyed her. She had seen the family go through various ups and downs, but never ever quit from her roles and responsibilities. She used to get offended when others made fun of her husband's dark brown complexion as compared to her pale yellow skin. Back then when Sanat's brothers were young and unmarried, she enjoyed all the attention of being an elder figure to them. And after the demise of her mother-in-law she grew up to be a motherly figure to all her brothers-in-law.

Being from a well to do family she adjusted perfectly with her in-laws through thick and thin, experienced motherhood at the age of twenty, and cherished the moment when she held little Moulina in her arms for the first time – the cute angel was an emotional bliss along with unlimited joy. In the hour of crisis, she didn't hesitate to mortgage her jewellery inherited from her mother and help Sanat to clear his debts and pay off the creditors. It was a testing time for the Chells when Sanat was left out from the business and the entire family was on the verge of separation – only Maya managed to keep everything intact like an epoxy glue while her husband gracefully exited from the venture.

The gorgeous, humble lady, with progressive thoughts and positive attitude, however remained overshadowed by her husband's orthodox approaches, cynical attitude, narcissistic ego and conniving mentality. When the kids were young, she used to revolt and voice out her concerns, but her husband's adamancy eventually muted her.

At the crematorium when the burning pyre paced up to reduce the corpse into mere ashes, grief surged to new heights with every expelled breath, never sufficiently soothed by Sanat's long intakes of the damp spring air. Tears began to spill from his helpless eyes onto the floor. Life without his significant other was unimaginable and undid him completely. Everybody except Maya misunderstood him. He would be incomplete without her and from here on life would be meaningless. He would rather opt for a life in solitary confinement of the prison than coping up with the memory of this loss silently in despondency.

After days of mourning, Lokesh had to head back to Faridabad and Lina joined her post-graduate college in Raipur leaving Moulina all alone to take control over things back home. With just two days left for her father's parole to end, Moulina was a worried soul. She had always been her daddy's girl and never been too close to her mother. But haunting memories of *Maa* often brought tears in her eyes – those *champis* on a winter afternoon, tasting of tangy pickle on a summer morning and learning to get those perfect poached eggs in the kitchen would never be the same again. She still couldn't come to terms with her mother's sudden absence from her life. She flipped the pages of their family album and stared at those old, faded, black and white childhood photographs with her mom that gave her cold shivers. Losing *Maa* left her in shambles and now she couldn't afford to lose her daddy dear in his world of loneliness and depression. She was determined to secure a bail for him from the honourable HC.

Chandrakar was on time. He wanted few vital inputs from Chell as well as spend some time talking to his beautiful daughter on the pretext of finalizing the bail application. Thereafter he had plans to expedite the hearing process and engage a senior lawyer for an assured result at the HC.

Sanat was inattentively browsing few Hindi channels before he settled for *News18 Odia*. Seeing Chandrakar open his laptop, he lowered the volume of the TV and waited for the lawyer to clear his queries. Just above him was a large ever-smiling portrait of Maya, newly framed and garlanded. Her lively eyes seemed to be overseeing every activity under the roof.

After an initial conversation, the defence lawyer asked few of the most anticipated and pertinent questions to his client. "Sir, were you aware of the content of the packet? Who came to see you that night? What did he say while handing over the packet? Did he or they try to contact you after your arrest?"

For a moment, Sanat pretended to remain busy with the TV remote and deliberately ignored Chandrakar's query. And later, recapitulation of same set of questions by the lawyer irked him. With much displeasure, Sanat rose from his chair and walked out of the room murmuring to himself.

Taken aback by such bizarre behaviour, Chandrakar voiced his concern to Moulina "How do you expect me to defend this case unless your father cooperates with me. I can't just cook-up stories for his bail application!"

"I understand your frustration. But that's how he has been reacting to such questions whenever asked about that night's incident. Actually, repeated questioning in police custody has made him go restless and behave so weirdly. Nonetheless we owe you an apology." Moulina tried convincing Chandrakar and begged his forgiveness.

But deep inside the corner of her mind, she knew something was definitely wrong. Her father was simply exaggerating it and trying to avoid those uncomfortable questions. He wasn't that faint-hearted to wither away so easily. There must have been some deep-rooted trouble which he wanted to avoid, a Pandora's Box which he preferred not to unlatch. At many instances he had faked his emotions to gain sympathy and diverted attention of others.

At a time when her cousin was set to have a fairytale engagement with her boyfriend, they remained uninvited and debarred. But this wasn't what she expected. This wasn't what her father promised when she decided to leave behind her in-laws and file an FIR. Sanat always assured her a better future. In spite of having every little happiness in her husband's company, she was indoctrinated and convinced to go against Sumit. She was happy in her swaddled world of Birmirpur, yet her father persuaded her to get married in Mumbai for a better future. She had always been pawned and lured for something bigger and better but every time remained betrayed. And why did she have to suffer always? Why did things turn ugly whenever she was involved, her siblings were all on the right track whereas she got trapped in the maze of life's complexities. Between right and wrong, probably she always chose the wrong path or may be, she was misguided often. And today at this juncture of her life, she stood all alone…the future looked bleak along with a haunted past and an equally frustrated present.

Suddenly every wrong started happening to her. As compared to her cousins and friends, she had a stringent childhood followed by a boring youth and then an unsuccessful marriage – but who should be blamed? She tried hard to keep up with everybody's expectations, specifically her father's. Yet the society would keep her at arm's length and tag her as a divorcee and a drug trafficker's daughter. This wasn't what she had envisaged. It would be like dying a thousand deaths every day.

Conflicting thoughts clung on to her with no one to express herself to. Acute loneliness enwreathed her and pushed to the brink of depression. She even contemplated felo-de-se but somehow retracted…loneliness was eating her alive, swallowing every ounce of hope left in her. It feasted upon her, leaving behind the empty carcass of despair and memories of her past. It took away her heart into its claws and squeezed out every bit of life she had left. It craved her to suffer a life without any warm hands embracing her or any shoulder to lean on. Loneliness made her life miserable and left her suffocating. She wanted to breathe some fresh air, but terrace moments weren't the same anymore – the darkness of the sky frightened her and she feared getting lost in its vastness. The presence of fireflies irritated her and the latest menace of rats frequenting the terrace restricted her evening stroll. One corner of the terrace was annexed by the rodents' brigade which often climbed the pipes connecting the kitchen. Nuisance caused by these pests is why Moulina avoided terrace in the evenings. Slowly and steadily, unpleasant circumstances took over all that she enjoyed doing in the past.

Of late she realised, that she was never in control of herself. It was her father who pulled the strings instead. And somewhere deep inside, she felt that he gambled away her life in order to cover-up his own failure and misdeeds. Or may be, the flip-side of being *daddy's girl* who blindly followed every instruction without pondering over it. Sanat Chell basically botched up his life miserably – improper family planning followed by unsuccessful business venture led to financial hardship. And in lieu of focusing on gradual improvement, he unsuccessfully attempted all shortcuts in life, while his toxic ego shoved him down the drain and ruined everything. Further his orthodox approach made life hell. He faked his responsibilities and never thought about the repercussions. Today, when Moulina's uncles and aunts were smoothly navigating the challenging course of life, she was in the middle of a sea-storm finding it hard to keep their sinking boat afloat. Sanat completely failed as a father making Moulina a victim of his whimsical decisions that satiated his ego. The emotional exploitation she underwent all these years, shouldn't have happened. Had she realised it earlier, she could have attempted to stop it. Better late than never – atleast from now on she vowed to be more practical rather than being swayed away by her emotions.

In the kitchen, just when Moulina sank into these deep thoughts, a mid-sized rat raced over her toes and left her screeching aloud. She lost her balance but timely grabbed the kitchen counter and avoided a fall. In the process, her elbow hit a bowl full of curry kept on the edge of the countertop and turned it turtle. The spilled curry led to a messy kitchen floor leaving behind stains on her pyjama. Irked with the nuisance caused, she swore to end this once and for all. Even the rodents took her for granted and didn't pay a heed to her presence in the kitchen. Fuming with rage, she rushed downstairs to get a pack of *Celphos* pellets.

It was a hot yet windy morning of early March, the discoloured Chell mansion stood etiolated while a few playful sparrows fluttered and chirped harmoniously at the edge of the terrace. Though it was a normal Friday outside, a vacuous spectral silence prevailed inside the two storeyed building until a police jeep arrived honking infrequently. Two constables stood guard outside the main gate while other two accompanied the Sub-Inspector, who headed towards the door that had a collapsible gate locked from inside. Morning newspaper tucked into the metallic handle was still waiting to be collected by the residents. The visiting men in uniform grew suspicious of the haunted silence that reigned. Something wasn't right, felt the duty officer before he decided to break in.

To know exactly what was happening, few passers-by gathered near the police vehicle out of sheer curiosity. Whereas the neighbours peeped out of their window and leaned over their balcony to witness the police operation at the Chell residence.

Birmirpur police had no other option but to come searching for Sanat, when he failed to appear before the police station and surrender himself even after a day of his parole expiry. After banging the door haphazardly along with continuous doorbell rings, when the cops failed to get any response, they forced their way into the house. There wasn't anything unusual at the ground floor but on reaching the first floor they were shocked to find Sanat lie prostrate on the floor. His motionless body was immediately inspected and declared dead. There was a bottle of water next to the body which might have rolled down from its original position on the side table of the room. The deceased might have tried to reach out for a glass of water before he succumbed. The shelves of the room were untouched and didn't raise any suspicion of burglary. Sensing a foul play, the SI sealed the entire building and deputed his men at the crime spot. He also carried out a recce of the entire premises and questioned the neighbours. Surprisingly Sanat's elder daughter was missing and the back door was left ajar. On visiting Moulina's room, the duty officer found nothing unusual apart from the fact that a duffle-bag might have been packed with few random clothes which were missing from the wardrobe. Her mobile phone was left to charge in a switched off condition. In the kitchen, a pile of dirty utensils from last night's supper remained unwashed inside the sink; the refrigerator was stacked up with vegetables, milk, bread and some leftover curries – nothing seemed anomalous. The terrace door was however kept wide open. Few crows were seen to feast on a couple of dead rats that laid on the left end of the terrace floor, while few others hovered over the building with their grating caws. From the terrace a few more rodents could be spotted lying lifeless in the backyard.

In a bid to unearth reasons behind the mysterious death of Sanat, the SI started questioning the neighbours and recorded their statements. The housemaid was summoned and Chell's relatives in Rourkela were informed about this unfortunate incident.

After spending the entire day enquiring, when nothing emerged to substantiate several hypotheses behind the untimely demise of Sanat, the SI left it to the autopsy report to determine the cause of death and preferred continuing with his investigation then. Meanwhile the housemaid didn't turn up as she had gone to her native village and wasn't even attending work for last ten days. Nothing unusual was observed by the neighbours, except for one who heard the father-daughter squabble a little past midnight. The gentleman also remembered seeing the light in Moulina's room remain switched on till the wee hours of the morning.

It got late, and on their way back home after a tough day's work, the exhausted constable who was keen to know the initial thoughts of his senior, asked him hesitantly, "Sir, what do you feel? What could be the real reason behind this death?"

"Too early to comment. *Kuch bhi ho sakta hai…*it's a kind of a mystery for the time being. Let the post-mortem report come in, we'll be in a better position then. Oh, by the way, first thing in the morning tomorrow – publish a look out notice for Sanat's daughter and circulate it to all the police stations in and around Rourkela and Birmirpur. Activate the local informants so that the lady can be traced." The SI instructed his subordinate before signing off for the day.

Back in Mumbai's suburban Tilaknagar, the Ghosh family was all set to go out on a family dinner in order to celebrate Sumit's new job. After a prolonged gap he finally managed to fetch a corporate job and was excited to start afresh. Even though the company offered him a lower package compared to what his experience and qualifications demanded, Sushil and Chitra were elated to see their son get back to normalcy. It was indeed a long struggle, an unending nightmare for Sumit, who was slowly recuperating from the toxic effect of the fake cases.

The next morning was very critical to the investigating team at Birmirpur PS as they were completely baffled with the post-mortem findings followed by some inputs from a local informant. They tried hard to put two and two together and yet couldn't connect the dots. The autopsy report clearly stated that Sanat's death occurred somewhere around 1:30 am due to aluminium-phosphide overdose. Ingestion of the fumigant had lethal consequences in form of arrhythmias which led to a circulatory collapse. Upon contact with moisture, aluminium-phosphide released phosphine which was detected in the tissues of brain, liver, and kidneys. The chemical in its solid state is sold as a pesticide and is often available as pellets of *Celphos, Alphos, Quick-Phos and Phostoxin* in the open market, and is considered to be a sure shot death agent. With specific inputs from the autopsy report along with a few circumstantial evidences, the police team initiated the probe to establish Sanat's death. However, the mysterious disappearance of Moulina raised several eye brows and the police aren't discounting her involvement either. As per a local resident, she was last seen waiting at the *Chowk-Bazar* bus stop; and appeared quite calm and composed. At the break of dawn, she was seen to board a Ranchi bound bus which honked its way through the foggy morning...